'P. D. James brings a vigour of intellect and insight to proceedings that should embarrass some young enough to be to be her grandchildren . . . The greatest joy of a P. D. James novel lies in her cool, painterly descriptions of landscapes. She is also excellent at female characters . . . The serenity and sophistication of James's imagination, and the bigger picture that dwarfs her stories, placing them within a timeless sense of order, are a perpetual pleasure.' *Herald*

'Once again James proves to be a mistress of suspense.' *Tatler*

'In *The Private Patient* we get the full works of the classic crime novel, from questioning of the whole household gathered in the library, to the possible forging of a will. But it is the incidentals that remain most delectable.' *Evening Standard*

'P. D. James doesn't just draw her characters, even the minor ones. She walks all round them, sculpting them lovingly, delving into their past.' *Daily Express*

'You know you're in the company of P. D. James from the first sentence: elegantly phrased, plot-driven, multi-layered and laced with menace . . . The story rattles along, propelled as always by James's eloquent way with words. . . Eloquent description and fine scene setting, graceful sentences and moral nuances.' *Observer*

'No one is better than James at maintaining the tension between the cosy and the frightful.' *Washington Post*

'[James is] a master . . . Nothing is as it first appears.' *Boston Globe*

'Elegant . . . compelling . . . She comfortably tackles timeless concerns.' *Chicago Tribune*

by the same author

COVER HER FACE
A MIND TO MURDER
UNNATURAL CAUSES
SHROUD FOR A NIGHTINGALE
AN UNSUITABLE JOB FOR A WOMAN
THE BLACK TOWER
DEATH OF AN EXPERT WITNESS
INNOCENT BLOOD
THE SKULL BENEATH THE SKIN
A TASTE FOR DEATH
DEVICES AND DESIRES
THE CHILDREN OF MEN
ORIGINAL SIN
A CERTAIN JUSTICE
DEATH IN THE HOLY ORDERS
THE MURDER ROOM
THE LIGHTHOUSE
DEATH COMES TO PEMBERLEY
THE MISTLETOE MURDER AND OTHER STORIES
SLEEP NO MORE

non-fiction
TIME TO BE IN EARNEST
A Fragment of Autobiography

THE MAUL AND THE PEAR TREE
The Ratcliffe Highway Murders 1811
(by P. D. James and T. A. Critchley)

TALKING ABOUT DETECTIVE FICTION

P. D. James

The Private Patient

FABER & FABER

First published in 2008
Faber & Faber Limited
The Bindery, 51 Hatton Garden,
London ECIN 8HN

Penguin Books paperback 2009
This Faber & Faber paperback edition first published in 2018

Typeset by Faber & Faber Limited
Printed and bound by CPI Group (UK) Ltd, Croydon, CR0 4YY

A CIP record for this book
is available from the British Library
ISBN 978–0–571–34512–0

FSC
www.fsc.org
MIX
Paper | Supporting
responsible forestry
FSC® C013604

Printed and bound in the UK on FSC® certified paper in line with our continuing
commitment to ethical business practices, sustainability and the environment.
For further information see faber.co.uk/environmental-policy

8 10 9 7

This book is dedicated to
Stephen Page, publisher,
and to all my friends, old and new, at Faber and Faber
in celebration of my forty-six unbroken years
as a Faber author

CONTENTS

AUTHOR'S NOTE
page xi

BOOK ONE
21 November–14 December: London, Dorset
page 3

BOOK TWO
15 December: London, Dorset
page 105

BOOK THREE
16–18 December: London, Dorset, Midlands, Dorset
page 209

BOOK FOUR
19–21 December: London, Dorset
page 317

BOOK FIVE
Spring: Dorset, Cambridge
page 383

AUTHOR'S NOTE

Dorset is notable for the history and variety of its manor houses, but travellers to that beautiful county will not find Cheverell Manor among them. The Manor and all connected with it, and the deplorable events which take place there, exist only in the imagination of the author and of her readers and have no connection with any person past or present, living or dead.

P. D. James

BOOK ONE

21 November–14 December
London, Dorset

On November the 21st, the day of her forty-seventh birthday, and three weeks and two days before she was murdered, Rhoda Gradwyn went to Harley Street to keep a first appointment with her plastic surgeon, and there in a consulting room designed, so it appeared, to inspire confidence and allay apprehension, made the decision which would lead inexorably to her death. Later that day she was to lunch at the Ivy. The timing of the two appointments was fortuitous. Mr Chandler-Powell had no earlier date to offer and the luncheon later with Robin Boyton, booked for twelve forty-five, had been arranged two months previously; one did not expect to get a table at the Ivy on impulse. She regarded neither appointment as a birthday celebration. This detail of her private life, like much else, was never mentioned. She doubted whether Robin had discovered her date of birth or would much care if he had. She knew herself to be a respected, even distinguished journalist, but she hardly expected her name to appear in the *Times* list of VIP birthdays.

She was due at Harley Street at eleven fifteen. Usually with a London appointment she preferred to walk at least part of the way, but today she had ordered a taxi for ten thirty. The journey from the City shouldn't take three-quarters of an hour but the London traffic was unpredictable. She was entering a world that was strange to her and had no wish to jeopardise her relationship with her surgeon by arriving late for this their first meeting.

Eight years ago she had taken a lease on a house in the City, part of a narrow terrace in a small courtyard at the end of Absolution Alley near Cheapside, and knew as soon as she moved in that this was the part of London in which she would always choose to live. The lease was long and renewable; she would have liked to buy the house, but knew that it would never be for sale. But the fact that she couldn't hope to call it entirely her own didn't distress her. Most of it dated back to the seventeenth century. Many generations had lived in it, been born and died there, leaving behind nothing but their names on browning and archaic leases, and she was content to be in their company. Although the lower rooms with their mullioned windows were dark, those in her study and sitting room on the top storey were open to the sky, giving a view of the towers and steeples of the City and beyond. An iron staircase led from a narrow balcony on the third floor to a secluded roof, which held a row of terracotta pots and where on fine Sunday mornings she could sit with her book or newspapers as the Sabbath calm lengthened into midday and the early peace was broken only by the familiar peals of the City bells.

The City which lay below was a charnel house built on multi-layered bones centuries older than those which lay beneath the cities of Hamburg or Dresden. Was this knowledge part of the mystery it held for her, a mystery felt most strongly on a bell-chimed Sunday on her solitary exploration of its hidden alleys and squares? Time had fascinated her from childhood, its apparent power to move at different speeds, the dissolution it wrought on minds and bodies, her sense that each moment, all moments past and those to come, were fused into an illusory present which with every breath became the unalterable, indestructible past. In the City of London these moments were caught and solidified in stone and brick, in churches and monuments and in bridges which spanned the grey-brown ever-flowing Thames. She would walk out in spring or summer as early as six o'clock, double locking the front door behind her, stepping into a silence more profound and mysterious than the absence of noise. Sometimes in this solitary perambulation it seemed that her own footsteps were muted, as if some part of her were afraid to waken the dead who had walked these streets and had known the same silence. She knew that on summer weekends, a few hundred yards away, the tourists and crowds would soon be pouring over the Millennium Bridge, the laden river steamers would move with majestic clumsiness from their berths, and the public city would become raucously alive.

But none of this business penetrated Sanctuary Court. The house she had chosen could not have been more different from that curtained, claustrophobic semi-detached suburban villa in Laburnum Grove, Silford Green, the east London suburb where she had been born and in which she had spent the first sixteen years of her life. Now she would take the first step on a path which might reconcile her to those years or, if reconciliation were impossible, at least rob them of their destructive power.

It was now eight thirty and she was in her bathroom. Turning off the shower, she moved, towel-wrapped, to the mirror over the washbasin. She put out her hand and smoothed it over the steam-smeared glass and watched her face appear, pale and anonymous as a smudged painting. It was months since she had deliberately touched the scar. Now, slowly and delicately, she ran a fingertip down its length, feeling the silver shininess at its heart, the hard bumpy outline of its edge. Placing her left hand over her cheek, she tried to imagine the stranger who, in a few weeks' time, would look into the same mirror and see a doppelgänger of herself, but one incomplete, unmarked, perhaps with only a thin white line to show where this puckered crevice had run. Gazing at the image which seemed no more than a faint palimpsest of her former self, she began slowly and deliberately to demolish her carefully constructed defences and let the turbulent past, first like a swelling stream and then a river in spate, break through unresisted and take possession of her mind.

She was back in that small rear room, both kitchen and sitting room, in which she and her parents colluded in their lies and endured their voluntary exile from life. The front room, with its bay window, was for special occasions, for family celebrations never held and for visitors who never came, its silence smelling faintly of lavender furniture polish and stale air, an air so portentous that she tried never to breathe it. She was the only child of a frightened and ineffective mother and a drunken father. That was how she had defined herself for more than thirty years and how she still defined herself. Her childhood and adolescence had been circumscribed by shame and guilt. Her father's periodic bouts of violence were unpredictable. No school friends could safely be brought home, no birthday or Christmas parties arranged and, since no invitations were ever given, none was received. The grammar school to which she went was single sex and friendships between the girls were intense. A special mark of favour was to be invited to spend the night at a friend's house. No guest ever slept at 239 Laburnum Grove. The isolation didn't worry her. She knew herself to be more intelligent than her fellows and was able to persuade herself that she had no need of a companionship which would be intellectually unsatisfying and which she knew would never be offered.

It was eleven thirty on a Friday, the night her father got paid, the worst day of the week. And now there came the sound she dreaded, the sharp closing of the front door. He came blundering in and she saw her mother move in front of the armchair, which Rhoda knew would awaken his fury. It was to be her father's chair.

He had chosen it, paid for it, and it had been delivered that morning. Only after the van had left had her mother discovered it was the wrong colour. It would have to be changed, but there had been no time before the shop closed. She knew that her mother's querulous, apologetic, half-whining voice would enrage him, that her own sullen presence would help neither of them, but she couldn't go up to bed. The noise of what would happen beneath her room would be more terrifying than to be part of it. And now the room was full of him, his blundering body, the stink of him. Hearing his bellow of outrage, his ranting, she felt a sudden spurt of fury, and with it came courage. She heard herself saying, 'It isn't Mother's fault. The chair was wrapped up when the man left it. She couldn't see it was the wrong colour. They'll have to change it.'

And then he turned on her. She couldn't recall the words. Perhaps at the time there had been no words, or she hadn't heard them. There was only the crack of the smashed bottle, like a pistol shot, the stink of whisky, a moment of searing pain which passed almost as soon as she felt it and the warm blood flowing from her cheek, dripping onto the seat of the chair, her mother's anguished cry. 'Oh God, look what you've done, Rhoda. The blood! They'll never take it back now. They'll never change it.'

Her father gave her one look before stumbling out and hauling himself up to bed. In the seconds in which their eyes met she thought she saw a confusion of emotions: bafflement, horror and disbelief. Then her mother finally turned her attention to her child. Rhoda had been trying to hold the edges of the wound together, the blood sticky on her hands. Her mother fetched towels and a packet of sticking plasters and tried with shaking hands to open it, her tears mixing with the blood. It was Rhoda who gently took the packet from her, unpeeled the plasters from their covers and managed at last to close most of the wound. By the time, less than an hour later, she was lying stiffly in bed the bleeding had been staunched and the future mapped out. There would be no visit to the doctor and no truthful explanation ever; she would stay away from school for a day or two, her mother would telephone, saying she was unwell. And when she did go back, her story would be ready: she had crashed against the edge of the open kitchen door.

And now the sharp-edged memory of that single slashing moment softened into the more mundane recollection of the following years. The wound, which became badly infected, healed painfully and slowly, but neither parent spoke of it. Her father had always found it difficult to meet her eyes; now he hardly ever came near her. Her classmates averted their gaze, but it seemed to her that fear had replaced active dislike. No one at school ever mentioned the disfigurement in her presence until she was in the sixth form and was sitting with her English mistress who was trying to persuade her to try for Cambridge – her own university – instead of London. Without looking up from her papers Miss Farrell had said, 'Your facial scar, Rhoda. It's wonderful what plastic surgeons can do today. Perhaps it would be sensible to make an appointment with your GP before you go up.' Their eyes had met, Rhoda's mutinous with outrage, and after four seconds of silence, Miss Farrell, cringing in her chair, her face an angry rash of mottled scarlet, had bent again to her papers.

She began to be treated with wary respect. Neither dislike nor respect worried her. She had her own private life, an interest in finding out what others kept hidden, in making discoveries. Probing into other people's secrets became a lifelong obsession, the substratum and direction of her whole career. She became a stalker of minds. Eighteen years after she had left Silford Green, the suburb had been enthralled by a notorious murder. She had studied the grainy pictures of victim and killer in the papers with no particular interest. The killer confessed within days, was taken away, the case closed. As an investigative journalist, by now becoming increasingly successful, she was interested less by Silford Green's brief notoriety than by her own more subtle and more lucrative and fascinating lines of enquiry.

She had left home on her sixteenth birthday and found a bed-sit in the next suburb. Every week until he died her father sent her a five-pound note. She never acknowledged it but took the money because she needed it to supplement the cash she earned in the evenings and at weekends working as a waitress, telling herself that it was probably less than her food would have cost at home. When, five years later, with a first in History and established in her first job, her mother phoned to say that her father had died, she felt an absence of emotion that paradoxically seemed stronger and more irksome than regret. He had been found drowned, slumped in an Essex stream whose name she could never remember, with an alcohol level in his blood which proved that he had been intoxicated. The coroner's verdict of accidental death was expected and, she thought, probably correct. It was the one she had hoped for. She told herself, not without a small flicker of shame which quickly died, that suicide would have been too rational and momentous a final judgement on such an ineffectual life.

3

The cab ride was quicker than she had expected. She arrived too early at Harley Street and asked the driver to stop at the Marylebone Road end of the street, then walked to her appointment. As on the rare occasions when she had passed this way, she was struck by the street's emptiness, the almost uncanny calm which hung over these formal eighteenth-century terraces. Almost every door bore a brass plate with a list of names confirming what surely every Londoner would know, that this was the hub of medical expertise. Somewhere behind these gleaming front doors and discreetly curtained windows patients must be waiting in various stages of anxiety, apprehension, hope or despair, yet she seldom saw any of them arriving or departing. The occasional tradesman or messenger would come and go, but otherwise the street could have been an empty film set, awaiting the arrival of director, cameraman and players.

Arriving at the door, she studied the panel of names. There were two surgeons and three physicians, and the name she expected to see was there at the top. Mr G. H. Chandler-Powell, FRCS, FRCS (Plast), MS – the last two letters which proclaimed that a surgeon had reached the summit of expertise and reputation. Master of Surgery. It had, she thought, a fine ring to it. The barber-surgeons awarded their licences by Henry VIII would be surprised to know how far they had come.

The door was opened by a serious-faced young woman in a white coat cut to compliment her figure. She was attractive but not disconcertingly so, and her brief welcoming smile was more minatory than warm. Rhoda thought, *Head girl. Girl Guide patrol leader. There was one in every sixth form.*

The waiting room into which she was shown so matched her expectations that momentarily she had the impression that she had been there before. It managed to achieve a certain opulence while containing nothing of real quality. The large central mahogany table, with its copies of *Country Life*, *Horse and Hounds* and the more upmarket women's magazines so carefully aligned as to discourage reading, was impressive but not elegant. The assorted chairs, some upright, others more comfortable, looked as if they had been acquired in a country-house sale but had seldom been used. The hunting prints were large and undistinguished enough to inhibit theft and she doubted whether the two high-baluster vases on the mantelpiece were genuine.

None of the patients except herself gave any clue to the particular expertise they required. As always, she was able to observe them knowing that no curious eyes would be fixed for long on her. They glanced up as she entered but there were no brief nods of acknowledgement. To become a patient was to relinquish a part of oneself, to be received into a system which, however benign, subtly robbed one of initiative, almost of will. They sat, patiently acquiescent, in their private worlds. A middle-aged woman, a child in the chair beside her, gazed expressionlessly into space. The child, bored, restless eyed, began gently knocking her feet against the chair legs until, without looking at her, the woman put out a restraining hand. Opposite them a young man who looked in his formal suit the epitome of a City financier took the *Financial Times* from his briefcase and, unfolding it with practised expertise, concentrated his attention on the page. A fashionably dressed woman moved silently to the table and studied the magazines then, rejecting the choice, returned to her seat next to the window and continued her stare at the empty street.

Rhoda was not kept waiting for long. The same young woman who had let her in came over to her, speaking softly and saying that Mr Chandler-Powell could see her now. With his speciality, discretion obviously started in the waiting room. She was shown into a large, light room across the hall. The two tall double windows facing the street were curtained in heavy linen and with white, almost transparent net softening the winter sunlight. The room had none of the furniture or equipment she had half-expected, a drawing room rather than an office. An attractive lacquer screen decorated with a rural scene of meadows, river and distant mountains stood in the angle to the left of the door. It was obviously old, possibly eighteenth century. Perhaps, she thought, it concealed a washbasin or even a couch, although this seemed unlikely. It was difficult to imagine anyone taking his or her clothes off in this domestic if opulent setting. There were two armchairs, one each side of the marble fireplace, and a mahogany pedestal desk facing the door, two upright chairs before it. The only oil picture was over the mantelpiece, a large painting of a Tudor house with an eighteenth-century family carefully grouped in front of it, the father and two sons mounted, the wife and three young daughters in a phaeton. On the opposite wall was a row of coloured prints of eighteenth-century London. They and the oil added to her sense of being subtly out of time.

Mr Chandler-Powell had been sitting at the desk and, as she entered, he rose and came to shake her hand, indicating one of the two chairs. His grasp was firm but momentary, his hand cool. She had expected him to be wearing a dark suit. Instead he was in very pale grey fine tweed, beautifully cut, which paradoxically gave a greater impression of formality. Facing him, she saw a strong bony face with a long mobile mouth and bright hazel eyes under well-marked brows. His brown hair, straight and a little unruly, was brushed over a high forehead, a few strands falling almost into his right eye. The immediate impression he gave was of confidence and she recognised it at once: a patina which had something, but not everything, to do with success. It was different from the confidence with which as a journalist she was familiar: celebrities, their eyes always avid for the next photographer, at the ready to assume the right stance; nonentities who seemed to know that their notoriety was a concoction of the media, a transitory fame which only their desperate self-belief could maintain. The man before her had the inner assurance of someone at the top of his profession, secure, inviolable. She detected, too, a hint of arrogance not altogether successfully concealed, but told herself that this could be prejudice. Master of Surgery. Well, he looked the part.

'You come, Miss Gradwyn, without a letter from your GP.' It was stated as a fact not a reproach. His voice was deep and attractive but with a trace of a country accent which she couldn't identify and hadn't expected.

'It seemed a waste of his time and mine. I registered with Dr Macintyre's practice about eight years ago as an NHS patient and I have never needed to consult either him or any of his partners. I only go to the surgery twice a year to have my blood pressure taken. That's usually done by the practice nurse.'

'I know Dr Macintyre. I'll have a word with him.'

Without speaking he came up to her, turning the desk lamp so that its bright beam shone full on her face. His fingers were cool as they touched the skin on each cheek, pinching it into folds. The touch was so impersonal that it seemed an insult. She wondered why he hadn't disappeared behind the screen to wash his hands, but perhaps, if he considered it necessary for this preliminary appointment, this had been done before she entered the room. There was a moment in which, not touching the scar, he scrutinised it in silence. Then he switched off the light and sat again behind the desk. His eyes on the file before him, he said, 'How long ago was this done?'

She was struck by the phrasing of the question. 'Thirty-four years ago.'

'How did it happen?'

She said, 'Is that a necessary question?'

'Not unless it was self-inflicted. I assume it wasn't.'

'No, it wasn't self-inflicted.'

'And you have waited thirty-four years to do something about it. Why now, Miss Gradwyn?'

There was a pause, then she said, 'Because I no longer have need of it.'

He didn't reply, but the hand making notes in the file was for a few seconds stilled. Looking up from his papers, he said, 'What are you expecting from this operation, Miss Gradwyn?'

'I should like the scar to disappear but I realise that's impossible. I suppose what I'm hoping for is a thin line, not this wide sunken cicatrice.'

He said, 'I think with the help of some make-up it could be almost invisible. After surgery, if necessary, you can be referred to a CC nurse for cosmetic camouflage. These nurses are very skilled. It's surprising what can be done.'

'I'd prefer not to have to use camouflage.'

'Very little or none may be necessary but it's a deep scar. As I expect you know, the skin is layered and it will be necessary to open up and reconstruct those layers. For a time after the operation the scar will look red and raw, a great deal worse before it gets better. We'll need to deal, too, with the effect on the naso-labial fold, that small droop of the lip, and the top of the scar where it pulls down the corner of the eye. At the finish I shall use a fat injection to plump up and correct any contour irregularities. But when I see you the day before the operation I shall explain in more detail what I propose to do and show you a diagram. The operation will be done under a general anaesthetic. Have you ever been anaesthetised?'

'No, this will be my first time.'

'The anaesthetist will see you before the operation. There are some tests I would like done, including blood tests and an ECG, but I would prefer those to be carried out at St Angela's. The scar will be photographed before and after the operation.'

She said, 'The injection of fat you mentioned, what kind of fat?'

'Yours. Harvested by syringing it from your stomach.'

Of course, she thought, a silly question.

He said, 'When were you thinking of having it done? I have private beds at St Angela's, or you could come to Cheverell Manor, my clinic in Dorset, if you prefer to be out of London. The earliest date I can offer you this year is Friday the 14th of December. That would have to be at the Manor. You would be one of only two patients at that time, as I shall be running down the clinic for the Christmas break.'

'I'd prefer to be out of London.'

'Mrs Snelling will take you to the office after this consultation. My secretary there will give you a brochure about the Manor. How long you stay there is up to you. The stitches will probably come out on the sixth day and very few patients need or wish to stay post-operative for more than a week. If you do decide on the Manor, it's helpful if you can find time for a preliminary visit either for a day or overnight. I like patients to see where they're to be operated on if they can spare the time. It's disconcerting to arrive at a totally strange place.'

She said, 'Is the wound likely to be painful, after the operation I mean?'

'No, it's unlikely to be painful. A little sore perhaps, and there may be considerable swelling. If there is pain we can deal with it.'

'A bandage over my face?'

'Not a bandage. A dressing which will be taped.'

There was one more question and she had no inhibition in asking it although she thought she knew the answer. She wasn't asking out of fear and hoped that he would understand this without greatly caring if he didn't. 'Would this be described as a dangerous operation?'

'There is always some risk with a general anaesthetic. As far as the surgery is concerned, it will be time consuming, delicate and likely to present some problems. Those will be my responsibility, not yours. It would not be described as surgically dangerous.'

She wondered whether he was implying that there might be other dangers, psychological problems arising from a complete alteration in appearance. She didn't expect any. She had coped with the implications of the scar for thirty-four years. She would cope with its disappearance.

He had asked whether she had any other questions. She said she had none. He rose and they shook hands, and for the first time he smiled. It transformed his face. He said, 'My secretary will send you the dates when I can fit you in at St Angela's for the tests. Will that present a problem? Will you be in London in the next two weeks?'

'I'll be in London.'

She followed Mrs Snelling into an office at the rear of the ground floor where a middle-aged woman gave her a brochure about the facilities at the Manor and set out the cost, both of the preparatory visit which, she explained, Mr Chandler-Powell thought would be helpful to patients but which wasn't, of course, obligatory, and the greater cost of the operation and a week's post-operative stay. She had expected the price to be high but the reality was beyond her estimate. No doubt the figures represented a social rather than a medical advantage. She seemed to remember over-hearing a woman say, 'Of course, I always go to the Manor,' as if this admitted her to a coterie of privileged patients. She knew she could have the operation under the NHS but there was a waiting list for non-urgent cases and she needed privacy. Speed and pri-vacy, in all fields, had become an expensive luxury.

She was shown out within half an hour of arriving. There was an hour to spare before she was due at the Ivy. She would walk.

4

The Ivy was too popular a restaurant to ensure anonymity but social discretion, in all other areas important to her, had never worried her where Robin was concerned. In an age where notoriety required increasingly scandalous indiscretions, even the most desperate gossip page would hardly waste a paragraph on the disclosure that Rhoda Gradwyn, the distinguished journalist, was lunching with a man twenty years younger than herself. She was used to him; he amused her. He opened up for her areas of life which she needed, however vicariously, to experience. And she was sorry for him. It was hardly the basis for intimacy and on her part there was none. He confided; she listened. She supposed that she must be gaining some satisfaction from the relationship or why was she still willing to let him appropriate even a restricted area of her life? When she thought about the friendship, which was seldom, it seemed a habit which imposed no more arduous obligations than an occasional lunch or dinner at her expense, and which it would be more time consuming and awkward to end than to continue.

He was waiting for her, as always, at his favourite table by the door, which she had booked, and as she entered she was able to observe him for half a minute before he raised his eyes from studying the menu and saw her. She was struck, as she always was, by his beauty. He himself seemed unconscious of it, yet it was difficult to believe that anyone so solipsistic could be unaware of the prize which genes and fate had bestowed on him or fail to take advantage of it. To an extent he had, but seeming hardly to care. She had always found it difficult to believe what experience had taught her, that men and women could be physically beautiful without also possessing some comparable qualities of mind and spirit, that beauty could be wasted on the mundane, the ignorant or the stupid. It was his looks, she suspected, which had helped gain Robin Boyton his place at drama school, his first engagements, his brief appearance in a television serial which promised much but ended after three episodes. Nothing ever lasted. Even the most indulgent or susceptible producer or director eventually became frustrated at lines not learnt, rehearsals not attended. When the acting failed, he pursued a number of imaginative initiatives, some of which might have succeeded had his enthusiasm lasted for more than six months. She had resisted his blandishments to invest in any of them and he took refusals without resentment. But refusals had never prevented him from trying again.

He got to his feet as she approached the table and, holding her hand, kissed her decorously on the cheek. She saw that the bottle of Meursault for which she, of course, would pay was already in the cooler, a third of it drunk.

He said, 'Lovely to see you, Rhoda. How did you get on with the great George?'

They never used endearments. Once he had called her darling but it was not a word he had ever dared to repeat. She said, 'The great George? Is that what they call Chandler-Powell at Cheverell Manor?'

'Not to his face. You look remarkably calm after your ordeal, but then you always do. What happened? I've been sitting here avid with anxiety.'

'Nothing happened. He saw me. He looked at my face. We made an appointment.'

'Didn't he impress you? He usually does.'

'His appearance is impressive. I wasn't with him long enough to make a character assessment. He seemed competent. Have you ordered?'

'Do I ever before you arrive? But I've concocted an inspired menu for both of us. I know what you like. I've been more imaginative than usual about the wine.'

Studying the wine list, she saw that he had been imaginative also about the cost.

They had hardly started on their first course when he introduced what was for him the purpose of the meeting. He said, 'I'm looking for some capital. Not much, a few grand. It's a first-rate investment opportunity, small risk – well, none really – and a guaranteed return. Jeremy estimates about ten per cent per annum. I wondered if you'd be interested.'

He described Jeremy Coxon as his business partner. Rhoda doubted whether he had ever been more than that. She had only met him once and had found him garrulous but harmless and not without sense. If he had any influence over Robin it was probably for the good.

She said, 'I'm always interested in a no-risk investment with a guaranteed return of ten per cent. I'm surprised you're not over-subscribed. What is it, this business you're involved in with Jeremy?'

'The same as I told you about when we had dinner in September. Well, things have moved on since then, but you remember the basic idea? It's really mine not Jeremy's, but we've worked on it together.'

'You mentioned that you and Jeremy Coxon were thinking of setting up some classes on etiquette for the newly rich who are socially insecure. Somehow I can't see you as a teacher – or indeed as an expert on etiquette.'

'I mug it up from books. It's surprisingly easy. And Jeremy is the expert so he has no trouble.'

'Couldn't your social incompetents get it from books themselves?'

'I suppose they could but they like the human touch. We give them confidence. That's what they're paying for. Rhoda, we've identified a real market opportunity. A lot of young people – well, young men mainly, and not only the rich – worry that they don't know what to wear for particular occasions, what to do if they're taking a girl out to a good restaurant for the first time. They're unsure about how to behave in company, how to impress the boss.

Jeremy has this house in Maida Vale which he bought with the money a rich aunt left him, so we're using it at present. We have to be discreet, of course. Jeremy isn't sure it can legitimately be used for business. We live in fear of the neighbours. One of the ground-floor rooms is set up as a restaurant and we use play-acting. After a bit, when they've got confidence, we take the clients to a genuine restaurant. Not this place, but others not too downmarket which give us special rates. The clients pay, of course. We're doing pretty well and the business is growing, but we need another house, or at least a flat. Jeremy is fed up with giving up virtually his ground floor and having these odd characters turning up when he wants to entertain his friends. And then there's the office. He's had to adapt one of the bedrooms for that. He's getting three-quarters of the profits because of the house but I know he feels it's time I paid him my share. Obviously we can't use my place. You know what the flat's like, hardly the ambiance we're looking for. Anyway, I may not be there for long. The landlord's becoming very disobliging about the rent. Once we get a separate address we'll be forging ahead. Well, what do you think, Rhoda? Interested?'

'Interested in hearing about it. Not interested in parting with any money. But it could succeed. It's more reasonable than most of your previous enthusiasms. Anyway, good luck.'

'So the answer's no.'

'The answer's no.' She added on impulse, 'You must wait for my will. I prefer to dispose of my charity after death. It's easier to contemplate parting with money when you'll have no further use for it yourself.'

She had left him twenty thousand pounds in her will, not sufficient to finance one of his more eccentric enthusiasms but enough to ensure that relief at being left anything would survive disappointment at the amount. It gave her pleasure to watch his face. She felt a small regret, too close to shame to be comfortable, that she had mischievously provoked and was enjoying his first flush of surprise and pleasure, the gleam of greed in his eyes and then the swift descent into realism. Why had she bothered merely to confirm once again what she already knew about him?

He said, 'You've definitely decided on Cheverell Manor, not one of Chandler-Powell's private beds at St Angela's?'

'I prefer to be out of London where there's a greater chance of peace and privacy. I'm making a preliminary overnight stay on the 27th. Apparently that's on offer. He likes his patients to be familiar with the place before he operates.'

'He likes the money, too.'

'So do you, Robin, so don't be censorious.'

Keeping his eyes on his plate, he said, 'I'm thinking of visiting the Manor while you're in residence. I thought you'd welcome a gossip. Convalescence is madly boring.'

'No, Robin, I won't welcome a gossip. I booked into the Manor specifically to ensure I'll be left alone. I imagine the staff there will see to it that I'm undisturbed. Isn't that the whole purpose of the place?'

'That's rather grudging of you, considering I recommended the Manor to you. Would you be going there if it weren't for me?'

'As you're not a doctor and have never had cosmetic surgery, I'm not sure what your recommendation would be worth. You have mentioned the Manor occasionally, but that's all. I had already heard of George Chandler-Powell. As he's recognised as one of the six best plastic surgeons in England, probably in Europe, and cosmetic surgery is becoming as fashionable as health farms, that's hardly surprising. I looked him up, compared his record, took expert advice and chose him. But you haven't told me what your connection is with Cheverell Manor. I'd better know in case I mention casually that I know you and am met with stony stares and relegation to the worst bedroom.'

'That could happen. I'm not exactly their favourite visitor. I don't actually stay in the house – that would be going a bit far for both parties. They've got a cottage for visitors, Rose Cottage, and I book in there. I have to pay, too, which I think is a bit much. They don't even send over the food. I don't usually get a vacancy in summer but they can hardly claim the cottage isn't free in December.'

'You said you were some kind of relation.'

'Not of Chandler-Powell. His surgical assistant, Marcus Westhall, is my cousin. He assists with the operations and looks after the patients when the great George is in London. Marcus lives there with his sister, Candace, in the other cottage. She doesn't have anything to do with the patients; she helps in the office. I'm their only living relation. You'd have thought that that would mean something to them.'

'And it doesn't?'

'I'd better tell you some family history if it won't bore you. It goes back a long way. I'll try to make it brief. It's about money, of course.'

'It usually is.'

'It's a sad, sad story about a poor orphan boy who's thrown penniless on the world. It's a pity to wrench your heart with it now. I wouldn't like salt tears to fall into your delicious dressed crab.'

'I'll take the risk. It's as well to know something about the place before I go.'

'I wondered what lay behind this invitation to lunch. If you want to go prepared, you've come to the right person. Well worth the cost of a good meal.'

He spoke without rancour but his smile was amused. She reminded herself that it was never prudent to underestimate him. He had never before spoken to her about his family history or his past. For a man so ready to communicate the minutiae of his daily existence, his small triumphs and more common failures in love and business, recounted usually with humour, he was remarkably unforthcoming about his early life. Rhoda suspected that his childhood might have been deeply unhappy and that this early trauma, from which no one totally recovers, could be at the root of his insecurity. Since she had no intention of responding to confidences with a reciprocal candour, his was a life she had had no compulsion to explore. But there were things about Cheverell Manor which it would be useful to know in advance. She would come to the Manor as a patient and, for her, this implied vulnerability and a certain physical and emotional subservience. To arrive unbriefed was to put oneself at a disadvantage from the start.

She said, 'Tell me about your cousins.'

'They're comfortably off, at least by my standards, and about to be very rich by anyone's standards. Their father, my Uncle Peregrine, died nine months ago and left them about eight million between them. He inherited from his father, Theodore, who died only a few weeks before him. The family fortune came from him. You have probably heard of T. R. Westhall's *Latin Primer* and *First Steps in Learning Greek* – something like that anyway. I didn't come across them myself, I wasn't at that kind of school. Anyway, textbooks, if they become standard, hallowed by long use, are amazingly good earners. Never out of print. And the old man was good with money. He had the knack of making it grow.'

Rhoda said, 'I'm surprised there's so much for your cousins to inherit with two deaths so close together, father and grandfather. The death duties must have been horrendous.'

'Old Grandfather Theodore had thought of that. I told you he was clever with money. He took out some form of insurance before his last illness started. Anyway, the money's there. They'll get it as soon as probate is granted.'

'And you'd like a part of it.'

'Frankly, I think I deserve a part of it. Theodore Westhall had two children, Peregrine and Sophie. Sophie was my mother. Her marriage to Keith Boyton was never popular with her father, in fact I believe he tried to stop it. He thought Keith was a gold-digging indolent nonentity who was only after the family money, and to be honest he probably wasn't far wrong. Poor Mummy died when I was seven. I was brought up – well, it was more like being dragged around – by my dad. Anyway, in the end he gave up and dumped me into that Dotheboys Hall of a boarding school. An improvement on Dickens, but not much. A charity paid the fees, such as they were. It was no school for a pretty boy, particularly one with the label *charity child* hung round his neck.'

He was grasping his wineglass as if it were a grenade, his knuckles white. For a moment Rhoda feared that it would shatter in his hand. Then he loosened his grip, smiled at her and raised the glass to his lips. He said, 'From the time of Mummy's marriage the

Boytons were cut off from the family. The Westhalls never forget and they never forgive.'

'Where is he now, your father?'

'Frankly, Rhoda, I haven't the slightest idea. He emigrated to Australia when I won my scholarship to drama school. We haven't been in touch since. He may be married or dead or both for all I know. We were never what you'd call close. And he didn't even support us. Poor Mummy learnt to type and went out to earn a pittance in a typing pool. An odd expression, typing pool. I don't think they have them now. Poor Mummy's was particularly muddy.'

'I thought you said you were an orphan.'

'Possibly I am. Anyway, if my father's not dead, he's hardly present. Not even a postcard for eight years. If he isn't dead he'll be getting on. He was fifteen years older than my mother, so that makes him over sixty.'

'So he's unlikely to appear demanding a little financial help from the legacy.'

'Well, he wouldn't get it if he did. I haven't seen the will but when I rang the family solicitor – just out of interest, you understand – he told me he wouldn't give me a copy of it. He said I could get a copy when probate had been granted. I don't think I'll bother. The Westhalls would leave money to a cats' home before they left a penny to a Boyton. My claim is on the grounds of justice, not legality. I'm their cousin. I've kept in touch. They've got more than enough cash to spare and they'll be very rich once probate is granted. It wouldn't hurt them to show a little generosity now. That's why I visit. I like to remind them that I exist. Uncle Peregrine only survived thirty-five days after Grandfather. I bet old Theodore hung on as long as he could just in the hope of outliving his son. I don't know what would have happened if Uncle Peregrine had died first, but whatever the legal complications, nothing would have come to me.'

Rhoda said, 'Your cousins must have been anxious though. There's a clause in all wills saying that the legatee has to survive twenty-eight days after the death of the testator if he is to inherit.

I imagine they took good care to keep their father alive – that is if he did survive for those vital eight days. Perhaps they popped him into a freezer and produced him nice and fresh on the appropriate day. That's the plot of a book by a detective novelist, Cyril Hare. I think it's called *Untimely Death*, but it may have been published originally under a different name. I can't remember much about it. I read it years ago. He was an elegant writer.'

He was silent and she saw that he poured the wine as if his thoughts were elsewhere. She thought with amusement and some concern, *My God, is he really taking this nonsense seriously?* If so, and he started pursuing it, the accusation was likely to finish him with his cousins. She could think of few allegations more likely to close Rose Cottage and Cheverell Manor to him for ever than an accusation of fraud. The novel had come unexpectedly to mind and she had spoken without thinking. That he should take her words seriously was bizarre.

He said, as if shaking it off, 'The idea is daft, of course.'

'Of course it is. What do you envisage, Candace and Marcus Westhall turning up at the hospital while their father is *in extremis*, insisting on taking him home and popping him into a convenient freezer the moment he dies, then thawing him out eight days later?'

'They wouldn't need to go to hospital. Candace nursed him at home for the last two years. The two old men, Grandfather Theodore and Uncle Peregrine, were in the same nursing home outside Bournemouth but were such a trial to the nursing staff that the management said one of them would have to go. Peregrine demanded to be taken in by Candace and there he stayed to the last, looked after by a doddery local GP. I never saw him during those last two years. He refused all visitors. It could have worked.'

She said, 'Not really. Tell me about the other people at the Manor apart from your cousins. The main ones, anyway. Whom shall I meet?'

'Well, there's the great George himself, naturally. Then there's the queen bee of the nursing services, Sister Flavia Holland – very sexy if uniforms turn you on. I won't worry you with the other nursing staff. Most of them come in by car from Wareham, Bournemouth or Poole. The anaesthetist was an NHS consultant who took as much as he could stomach from the Health Service and retired to an agreeable little cottage on the Purbeck coast. A part-time job at the Manor suits him very well. And then, more interestingly, there's Helena Haverland, née Cressett. She's called the general administrator, which covers practically everything from housekeeping to keeping an eye on the books. She came to the Manor after her divorce six years ago. The intriguing thing about Helena is her name. Her father, Sir Nicholas Cressett, sold the Manor to George after the Lloyd's debacle. He was in a wrong syndicate and lost everything. When George advertised the job of general administrator Helena Cressett applied and got it. Anyone more sensitive than George wouldn't have taken her on. But she knew the house intimately and, I gather, she's made herself indispensable, which is clever of her. She disapproves of me.'

'How unreasonable of her.'

'Yes, isn't it? But then I think she disapproves of practically everyone. There's a certain amount of family hauteur there. After all, her family owned the Manor for nearly four hundred years. Oh, and I should mention the two cooks, Dean and Kim Bostock. George must have filched them from somewhere rather good, I'm told the food is excellent, but I've never been invited to taste it. Then there's Mrs Frensham, Helena's old governess, who's in charge of the office. She's the widow of a C-of-E priest and looks the part, so it's rather like having an uncomfortable public conscience on two legs stalking the place to remind one of one's sins. And there's a strange girl they've picked up from somewhere, Sharon Bateman, who's a kind of runner doing unspecified jobs in the kitchen and for Miss Cressett. She mooches around carrying trays. That's about all as far as you'll be concerned.'

'How do you know all this, Robin?'

'By keeping eyes and ears open when I'm drinking with the locals in the village pub, the Cressett Arms. I'm the only one who does. Not that they're given to gossiping with strangers. Contrary to common belief, villagers don't. But I pick up a few unconsidered trifles. The Cressett family in the late seventeenth century had a fiendish row with the local parson and no longer went to church. The village sided with the parson and the feud continued down the centuries, as they often do. George Chandler-Powell has done nothing to heal it. Actually it suits him. The patients go there for privacy and he doesn't want a lot of chat about them in the village. A couple of village women come in as part of the house-cleaning team, but most of the staff come from further afield. And then there's old Mog – Mr Mogworthy. He worked as gardener-handy-man for the Cressetts and George has kept him on. He's a mine of information if you know how to get it out of him.'

'I don't believe it.'

'Believe what?'

'I don't believe that name. It's totally fictitious. Nobody can be called Mogworthy.'

'He is. He tells me there was a parson of that name at Holy Trinity Church, Bradpole, in the late fifteenth century. Mogworthy claims to be descended from him.'

'He could hardly be. If the first Mogworthy was a priest, he would be a Roman Catholic celibate.'

'Well, descended from the same family. Anyway, there he is. He used to live in the cottage which Marcus and Candace now occupy, but George wanted the cottage and kicked him out. He's now with his aged sister in the village. Yes, Mog's a mine of information. Dorset is full of legends, most of them horrific, and Mog is the expert. Actually he wasn't born in the county. All his forebears were but his dad moved to Lambeth before Mog was born. Get him to tell you about the Cheverell Stones.'

'I've never heard of them.'

'Oh, you will if Mog's around. And you can hardly miss them. It's a Neolithic circle in a field next to the Manor. The story is rather horrible.'

'Tell me.'

'No, I'll leave it to Mog or Sharon. Mog says she's obsessed with the stones.'

The waiter was serving their main courses and Robin was silent, contemplating the food with gratified approval. She sensed he was losing interest in Cheverell Manor. The talk became desultory, his mind obviously elsewhere until they were drinking their coffee. Then he turned his eyes on her and she was struck again by the depth and clarity of their almost inhuman blueness. The power of his concentrated gaze was unnerving. Stretching his hand across the table, he said, 'Rhoda, come back to the flat this afternoon. Now. Please. It's important. We need to talk.'

'We have been talking.'

'Mostly about you and the Manor. Not about us.'

'Isn't Jeremy expecting you? Shouldn't you be instructing your clients on how to cope with terrifying waiters and corked wine?'

'The ones I teach mostly come in the evening. Please, Rhoda.'

She bent to pick up her bag. 'I'm sorry, Robin, but it's not possible. I've a lot to get through before I go to the Manor.'

'It is possible, it's always possible. You mean you don't want to come.'

'It's possible, but at the moment it isn't convenient. Let's talk after the operation.'

'That might be too late.'

'Too late for what?'

'For a lot of things. Can't you see that I'm terrified that you might be planning to chuck me? You're making a big change, aren't you? Perhaps you're thinking of getting rid of more than your scar.'

It was the first time in the six years of their relationship that they had ever spoken the word. A taboo never acknowledged between them had been broken. Getting up from the table, the bill paid, she tried to keep the note of outrage from her voice. Without looking at him, she said, 'I'm sorry, Robin. We'll talk after the operation. I'll be taking a cab back to the City. Is there anywhere that you would like to be dropped?' That was usual. He never travelled by underground.

The word, she realised, had been unfortunate. He shook his head but didn't reply and followed her in silence to the door. Outside, turning to take their different ways, he suddenly said,

'When I say goodbye I always fear that I may not see that person again. When my mother went to work I used to watch from the window. I was terrified that she might never come home. Do you ever feel that?'

'Not unless the person I'm parting from is over ninety and frail or suffering from a terminal illness. I'm neither.'

But as they finally parted she paused and for the first time turned to watch his retreating back until he was out of sight. She had no dread of the operation, no premonition of death. Mr Chandler-Powell had said that there was always some risk in a general anaesthetic, but in expert hands that could be discounted. Yet, as he disappeared and she turned away, she shared for a moment Robin's irrational fear.

5

By two o'clock on Tuesday 27 November Rhoda was ready to leave for her first visit to Cheverell Manor. Her outstanding assignments had been completed and delivered on time, as they always were. She was never able to leave home even for a single night without rigorous cleaning, tidying, emptying of bins, locking up of papers in her study and a final check of internal doors and windows. Whatever place she called home had to be immaculate before she left, as if this punctiliousness could guarantee that she would return safely.

She had been sent instructions for the drive to Dorset with the brochure about the Manor, but as always with an unfamiliar route, she listed the route on a card to be placed on the dashboard. The morning had been fitfully sunny but, despite her late start, getting out of London had been slow and by the time, nearly two hours later, she left the M3 and had joined the Ringwood road, darkness was already falling and with it came heavy squalls of rain which within seconds became a downpour. The windscreen wipers, jerking like living things, were powerless to cope with the flood. She could see nothing ahead but the shine of her headlights on rippling water which was fast becoming a small torrent. She saw few other car lights. It was hopeless to try to drive on and she peered out through a wall of rain, looking for a grass verge which might offer firm standing. Within minutes she was able to drive cautiously on to a few yards of level ground fronting a heavy farm gate. At least here there would be no risk of a hidden ditch or soft wheel-sucking mud. She turned off the engine and listened to the rain battering the roof like a hail of bullets. Under the assault the

BMW held a cloistered metallic peace which intensified the tumult outside. She knew that beyond the cropped invisible hedgerows lay some of the most beautiful countryside in England, but now she felt immured in an immensity both alien and potentially unfriendly. She had switched off her mobile phone, as always with relief. No one in the world knew where she was or could reach her. No cars passed and, peering through the windscreen, she saw only the wall of water and, beyond it, trembling smudges of light which marked the distant houses. Usually she welcomed silence and was able to discipline her imagination. She contemplated the coming operation without fear while recognising that she had some rational cause for anxiety; to be given a general anaesthetic was never without risk. But now she was aware of an unease which went deeper than worry about either this preliminary visit or the impending surgery. It was, she realised, too close to superstition to be comfortable, as if some reality formerly unknown to her or thrust out of consciousness was gradually making its presence felt and demanding to be recognised.

It was useless to listen to music above the competing tumult of the storm, so she slid back her seat and closed her eyes. Memories, some old, some more recent, flooded into her mind unresisted. She relived once again the day in May six months ago which had brought her to this journey, this stretch of deserted road. Her mother's letter had arrived with a delivery of boring post: circulars, notifications of meetings she had no intention of attending, bills. Letters from her mother were even rarer than their brief telephone conversations and she took up the envelope, more square and thicker than the ones her mother normally used, with a slight foreboding that something could be wrong – illness, problems with the bungalow, her presence needed. But it was a wedding invitation. The card, printed in ornate script surrounded by pictures of wedding bells, announced that Mrs Ivy Gradwyn and Mr Ronald Brown hoped that their friends would join them to celebrate their wedding. The date, time and name of the church were given and a hotel at which guests would be welcome at the reception. A note in her mother's handwriting said, *Do come if you can,*

Rhoda. I don't know whether I've mentioned Ronald in my letters. He's a widower and his wife was a great friend of mine. He's looking forward to meeting you.

She remembered her emotions, surprise followed by relief, of which she was slightly ashamed, that this marriage could remove a part of her responsibility for her mother, might lessen her guilt over her infrequent letters and telephone calls and even rarer meetings. They met as polite but wary strangers still inhibited by the things they couldn't say, the memories they took care not to provoke. She couldn't remember hearing about Ronald and had no desire to meet him, but this was an invitation she had an obligation to accept.

And now she consciously relived that portentous day which had promised only boredom dutifully endured but which had led her to this rain-lashed moment and to all that lay ahead. She had set off in good time but a lorry had overturned, shedding its load on the motorway, and when she arrived outside the church, a gaunt Victorian Gothic building, she heard the reedy uncertain singing of what must be the last hymn. She waited in the car a little way down the street until the congregation, mainly middle aged or elderly, had emerged. A car with white ribbons had drawn up but she was too distant to see her mother or the bridegroom. She followed the car, with others leaving the church, to the hotel, which was some four miles further down the coast, a much-turreted Edwardian building flanked by bungalows and backed by a golf course. A profusion of dark beams on the façade suggested that the architect had intended mock Tudor but had been seduced by hubris to add a central cupola and a Palladian front door.

The reception hall had an air of long-faded grandeur, curtains of red damask hung in ornate pleats and the carpet looked grimed as with decades of dust. She joined the stream of fellow guests who, a little uncertainly, were moving to a room at the rear which proclaimed its function by a board and printed notice: *Function room available for private parties.* For a moment she paused in the doorway, irresolute, then entered and saw her mother at once. She was standing with her bridegroom surrounded by a little group of chattering women. Rhoda's entrance was almost unnoticed, but she edged through them and saw her mother's face breaking into a tentative smile. It had been four years since they had met but she looked younger and happier, and after a few seconds kissed Rhoda on the right cheek a little hesitantly then turned to the man at her side. He was old – at least seventy, Rhoda judged – rather shorter than her mother with a soft round-cheeked, pleasant but anxious face. He seemed a little confused and her mother had to repeat Rhoda's name twice before he smiled and held out his hand. There were general introductions. The guests resolutely ignored the scar. A few scampering children gazed at it boldly, then ran off shouting through the French windows to play outside. Rhoda remembered snatches of conversation. 'Your mother speaks of you so often.' 'She's very proud of you.' 'It's good of you to come so far.' 'Lovely day for it, isn't it? Nice to see her so happy.'

The food and the service were better than she had expected. The cloth on the long table was immaculate, the cups and plates shone and her first bite confirmed that the ham in the sandwiches was fresh off the bone. Three middle-aged women dressed as parlour maids served them with a disarming cheerfulness. Strong tea was poured from an immense pot and, after a certain amount of whispering between the bride and groom, a variety of drinks was brought in from the bar. The conversation, which had so far been as hushed as if they had recently attended a funeral, became more lively and glasses, some containing liquids of a highly ominous hue, were raised. After much anxious consultation between her mother and the barman, champagne flutes were brought in with some ceremony. There was to be a toast.

The proceedings were in the hands of the vicar who had conducted the service, a red-haired young man who, divested of his cassock, now wore a dog collar with grey trousers and a sports jacket. He gently patted the air as if to subdue a hubbub and made a brief speech. Ronald, apparently, was the church organist and there was some laboured humour about pulling out all the stops and the two of them living in harmony to their lives' end, interspersed with small harmless jokes, now unremembered, which had been greeted by the braver of the guests with embarrassed laughter.

There was a crush at the table so, plate in hand, she moved over to the window, grateful for the moment when the guests, obviously hungry for the food, were unlikely to accost her. She watched them with a pleasurable mixture of critical observation and sardonic amusement – the men in their best suits, some now a little stretched over rounded stomachs and broadening backs; the women, who had obviously made efforts and had seen an opportunity for a new outfit. Most, like her mother, were wearing floral summer dresses with matching jackets, their straw hats in pastel colours sitting incongruously on newly set hair. They could, she thought, have looked much the same in the 1930s and '40s. She was discomforted by a new and unwelcome emotion compounded of pity and anger. She thought, *I don't belong here, I'm not happy with them, nor they with me. Their embarrassed mutual politeness can't bridge the gap between us. But this is where I came from, these are my people, the upper working class merging into the middle class, that amorphous unregarded group who fought the country's wars, paid their taxes, clung to what remained of their traditions.* They had lived to see their simple patriotism derided, their morality despised, their savings devalued. They caused no trouble. Millions of pounds of public money wasn't regularly siphoned into their neighbourhoods in the hope of bribing, cajoling or coercing them into civic virtue. If they protested that their cities had become alien, their children taught in overcrowded schools where ninety per cent of the children spoke no English, they were lectured about the cardinal sin of racism by those more expensively and comfortably circumstanced. Unprotected by accountants, they were the milch-cows of the rapacious Revenue. No lucrative industry of social concern and psychological analysis had grown up to analyse and condone their inadequacies on the grounds of deprivation or poverty. Perhaps she should write about them before she finally relinquished journalism, but she knew that, with more interesting and lucrative challenges ahead, she never would. They had no place in her plans for her future just as they had no place in her life.

Her last memory was of standing alone with her mother in the women's cloakroom, gazing at their two profiles in a long mirror above a vase of artificial flowers.

Her mother said, 'Ronald likes you, I could see that. I'm glad you could come.'

'So am I. I liked him too. I hope you'll both be very happy.'

'I'm sure we shall. We've known each other for four years now. His wife sang in the choir. Lovely alto voice – unusual in a woman really. We've always got on, Ron and I. He's so kind.' Her voice was complacent. Gazing critically into the mirror she adjusted her hat.

Rhoda said, 'Yes, he looks kind.'

'Oh he is. He's no trouble. And I know that this is what Rita would have wanted. She more or less hinted at it to me before she died. Ron has never been good at being alone. And we shall be all right – for money I mean. He's going to sell his house and move into the bungalow with me. That seems sensible now that he's seventy. So that standing order you have – the five hundred pounds a month – you don't have to go on with that, Rhoda.'

'I should leave it as it is, that is unless Ronald isn't happy about it.'

'It isn't that. A little bit extra always comes in useful. I just thought you might need it yourself.'

She turned and touched Rhoda's left cheek, a touch so soft that Rhoda was only conscious of the fingers shaking in a gentle tremble against the scar. She closed her eyes, willing herself not to flinch. But she didn't draw back.

Her mother said, 'He wasn't a bad man, Rhoda. It was the drink. You oughtn't to blame him. It was an illness, and he loved you really. That money he sent you after you left home – it wasn't easy finding it. He spent nothing on himself.'

Rhoda thought, *Except on drink*, but she didn't speak the words. She had never thanked her father for that weekly five pounds, had never spoken to him after she left home.

Her mother's voice seemed to come out of a silence. 'Remember those walks in the park?'

She remembered the walks in the suburban park when it seemed always autumn, the straight gravelled paths, the rectangular or round flowerbeds thick with the discordant colours of dahlias, a flower she hated, walking beside her father, neither speaking.

Her mother said, 'He was all right when he wasn't drinking.'

'I don't remember him when he wasn't drinking.' Had she spoken those words or only thought them?

'It wasn't easy for him, working for the council. I know he was lucky to get that job after he'd been sacked from the law firm, but it was beneath him. He was clever, Rhoda, that's where you get your brains. He won a scholarship to university and he came in first.'

'You mean he got a first?'

'I think that's what he said. Anyway, it means he was clever. That's why he was so proud when you got into the grammar school.'

'I never knew he'd been to university. He never told me.'

'Well he wouldn't, would he? He thought you weren't interested. He wasn't one for talking, not about himself.'

None of them had been. Those outbursts of violence, the impotent rage, the shame, had done for them all. The important things had been unsayable. And looking into her mother's face, she asked herself how could she begin now? She thought her mother was right. It couldn't have been easy for her father to find that five-pound note week after week. It had come with a few words, sometimes in shaky handwriting, which simply said, *With love from Father*. She had taken the money because she needed it and had thrown away the paper. With the casual cruelty of an adolescent she had judged him unworthy to offer her his love, which she had always known was a more difficult gift than money. Perhaps the truth was that she hadn't been worthy to receive it. For over thirty years she had nursed her contempt, her resentment and, yes, her hatred. But that muddy Essex stream, that lonely death, had put him out of her power for ever. It was herself she had harmed and to recognise this might be the beginning of healing.

Her mother said, 'It's never too late to find someone to love.

36

You're a handsome woman, Rhoda, you should do something about that scar.'

Words she had never expected to hear. Words which no one since Miss Farrell had dared to speak. She remembered little of what happened afterwards, only her own reply spoken quietly and without emphasis.

'I shall get rid of it.'

She must fitfully have dozed. Now she woke into full consciousness with a start to find that the rain had passed. Darkness had fallen. Glancing at the dashboard, she saw that it was four fifty-five. She had been on the road for nearly three hours. In the unexpected quiet the noise of the engine as she bumped cautiously from the verge jarred the silent air. The rest of the journey was easy. The turns of the road came where expected and her headlights on the signposts lit up reassuring names. Sooner than expected she saw the name Stoke Cheverell, and turned right for the final mile. The village street was deserted, lights shone behind drawn curtains and only the corner shop with its bright crowded window, through which two or three late shoppers could be dimly seen, showed signs of life. And now there was the sign she was looking for, Cheverell Manor. The great iron gates stood open. She was expected. She drove down the short avenue which widened into a half-circle, and the house was before her.

There had been a picture of Cheverell Manor in the brochure handed to her after her first consultation, but it was only a pale-coloured similitude of the reality. In her headlights she saw the outline of the house, seeming larger than she had expected, a dark mass against the darker sky. It stretched each side of a large central gable with two windows above. These showed a pale light, but most were blank except for four large mullioned windows to the left of the door which were brightly lit. As she drove carefully and parked under the trees the door opened and a strong light streamed out over the gravel.

Switching off the engine, she got out and opened the back door for her overnight case, the cold damp air a welcome release after the drive. A male figure appeared in the doorway and moved towards her. Although the rain had stopped, he was wearing a plastic mackintosh with a hood that reached over his head like a baby's bonnet, giving him the look of a malevolent child. He walked firmly and his voice was strong but she could see that he was no longer young. He took the case firmly from her and said, 'If you give me the key, madam, I'll park the car for you. Miss Cressett doesn't like to see cars parked outside. They're expecting you.'

She handed over the key and followed him into the house. The unease, the slight sense of disorientation she had felt sitting alone in the storm, was still with her. Drained of emotion, she felt only a mild relief at having arrived and, as she passed into the wide hall with its central staircase, she was aware of a need to be again solitary, relieved of the necessity of shaking hands, of a formal welcome, when all she wanted was the silence of her own home and, later, the familiar comfort of her bed.

The entrance hall was impressive – she had expected it to be – but it was not welcoming. Her suitcase was placed at the foot of the stairs and then, opening a door to the left, the man announced loudly, 'Miss Gradwyn, Miss Cressett,' and, picking up her suitcase, made for the stairs.

She entered the room and found herself in a great hall which brought back pictures seen perhaps in childhood or on visits to other country houses. After the darkness outside, it was full of light and colour. High above, the arched timbers were blackened with age. Linen-fold panelling covered the lower part of the walls and, above it, a row of portraits, Tudor, Regency, Victorian faces, celebrated with varying talents, some, she suspected, owing their place more to family piety than artistic merit. Facing her was a stone fireplace with a coat of arms, also in stone, above it. A wood fire was crackling in the grate, the dancing flames casting gules over the three figures who rose to meet her.

They had obviously been sitting having tea, the two linen-covered armchairs set at right angles to the fire, the only modern furniture in the room. Between them a low table held a tray with the remains of the meal. The welcoming party consisted of a man and two women, although the word 'welcome' was hardly appropriate since she felt like an intruder inconveniently late for tea and awaited without enthusiasm.

The taller of the two women made the introduction. She said, 'I'm Helena Cressett. We have spoken. I'm glad you've got here safely. We've had a bad storm but sometimes they're very local. You may have escaped it. May I introduce Flavia Holland, the theatre sister, and Marcus Westhall who will assist Mr Chandler-Powell with your operation.'

They shook hands, faces creased into smiles. Rhoda's impression of new people was always immediate and strong, a visual image implanted on her mind, never to be totally erased, bringing with it a perception of basic character which time and closer acquaintanceship might, as she knew, be shown to be perversely and sometimes dangerously misleading, but which rarely was. Now, tired, her perception a little dulled, she saw them almost as stereotypes. Helena Cressett in a well-tailored trouser suit with a turtleneck jumper which avoided looking too smart for wearing in the country while proclaiming that it hadn't been bought off a peg. No make-up except for lipstick; fine pale hair with a hint of auburn framing high prominent cheekbones; a nose a little too long for beauty; a face one might describe as handsome but certainly not pretty. Remarkable grey eyes regarded her with more curiosity than formal kindliness. Rhoda thought, *ex-head girl, now headmistress – or, more probably, principal of an Oxbridge college*. Her handshake was firm, the new girl being welcomed with circumspection, all judgement deferred.

Sister Holland was less formally dressed in jeans, a black jumper and a suede jerkin, comfort clothes proclaiming that she had been released from the impersonal uniform of her job and was now off duty. She was dark haired, with a bold face that conveyed a confident sexuality. Her glance, from bright large-pupilled eyes so dark that they were almost black, took in the scar as if mentally assessing how much trouble could be expected from this new patient.

Mr Westhall was surprising. He was slightly built with a high forehead and a sensitive face, the face of a poet or academic rather than a surgeon. She felt none of the power or confidence which had so strongly emanated from Mr Chandler-Powell. His smile was warmer than those of the women but his hand, despite the warmth of the fire, was cold.

Helena Cressett said, 'You must be ready for tea, or perhaps for something stronger. Would you like it here or in your own sitting room? Either way, I'll take you there now so that you can settle in.'

Rhoda said that she would prefer to have tea in her room. They mounted the broad uncarpeted stairs together and passed down a corridor lined with maps and what looked like earlier pictures of the house. Rhoda's suitcase had been placed outside a door midway down the patients' corridor. Picking it up, Miss Cressett opened the door and stood aside as Rhoda entered. The two rooms allocated to her were shown to her by Miss Cressett rather, she thought, as a hotelier might briefly indicate the conveniences of a hotel suite, a routine too often undertaken to be more than a duty.

Rhoda saw that the sitting room was both agreeable in its proportions and beautifully furnished, obviously in period furniture. Most of it looked Georgian. There was a mahogany bureau with a desk large enough for comfortable writing. The only modern furniture were the two armchairs before the fireplace and a tall angled reading lamp beside one of them. To the left of the fire there was a modern television on a stand with a DVD player on a shelf beneath it, an incongruous but presumably necessary addition to a room which was both distinctive and welcoming.

They moved next door. Here was the same elegance, with any suggestion of a sickroom rigorously excluded. Miss Cressett placed Rhoda's suitcase on a folding stand, then, walking over to the window, drew the curtains. She said, 'At present it's too dark to see anything but you'll be able to in the morning. We'll meet again then. Now, if you have everything you want, I'll send up the tea and the menu for breakfast tomorrow. If you prefer to come down rather than have it in your room, dinner is served in the dining room at eight o'clock but we meet in the library at seven thirty for a pre-dinner drink. If you'd like to join us, ring my number – all the extensions are on the card by the telephone – and someone will come up to escort you down.' And then she was gone.

But for now Rhoda had seen enough of Cheverell Manor and hadn't the energy to engage in the to and fro of dinner conversation. She would request dinner in her room and have an early night. Gradually she took possession of a room to which, she already knew, she would return in just over two weeks' time without foreboding or apprehension.

6

It was six forty on the same Tuesday before George Chandler-Powell had finished his list of private patients at St Angela's Hospital. Pulling off his operating gown, he felt paradoxically both exhausted and restless. He had started early and worked without a break, which was unusual but necessary if he were to get through his London list of private patients before leaving for his customary Christmas holiday in New York. Since his early childhood Christmas had become a horror to him and he never spent it in England. His ex-wife, now married to an American financier well able to maintain her in the state both she and he regarded as reasonable for a very beautiful woman, held strong views about the necessity of all divorces being what she described as 'civilised'. Chandler-Powell suspected that the word applied solely to the generosity or otherwise of the financial settlement, but with the USA fortune secured she had been able to substitute the public appearance of generosity for the more mundane satisfaction of monetary gain. They liked seeing each other once a year and he enjoyed New York and the programme of civilised entertainment Selina and her husband organised for him. He never stayed longer than a week before flying to Rome where he stayed in the same *pensione* outside the city he had first visited when at Oxford, was quietly welcomed and saw no one. But the annual visit to New York had become a habit, and one which at present he saw no reason to break.

He was not due to arrive at the Manor until Wednesday night for the first operating session on Thursday morning but two NHS wards had that morning been closed because of infection and the next day's list had had to be postponed. Now, back in his Barbican flat and looking out at the lights of the City, the wait seemed interminable. He needed to get out of London, to sit in the great hall at the Manor before a wood fire, to walk in the lime avenue, to breathe a less cluttered air, with the taste of wood smoke, earth and mulched leaves on the unencumbered breeze. He flung what he needed for the next few days into a grip with the careless exhilaration of a schoolboy released for the holidays and, too impatient to wait for the lift, ran down the stairs to the garage and his waiting Mercedes. There was the usual problem getting free of the City but once on the motorway the pleasure and relief of movement took over, as it invariably did when he drove alone at night, and disconnected thoughts of the past, like a series of brown and fading photographs, came untroubling to mind. He slotted a CD of Bach's Violin Concerto in D Minor into the player and, with his hands lightly on the wheel, let the music and the memories merge in a contemplative calm.

On his fifteenth birthday he had come to conclusions about three matters which from childhood had increasingly exercised his thoughts. He decided that God didn't exist, that he didn't love his parents and that he would become a surgeon. The first required no action on his part, merely the acceptance that since neither help nor comfort could be expected from a supernatural being, his life was subject like any other to time and chance and that it was up to him to take such control as he could. The second required little more of him. And when, with some embarrassment – and on his mother's part some shame – they broke the news to him that they were thinking of divorce, he expressed regret – that seemed only proper – while subtly encouraging them to end a marriage that was obviously producing unhappiness for all three of them. The school holidays would be a great deal more pleasant if not disrupted by sullen silences or rancorous outbursts. When they were killed in a road accident while on a holiday planned in the hope of a reconciling fresh start – there had been several such – he was visited for a moment by a fear that there might be a power as strong as the one he had rejected, but more ruthless and possessed of a certain sardonic humour, before telling himself that it was folly to abandon a benign superstition in favour of one less accommodating, possibly even malign. His third conclusion remained as an ambition: he would rely on the ascertainable facts of science and concentrate on becoming a surgeon.

His parents had left him little but their debts. That hardly mattered. He had always spent most of his summer holidays with his widowed grandfather in Bournemouth and now this became his home. As far as he was capable of strong human affection, it was Herbert Chandler-Powell that he loved. He would have been fond of him even had the old man been poor, but was glad that he was rich. He had made a fortune by a talent for designing elegant and original cardboard boxes. It became prestigious for a company to deliver its goods in a Chandler-Powell container, for presents to be wrapped in a box with the distinctive C-P colophon. Herbert discovered and promoted new young designers and some of the boxes, issued in limited numbers, became collectors' items. His firm needed no advertisement beyond the goods they produced. When he was sixty-five and George was ten he sold the business to his largest competitor and retired with his millions. It was he who paid for George's expensive education, saw him through Oxford, required nothing in return but his grandson's company in the holidays from school and university, and later for three or four visits a year. For George these requirements had never been an imposition. Walking or driving together he would listen to his grandfather's voice reciting stories of his depressed childhood, commercial triumphs, the Oxford years. Before George himself went up to Oxford his grandfather had been more specific. Now that remembered voice, strong and authoritative, broke through the high trembling beauty of the violins.

'I was a grammar-school boy, you see, there on a county scholarship. Difficult for you to understand. Things may be different now, although I doubt it. Not that different. I wasn't mocked or despised or made to feel different, I just *was* different. I never felt I belonged there – and, of course, I didn't. I knew from the first that I had no right to be there, that something in the air of those quads rejected me. I wasn't the only one to feel that, of course. There were boys not from grammar schools but from the less prestigious public schools, places they tried not to mention. I could see it. They were the ones avid to be admitted to that golden group of the privileged upper class. I used to imagine them, edging their way with brains and talent into the Boars Hill academic dinner parties, performing like court jesters at the country weekend parties, offering their pathetic verses, their wit and their cleverness to buy their way in. I hadn't any talent except intelligence. I despised them, but I knew what they respected, all of them. Money, my boy, that's what mattered. Breeding was important, but breeding with money was better. And I made money. It will come to you in time, what's left after a rapacious government has extracted its loot. Make good use of it.'

Herbert's hobby was visiting stately homes open to the public, motoring to them by carefully devised circuitous routes with the aid of unreliable maps, driving his immaculate Rolls-Royce, as upright as the Victorian general he resembled. He travelled magisterially down country roads and little-used lanes, George at his side reading aloud from the guidebook. He thought it strange that a man so responsive to Georgian elegance and Tudor solidity should live in a penthouse in Bournemouth, even if the sea view was spectacular. In time he came to understand why. His grandfather, approaching old age, had simplified his life. He was looked after by a generously paid cook, housekeeper and general cleaner who came in by the day, did their work efficiently and quietly and left. His furniture was expensive but minimal. He neither collected nor coveted the artefacts which were his enthusiasm. He could admire without wanting to possess. George from an early age knew himself to be a possessor.

And the first time they visited Cheverell Manor he knew that this was the house he wanted. It lay before him in the mellow sunshine of an early autumn day when the shadows were beginning to lengthen and trees, lawns and stone took on a richer intensity of colour from the dying sun, so that there seemed only a moment in which everything – the house, gardens, the great wrought-iron gates – were held in a calm, almost unearthly perfection of light, form and colours which caught at his heart. At the end of their visit, turning to take a last look, he said, 'I want to buy that house.'

'Well one day, George, perhaps you will.'

'But people don't sell houses like that. I wouldn't.'

'Most don't. Some may have to.'

'But why, Grandfather?'

'The money runs out, they can't afford to maintain it. The heir makes millions in the City and has no interest in his heritage. Or the heir may be killed in a war. The landed class have a propensity for getting themselves killed in wars. Or the house is lost through folly – women, gambling, drink, drugs, speculation, extravagance. You never know.'

And in the end it had been the owner's misfortune that had gained George the house. Sir Nicholas Cressett was ruined in the 1990s Lloyd's disaster. George only knew that the house was coming on the market by alighting upon an article in a financial broadsheet about the Lloyd's Names who had suffered the most, and Cressett was prominent among them. He couldn't remember now who had written it – some woman with a name for investigative journalism. It had not been a kind article, focusing more on folly and greed than on ill luck. He had moved quickly and acquired the Manor, driving a hard bargain, knowing exactly what possessions he wanted included in the sale. The best pictures had been reserved for auction, but he wasn't greedy for those. It was the contents which had caught his eye as a boy on that first visit that he was determined to collect, among them a Queen Anne armchair. He had been moving a little ahead of his grandfather into the dining room and had seen the chair. He was sitting on it when a girl, a plain serious child who looked no more than six years old, wearing jodhpurs and an open-necked shirt, came up and said aggressively, 'You're not allowed to sit on that chair.'

'Then you ought to have a cord round it.'

'There should be a cord. There usually is.'

'Well there isn't now.' After five seconds of silent staring, George stood up.

Without speaking she lugged the chair with surprising ease over the white cord separating the dining room from the narrow strip available for visitors to walk and sat firmly down, her legs dangling, then stared fixedly at him as if challenging him to object. She said, 'What's your name?'

'George. What's yours?'

'Helena. I live here. You're not supposed to cross over the white cords.'

'I didn't. The chair was on this side.'

The encounter was too boring to be lengthened, the child too young and too plain to excite interest. He had shrugged his shoulders and moved away.

And now the chair was in his study, and Helena Haverland, née Cressett, was his housekeeper, and if she remembered that first childhood encounter she never mentioned it, and nor did he. He had used the whole of his grandfather's legacy to purchase the Manor and had planned to maintain it by converting the west wing into a private clinic, spending from Monday to Wednesday each week in London operating on his NHS patients and those in his private beds at St Angela's, and returning to Stoke Cheverell on Wednesday nights. The work of adapting the wing was done sensitively, the changes minimal. The wing was a twentieth-century restoration following an earlier replacement in the eighteenth century, and no other original part of the Manor had been touched. Staffing the clinic had never been a problem; he knew whom he wanted and was prepared to pay over the odds to get them. But staffing the operating suite had proved easier than staffing the Manor. The months while he awaited planning consent and when the work was in progress presented no problem. He camped in the Manor, often with the house to himself, looked after by an elderly cook, the only member of the Cressett staff, apart from the gardener, Mogworthy, who stayed on. He looked back now on that year as one of the most contented and happiest that he had ever known. He rejoiced in his possession, moving daily in the silence from the great hall to the library, from the long gallery to his rooms in the east wing with a quiet undiminished triumph. He knew that the Manor couldn't hope to rival the magnificent great hall or the gardens of Athelhampton, the breathtaking beauty of the setting of Encombe, or the nobility and history of Wolfeton. Dorset was rich in great houses. But this was his place and he wanted no other.

The problems began after the clinic had opened and the first patients arrived. He advertised for a housekeeper but, as acquaintances in similar need had prophesied, none proved satisfactory. The old servants from the village whose forebears had worked for the Cressetts were not seduced from old loyalties by the high wages offered by the interloper. He had thought that his secretary in London would have time to cope with the bills and bookkeeping. She hadn't. He had hoped that Mogworthy, the gardener now relieved by an expensive firm who came in weekly to cope with the heavy work, would condescend to help more in the house. He wouldn't. But the second advertisement for a housekeeper, this time differently placed and worded, had produced Helena. She had, he remembered, interviewed him rather than he her. She said that she was recently divorced, independent with a flat in London, but wanted something to do while she considered her future. It would be interesting to return, even temporarily, to the Manor.

She had returned six years ago and was still there. Occasionally he wondered how he would manage when she decided to leave, which she would probably do as unfussily and determinedly as she had arrived. But he was too busy. There were problems, some of his own making, with the theatre sister, Flavia Holland, and with his assistant surgeon, Marcus Westhall, and although by nature a planner, he had never seen sense in anticipating a crisis. Helena had recruited her old governess, Letitia Frensham, as a bookkeeper. She was presumably either a widow, or divorced or separated, but he made no enquiry. The accounts were meticulously kept, in the office order was produced out of chaos. Mogworthy ceased his irritating threats to resign and became accommodating. Part-time staff from the village became mysteriously available. Helena said that no good cook would tolerate the kitchen and, ungrudgingly, he provided the money required for its upgrading.

Fires were lit, flowers and greenery found for the rooms in use, even in the winter. The Manor became alive.

When he drew up at the locked gates and got out of the Mercedes to open them, he saw that the avenue to the house was in darkness. But as he drove past the east wing to park, lights came on and he was greeted at the open front door by the cook, Dean Bostock. He was wearing checked blue trousers and his short white jacket, as was usual when he expected to serve dinner.

He said, 'Miss Cressett and Mrs Frensham went out for dinner, sir. They said to tell you they were visiting some friends in Weymouth. Your room is ready, sir. Mogworthy has lit the fire in the library as well as in the great hall. We thought, being alone, you might prefer to have dinner served there. Shall I bring in the drinks, sir?'

They moved through the great hall. Chandler-Powell tore off his jacket and, opening the library door, threw it and his evening paper on a chair. 'Yes. Whisky please, Dean. I'll have it now.'

'And dinner in half an hour?'

'Yes, that'll be fine.'

'You won't be going out before dinner, sir?'

There was a note of anxiety in Dean's voice. Recognising the cause, Chandler-Powell said, 'So what is it you and Kimberley have cooked between you?'

'We thought cheese soufflé, sir, and a beef stroganoff.'

'I see. The first requires me to be sitting waiting for it and the second is quickly cooked. No, I shan't be going out, Dean.'

The dinner, as usual, was excellent. He wondered why he should so look forward to his meals when the Manor was at its quietest. During his operating days, when he ate with the medical and nursing staff, he hardly noticed what was on his plate. After dinner he sat and read for half an hour beside the library fire then, fetching his jacket and a torch, went out by the door in the west wing, unlocking and unbolting it, and then walked in the star-pricked darkness down the lime avenue to the pale circle of the Cheverell Stones.

A low wall, more landmark than barrier, separated the Manor garden from the stone circle and he hauled himself over without

49

difficulty. As usual after dark, the circle of twelve stones seemed to become paler, more mysterious and more impressive, even to take on a faint gleam from the moonlight or stars. Seeing them in daylight they were clumps of ordinary stone, as commonplace as any large boulder seen on a hillside, uneven in size and oddly shaped, their only distinction the highly coloured lichen creeping in the crevices. A note on the door of the hut beside the parking space instructed visitors that the stones were not to be stood on or damaged and explained that the lichen was both old and interesting and should not be touched. To Chandler-Powell, approaching the circle, even the tallest central stone standing as an evil omen in its ring of dead grass induced little emotion. He thought briefly of the long-dead woman bound to this stone in 1654 and burnt alive as a witch. And for what? An over-sharp tongue, delusions, mental eccentricity, to satisfy a private vengeance, the need for a scapegoat in times of sickness or the failure of a harvest, or perhaps as a sacrifice to propitiate a malignant unnamed god? He felt only a vague unfocused pity, not strong enough to cause even a vestige of distress. She was only one of millions who down the ages had been the innocent victims of the ignorance and cruelty of mankind. He saw enough pain in his world. He had no need to stimulate pity.

He had intended to lengthen his walk beyond the circle but decided that this should be the limit of his exercise and, sitting on the lowest stone, gazed along the avenue to the west wing of the Manor, now in darkness. He sat absolutely still, listening intently to the noises of the night, the small scuffling in the high grasses on the fringe of the stones, a distant scream as some predator found its prey, the susurration of the drying leaves as a breeze suddenly gusted. The anxieties, petty irritations and rigours of the long day fell away. Here in no alien place he sat, so motionless that even his breathing seemed no more than an unheard, softly rhythmic affirmation of life.

Time passed. Glancing at his watch he saw that he had been sitting there for three-quarters of an hour. He became aware that he was getting chilled, that the hardness of the stone was becoming uncomfortable. Easing his cramped legs, he scaled the wall and entered the lime walk. Suddenly a light appeared in the middle window of the patients' floor, the window was opened and a woman's head appeared. She stood motionless looking out into the night. Instinctively he stopped walking and stared at her, both so motionless that for a moment he could believe that she could see him and that some communication was passing between them. He remembered whom she was, Rhoda Gradwyn, and that she was at the Manor for her preliminary stay. Despite his meticulous note taking and examination of patients before operating, few of them remained in mind. He could have described accurately the scar on her face but remembered little else about her except for one sentence. She had come to get rid of the disfigurement because she no longer had need of it. He had asked for no explanation and she had offered none. And in just over two weeks she would be rid of it, and how she would cope with its absence would not be his concern.

He turned to walk back to the house and, as he did, a hand half closed the window, the curtains were partly drawn and a few minutes later the light in the room went out and the west wing was in darkness.

7

Dean Bostock always felt a lift of the heart when Mr Chandler-Powell phoned to say that he would be arriving unexpectedly early in the week and would be at the Manor in time for dinner. This was a meal Dean enjoyed cooking, particularly when the boss had time and peace to enjoy and praise. Mr Chandler-Powell brought with him something of the energy and excitement of the capital, its smells, its lights, the sense of being at the heart of things. Arriving, he would almost bound through the great hall, strip off his jacket and toss the London evening paper on to a library chair as if released from a temporary bondage. But even the paper, which Dean would later retrieve to read at leisure, was for him a reminder of where essentially he, Dean, belonged. He had been born and brought up in Balham. London was his place. Kim was country born, coming to the capital from Sussex to begin her training at the cookery school where he had been a second-year student. And within two weeks of their first meeting he had known that he loved her. That was how he had always thought of it; he hadn't fallen in love, he wasn't in love, he loved. This was for life, his life and hers. And now, for the first time since their marriage, he knew that she was happier than she'd ever been. How could he miss London while Kim rejoiced in her Dorset life? She who was so nervous of new people and new places, felt no fear in the dark winter nights. The total blackness of starless nights disorientated and frightened him, nights made more terrifying by the half-human shrieks of animals in the jaws of their predators. This beautiful and apparently peaceful countryside was full of pain. He missed the lights, the night sky bruised by the grey, purple and blues of the city's ceaseless life, the changing pattern of traffic lights, light spilling from pubs and shops over glittering rain-washed pavements. Life, movement, noise, London.

He liked his job at the Manor but it didn't satisfy him. It made so few demands on his skill. Mr Chandler-Powell was discriminating about food but on his operating days meals were never lingered over. Dean knew he would have complained soon enough had the meal been below standard, but he took its excellence for granted, ate it quickly and was gone. The Westhalls usually took meals in their cottage, where Miss Westhall had been caring for their elderly father until his death in February, and Miss Cressett usually ate in her own apartment. But she was the only one who spent time in the kitchen talking to Kim and him, discussing menus, thanking him for special efforts made. The visitors were fussy but usually not hungry, and the non-resident staff who ate the midday meal at the Manor praised him perfunctorily, ate quickly and returned to work. It was all so different from his dream of his own restaurant, his menus, his customers, the ambiance which he and Kim would create. Occasionally, lying beside her wakeful, he would horrify himself with half-expressed hopes that somehow the clinic would fail, that Mr Chandler-Powell would find it too exhausting and not lucrative enough to work in both London and Dorset, that he and Kim would have to look for another job. And perhaps Mr Chandler-Powell or Miss Cressett would help them to gain a footing. But they couldn't return to work in the hectic kitchen of a London restaurant. Kim would never be suited to that life. He remembered still with horror that awful day on which she had been sacked.

Mr Carlos had called him into the cupboard-sized sanctum at the rear of the kitchen, which he dignified by the name of office, and had squeezed his ample buttocks into the carved desk chair inherited from his grandfather. It was never a good sign. Here was Carlos imbued with genetic authority. A year previously he had announced that he had been born again. It had been a regeneration profoundly uncomfortable for the staff and there had been general relief when, within nine months, the old Adam had mercifully reasserted himself and the kitchen was no longer a swear-free zone. But one relic of the new birth remained: no word stronger than 'bloody' was permitted, and now Carlos himself had made free use of it.

'It's no bloody use, Dean. Kimberley's got to go. Frankly I can't afford her, no restaurant could. Talk about bloody slow. Try to hurry her and she looks at you like a whipped puppy. Gets nervous and nine times out of ten spoils the whole bloody dish. And she affects the rest of you. Nicky and Winston are forever helping her to plate up. Most of the time you've only got half your bloody mind on what you're supposed to be doing. I'm running a restaurant, not a bloody kindergarten.'

'Kim's a good cook, Mr Carlos.'

'Of course she's a good cook. She wouldn't be here if she wasn't. She can go on being a good cook, but not here. Why not encourage her to stay at home? Get her pregnant, then you can go home to a decent meal you haven't had to cook yourself and she'll be happier. I've seen it time and time again.'

How could Carlos know that home was a bed-sitting room in Paddington, that this and the job were part of a carefully worked out plan, the putting aside each week of Kim's wages, the two of them working together, then, when the capital was sufficient, finding the restaurant? His restaurant. Their restaurant. And when they were established and she could be spared from the kitchen, there would be the baby she so longed for. She was only twenty-three; they had plenty of time.

The news having been broken, Carlos had settled himself back, prepared to be magnanimous. 'No point in Kimberley working out her notice. She may as well pack it in this week. I'll pay her a month's salary in lieu. You'll stay on, of course. You've got the makings of a bloody good chef. You've got the skills, the imagination. You're not afraid of hard work. You could go far. But another year of Kimberley in the kitchen and I'll be bloody bankrupt.'

Dean had found his voice, a cracked vibrato with its shaming note of entreaty. 'We've always planned to work together. I don't know that Kim would like to take a job on her own.'

'She wouldn't last a bloody week on her own. Sorry, Dean, but there it is. You might find a place to take the two of you, but not in London. Some small town in the country, maybe. She's a pretty lass, nice manners. Baking a few scones, home-made cakes, afternoon teas, nicely served with doilies, that kind of thing; that wouldn't stress her.'

The note of contempt in his voice had been like a slap across the face. Dean wished he wasn't standing there unsupported, vulnerable, diminished, that there was a chair-back, something solid that he could grip to help control this surging tumult of anger, resentment and despair. But Carlos was right. That summons to the office hadn't been unexpected. He had been dreading it for months. He made one more appeal. He said, 'I'd like to stay on, at least until we find somewhere to go.'

'Suits me. Haven't I told you you've got the makings of a bloody good chef?'

Of course he would stay on. The restaurant plan might be fading but they had to eat.

Kim had left at the end of the week and it was two weeks later to the day that they saw the advertisement for a married couple – cook and assistant cook – at Cheverell Manor. The day of the interview had been a Tuesday in mid-June of the previous year. They had been instructed to take a train from Waterloo to Wareham where they would be met. Looking back, it seemed to Dean that they had travelled in a trance, being borne onwards with no consent of will through a verdant and magical landscape to a distant and unimaginable future. Looking at Kim's profile against the rise and fall of the telegraph wires and, later, the green fields and hedges beyond, he longed for this extraordinary day to end well. He hadn't prayed since childhood, but found himself silently reciting the same desperate petition. 'Please God, make it all right. Please don't let her be disappointed.'

Turning to him as they approached Wareham, she said, 'You've got the references safe, darling?' She had asked about them every hour.

At Wareham a Range Rover was waiting in the forecourt with a stocky elderly man at the wheel. He didn't get out but beckoned them over. He said, 'You'll be the Bostocks, I'm thinking. My name's Tom Mogworthy. No luggage? No, there wouldn't be, would there? You'll not be staying. Climb in the back, then.'

It wasn't, thought Dean, a propitious welcome. But that hardly mattered when the air smelled so sweet and they were being driven through such beauty. It was a perfect summer day, the sky azure and cloudless. Through the open windows of the Range Rover a cooling breeze fell on their faces, not strong enough even to stir the delicate branches of the trees or rustle the grasses. The trees were in full leaf, still with the freshness of spring, their branches not yet stagnant with the dusty heaviness of August. It was Kim who, after ten minutes of a silent drive, leaned forward and said, 'Do you work at Cheverell Manor, Mr Mogworthy?'

'I've been there for just on forty-five years. Started as a boy in the grounds, clipping the knot garden. Still do. Sir Francis was the owner then, and after him Sir Nicholas. You'll be working for Mr Chandler-Powell now, if the women take you on.'

'Won't he be interviewing us?' asked Dean.

'He'll be in London. He operates there on Mondays, Tuesdays and Wednesdays. Miss Cressett and Sister Holland will be interviewing you. Mr Chandler-Powell doesn't bother himself with domestic matters. Satisfy the women and you're in. If not, pack your bags and you're out.'

It had not been a promising beginning, and on first sight even the beauty of the Manor, standing silent and silvery in the summer sun, was more intimidating than reassuring. Mogworthy left them at the front door, merely pointing at the bell, then returned to the Range Rover and drove it round the east wing of the house. Resolutely Dean tugged on the iron bell-pull. They heard no sound but within half a minute the door opened and they saw a young woman. She had shoulder-length blonde hair which Dean thought looked none too clean, heavily applied lipstick and wore jeans beneath a coloured apron. He put her down as someone from the village who helped out, a first impression which proved right. She regarded them with some distaste for a moment, then said, 'I'm

Maisie. Miss Cressett said I'm to give you tea in the great hall.'

Now, recalling the arrival, Dean was surprised that he had become so used to the magnificence of the great hall. He could understand now how people who owned such a house could get used to its beauty, could move confidently down its corridors and through its rooms hardly noticing the pictures and artefacts, the richness which surrounded them. He smiled, remembering how, after asking if they could wash their hands, they had been led through the hall to a room at the back which was obviously a lavatory and washroom. Maisie had disappeared and he waited outside while Kim went in first.

Three minutes later she was out, eyes wide with surprise, saying in a whisper, 'It's so strange. The lavatory bowl is painted inside. It's all blue with flowers and foliage. And the seat is huge – it's mahogany. And there's no proper flush at all. You have to pull on a chain like you do in my gran's loo. The wallpaper's lovely though, and there are lots of towels. I didn't know which to use. Expensive soap too. Hurry up, darling. I don't want to be left alone. Do you suppose the loo is as old as the house? It must be.'

'No,' he said, wanting to demonstrate superior knowledge, 'there wouldn't have been any lavatories when this house was built, not like that anyway. It sounds more Victorian. Early nineteenth century, I'd say.'

He spoke with a confidence he didn't feel, determined not to let the Manor intimidate him. It was to him Kim looked for reassurance and support. He mustn't show that he needed them himself.

Returning to the hallway, they found Maisie at the door of the great hall. She said, 'Your tea's in here. I'll come back in a quarter of an hour and take you to the office.'

At first the great hall overpowered them and they moved forward like children beneath the huge rafters, under the gaze, or so it seemed, of Elizabethan gentlemen in doublet and hose and young soldiers arrogantly posed with their steeds. Bemused by the size and grandeur, it was only later that he noticed details. Now he was aware of the great tapestry on the right wall and beneath it a long oak table holding a huge vase of flowers.

The tea was waiting for them, set out on a low table before the fireplace. They saw an elegant tea-service, a plate of sandwiches, scones with jam and butter and a fruit cake. They were both thirsty. Kim poured the tea with shaking fingers while Dean, having already had a surfeit of sandwiches on the train, took a scone and anointed it generously with butter and jam. After a bite he said, 'The jam's home made, the scone isn't. That's bad.'

Kim said, 'The cake's bought too. Rather good though, but it makes me wonder when the last cook left. I don't think we'd want to give them bought cake. And that girl who opened the door, she must be a temp. I can't see them taking on someone like that.' They found themselves whispering to each other like conspirators.

Maisie returned promptly. Still unsmiling, she said rather pompously, 'Will you follow me, please?' and led them through the square entrance hall to the opposite door, opened it and said, 'The Bostocks are here, Miss Cressett. I've given them tea,' and disappeared.

The room was small, oak panelled and obviously highly functional, the large desk in contrast to the linen-fold panelling and the row of smaller pictures above it. Three women were seated at the desk and motioned them to the chairs set ready.

The taller one said, 'My name is Helena Cressett and this is Sister Holland and Mrs Frensham. Did you have a comfortable journey?'

Dean said, 'Very comfortable, thank you.'

'Good. You'll need to see your accommodation and the kitchen before you make up your mind, but first we would like to explain about the job. In some ways it's very different from the usual work of a cook. Mr Chandler-Powell operates in London from Monday to Wednesday. That means that the beginning of each week will be comparatively easy for you. His assistant, Mr Marcus Westhall, lives in one of the cottages with his sister and his father, and I usually cook for myself in my flat here, although I may from time to time have a small dinner party and ask you to cook for me. The second half of the week will be very busy. The anaesthetist and all the additional nursing and ancillary staff will be here, either

58

overnight or returning to their homes at the end of the day. They have something when they arrive, a cooked lunch and a meal which one could describe as high tea before they leave. Sister Holland will also be in residence as, of course, will Mr Chandler-Powell and the patients. Mr Chandler-Powell sometimes leaves the Manor as early as five thirty to see his London patients. He's usually back by one and requires a good luncheon, which he likes served in his own sitting room. Because of his need sometimes to return for part of a day to London, his meals can be erratic but they are always important. I shall discuss the menus with you in advance. Sister is responsible for all the patients' needs so I'll ask her now to describe what she expects.'

Sister Holland said, 'The patients are required to fast before an anaesthetic and usually eat little until the first day after the operation, depending on its severity and what has been done. When they are well enough to eat, they tend to be demanding and fastidious. Some will be on diets and the dietician or I will supervise this. Patients usually eat in their rooms and nothing should be served to them without my approval.' She turned to Kimberley. 'Usually one of my nursing staff will take the food up to the patients' wing, but you may be required to serve tea or occasional drinks. You do understand that even these require approval?'

'Yes, Sister, I understand.'

'Apart from the patients' food, you will take your instructions from Miss Cressett, or if she isn't here, from her deputy, Mrs Frensham. And now Mrs Frensham has some questions for you.'

Mrs Frensham was a tall, elderly and angular lady with steel-grey hair curled into a bun. But her eyes were kind and Dean felt more at home with her than with the much younger, dark-haired and – he thought – rather sexy Sister Holland, or Miss Cressett with her extraordinary pale and distinctive face. He supposed some people might find her attractive, but no one could say she was pretty.

Mrs Frensham's questions were chiefly directed at Kim and were not difficult. What biscuits would she serve with coffee in the morning and how would she make them? Kim, immediately at ease, described her own recipe for thin spiced biscuits with currants. And how would she make profiteroles? Again Kim had no difficulty. Dean was asked which of three named wines he would serve with duck à l'orange, vichyssoise, and roast sirloin of beef, and what meals he would suggest serving for a very hot summer day or in the difficult days after Christmas. He gave replies which were obviously regarded as satisfactory. It had not been a difficult test and he could sense Kim relaxing.

It was Mrs Frensham who took them to the kitchen and afterwards turned to Kim and said, 'Do you think you could be happy here, Mrs Bostock?'

Dean decided then that he liked Mrs Frensham.

And Kim was happy. For her, getting this job had been a miraculous deliverance. He remembered that mixture of awe and delight with which she had moved about the large gleaming kitchen, then, as if in a dream, through the rooms above it, the sitting room, the bedroom and the luxurious bathroom which would be theirs, touching the furniture in incredulous wonder, running to look out of every window. Finally, they had gone into the garden and she had flung out her arms to the sunlit view, then taken his hand like a child and gazed at him with shining eyes. 'It's wonderful. I can't believe it. No rent to pay and we get our keep. We'll be able to save both our wages.'

For her it had been a new beginning, filled with hope, bright with pictures of them working together, becoming indispensable, the pram on the lawn, their child running about the garden watched from the kitchen windows. For him, looking into her eyes, he knew that it had been the beginning of the death of a dream.

8

Rhoda woke, as always, not to a slow rise to full consciousness, but to an instant wakefulness, senses alert to the new day. She lay quietly for a few minutes, relishing the warmth and comfort of the bed. Before sleep she had partly drawn the curtains and now a narrow band of pale light showed that she had slept longer than expected, certainly longer than was usual, and that a wintry dawn was breaking. She had slept well, but now the need for hot tea was imperative. She rang the number listed on the bedside table and heard a male voice. 'Good morning, Miss Gradwyn. Dean Bostock speaking from the kitchen. Is there anything we can bring you?'

'Tea please. Indian. A large pot, milk but no sugar.'

'Would you like to order breakfast now?'

'Yes, but bring it, please, in half an hour. Fresh pressed orange juice, one poached egg on white toast, then wholemeal toast and marmalade. I'll have it in my room.'

The poached egg was a test. If it came perfectly cooked, the toast lightly buttered and neither hard nor soggy, she could depend on good food when she returned for her operation and a longer stay. She would return – and to this room. Putting on her dressing gown, she went to the window and saw the landscape of wooded valleys and hills. A mist lay over the valley so that the rounded hill-tops looked like islands in a pale silver sea. It had been a clear and cold night. The grass on the narrow stretch of lawn under her windows was pale and stiffened by frost, but already the misty sun was beginning to green and soften it. On the high twigs of a leaf-denuded oak three rooks were perched, unusually silent and motionless, like carefully placed black portents. Below stretched a lime avenue which led to a low stone wall and beyond it a small circle of stones. At first only the tops of the stones were visible, but as she watched, the mist rose and the circle became complete. At this distance and with the ring partly obscured by the wall, she could see only that the stones were of different sizes, crude mis-shapen lumps around a central taller stone. They must, she thought, be prehistoric. As she gazed, her ears caught the soft closing of the sitting-room door. Tea had arrived. Still gazing, she saw in the far distance a narrow strip of silver light and, with a lifting of the heart, realised that it must be the sea.

Reluctant to leave the view, she stood for a few seconds before turning and saw, with a small shock of surprise, that a young woman had entered noiselessly and was standing silently regarding her. She was a slight figure wearing a blue checked dress with a shapeless fawn cardigan over it, which proclaimed an ambiguous status. She was obviously not a nurse yet had none of the assurance of a servant, the confidence born of a recognised and familiar job. Rhoda thought she was probably older than she looked, but the uniform, particularly the ill-fitting cardigan, diminished her into childhood. She had a pale face and straight brown hair drawn to one side in a long patterned slide. Her mouth was small, the top lip a perfect bow so full that it looked swollen, but the bottom thinner. Her eyes were pale blue and a little protuberant under straight brows. They were watchful, almost wary, even a little judgemental in their unblinking scrutiny.

She said, in a voice which was more town than country, an ordinary voice with a hint of deference which Rhoda thought deceptive, 'I've brought your morning tea, madam. I'm Sharon Bateman and I help in the kitchen. The tray's outside. Do you want it in here?'

'Yes, in a moment. Is the tea freshly made?'

'Yes, madam. I brought it up immediately.'

Rhoda was tempted to say the word 'madam' was inappropriate but let it pass. She said, 'Then leave it for a couple of minutes to brew. I've been looking at the stone circle. I've been told about it but didn't realise that it was so close to the Manor. Presumably it's prehistoric.'

'Yes, madam. The Cheverell Stones. They're quite famous. Miss Cressett says they're over three thousand years old. She says stone circles are rare in Dorset.'

Rhoda said, 'Last night when I was opening the curtain I saw a light flickering. It looked like a torch. It came from that direction. Perhaps someone was walking among the stones. Presumably the circle attracts a lot of visitors.'

'Not that many, madam. I don't think most people know they're here. The villagers keep away. It was probably Mr Chandler-Powell. He's fond of walking in the grounds at night. We didn't expect him but he arrived last night. No one from the village goes to the stones after dark. They're scared of seeing the ghost of Mary Keyte walking and watching.'

'Who is Mary Keyte?'

'The stones are haunted. She was tied to the middle stone and burnt there in 1654. It's different from all the other stones, taller and darker. She was condemned as a witch. It's usually old women who got burnt as witches but she was only twenty. You can still see the brown patch where the fire was. No grass ever grows in the middle of the stones.'

Rhoda said, 'No doubt because people over the centuries have ensured that it doesn't. Probably by pouring on something to kill the grass. Surely you don't believe that nonsense?'

'They say that her screams could be heard as far as the church. She cursed the village as she burnt, and afterwards nearly all the children died. You can see the remains of some of the gravestones in the churchyard, although the names are too faint now to be read. Mog says that on the date she was burnt you can still hear her screams.'

'On a windy night, presumably.'

The conversation was becoming tiresome but Rhoda felt it difficult to put a stop to it. The child – she looked little more and was probably not much older than Mary Keyte had been – was obviously morbidly obsessed with the burning. She said, 'The village children died of childhood infections, tuberculosis perhaps, or a fever. Before she was condemned they blamed Mary Keyte for the

63

illnesses, and after she was burnt they blamed her for the deaths.'

'So you don't believe that the spirits of the dead can come back to visit us?'

'The dead don't return to visit us either as spirits – whatever that means – or in any other form.'

'But the dead are here! Mary Keyte isn't at rest. The portraits in this house. Those faces – they haven't left the Manor. I know they don't want me here.'

She didn't sound hysterical or even particularly worried. It was a statement of fact. Rhoda said, 'That's ridiculous. They're dead. They're beyond thought. I have an old portrait in the house where I live. A Tudor gentleman. Sometimes I try to imagine what he would be thinking if he could see me living and working there. But the emotion is mine, not his. Even if I persuaded myself that I could communicate with him, he wouldn't speak to me. Mary Keyte is dead. She can't come back.' She paused and said authoritatively, 'I'll have my tea now.'

The tray was brought in, delicate china, a teapot of the same pattern, the matching milk jug. Sharon said, 'I need to ask you, madam, about lunch, whether you want it served here or in the patients' sitting room. That's in the long gallery below. There's a menu for you to choose.'

She took a paper from her cardigan pocket and handed it over. There were two choices. Rhoda said, 'Tell the chef I'll have the consommé, the scallops on creamed parsnips and spinach with duchesse potatoes, followed by the lemon sorbet. And I'd like a glass of chilled white wine. A Chablis would be fine. I'll have it in my sitting room at one o'clock.'

Sharon left the room. Drinking her tea, Rhoda contemplated what she recognised as confused emotions. She had never seen the girl before nor heard of her, and hers was a face she would not easily have forgotten. And yet she was, if not familiar, at least an uneasy reminder of some past emotion, not keenly felt at the time but still lodged in some recess of memory. And the brief encounter had reinforced a feeling that the house held more than the secrets enshrined in paintings or elevated into folklore. It would be interesting to do a little exploring, to indulge once more that lifelong passion to discover the truth about people, people as individuals or in their working relationships, the things they revealed about themselves, the carefully constructed carapaces they presented to the world. It was a curiosity she had now determined to discipline, a mental energy she planned to harness to a different purpose. This might well be her last investigation, if one could call it that; it was unlikely to be her last curiosity. And she realised that it was already losing its power, that it was no longer a compulsion. Perhaps when she had rid herself of the scar it would have gone for good or remained as no more than a useful adjunct to research. But she would like to know more about the inhabitants of Cheverell Manor, and if indeed there were interesting truths to be discovered Sharon, with her obvious need to chat, might well be the one most likely to reveal them. She had booked in only until after lunch, but half a day would be inadequate even to explore the village and the Manor grounds, particularly as she had an appointment with Sister Holland to look at the operating theatre and recovery suite. The early mist presaged a fine day and it would be good to walk in the gardens and perhaps beyond. She liked the place, the house, this room. She would ask if she could stay until the following afternoon. And in two weeks' time she would return for her operation and her new untried life would begin.

9

The chapel at the Manor stood some eighty yards from the east wing, half-obscured by a circle of speckled laurel bushes. Its early history and the date when it was built were unrecorded but it was certainly older than the Manor, a single plain rectangular cell with a stone altar under the eastern window. There was no means of lighting except by candles and a cardboard box of these was on a chair to the left of the door, together with an assortment of candlesticks, many wooden, which looked like discards from ancient kitchens and the bedrooms of Victorian servants. Since no matches were provided, the casual improvident visitor had to make his devotions, if any, without benefit of their light. The cross on the stone altar was crudely carved, perhaps by some estate carpenter either in obedience to orders or under some private compulsion of piety or religious affirmation. It could hardly have been on the order of some long-dead Cressett, who would surely have chosen silver or a more important carving. Except for the cross the altar was bare. No doubt its earlier furnishings had changed with the great upheavals of the Reformation, once elaborately festooned, later completely unadorned.

The cross was directly in Marcus Westhall's sightline and sometimes for long periods of silence he would fix his gaze on it as if expecting from it some mysterious power, an aid to resolution, a grace which he realised would always be withheld. Under this symbol battles had been fought, the great seismic upheavals of State and Church had changed the face of Europe, men and women had been tortured, burnt and murdered. It had been carried with its message of love and forgiveness into the darkest hells of human imagining. For him it served as an aid to concentration, the focus of the thoughts which crept and rose and whirled in his mind like brown brittle leaves in a gusting wind.

He had entered quietly and, seating himself as usual on the back wooden bench, gazed fixedly at the cross, but not in prayer since he had no idea how to begin praying or with whom precisely he would be attempting to communicate. He sometimes wondered what it would be like to find that secret door said to be open to the lightest touch, and to feel this burden of guilt and indecision fall from his shoulders. But he knew that one dimension of human experience was as closed to him as was music to the tone deaf. Lettie Frensham could have found it. Early on Sunday mornings he would see her cycling past Stone Cottage, woollen capped, her angular figure pushing against the slight incline to the road, summoned by unheard church bells to some distant village church unnamed by her and never spoken of. He had never seen her in the chapel. If she came it must be at times when he was with George in theatre. He thought that he wouldn't have minded if they had shared this sanctuary, if she had sometimes quietly entered to sit in companionable silence beside him. He knew nothing about her except that she had once been Helena Cressett's governess, and he had no idea why she should have returned to the Manor after all these years. But in her quietness and calm good sense she seemed to him like a still pool in a house where he sensed that turbulent undercurrents ran deep, not least in his own troubled mind.

Of the rest of the Manor, only Mog attended the village church and was indeed a stalwart of the choir. Marcus suspected that Mog's still powerful baritone at Evensong was his way of voicing an allegiance, at least partial, to the village against the Manor and to the old dispensation against the new. He would serve the interloper while Miss Cressett was in charge and the money was good, but Mr Chandler-Powell could buy only a carefully rationed part of his loyalty.

Apart from the altar cross, the only sign that this cell was in some sense set apart was a bronze commemorative tablet set in the wall beside the door:

TO THE MEMORY OF CONSTANCE URSULA 1896–1928,
WIFE OF SIR CHARLES CRESSETT BT, WHO FOUND PEACE IN
THIS PLACE.
BUT STRONGER STILL, IN EARTH AND AIR,
AND IN THE SEA, THE MAN OF PRAYER,
AND FAR BENEATH THE TIDE;
AND IN THE SEAT TO FAITH ASSIGNED,
WHERE ASK IS HAVE, WHERE SEEK IS FIND,
WHERE KNOCK IS OPEN WIDE.

Commemorated as wife, but not a beloved wife, and dead at thirty-two. A brief marriage, then. He had traced the verse, so different from the usual pieties, to a poem by the eighteenth-century poet Christopher Smart, but made no enquiries about Constance Ursula. Like the rest of the household, he was inhibited from speaking to Helena about her family. But he found the bronze a discordant intrusion. The chapel should be simply stone and wood.

No other place at the Manor held such peace, not even the library where sometimes he sat alone. Always there was the fear that solitude would be interrupted, that the door would be opened to the dreaded words so familiar from his childhood, 'Oh here you are, Marcus, we've been looking for you.' But no one had ever looked for him in the chapel. It was strange that this stone cell should be so peaceful. Even the altar was a reminder of conflict. In the uncertain days of the Reformation there had been theological disputes between the local priest, who adhered to the old religion, and the then Sir Francis Cressett, who was inclined to the new ways of thought and worship. Needing an altar for his chapel, he had sent the male members of the household at night to steal the one from the Lady Chapel, a sacrilege which had caused the rift between church and Manor for generations. Then, during the Civil War, the Manor had been briefly occupied by Parliamentary troops after a successful local skirmish and the Royalist dead had been laid out on this stone floor.

Marcus put thoughts and memories from him and concentrated on his own dilemma. He had to make a decision – and make it now – whether to remain at the Manor or to go with a surgical team to Africa. He knew what his sister wanted, what he had come to see as a solution for all his problems, but was this desertion a running away from more than his job? He had heard the mixture of anger and entreaty in his lover's voice. Eric, who worked as a theatre nurse at St Angela's, had wanted him to join a gay march. The quarrel was not unexpected. It wasn't the first time that conflict had arisen. He remembered his words.

'I don't see the point of it. If I were heterosexual you wouldn't expect me to go marching down the high street to proclaim that I was straight. Why do we need to do it? Isn't the whole point that we have a perfect right to be what we are? We don't need to justify it, or advertise it, or proclaim it to the world. I don't see why my sexuality should be of interest to anyone except you.'

He tried to forget the bitterness of the quarrel that followed, Eric's broken voice at the end, his face smeared with tears, the face of a child.

'It's nothing to do with being private; you're running away. You're ashamed of what you are, of what I am. And it's the same with the job. You stay with Chandler-Powell, wasting your skill on a bunch of vain extravagant rich women obsessed with their looks when you could be working full time up here in London. You'd find a job – of course you'd find a job.'

'Not so easily now, and I'm not proposing to waste my talent. I'm going to Africa.'

'To get away from me.'

'No, Eric, to get away from myself.'

'You'll never do that; never, never!' Eric's tears, the slamming of the door were the final memory.

He had been staring at the altar so intently that the cross seemed to blur and become a moving fuzz. He shut his eyes and breathed the damp, cold smell of the place, felt the hard wood of the bench against his back. He remembered the last major operation he had assisted at in St Angela's, an elderly NHS patient whose face had been savaged by a dog. She was already sick and, given her prognosis, there must only have been a year of life at most to save, but with what patience, what skill George had put together over long hours a face that could bear the unkind scrutiny of the world. Nothing was ever neglected, nothing hurried or forced. What right had George to waste that commitment and skill even for three days a week on wealthy women who disliked the shape of nose, or mouth, or breast, and who wanted the world to know that they could afford him? What was so important to him that he could spare time on work a lesser surgeon could do, and do as well?

But to leave him now would still be a betrayal of a man he revered. Not to leave him would be a betrayal of himself and of Candace, the sister who, loving him, knew that he had to break free and urged him to have the courage to act. She herself had never lacked courage. He had slept at Stone Cottage and spent enough time there during his father's last illness to have gained some idea of what she had to bear during those two years. And now she was left with her job ended, no other in sight, and the prospect of his leaving for Africa. It was what she wanted for him, had worked for and encouraged, but he knew it would leave her lonely. He was planning to desert the two people who loved him – Candace and Eric – and George Chandler-Powell, the man he most admired.

His life was a mess. Some part of his nature, timid, indolent, lacking in confidence, had led him into this pattern of indecision, of leaving things to sort themselves out, as if he put his faith in a benevolent providence which would operate on his behalf if left alone. In the three years he had spent at the Manor, how much of that was loyalty, gratitude, the satisfaction of learning from a man at the top of his profession, not wanting to let him down? All those had played a part, but essentially he had stayed because it was easier than facing up to the decision to leave. But he would face up to it now. He would break away, and not only physically. In Africa he could make a difference, more profound, more lasting than anything he had done at the Manor. He had to do something new, and if this were running away, he would be running away to people who desperately needed his skills, to wide-eyed children with appalling and untreated harelips, to the victims of leprosy who needed to be accepted and made whole, to the scarred, the disfigured and the rejects. He needed to smell a stronger air. If he didn't face Chandler-Powell now he would never have the courage to act.

He got up stiffly and walked like an old man to the door, then after pausing a moment, stepped with resolution towards the Manor like a soldier going into battle.

10

Marcus found George Chandler-Powell in the operating suite. He was alone and occupied in counting a new delivery of instruments, examining each carefully, turning it over in his hand and replacing it in its tray with a kind of reverence. This was a job for an operating department assistant, and Joe Maskell would arrive at seven o'clock next morning to prepare for the first operation of the day. Marcus knew that checking the instruments didn't mean that Chandler-Powell had little confidence in Joe – he employed no one whom he couldn't trust – but here he was at home with his two passions, his work and his house, and now he was like a child picking over his favourite toys.

Marcus said, 'I wanted to have a word with you, if you've got time.'

Even to his own ears his voice sounded unnatural, oddly pitched. Chandler-Powell didn't look up. 'That depends on what you mean by a word. A word or a serious talk?'

'I suppose a serious talk.'

'Then I'll finish here and we'll go to the office.'

For Marcus there was something intimidating in the suggestion. It was too reminiscent of boyhood summonses to his father's study. He wished he could speak now, get it over with. But he waited until the last drawer was shut and George Chandler-Powell led the way out of the door into the garden, through the back of the house and the hall, to the office. Lettie Frensham was seated at the computer but, as they entered, she muttered a low apology and quietly left. Chandler-Powell sat down at the desk, motioned Marcus to a chair and sat waiting.

Marcus tried to convince himself that the silence wasn't a carefully controlled impatience.

Since it seemed unlikely that George would speak first, Marcus said, 'I've come to a decision about Africa. I wanted to let you know that I've finally made up my mind to join Mr Greenfield's team. I'd be grateful if you could release me in three months' time.'

Chandler-Powell said, 'I take it you've been to London and spoken to Mr Greenfield. No doubt he pointed out some of the problems, your future career among them.'

'Yes, he did all that.'

'Matthew Greenfield is one of the best plastic surgeons in Europe, probably among the six best in the world. He's also a brilliant teacher. We can take his qualifications for granted – FRCS, FRCS (Plast), Master of Surgery. He goes to Africa to teach and to set up a centre of excellence. That's what Africans want, to learn how to cope for themselves, not to have white people going in to take over.'

'I wasn't thinking of taking over, just of helping. There's so much to be done. Mr Greenfield thinks I could be useful.'

'Of course he does; he wouldn't otherwise want to waste his time or yours. But what exactly do you think you're offering? You're an FRCS and a competent surgeon, but you're not qualified to teach, nor even to cope unaided with the most complicated cases. And even a year in Africa will interfere seriously with your career – that is if you see yourself as having one. It hasn't been helpful to you staying here and I pointed that out when you first came. This new MMC – Modernising Medical Careers – makes training schemes far more rigid. Housemen have become foundation-year doctors – and we all know what a mess the government have made there – senior house officers are out, registrars are specialist surgical trainees, and God knows how long all this will last before they think of something else, more forms to fill in, more bureaucracy, more interference with people trying to get on with their jobs. But one thing's certain, if you want to make a career in surgery, you need to be on the training scheme, and that's become pretty inflexible. It might be possible to get you back on stream and I will try to help, but it won't be if you're gadding off to Africa. And it's not as if you're going from religious motives. I wouldn't sympathise if you were but I could understand – well, if not understand, accept. There are people like that, but I have never thought of you as particularly devout.'

'No, I don't think I could claim to be.'

'Well, what are you claiming? Universal beneficence? Or post-colonial guilt? I understand that's still popular.'

'George, there's useful work for me to do. I'm not claiming anything except this strong conviction that Africa would be right for me. I can't stay here indefinitely, you said that yourself.'

'I'm not asking you to. I'm just asking you to consider carefully which way you want your future career to go. That is, if you want a career in surgery. But I'm not going to waste breath trying to persuade you if you've made up your mind. I suggest you think it over, and for the present I'll take it that I shall need a replacement for you in three months' time.'

'I know it will be inconvenient for you and I'm sorry about that. And I know what I owe you. I am grateful. I'll always be grateful.'

'I don't think you need to bleat on about gratitude. That's never an agreeable word between colleagues. We'll take it that you'll leave in three months' time. I hope you find in Africa whatever it is you're looking for. Or is it a case of finding relief from whatever it is you're running away from? And now, if that's all, I'd like the use of my office.'

There was one other thing and Marcus steeled himself to say it. Words had been spoken which had destroyed a relationship. Nothing could be worse. He said, 'It's about a patient, Rhoda Gradwyn. She's here now.'

'I know that. And she'll be back again in two weeks for her operation, unless she takes a dislike to the Manor and opts for a bed at St Angela's.'

'Wouldn't that be more convenient?'

'For her or for me?'

'I was wondering whether you really want to encourage investigative journalists at the Manor. And if one comes, others may

74

follow. And I can imagine what Gradwyn will write. *Rich women spending a fortune because they're dissatisfied with how they look. Valuable surgeons' skills which could be better used.* She'll find something to criticise, that's her job. Patients rely on our discretion and expect an absolute confidentiality. I mean, isn't that what this place is about?'

'Not altogether. And I don't intend to distinguish between patients on any grounds other than medical need. And frankly I wouldn't lift a finger to muzzle the popular press. When you consider the machinations and deviousness of governments we need some organisation strong enough to shout occasionally. I used to believe that I lived in a free country. Now I have to accept that I don't. But at least we have a free press and I'm willing to put up with a certain amount of vulgarity, popularisation, sentimentality and even misrepresentation to ensure it remains free. I suppose Candace has been getting at you. You'd hardly have thought this up on your own. If she has personal reasons for her antagonism to Miss Gradwyn she need have nothing to do with her. She's not required to, the patients are not her concern. She doesn't need to see her either now or when she returns. I don't select my patients to oblige your sister. And now, if you've nothing else to say, I'm sure both of us have work to do. I know I have.'

He got up and stood at the door. Without another word Marcus walked past him, brushing George's sleeve, and left. He felt like an incompetent servant, discharged in disgrace. This was the mentor he had revered, almost worshipped, for years. Now with horror he knew that what he felt was close to hatred. A thought, almost a hope, disloyal and shameful, took hold of his mind. Perhaps the west wing, the whole enterprise, would be forced to close if there were a disaster, a fire, infection, a scandal. If the supply of wealthy patients dried up, how could Chandler-Powell carry on? He tried to shut his mind against the most shameful imaginings but they were unstoppable even, to his disgust, the most shameful and terrible of all, the death of a patient.

Chandler-Powell waited until Marcus's footsteps had faded then left the Manor to see Candace Westhall. He hadn't intended to spend this Wednesday becoming embroiled in arguments with either Marcus or his sister, but now that a decision had been made it would be as well to see what Candace had in mind. It was going to be a nuisance if she too had decided to leave but presumably, now that her father was dead, she would want to return to her university post for the next term. Even if that wasn't the plan, her job at the Manor, taking over from Helena when Helena was in London and helping out in the office, was hardly a career. He disliked interfering in the domestic management of the Manor but if Candace now intended to leave, the sooner he knew the better.

He walked up the lane to Stone Cottage in the fitful winter sunshine and, approaching, saw that there was a dirty sports car parked outside Rose Cottage. So the Westhalls' cousin, Robin Boyton, had arrived. He remembered that Helena had said something about his visit with a marked lack of enthusiasm which, he suspected, was shared by both the Westhalls. Boyton tended to book the cottage at short notice, but as it was vacant, Helena obviously had found it difficult to refuse him.

He was always interested in how different Stone Cottage had looked since Candace and her father had arrived some two and a half years previously. She was an assiduous gardener. Chandler-Powell suspected that it had been one legitimate excuse for getting away from Peregrine Westhall's bedside. He had only visited the old man twice before his death, but he knew, as he suspected did the whole village, that he was a selfish, demanding and unrewarding patient to care for. And now that he was dead and Marcus about to leave England, no doubt Candace, released from what must have been servitude, would have her own plans for the future.

She was raking the back lawn, wearing her old tweed jacket, corduroy trousers and boots which she kept for gardening, her strong dark hair covered by a woollen cap pulled down to her ears. It emphasised the stark resemblance to her father, the dominant nose, the deep-set eyes under straight bushy brows, the length and thinness of the lips, a forceful uncompromising face which, with the hair concealed, looked androgynous. How oddly the Westhall genes had fallen so that it was Marcus, not she, in whom the old man's features were softened into an almost feminine gentleness. Seeing him, she propped the rake against a tree trunk and came to meet him. She said, 'Good morning, George. I think I know why you've come. I was just going to break for coffee. Come in, will you.'

She led him through the side door, the one commonly used, into the old pantry which, with its stone walls and floor, looked more like an outhouse, a convenient dump for worn-out equipment, dominated by a Welsh dresser hung with a miscellany of mugs and cups, bundles of keys and a variety of plates and dishes. They moved to the adjoining small kitchen. It was meticulously tidy but Chandler-Powell told himself that it was time something was done to enlarge and modernise the place, and wondered that Candace, reputed to be a good cook, hadn't complained about it.

She switched on a coffee percolator and took down two mugs from the cupboard, and they stood in silence until the coffee was ready. She had collected a jug of milk from the refrigerator and they passed into the sitting room. Seated opposite her at a square table, he thought again how little had been done to the cottage. Most of the furniture was hers, taken from store, some pieces enviable, others too large for the space. Three walls were lined with wooden bookshelves brought to the cottage by Peregrine Westhall as part of his library when the old man had moved from his nursing home. The library had been bequeathed by him to his old school and the books thought worth preserving had been collected, leaving the walls honeycombed with empty spaces on which the unwanted volumes fell against each other, sad symbols of rejection. The whole room had an air of impermanence and loss. Only the cushioned settle at right angles to the fireplace gave promise of comfort.

He said without preamble, 'Marcus has just given me the news that he's leaving for Africa in three months. I'm wondering how far you influenced that not very intelligent plan.'

'You're not suggesting that my brother isn't capable of making his own decisions about his life?'

'He can make them. Whether he feels free to carry them out is something else. Obviously you influenced him. It would be surprising if you hadn't. You're older by eight years. With your mother an invalid for most of his childhood, it's not surprising that he listens to you. Didn't you more or less bring him up?'

'You seem to know a great deal about my family. If I did influence him it's been to encourage him. It's time he left. I can see it's inconvenient for you, George, and he's sorry about that, we both are. But you'll find someone else. You've known about this possibility for a year now. You must have a replacement in mind.'

She was right, he had. A retired surgeon in his own field, highly competent if not brilliant, who would be glad to assist for three days a week. He said, 'That isn't what concerns me. What does Marcus propose? To stay in Africa permanently? That hardly seems feasible. To work there for a year or two and then come home? To what? He needs to think very clearly about what he wants to do with his life.'

Candace said, 'So do we all. He has thought. He's convinced this is something he has to do. And now that probate has been granted for Father's will, the money's there. He won't be a burden in Africa. He won't go empty handed. You surely understand one thing, the need to do what every instinct of your body tells you is ordained for you. Haven't you lived your life like that? Don't we all at some time or another make a decision which we know is absolutely right, the assurance that some enterprise, some change, is imperative? And even if it fails, to resist it will be a greater failure. I suppose some people would see that as a call from God.'

'In Marcus's case it seems to me more like an excuse for running away.'

'But there's a time for that too, for escape. Marcus needs to get away from this place, from the job, from the Manor, from you.'

'From me?' It was a quietly spoken response, without anger, as if this was a suggestion he needed to think over. His face gave nothing away.

She said, 'From your success, your brilliance, your reputation, your charisma. He has to be his own man.'

'I wasn't aware that I was stopping him from being his own man, whatever that means.'

'No, you aren't aware. That's why he has to go and I have to help him.'

'You'll miss him.'

'Yes, George, I'll miss him.'

He said, anxious not to sound intrusively curious but needing to know, 'Will you want to stay on here for a time? If you do, I know Helena will be glad of help. Someone has to take over when she makes her trips to London. But I suppose you'll want to get back to the university.'

'No, George, that isn't possible. They've decided to shut down the Classics Department. Not enough applicants. And they've offered me a part-time job in one of the new departments they're setting up – Comparative Religion or British Studies, whatever that may mean. As I'm not competent to teach either, I shan't be returning. I'm happy to stay on here for at least six months after Marcus leaves. In nine months I should have made up my mind what I'm going to do. But with Marcus gone I can't justify continuing to live here rent free. If you'll accept some rent, I'd be grateful to have this place until I've settled where I'll go.'

'That won't be necessary. I'd rather not establish any kind of tenancy here, but if you could stay on for nine months or so, that would be fine if Helena's happy about it.'

She said, 'I'll ask her, of course. I'd like to make some changes.

While Father was alive he so hated any fuss or noise, particularly workmen coming in, that there was no point in doing anything. But the kitchen is depressing and too small. If you're going to use this cottage for staff or visitors after I've left, I think you'll have to do something about it. The sensible thing would be to make the old pantry into a kitchen and enlarge the sitting room.'

Chandler-Powell had no wish now to discuss the state of the kitchen. He said, 'Well, have a word with Helena about it. And you'd better speak to Lettie about the cost of redecorating the cottage. It needs doing. I think we could manage some renovations.'

He had finished his coffee and discovered what he needed to know, but before he could get up she said, 'There's one other thing. You've got Rhoda Gradwyn here and I understand she's coming back in two weeks for her operation. You've got private beds at St Angela's. London's more appropriate for her anyway. If she stays here she'll get bored, and that's when women like her become most dangerous. And she is dangerous.'

So he had been right. Candace was at the back of this obsession with Rhoda Gradwyn. He said, 'Dangerous in what way? Dangerous to whom?'

'If I knew that I'd be less worried. You must know something of her reputation – that is if you read anything other than the surgical journals. She's an investigative journalist, one of the worst kind. She sniffs out gossip like a pig with truffles. She makes it her job to discover things about other people which give them distress or pain, or worse, and would titillate the great British public if they became known. She sells secrets for money.'

He said, 'Isn't that a gross exaggeration? And even if it's true, it wouldn't justify me in refusing to treat her where she chooses. Why the concern? She's unlikely to find anything here to whet her appetite.'

'Can you be sure of that? She'll find something.'

'And what excuse would I give for telling her she can't return?'

'You wouldn't need to antagonise her. Simply say that there's been a double booking and you find you haven't a bed.'

It was difficult to control his irritation. This was an unforgivable intrusion, interfering with the management of his patients. He said, 'Candace, what's all this about? You're usually rational. This seems close to paranoia.'

She led the way through to the kitchen and began washing the two mugs and emptying the percolator. After a moment's silence, she said, 'I sometimes wonder about that myself. I admit it does sound far-fetched and irrational. Anyway, I've no right to inter-fere, but I don't think patients who come here for privacy would be delighted to find themselves in the company of a notorious jour-nalist. But you needn't worry. I shan't see her, either now or when she returns. I'm not proposing to take a kitchen knife to her. Frankly she's not worth it.'

She saw him to the door. He said, 'I see Robin Boyton is back. I think Helena did mention that he'd booked in. What's he here for, do you know?'

'He said because Rhoda Gradwyn is here. Apparently they're friends and he thinks she might like company.'

'For a stay of one night? Does he plan to book into Rose Cottage when she returns? If he does he won't see her, and he won't see her now. She made it plain that she's coming here for absolute privacy and that's what I'll ensure she gets.'

Closing the garden gate behind him, he wondered what all that had been about. There must be some strong personal reason for an antipathy which seemed otherwise unreasonable. Was she perhaps focusing on Gradwyn the two years of frustration tied to a cantan-kerous unloving old man and the prospect of losing her job? And now there was Marcus's plan to go to Africa. She might support his decision but she could hardly welcome it. But striding purpose-fully back to the Manor he put Candace Westhall and her troubles out of mind and concentrated on his own. He would find a replacement for Marcus and, if Flavia decided it was time to leave, he would cope with that too. She was getting restless. There had been signs which even he, busy as he was, had noticed. Perhaps it was time the affair ended. Now, with the Christmas break coming and the work slowing down, he should steel himself to end it.

Back at the Manor he decided to speak to Mogworthy, who

would probably be working in the garden taking advantage of an uncertain period of winter sun. There were bulbs to be planted and it was time he showed an interest in Helena and Mog's plans for the spring. He passed through the north door leading to the terrace and the knot garden. Mogworthy was nowhere in sight but he saw two figures walking side by side towards the gap in the far beech hedge which led to the rose garden. The shorter was Sharon, her companion he recognised as Rhoda Gradwyn. So Sharon was showing her the garden, a task usually undertaken at a visitor's request by Helena or Lettie. He stood watching them, an odd couple, as they passed out of sight, walking in intimacy, obviously talking, Sharon looking up at her companion. For some reason the sight disconcerted him. Marcus and Candace's forebodings had irritated rather than worried him but now, for the first time, he felt a twinge of anxiety, a sense that something uncontrollable and possibly dangerous had entered his domain. The thought was too irrational, even superstitious, to be seriously examined and he thrust it aside. But it was odd that Candace, highly intelligent and usually so rational, had this obsession with Rhoda Gradwyn. Did she perhaps know something about the woman that he didn't, something she was unwilling to reveal?

He decided not to look for Mogworthy and, re-entering the Manor, he closed the door firmly behind him.

12

Helena knew that Chandler-Powell had gone to Stone Cottage and was unsurprised when, twenty minutes after his return, Candace arrived in the office.

Without preamble she said, 'There's something I wanted to discuss with you. Two things actually. Rhoda Gradwyn. I saw her arriving yesterday – at least I saw a BMW being driven past and I assumed it was hers. When is she leaving?'

'She isn't, at least not today. She's booked in for a second night.'

'And you agreed?'

'I could hardly refuse, not without an explanation and there wasn't one. The room was vacant. I phoned George and he didn't seem worried.'

'He wouldn't be. An extra day's income and at no trouble to him.'

Helena said, 'And no trouble for us either.'

She spoke without resentment. For her George Chandler-Powell was behaving reasonably. But she would find a time to have a word with him about these one-nighters. Was it really necessary to have to take a preliminary look at the facilities? She didn't want the Manor degenerating into a bed-and-breakfast hotel. On second thoughts, perhaps it would be wiser not to raise the matter. He had always been adamant that patients should be given the opportunity to see in advance where their operation was to take place. He would see any interference with his clinical judgement as intolerable. Their relationship had never been clearly defined but both knew how they stood. He never interfered with her domestic running of the Manor; she took no part in the clinic.

Candace said, 'And she's coming back?'

'I presume so, in just over two weeks' time.' There was a silence. Helena said, 'Why do you feel so strongly about it? She's a patient much like the others. She's booked in for a week's convalescence after surgery, but I doubt whether she'll stay the course, not in December. She'll probably want to get back to town. Whether she does or not, I can't see her being more of a nuisance than the other patients. Probably less.'

'It depends on what you mean by a nuisance. She's an investigative journalist. She'll always be on the lookout for a story. And if she wants material for a new article, she'll find it, even if she does no more than write a diatribe about the vanity and silliness of some of our patients. After all, they're guaranteed secrecy as well as security. I don't see how you can hope for secrecy with an investigative journalist in residence, particularly this one.'

Helena said, 'With only herself and Mrs Skeffington in residence, she's hardly likely to encounter more than one example of vanity and silliness to write about.'

She thought, *But it's more than that. Why should she worry whether the clinic flourishes or fails once her brother has gone?* She said, 'But with you it's personal, isn't it? It has to be.'

Candace turned away. Helena regretted the sudden impulse which had prompted the question. The two of them worked well together, respected each other, at least professionally. Now wasn't the time to start exploring those private areas which she knew, like her own, were barred by a keep-out notice.

There was silence, then Helena said, 'You said there were two things.'

'I've asked George if I can stay on here for another six months, perhaps as long as a year. I would continue to help with the accounts and in the office generally, if you think I could be useful. Obviously once Marcus has left I'd pay a proper rent. I don't want to stay on if you're not happy about it. I ought to mention that I shan't be here for three days next week. I'm flying to Toronto to arrange some kind of pension for Grace Holmes, the nurse who helped me with Father.'

So Marcus was going. It was about time he made up his mind. His loss would be a major inconvenience for George, but no doubt he'd find a substitute. Helena said, 'We wouldn't find it easy to do without you. I'd be grateful if you could stay on, at least for a time. I know that Lettie will feel the same. So you've finished with the university?'

'The university has finished with me. There are not enough students to justify a Classics Department. I saw it coming, of course. They closed the Physics Department last year to enlarge Forensic Science, and now the Classics Department is to close and Theology will become Comparative Religion. When that's judged to be too difficult – and with our intake it undoubtedly will be – then no doubt Comparative Religion will become Religion and Media Studies. Or Religion and Forensic Sciences. The government, which proclaims a target of fifty per cent of young people going to university, and at the same time ensures that forty per cent are uneducated when they leave secondary school, lives in a fantasy world. But don't let me get on to the subject of higher education. I've become a bore about it.'

So, Helena thought, *she's lost her job, is losing her brother and is now facing six months stuck in this cottage with no clear idea of her future.* Looking at Candace's profile, she felt an onrush of pity. The emotion was transitory but surprising. She couldn't imagine letting herself drift into Candace's situation. It was that dreadful, domineering old man, dying so slowly for two years, who had caused the mischief. Why hadn't Candace broken free of him? She had nursed him as conscientiously as might a Victorian daughter, but there had been no love. It hadn't needed any perception to see that. She herself had kept away from the cottage as much as possible, as indeed did most of the staff, but the truth of what was going on was known, by gossip, innuendo and by what they saw and heard. He had always despised his daughter, destroyed her confidence as a woman and a scholar. Why, with her ability, hadn't she applied for a job at a prestigious university instead of one near the bottom of the pecking order? Had that old tyrant made it clear to her that she deserved nothing better? And he had needed more care than she could reasonably provide, even with the help of the district nurse. Why hadn't she put him in a nursing home? He hadn't been happy in the one at Bournemouth where his father had been nursed but there were other nursing homes and there was no lack of family money. The old man was rumoured to have been left close on eight million pounds by his father who predeceased him by only a few weeks. Now that probate had been granted, Marcus and Candace were wealthy.

Five minutes later Candace had left. Helena thought over their conversation. There was something she had not told Candace. She couldn't imagine that it was particularly important, but it might have proved an added source of irritation. It would hardly have lightened Candace's mood to be told that Robin Boyton had also booked himself in at Rose Cottage for the day before Miss Gradwyn's operation and the week of her convalescence.

13

By eight o'clock on Friday 14 December, the operation on Rhoda Gradwyn satisfactorily completed, George Chandler-Powell was alone in his private sitting room in the east wing. It was a solitude he often sought at the end of an operating day, and although there had only been one patient, dealing with her scar had been more complicated and time consuming than he had expected. At seven Kimberley had brought him a light supper and by eight o'clock evidence of the meal had been removed and the small dining table folded away. He could be confident of two hours of solitude. He had seen his patient and checked on her progress at seven o'clock and would do so again at ten. Immediately after the operation Marcus had left to spend the night in London and now, knowing Miss Gradwyn to be in the experienced hands of Flavia, and with himself on call, George Chandler-Powell turned his mind to private pleasures. Not least among them was the decanter of Château Pavie on a small table before the fire. He prodded the burning logs into greater life, checked they were carefully aligned and settled into his favourite chair. Dean had decanted the wine and Chandler-Powell judged that in another half-hour it would be right for drinking.

Some of the best pictures, bought when he purchased the Manor, hung in the great hall and the library, but here were his favourites. They included six watercolours bequeathed to him by a grateful patient. The bequest had been totally unexpected and it had taken some time for him to remember her name. He was grateful that she had obviously shared his prejudice against foreign ruins and alien landscapes, and all six showed English scenes.

Three views of cathedrals: Albert Goodwin's watercolour of Canterbury, a Peter de Wint of Gloucester and Girtin's Lincoln. On the opposite wall he had hung Robert Hills's painting of a view in Kent and two seascapes, one by Copley Fielding and Turner's study for his watercolour of the arrival of the English packet at Calais, which was his favourite.

He let his eyes rest on the Regency bookcase with the books he most often promised himself to re-read, some childhood favourites, others from his grandfather's library, but now, as often at the end of the day, he was too tired to summon energy for the symbiotic satisfaction of literature and turned to music. Tonight a particular pleasure awaited him, a new recording of Handel's *Semele*, conducted by Christian Curnyn with his favourite mezzo-soprano, Hilary Summers, glorious sensual music as joyous as a comic opera. He was putting the first CD into the player when there was a knock on the door. He felt an irritation close to anger. Very few people disturbed him in his private sitting room and fewer knocked. Before he could answer, the door opened and Flavia came in, shutting the door sharply behind her and leaning against it. Apart from her cap she was still in uniform and his first words were instinctive.

'Miss Gradwyn. Is she all right?'

'Of course she's all right. If she weren't, would I be here? At six fifteen she said she was hungry and ordered supper – consommé, scrambled egg and smoked salmon, followed by lemon mousse, if you're interested. She managed to get most of it down and seemed to enjoy it. I've left Nurse Frazer in charge until I return, then she'll be off duty and will drive back to Wareham. Anyway, I'm not here to discuss Miss Gradwyn.'

Nurse Frazer was one of his part-time staff. He said, 'If it's not urgent, can't it wait until tomorrow?'

'No, George, it can't. Not until tomorrow, nor the day after, nor the day after that. Not until any day when you condescend to find time to listen.'

He said, 'Will it take much time?'

'More time than you are usually willing to give.'

He could guess what was coming. Well, the future of their affair had to be settled sooner or later and with his evening already ruined it might as well be now. Her outbursts of resentment had become more common of late but had never before occurred while they were at the Manor. He said, 'I'll get my jacket. We'll walk under the limes.'

'In the dark? And the wind's rising. Can't we talk here?'

But he was already fetching his jacket. Returning and putting it on, he patted the pocket for his keys. He said, 'We'll talk outside. I suspect that the discussion will be disagreeable and I'd prefer a disagreeable conversation to take place outside this room. You'd better get a coat. I'll see you at the door.'

There was no need to specify which door. Only that on the ground floor of the west wing led directly to the terrace and to the lime walk. She was waiting for him, coated and with a woollen scarf tied over her head. The door was locked but unbolted, and he locked it behind them. They walked for a minute in silence which Chandler-Powell had no intention of breaking. Still annoyed at the loss of his evening, he was disinclined to be helpful. Flavia had asked for this meeting. If she had anything to say, let her say it.

It wasn't until they had reached the end of the lime walk, and after a few seconds of indecision had turned back, that she stopped walking and faced him. He couldn't see her face clearly, but her body was rigid and there was a harshness and a resolution in her voice that he had never heard before.

'We can't go on as we are. We have to make a decision. I'm asking you to marry me.'

So it had come, the moment he had dreaded. But it was meant to be his decision, not hers. He wondered why he hadn't seen it coming, then realised that the demand, even in its brutal explicitness, wasn't totally unexpected. He had chosen to ignore the hints, the moodiness, the sense of a grievance unexpressed amounting almost to rancour. He said calmly, 'I'm afraid that isn't possible, Flavia.'

'Of course it's possible. You're divorced, I'm single.'

'I mean that it wasn't something I've ever considered. From the beginning our relationship was never on that footing.'

'What footing exactly did you think it was on? I'm speaking of when we first became lovers – eight years ago, in case you've forgotten. On what footing was it then?'

'I suppose sexual attraction, respect, affection. I know I felt all those things. I never said I loved you. I never mentioned marriage. I wasn't looking for marriage. One failure is enough.'

'No, you were always honest – honest or careful. And you couldn't even give me fidelity, could you? An attractive man, a distinguished surgeon, divorced, eligible. Do you think I don't know how often you've relied on me – on my ruthlessness, if you like – to get rid of those avaricious little gold-diggers who were trying to get their claws into you? And I'm not talking about a casual affair. For me it was never that. I'm talking about eight years of commitment. Tell me, when we're apart, do I ever enter your mind? Do you ever picture me except gowned and masked in the theatre, anticipating your every need, knowing what you like and what you don't like, what music you want played while you work, available when wanted, discreetly on the margin of your life? Not so very different from being in bed, is it? But at least in the operating theatre there was no easy substitute.'

His voice was calm but he knew with some shame that Flavia wouldn't miss the clear note of insincerity. 'Flavia, I'm sorry. I'm sure I've been thoughtless and unintentionally unkind. I had no idea you felt like this.'

'I'm not asking for pity. Spare me that. I'm not even asking for love. You haven't got it to give. I'm asking for justice. I want marriage. The status of being a wife, the hope of children. I'm thirty-six. I don't want to work until I retire. And what then? Using my retirement lump sum to buy a cottage in the country, hoping the villagers will accept me? Or a one-bedded flat in London when I'll never be able to afford a decent address? I have no siblings. I've neglected friends to be with you, to be available when you have time for me.'

He said, 'I never asked you to sacrifice your life for me. That is, if you say it's a sacrifice.'

But now she went on as if he hadn't spoken. 'In eight years

we've never had a holiday together, in this country or abroad. How often have we been to a show, a film, dined in a restaurant except one where there'll be no risk of meeting someone you know? I want these ordinary companionable things that other people enjoy.'

He said again, and with some sincerity, 'I'm sorry. Obviously I've been selfish and unthinking. I think in time you'll be able to look back on these eight years more positively. And it isn't too late. You're very attractive and you're still young. It's sensible to recognise when a stage of life has come to an end, when it's time to move on.'

And now, even in the darkness, he thought he could see her contempt. 'You mean to throw me over?'

'Not that. To move on. Isn't that what you've been saying, what this talk is all about?'

'And you won't marry me? You won't change your mind?'

'No, Flavia, I won't change my mind.'

She said, 'It's the Manor, isn't it? It isn't another woman who's come between us, it's this house. You've never made love to me here, ever, have you? You don't want me here. Not permanently. Not as your wife.'

'Flavia, that's ridiculous. I'm not looking for a chatelaine.'

'If you lived in London, in the Barbican flat, we wouldn't be having this conversation. We could be happy there. But here at the Manor I don't belong, I can see it in your eyes. Everything about this place is against me. And don't think that the people here don't know that we're lovers – Helena, Lettie, the Bostocks, even Mog. They're probably wondering when you're going to chuck me. And if you do, I'll have to endure the humiliation of their pity. I'm asking you again, will you marry me?'

'No, Flavia. I'm sorry but I won't. We wouldn't be happy and I'm not going to risk a second failure. You have to accept that this is the end.'

And suddenly, to his horror, she was crying. She grasped his jacket and leaned against him and he could hear the great gasping sobs, feel the pulse of her body against him, the soft wool of her scarf brushing his cheek, sense the familiar smell of her, of her breath. Taking her by the shoulders, he said, 'Flavia, don't cry. This is a liberation. I'm setting you free.'

She drew apart, making a pathetic attempt at dignity. Controlling her sobs, she said, 'It'll look odd if I disappear suddenly, and there's Mrs Skeffington to be operated on tomorrow, Miss Gradwyn here to be cared for. So I'll stay until you leave for the Christmas break, but when you return I won't be here. But promise me one thing. I've never asked for anything, have I? Your presents on birthdays and Christmases were chosen by your secretary or posted from a shop, I always knew that. Come to me tonight, come to my room. It'll be for the first and last time, I promise. Come late, about eleven. It can't end like this.'

And now he was desperate to get rid of her. He said, 'Of course I'll come.'

She murmured a thank you and, turning, began walking quickly back towards the house. From time to time she half-stumbled and he had to resist the urge to catch her up, to find some final word which could assuage her. But there was none. He knew that already he was turning his mind to find a replacement as theatre sister. He knew, too, that he had been seduced into a disastrous promise, but it was one he had to keep.

He waited until her figure became faint, then merged into the darkness. And still he waited. Looking up at the west wing, he saw the faint blur of two lights, one in Mrs Skeffington's room, one next door in Rhoda Gradwyn's. So her bedside lamp must be on and she was not yet settled for sleep. He thought back to that night just over two weeks ago when he had sat on the stones and watched her face at the window. He wondered what it was about this particular patient that had so caught his imagination. Perhaps it was that enigmatic, still unexplained response when, in his Harley Street consulting room, he had asked her why she had waited so long to get rid of her scar. *Because I no longer have need of it.*

14

Four hours earlier Rhoda Gradwyn had slowly drifted back to consciousness. The first object she saw on opening her eyes was a small circle. It hung suspended in air immediately in front of her, like a floating full moon. Her mind, puzzled but transfixed, tried to make sense of it. It couldn't, she thought, be the moon. It was too solid and unmoving. And then the circle became clear and she saw that it was a wall clock with a wooden frame and a narrow inner rim of brass. Although the hands and numerals were becoming clearer she couldn't read the time; deciding that it didn't matter, she quickly gave up the attempt. She became aware that she was lying on a bed in an unfamiliar room and that other people were with her, moving like pale shadows on silent feet. And then she remembered. She was to have her scar removed and they must have prepared her for the operation. She wondered when it would take place.

And then she became aware that something had happened to the left side of her face. She felt a soreness and an aching heaviness, like a thick plaster. It was partly obscuring the edge of her mouth and dragging at the corner of her left eye. Tentatively she raised her hand, uncertain whether she had the power to move, and carefully touched her face. The left cheek was no longer there. Her exploring fingers found only a solid mass, a little rough to the touch and criss-crossed with something that felt like tape. Someone was gently lowering her arm. A reassuring familiar voice said, 'I shouldn't touch the dressing for a time.' And then she knew that she was in the recovery room and the two figures taking shape by her bed must be Mr Chandler-Powell and Sister Holland.

She looked up and tried to form words from her impeded mouth. 'How did it go? Are you pleased?'

The words were a croak but Mr Chandler-Powell seemed to understand. She heard his voice, calm, authoritative, reassuring. 'Very well. I hope that in a little time you will be pleased too. Now you must rest here for a while and then Sister will wheel you up to your room.'

She lay unmoving as objects solidified round her. How many hours, she wondered, had the operation taken? One hour, two, three? However long, time had been lost to her in a semblance of death. It must be as like death as any human imagining could be, a total annihilation of time. She pondered the difference between this temporary death and sleep. To wake after sleeping, even a deep sleep, was always to be aware that time had passed. The mind grasped at the tatters of waking dreams before they faded beyond recall. She tried to test memory by reliving the previous day. She was sitting in a rain-lashed car, then arriving at the Manor, entering the great hall for the first time, unpacking in her room, talking to Sharon. But that surely had all been on her first visit over two weeks ago. The recent past began to come back. Yesterday had been different, a pleasant uncomplicated drive, the winter sunlight interspersed with brief and sudden showers. And this time she had brought with her to the Manor some patiently acquired knowledge which she could make use of or could let go. Now in sleepy contentment she thought she would let it go as she was letting go of her own past. It couldn't be relived, none of it could be changed. It had done its worst but its power would soon be over.

Closing her eyes and drifting into sleep, she thought of the peaceful night ahead and of the morning which she would never live to see.

15

Seven hours later, back in her bedroom, Rhoda stirred into drowsy wakefulness. She lay for a few seconds, motionless in that brief confusion which attends the sudden awakening from sleep. She was aware of the comfort of the bed and the weight of her head against the raised pillows, of the smell of the air – different from that in her London bedroom – fresh but faintly pungent, more autumnal than wintry, a smell of earth and grass borne to her on the erratic wind. The darkness was absolute. Before finally accepting Sister Holland's advice that she should settle herself for the night, she had asked for the curtains to be pulled back and the lattice window slightly opened; even in winter she disliked sleeping without fresh air. But perhaps it had been unwise. Gazing fixedly at the window, she could see that the room was darker than the night outside and that high constellations were patterning the faintly luminous sky. The wind was gusting more strongly and she could hear its hiss in the chimney and feel its breath on her right cheek.

Perhaps she should stir herself from this unwonted lassitude and get up to close the window. The effort seemed beyond her. She had declined the offer of a sedative and found it strange, but not worrying, that she should feel this heaviness, this urge to stay where she was, cocooned in warmth and comfort, awaiting the soft boom of the next gust of wind, her eyes fixed on that narrow oblong of starlight. She felt no pain and, putting up her left hand, gently touched the padded dressing and the adhesive tape which secured it. She was used now to the weight and stiffness of the dressing, and would find herself touching it with something like a caress, as if it were becoming as much a part of her as the imagined wound which it covered.

And now, in a lull in the wind, she heard a sound so faint that only the stillness of the room could have made it audible. She sensed rather than heard a presence moving round the sitting room. At first, in her sleepy half-consciousness, she felt no fear, only a vague curiosity. It must be early morning. Perhaps it was seven o'clock and the arrival of her tea. And now there was another sound, no more than a gentle squeak but unmistakable. Someone was closing the bedroom door. Curiosity gave way to the first cold clutch of unease. No one spoke. No light was turned on. She tried to call out in a cracked voice made ineffectual by the obstructive dressing, 'Who are you? What are you doing? Who is it?' There was no reply. And now she knew with certainty that this was no friendly visitor, that she was in the presence of someone or something whose purpose was malignant.

As she lay rigid the pale figure, white-clad and masked, was at her bedside. Arms moved above her head in a ritual gesture like an obscene parody of a benediction. With an effort she tried to struggle up – the bedclothes seemed suddenly to weigh her down – and stretched out a hand for the bell pull and the lamp. The bell pull wasn't there. Her hand found the light switch and clicked it on, but there was no light. Someone must have hooked the bell pull out of reach and taken the bulb from the lamp. She didn't cry out. All those early years of self-control against betraying fear, against finding relief in shouting and yelling, had inhibited her power to scream. And she knew screaming would be ineffective; the dressing made even speech difficult. She struggled to get out of bed but found herself unable to move.

In the darkness she could vaguely make out the whiteness of the figure, the covered head, the masked face. A hand was passing across the pane of the half-open window – but it was not a human hand. No blood had ever flowed in those boneless veins. The hand, so pinkly white that it might have been severed from the arm, was moving slowly through space on its mysterious purpose. Soundlessly it closed the window latch and, with a gesture delicate and elegant in its controlled motion, it slowly drew the curtain across the window. The darkness in the room intensified, no longer just the shutting out of light, but an occluding thickening of the air which made it difficult to breathe. She told herself that it must be a hallucination conjured from her half-sleeping state and for one blessed moment she gazed at it, all terror past, waiting for the vision to fade into the surrounding darkness. And then all hope faded.

The figure was at the bedside, looking down on her. She could discern nothing but a white formless shape, the eyes looking into hers might be merciless but all she could make out was a black slit. She heard words, quietly spoken but she could make no sense of them. With an effort she raised her head from the pillow and tried to croak out a protest. Immediately time was suspended and in her vortex of terror she was aware only of smell, the faintest smell of starched linen. Out of the darkness, leaning over her, was her father's face. Not as she had remembered him for over thirty years, but the face she had briefly known in early childhood, young, happy, bending over her bed. She lifted her arm to touch the dressing but the arm was too weighty and fell back. She tried to speak, to move. She wanted to say, 'Look at me, I've got rid of it.' Her limbs felt encased in iron, but now she managed, trembling, to lift her right hand and touched the dressing over the scar.

She knew that this was death, and with the knowledge came an unsought peace, a letting go. And then the strong hand, skinless and inhuman, closed round her throat, forcing her head back against the pillows and the apparition flung its weight forward. She wouldn't shut her eyes in the face of death, nor did she struggle. The darkness of the room closed in on her and became the final blackness in which all feeling ceased.

16

At twelve minutes past seven, in the kitchen Kimberley was becoming anxious. She had been told by Sister Holland that Miss Gradwyn had asked for her early morning tea tray to be brought up at seven o'clock. That was earlier than the first morning she had been at the Manor, but seven o'clock was the time Sister had told Kim to be ready to make it, and she had set the tray by six forty-five and placed the teapot on top of the Aga to warm.

And now it was twelve minutes after seven, and no ring. Kim knew that Dean needed her help with the breakfast, which was proving unexpectedly aggravating. Mr Chandler-Powell had asked for his to be served in his apartment, which was unusual, and Miss Cressett, who usually prepared what she wanted in her own small kitchen and rarely ate a cooked breakfast, had rung to say that she would join the household in the dining room at seven thirty and had been unusually fussy about the required crispness of the bacon and the freshness of the egg – as if, thought Kim, any egg served at the Manor would be other than free range and fresh, and Miss Cressett knew that as well as she. An added irritation was the non-appearance of Sharon, whose duty it was to lay the breakfast table and turn on the hotplates. Kim was reluctant to go upstairs and rouse her in case Miss Gradwyn rang her bell.

Fretting once again over the exact alignment of the cup, saucer and milk jug on the tray, she turned to Dean, her face puckered with anxiety. 'Perhaps I ought to take it up. Sister said seven. Perhaps she meant that I needn't wait for the ring, that Miss Gradwyn would expect it promptly at seven.'

Her face, looking like that of a troubled child, induced as

always Dean's love and pity tinged with irritation. He moved to the telephone. 'Sister, this is Dean. Miss Gradwyn hasn't rung for her tea. Shall we wait or do you want Kim to make it now and take it up?'

The call took less than a minute. Replacing the receiver, Dean said, 'You're to take it up. Sister says to knock on her door before you go in. She'll take it in to Miss Gradwyn.'

'I suppose she'll have the Darjeeling as she did before, and the biscuits. Sister didn't say any different.'

Dean, busy at the Aga frying eggs, said shortly, 'If she doesn't want the biscuits she'll leave them.'

The kettle boiled quickly and within minutes the tea was made. Dean, as usual, came to the lift with her and, holding the door open, pressed the button so that she had both hands free to carry the tray. Emerging from the lift, Kim saw Sister Holland coming out of her sitting room. She expected the tray to be taken from her, but instead Sister, after a cursory glance, opened the door to Miss Gradwyn's suite, obviously expecting Kim to follow. Perhaps, Kim thought, that wasn't surprising; it wasn't Sister's job to carry early morning tea to the patients. She was carrying her torch so it wouldn't in any case have been easy.

The sitting room was in darkness. Sister switched on the light and they moved to the bedroom door, which Sister opened slowly and quietly. This room, too, was in darkness, and there was no sound, not even the soft noises of someone breathing. Miss Gradwyn must be sleeping soundly. Kim thought it was an eerie silence, like entering an empty room. She wasn't usually conscious of the weight of the tray, but now it seemed to grow heavier by the second. She stayed in the open doorway holding it. If Miss Gradwyn was sleeping late, she would have to make another pot later. No good leaving this to get over-stewed and cold.

Sister said, her voice unworried, 'If she's still asleep, there's no point in waking her. I'll just check that she's all right.'

She moved to the bed and swept the pale moon of her torch over the supine figure, then switched it to a powerful beam. Then she switched it off, and in the darkness Kim heard her high urgent voice, which didn't sound like Sister's. She said, 'Get back, Kim. Don't come in. Don't look! Don't look!'

But Kim had looked, and for those disorientating seconds before the torchlight went out, she had seen the bizarre image of death: dark hair sprawled on the pillow, the clenched fists raised like those of a boxer, the one open eye and the livid mottled neck. It wasn't Miss Gradwyn's head – it was nobody's head, a bright red severed head, a dummy which had nothing to do with anything living. She heard the crash of falling china on the carpet and, stumbling to an easy chair in the sitting room, she leaned over and was violently sick. The stink of her vomit rose to her nostrils and her last thought before she fainted was a new horror: what would Miss Cressett say about the ruined chair?

When she came round she was lying on the bed in her and Dean's bedroom. Dean was there and behind him Mr Chandler-Powell and Sister Holland. She lay for a moment with her eyes closed and heard Sister's voice and Mr Chandler-Powell's reply.

'Didn't you realise, George, that she was pregnant?'

'How the hell should I? I'm not an obstetrician.'

So they knew. She wouldn't have to break the news. All she cared about was the baby. She heard Dean's voice. 'You've been asleep after you fainted. Mr Chandler-Powell carried you here and you were given a sedative. It's nearly lunchtime.'

Mr Chandler-Powell came forward and she could feel his cool hands on her pulse.

'How do you feel, Kimberley?'

'I'm all right. Better, thank you.' She sat up quite vigorously and looked at Sister. 'Sister, will the baby be all right?'

Sister Holland said, 'Don't worry. The baby will be fine. You could have your lunch in here if you prefer and Dean will stay with you. Miss Cressett, Mrs Frensham and I will cope in the dining room.'

Kim said, 'No, I'm all right. Really. I'll be better working. I want to get back to the kitchen. I want to be with Dean.'

Mr Chandler-Powell said, 'Good girl. We must all get on with our usual routine as far as we can. But there's no hurry. Take things gently. Chief Inspector Whetstone has been here but apparently he's expecting a special squad from the Metropolitan Police. In the meantime I've asked everyone not to discuss what happened last night. Do you understand, Kim?'

'Yes, sir, I understand. Miss Gradwyn was murdered, wasn't she?'

'I expect we shall know more when the London squad arrive. If she was, they'll find out who was responsible. Try not to be frightened, Kimberley. You're among friends, as you and Dean always have been, and we shall look after you.'

Kim muttered her thanks. And now they were gone and, sliding out of bed, she moved into the comfort of Dean's strong arms.

BOOK TWO

15 December
London, Dorset

I

At half past ten on that Saturday morning, Commander Adam Dalgliesh and Emma Lavenham had an appointment to meet her father. To meet a future father-in-law for the first time, especially with the purpose of informing him that one is shortly to marry his daughter, is seldom an enterprise undertaken without some misgivings. Dalgliesh, with a vague recollection of similar fictional encounters, had somehow envisaged that, as the suppliant, he was expected to see Professor Lavenham on his own, but was easily persuaded by Emma that they should visit her father together. 'Otherwise, darling, he'll keep asking what my views are. After all, he's never yet seen you and I've hardly mentioned your name. If I'm not there I won't be sure he's taken it in. He does have a tendency to vagueness although I'm never sure how much of that is genuine.'

'Are his vague moods frequent?'

'They are when I'm with him, but there's nothing wrong with his brain. He does rather like to tease.'

Dalgliesh thought that vagueness and teasing would be the least of his problems with his prospective father-in-law. He had noticed that men of distinction in old age were given to exaggerating the eccentricities of youth and the middle years, as if these self-defining quirks of personality were a defence against the draining away of physical and mental powers, the amorphous flattening of the self in its last years. He was uncertain what Emma and her father felt for each other, but surely there must have been love – in memory at least – and affection. Emma had told him that her younger sister, playful, biddable and prettier than she and killed in childhood by a speeding car, had been his favourite child, but she had spoken without a note of criticism and no resentment. Resentment was not an emotion he associated with Emma. But however difficult the relationship, she would want this meeting between father and lover to be a success. It was his job to ensure that it was, that it didn't remain an embarrassment or a lasting disquietude in her memory.

All that Dalgliesh knew of Emma's childhood had been told in those desultory snatches of conversation in which each explored with tentative footsteps the hinterland of the other's past. On his retirement, Professor Lavenham had rejected Oxford in favour of London and lived in a spacious flat in one of Marylebone's Edwardian blocks dignified, as most of them were, by the description 'mansions'. The block was not too distant from Paddington station, with its regular train service to Oxford where the professor was a frequent – and, his daughter suspected, occasionally too frequent – diner at his college's high table. An ex-college servant and his wife, who had moved to Camden Town to live with a widowed daughter, came in daily to do the necessary cleaning and returned later to cook the professor's dinner. He had been over forty at the time of his marriage and, although now just over seventy, was perfectly competent to look after himself, at least in essentials. But the Sawyers had convinced themselves, with some conniving on his part, that they were devotedly caring for a helpless and distinguished old gentleman. Only the final adjective was appropriate. The view of his former colleagues visiting Calverton Mansions was that Henry Lavenham had done very well for himself.

Dalgliesh and Emma drove to the Mansions, arriving as arranged with the professor, at half past ten. The block had recently been repainted, the brickwork an unfortunate colour which Dalgliesh thought could most accurately be described as fillet steak. The commodious lift, mirror panelled and smelling strongly of furniture polish, took them up to the third floor.

The door to number 27 was opened so promptly that Dalgliesh suspected that their host had been watching for their cab from his windows. The man facing him was almost as tall as he with a strong-boned handsome face under a thatch of steel-grey undisciplined hair. He was supported by a stick but his shoulders were only slightly bent and the dark eyes, the only resemblance to his daughter, had lost their lustre but regarded Dalgliesh with a look that was surprisingly keen. He was slippered and informally dressed but looked immaculate. He said, 'Come in, come in,' with an impatience which implied that they were lingering at the door.

They were led into a large front room with a bay window. It was obviously a library; indeed, given the fact that every wall was a mosaic of book spines and that the desktop and practically all other surfaces were heaped with journals and paperbacks, there was room for no other function than reading. An upright chair facing the desk had been cleared by piling the papers beneath it, giving it, in Dalgliesh's eyes, a naked and somehow ominous singularity.

Professor Lavenham, having pulled out his chair from the desk and seated himself, motioned Dalgliesh to take the empty chair. The dark eyes, under brows now grey but disconcertingly shaped like Emma's, stared at Dalgliesh over half-moon spectacles. Emma walked over to the window. Dalgliesh suspected that she was preparing to enjoy herself. After all, her father couldn't forbid the marriage. She would like his approval but had no intention of being influenced by either approbation or dissent. But it was right that they should be there. Dalgliesh had an uneasy awareness that he should have come earlier. The start was not propitious.

'Commander Dalgliesh, I hope I have your rank correctly.'

'Yes, thank you.'

'I thought that was what Emma told me. I have guessed why you are making what, for a busy man like yourself, must be a somewhat inconveniently timed visit. I feel bound to tell you that you are not down on my list of eligible young men. However, I am quite ready to enter your name should your answers be what an affectionate father requires.'

So they were to be indebted to Oscar Wilde for the dialogue of this personal inquisition. Dalgliesh felt grateful; the professor might well have dredged from his obviously still lively memory some recondite passage from drama or fiction, probably in Latin. As it was he thought he could keep his end up. He said nothing.

Professor Lavenham went on. 'I think it is usual to enquire whether you have an income sufficient to keep my daughter in the manner to which she has become accustomed. Emma has supported herself since she got her PhD, apart from irregular and occasional generous subventions from myself, probably meant to compensate for previous delinquencies as a father. Should I take it you have sufficient money for the two of you to live comfortably?'

'I have my salary as a commander of the Metropolitan Police, and my aunt left me her considerable fortune.'

'In land or in investments?'

'In investments.'

'That is satisfactory. What between the duties expected of one during one's lifetime, and the duties exacted from one after one's death, land has ceased to be either a profit or a pleasure. It gives one position and prevents one from keeping it up. That's all that can be said about land. You have a house?'

'I have a flat overlooking the Thames at Queenhithe with a lease of over one hundred years. I have no house, not even on the unfashionable side of Belgrave Square.'

'Then I suggest you acquire one. A girl with a simple unspoilt nature like Emma could hardly be expected to reside in a flat at Queenhithe, overlooking the Thames, even with a lease of over one hundred years.'

Emma said, 'I love the flat, Papa.' The remark was ignored.

The professor had obviously decided that the effort to continue the tease was disproportionate to the pleasure it gave him. He said, 'Well, that seems satisfactory. And now I believe it is customary to offer you both a drink. Personally I dislike champagne, and white wine disagrees with me, but there is a bottle of burgundy on the kitchen table. Ten forty in the morning is hardly an appropriate time to begin imbibing so I suggest you take it with you. I don't suppose you'll be staying long. Or' – he said hopefully – 'you could have coffee. Mrs Sawyer tells me that she has left everything ready.'

Emma said firmly, 'We'd like the wine, Papa.'

'Then perhaps you could see to it.'

They went together into the kitchen. It seemed discourteous to shut the door so both managed to restrain an impulse to erupt into laughter. The wine was a bottle of Clos de Bèze.

Dalgliesh said, 'This is an impressive bottle.'

'Because he liked you. I wonder if a bottle of plonk is waiting in his desk drawer in case he didn't. I wouldn't put it past him.'

They returned to the library, Dalgliesh carrying the bottle. He said, 'Thank you, sir. We'll save this for a special occasion, which we hope will be when you're able to join us.'

'Maybe, maybe. I don't often dine out except in college. Perhaps when the weather improves. The Sawyers don't like my venturing out on cold nights.'

Emma said, 'We hope you'll come to the wedding, Papa. It will be in the spring, probably May, in the College Chapel. I'll let you know as soon as we have a date.'

'Certainly I'll come, if I'm well enough. I regard it as my duty. I gather by referring to the Book of Common Prayer – not my customary reading – that I shall be expected to take some non-verbal and ill-defined part in the proceedings. That certainly was the case with my own father-in-law at our wedding, also in the College Chapel. He rushed your poor mother up the aisle as if afraid that I might change my mind if kept waiting. Should my participation be required I hope to do better, but perhaps you will reject the idea of a daughter being formally handed over to the possession of another. I expect you are anxious to be on your way, Commander. Mrs Sawyer said that she might arrive this morning with some things I need. She will be sorry to have missed you.'

At the door Emma moved up to her father and kissed him on both cheeks. Suddenly he clutched her and Dalgliesh saw his knuckles whiten. The grasp was so strong that it looked as if the old man needed support. In the seconds when they were clasped together, Dalgliesh's mobile phone rang. Not in any previous summons had its low but distinctive peal seemed more inappropriate.

Releasing his hold on Emma, her father said irritably, 'I have a particular abhorrence of mobile telephones. Couldn't you have switched that thing off?'

'Not this one, sir. Will you excuse me?'

He moved towards the kitchen. The professor called, 'You'd better close the door. As you've probably discovered, my hearing is still acute.'

Geoffrey Harkness, Assistant Commissioner of the Metropolitan Police, was experienced in conveying information concisely and in terms designed to inhibit question or discussion. Now within six months of retirement, he relied on well-tested stratagems for ensuring that his professional life moved gently to its final celebrations without major disruption, public embarrassment or disaster. Dalgliesh knew that Harkness had his retirement job as security adviser to a large international corporation comfortably settled and at three times his present salary. Good luck to him. Between him and Dalgliesh there was respect – sometimes grudging on Harkness's part – but not friendship. His voice now sounded as it often did: abrupt, impatient but with its urgency controlled.

'A case for the Squad, Adam. The address is Cheverell Manor in Dorset, some ten miles west of Poole. It's run by a surgeon, George Chandler-Powell, as something between a clinic and a nursing home. Anyway, he operates on rich patients who want cosmetic surgery. One of them is dead, a Rhoda Gradwyn, apparently strangled.'

Dalgliesh asked the obvious question. It wasn't the first time he had had to ask it and it was never well received. 'Why the Squad? Can't the local force take it on?'

'They could take it on, but we've been asked for you. Don't ask me why; it's come from Number Ten, not here. Look Adam, you know how things are between us and Downing Street at present. It's not the time to start making difficulties. The Squad was set up to investigate cases of particular sensitivity and Number Ten takes the view that this case falls into that category. The Chief Constable, Raymond Whitestaff – I think you know him – is reasonably happy about it, and he'll provide the SOCOs and the photographer, if you're happy with that. It will save time and money. It hardly warrants a helicopter, but it's urgent of course.'

'It always is. What about the pathologist? I'd like Kynaston.'

'He's already on a case, but Edith Glenister is free. You had her for the Combe Island murder, remember?'

'I'm hardly likely to forget. I suppose the force can provide the incident room and some backup?'

'They've got a cottage free some hundred yards or so from the Manor. It used to be the house of the village constable but they didn't replace him when he retired and at present it's empty awaiting sale. There's a B & B further down the road, so I suppose Miskin and Benton-Smith can make themselves comfortable there. There'll be Chief Inspector Keith Whetstone from the local force to meet you at the scene. They're not removing the body until you and Doc Glenister arrive. Do you want me to do anything more this end?'

Dalgliesh said, 'No. I'll get on to Inspector Miskin and Sergeant Benton-Smith. But it will save time if someone could speak to my secretary. There are meetings on Monday which I'll have to miss, and Tuesday's had better be cancelled. After that I'll be in touch.'

Harkness said, 'Right, I'll see to it. Good luck', and replaced the receiver.

He returned to the library. Professor Lavenham said, 'Not bad news, I hope. Your parents are well?'

'Both have died, sir. That was an official call. I'm afraid that I shall have to leave urgently.'

'Then I mustn't keep you.'

They were being hastened to the door with what seemed unnecessary speed. Dalgliesh feared that the Professor might comment that to lose one parent may be regarded as a misfortune, but to lose both looked very like carelessness, but it was apparent that there were some remarks that even his future father-in-law baulked at.

They walked swiftly to the car. Dalgliesh knew that Emma, whatever her plans, wouldn't expect him to go out of his way to drop her. He needed to get to his office without a minute's delay.

He didn't need to express his disappointment; Emma understood both its depth and its inevitability. As they walked together he asked about her plans for the next two days. Would she stay in London or return to Cambridge?

'Clara and Annie have said that, if our plans come unstuck, they'd love me to stay for the weekend. I'll give them a ring.'

Clara was Emma's best friend and Dalgliesh understood what she valued in her: honesty, intelligence and a sturdy common sense. He had met Clara and now they were at ease with each other, but the early days of his love for Emma hadn't been easy. Clara had made it plain that she considered him to be too old, too absorbed in his job and his poetry to make a serious commitment to any woman, and simply not good enough for Emma. Dalgliesh agreed with the last indictment, a self-incrimination which didn't make it any more agreeable to hear it from another, particularly not from Clara. Emma must lose nothing by her love for him.

Clara and Emma had known each other from their schooldays, had gone in the same year to the same Cambridge college and, though subsequently taking very different paths, had never lost touch. It was on the face of it a surprising friendship, commonly explained by the attraction of opposites. Emma, heterosexual with her disturbing heart-stirring beauty which Dalgliesh knew could be more a burden than the envied and unmixed blessing of popular imagination; Clara, short with a round cheerful face, bright-eyed behind large spectacles and with the stumpy walk of a ploughman. That she was attractive to men was to Dalgliesh one more example of the mystery of sexual appeal. He had sometimes wondered whether Clara's first response to him had been activated by jealousy or regret. Both seemed unlikely. Clara was so obviously happy with her partner, the frail gentle-faced Annie who, Dalgliesh suspected, was tougher than she looked. It was Annie who made their Putney flat a place where no one entered without – in Jane Austen's words – the sanguine expectation of happiness. After achieving a first in Mathematics, Clara had begun working in the City, where she was a highly successful fund manager. Colleagues came and went but Clara was retained. Emma had told him that she planned to leave the job in three years' time, when she and Annie would use the considerable capital accrued to begin a very different life. In the meantime much of what she earned was spent on good causes close to Annie's heart.

Three months earlier Emma and he had attended the ceremony of Clara and Annie's civil partnership, a quietly satisfying celebration at which only Clara's parents, Annie's widowed father and a few close friends had been guests. Afterwards there had been a lunch cooked by Annie in the flat. After the second course was finished Clara and Dalgliesh together carried plates into the kitchen to bring in the pudding. It was then she had turned to him with a resolution which suggested that she had been waiting for this opportunity.

'It must seem perverse in us to tie a legal knot when you heteros are scrambling in thousands to divorce, or living together without benefit of marriage. We were perfectly happy as we were but we needed to ensure that each is the other's recognised next of kin. If Annie is ever in hospital, I need to be there. And then there's the property. If I die first, it must go untaxed to Annie. I expect she'll spend most of it on lame ducks but that's up to her. It won't be wasted. Annie is very wise. People think that our partnership lasts because I'm the stronger and Annie needs me. Actually the reverse is true, and you're one of the rare people who've seen that from the start. Thank you for being with us today.'

Dalgliesh knew those last gruffly spoken words had been the confirmation of an acceptance which, once given, would be unassailable. He was glad that whatever the unknown faces, problems and challenges that lay ahead for him in the next few days, Emma's weekend would be lively in his imagination and for her would be happy.

2

For Detective Inspector Kate Miskin, her flat on the north bank of the Thames, downstream from Wapping, was a celebration of achievement in the only form which, for her, had any hope of permanence, solidified in steel, bricks and wood. She had known when first taking possession of the flat that it was too expensive for her and the first few years of paying the mortgage had meant sacrifices. She had made them willingly. She had never lost that first excitement of walking through rooms full of light, of waking and falling asleep to the changing but never-ending pulsation of the Thames. Hers was the top-floor corner flat with two balconies giving wide views upstream and to the opposite bank. Except in the worst weather, she could stand silently contemplating the changing moods of the river, the mystic power of T. S. Eliot's brown god, the turbulence of the inrushing tide, the glittering stretch of pale blue under hot summer skies, and after dark the black viscous skin slashed with light. She watched for the familiar vessels as if they were returning friends: the launches of the Port of London Authority and the river police, the dredgers, the low-laden barges, in the summer the pleasure boats and the small cruise ships and, most exciting of all, the tall sailing ships, their young crews lining the rails as they moved with majestic slowness upstream to pass under the great raised arms of Tower Bridge into the Pool of London.

The flat could not be more different from those claustrophobic rooms on the seventh floor of Ellison Fairweather Buildings where she had been brought up by her grandmother, from the smell, the vandalised lifts, the overturned rubbish bins, the screaming voices, the ever-constant awareness of danger. As a small child she had walked frightened and wary-eyed in an urban jungle. Her childhood had been defined for her by the words of her grandmother to a neighbour, overheard when she was seven and never forgotten. 'If her ma had to have an illegitimate kid, at least she could have stayed alive to look after it, not dumped it on me! She never knew the father, or if she did she wasn't saying.' In adolescence she had taught herself to forgive her grandmother. Tired, overworked, poor, she was coping unaided with a burden she hadn't expected and didn't want. What remained with Kate, and always would, was the knowledge that never to have known either parent was to live life with some essential part of you missing, a hole in the psyche which could never be filled.

But she had her flat, a job she loved and was good at, and until six months ago there had been Piers Tarrant. They had been so close to love, although neither of them ever spoke the word, but she knew how much he had enhanced her life. He had left the Special Investigation Squad to join the Met's Anti-terrorist Branch and although much of his present work was secret, they could relive the old days when they had been colleagues. They used the same language, he understood the ambiguities of policing as no civilian ever could. She had always found him sexually attractive but, while they were colleagues, knew that an affair would be disastrous. AD was intolerant of anything which could damage the effectiveness of the Squad and one, or probably both of them, would have been reallocated. But it seemed to her that the years of working alongside each other, the shared danger, disappointments, exhaustion and successes, even at times the rivalry for AD's approbation, had so bound them together that, when they became lovers, it was a natural and happy confirmation of something which had always existed.

But six months ago she had ended the affair and she couldn't regret her decision. For her it was insupportable to have a partner who was unfaithful. She had never expected permanence in any relationship; nothing in her childhood and youth had ever promised that. But what for him had been a bagatelle had for her been betrayal. She had sent him away and she had heard and seen nothing of him since. Looking back she told herself that from the start she had been naïve. After all, she had known his reputation. The break had happened when at the last moment she had decided to attend Sean McBride's farewell party. It threatened to be the usual boozy affair and she had long outgrown farewell parties, but she had worked with Sean for a short time when she was a detective constable and he had been a good boss, helpful and without the then all too common prejudice against female officers. She would put in an appearance to wish him good luck.

Fighting her way through the crowd, she had seen Piers at the centre of a raucous group. The blonde who was winding herself round him was so scantily dressed that the men had difficulty in deciding whether to focus on her crotch or her breasts. There had been no doubt of their relationship; this had been a trophy lay and they were both happy to demonstrate it. He had seen Kate through the gap in the close-packed jostling crowd. Their eyes had briefly met, but before he had time to break through and approach her she had left.

Early the next morning he had arrived and the break had been formalised. Much of what they had said was now forgotten but disconnected snatches still echoed in her mind like a mantra.

'Look, Kate, it's unimportant. It didn't mean anything. She doesn't mean anything.'

'I know. That's what I object to.'

'You're asking a lot of me, Kate.'

'I'm not asking anything of you. If that's how you want to live, that's your affair. I'm simply telling you that I don't want to have sex with a man who's sleeping with other women. That may sound unfashionable in a world where a one-night stand means another score on your truncheon, but that's how I am and I can't change, so for us it's the end. It's a good thing neither of us is in love. We'll be spared the usual tedium of tears and recriminations.'

'I could give her up.'

'And the next one, and the one after that? You haven't begun to understand. I'm not offering sex as a good-conduct prize. I don't want explanations, excuses, promises. It's the end.'

And it had been the end. For six months he had disappeared completely from her life. She told herself she was getting used to being without him, but it hadn't been easy. She missed more than the mutual fulfilment of their lovemaking. The laughter, the drinks in their favourite riverside pubs, the stress-free companionship, the meals in her flat which they cooked together, all had released in her a light-hearted confidence in life which she had never before known.

She wanted to talk to him about the future. There was no one else in whom she could confide. The next case might well be her last. It was certain that the Special Investigation Squad wouldn't continue in its present form. Commander Dalgliesh had so far managed to thwart official plans to rationalise the maverick staffing, define its functions in contemporary jargon devised to obscure rather than illumine, and incorporate the Squad in some more orthodox bureaucratic structure. The SIS had survived because of its undoubted success, relative cheapness – not in some eyes a convenient virtue – and because it was headed by one of the country's most distinguished detectives. The rumour mill of the Met ground incessantly and more often than not produced a kernel of wheat among the chaff. The present rumours had all come to her ears: Dalgliesh, deploring the politicisation of the Met and much else, himself wanted to retire; AD had no intention of retiring and would shortly take over a special inter-force department concerned with detective training; approaches had been made to him from two university departments of criminology; someone in the City wanted him for an unspecified job at a salary four times that at present enjoyed by the Commissioner.

Kate and Benton had countered all questions with silence. It had required no self-discipline. They knew nothing but were confident that when AD had made his choice they would be among the first to be told. The chief for whom she had worked since she became a detective sergeant would be marrying his Emma in a few months. After the years together, he and she would no longer be part of the same team. She would get her promised promotion to detective chief inspector, perhaps within weeks, and could hope to rise even higher. The future might be lonely, but if it were, she had her job, the only one she had ever wanted, the one which had given her all she now possessed. And she knew better than most that there were worse fates than loneliness.

The call came at ten fifty. She wasn't due in the office until one thirty and was about to leave the flat to deal with the routine chores which always took hours out of her free half-day: a visit to the supermarket to buy food, a watch that was being mended to collect, some clothes to be taken to the dry-cleaners. The call came on her dedicated mobile and she knew whose voice she would hear. She listened closely. It was, as she had expected, a murder case. The victim, Rhoda Gradwyn, an investigative journalist, found dead in her bed at seven thirty, apparently strangled, after an operation at a private clinic in Dorset. He gave the address as Cheverell Manor, Stoke Cheverell. No explanation of why the Squad were taking over, but apparently Number Ten was involved. They were to travel by car, either hers or Benton's, and the team would aim to arrive together.

She said, 'Yes, sir. I'll ring Benton now and meet him at his flat. I think we'll take his car. Mine's due for a service. I have my murder bag and I know he has his.'

'Right. I need to call in at the Yard, Kate, and I'll meet you at Shepherd's Bush, I hope by the time you get there. I'll give you further details as far as I know them when we meet.'

She ended the call then rang Benton, and within twenty minutes had changed into the tweed trousers and jacket she wore for a country case. Her grip with other clothes she might need was always packed and ready. Swiftly she checked windows and power plugs and, picking up her murder bag, turned the keys in the two security locks and was on her way.

3

Kate's call to Sergeant Francis Benton-Smith came while he was shopping in the Notting Hill farmers' market. His day had been carefully planned and he was in the excellent spirits of a man who could look forward to a well-earned rest day which presaged more energetic pleasure than rest. He had promised to cook lunch for his parents in the kitchen of their South Kensington home, would later spend the afternoon in bed with Beverley in his Shepherd's Bush flat, and planned to end a perfect mixture of filial duty and pleasure by taking her to see the new film at the Curzon. The day would also be for him a private celebration of his recent reinstatement as Beverley's boyfriend. The ubiquitous word slightly irritated him but it seemed inappropriate to describe her as his lover, which to his mind suggested a greater degree of commitment.

Beverley was an actor – she insisted that she should not be described as an actress – and was making a career for herself on television. She had from the start made it clear where her priority lay. She liked variety in her boyfriends but was as intolerant of promiscuity as any fundamentalist preacher. Her sex life was a strictly time-enforced procession of single affairs, few, as she was considerate enough to inform Benton, with any hope of lasting for more than six months. Despite the slenderness of her neat, tough little body she loved food and he knew that part of his attraction had been the meals, either in carefully chosen restaurants which he could ill afford or, as she preferred, cooked by him at home. This lunch, to which she had been invited, was planned in part to remind her what she had been missing.

He had met her parents once and only briefly, and was surprised that this solidly fleshed couple, conventional, well dressed and physically unremarkable, should have produced such an exotic child. He loved to look at her, the pale oval face, dark hair cut in a fringe over slightly slanted eyes which gave her a faintly oriental attraction. She came from a background as privileged as his and, despite her efforts, had never succeeded in losing all evidence of a good general education. But the despised bourgeois values and appurtenances had been rejected in the service of her art, and in speech and appearance she had become Abbie, the wayward daughter of a publican, in a television soap set in a Suffolk village. When they had first come together her acting prospects had been bright. There were then plans for an affair with the church organist, a pregnancy and an illegal operation, and general mayhem in the village. But there had been complaints from viewers that this country idyll was beginning to compete with *EastEnders* and the rumour now was that Abbie was to be redeemed. There was even a suggestion of a faithful marriage and virtuous motherhood. As Beverley complained, it was a disaster. Already her agent was putting out feelers to capitalise on her present notoriety while it lasted. Francis – he was only Benton to his colleagues at the Met – had no doubt that the lunch would be a success. His parents were always curious to learn about the mysterious worlds to which they had no access and Beverley would be happy to provide a spirited rendering of the latest plot, probably with dialogue.

His own appearance was, he felt, as misleading as Beverley's. His father was English, his mother Indian, and he had inherited her beauty but none of the deep attachment to her country which she had never lost and which her husband shared. They had married when she was eighteen and he twelve years older. They had been passionately in love and remained in love, and their annual visits to India were the highlight of their year. Throughout boyhood he had accompanied them but always with a sense of being an alien, ill at ease, unable to participate in a world to which his father, who seemed happier, more light hearted, in India than in England, readily adapted himself in speech, dress and food. He had felt, too, from early childhood that his parents' love was too all-consuming to admit of a third person, even an only child. He knew he was loved, but in the company of his father, a retired headmaster, had always felt more like a promising and valued sixth-former than a son. Their benign non-interference was disconcerting. When he was sixteen, listening to the complaints of a school friend about his parents – the ridiculous rule about coming home before midnight, the warnings about drugs, heavy drinking, AIDS, their insistence that homework should take precedence over pleasure, niggling complaints about hairstyle, clothes and the state of his room which, after all, was supposed to be private – had made Francis feel that his parents' tolerance amounted to an uninterest which was close to emotional neglect. This was not what parenting was supposed to be.

His father's response to his choice of career had been one that he suspected had been used before. 'There are only two important things about one's choice of job: that it should promote the happiness and well-being of others and give satisfaction to you. The police service fulfils the first and I hope that it will fulfil the second.' He had almost had to stop himself from saying, 'Thank you, sir.' But he knew that he loved his parents and was sometimes quietly aware that the distancing was not all on their side and that he saw them too seldom. This lunch was to be some small atonement for neglect.

The call came on his dedicated mobile at ten fifty-five while he was adding to his selection of organic vegetables, and was Kate's voice. 'We have a case. The apparent murder of a patient at a private clinic in Stoke Cheverell in Dorset. It's in a manor house.'

'That makes a change, ma'am. But why the Squad? Why not Dorset Constabulary?'

Her voice sounded impatient. This was no time for chattering. 'Heaven knows. They're being coy about it as usual, but I gather it's something to do with Number Ten. I'll give you all the information I have when we're on the way. I suggest we take your car and Commander Dalgliesh wants us to arrive at the Manor at the same time. He'll have his Jag. I'll be with you as soon as I can. I'll leave my car in your garage and he'll join us there. I take it you've got your murder kit? And bring your camera. It could be useful. Where are you now?'

'At Notting Hill, ma'am. With luck I'll be back at the flat in under ten minutes.'

'Good. You may as well pick up some sandwiches or wraps and something to drink. AD won't want us to arrive hungry.'

As Kate rang off, Benton reflected that he already knew that. He had only two calls to make, one to his parents and one to Beverley. His mother took the call and, wasting no time, quickly expressed her regrets and rang off. Beverley didn't answer her mobile, which he felt was just as well. He left a simple message that their plans would have to be cancelled and said he would call later.

It took him only minutes to buy the sandwiches and drink. Running from the market to Holland Park Avenue, he saw that a number 94 bus was just slowing at the stop and, sprinting, managed to leap in before the doors closed. Already his plans for the day were forgotten and he was looking ahead to the more demanding task of enhancing his reputation with the Squad. It worried him, but only slightly, that this exhilaration, the sense that the immediate future was full of excitement and challenge, depended on an unknown body stiffening in a Dorset manor house, on grief, anguish and fear. He admitted, and not without a small spasm of conscience, that it would be disappointing to arrive in Dorset to find that, after all, this was only a commonplace murder and that the perpetrator had already been identified and arrested. It had never yet happened and he knew that it was unlikely. The Squad was never called in to a commonplace murder.

Standing at the bus doors he waited impatiently for them to open, then sprinted to his block of flats. Stabbing the lift button, he stood breathless listening for its descent. It was then that he realised, without in the least caring, that he had left his bag of carefully selected organic vegetables in the bus.

4

It was one thirty, six hours after the finding of the body, but for Dean and Kimberley Bostock, waiting in the kitchen until someone arrived to tell them what to do, the morning seemed unending. This was their domain, the place where they were at home, in control, never harassed, knowing that they were valued even if the words weren't often spoken, confident in their professional skills and, above all, together. But now they drifted from table to stove like disorganised amateurs abandoned in an unfamiliar and intimidating environment. Like automata they had slipped the cords of their cooks' aprons over their heads and put on their white caps, but little work had been done. At half past nine, at Miss Cressett's request, Dean had taken croissants, jam and marmalade and a large jug of coffee into the library but, removing the plates later, found that little had been eaten, although the coffee jug was empty and the demand for it seemed unending. Sister Holland regularly appeared to bear off another thermos. Dean was beginning to feel that he was imprisoned in his own kitchen.

They could sense that the house was locked in an eerie silence. Even the wind had dropped, its dying gusts like despairing sighs. Kim was ashamed of her faint. Mr Chandler-Powell had been very kind to her and had said that she wasn't to return to work until she felt ready, but she was glad to be back where she belonged with Dean in the kitchen. Mr Chandler-Powell had been grey faced and looked much older and somehow different. He reminded Kim of how her dad had looked when he came home after his operation, as if strength and something more vital than strength, something that made him uniquely her dad, had drained out of him. Everyone had been kind to her but she felt that the sympathy had been carefully voiced as if any words could be dangerous. If a murder had happened at home in her village, how different it would have been. The cries of outrage and horror, the comforting arms round her, the whole street pouring into the house to see, hear and lament, a jumble of voices questioning and speculating. The people at the Manor weren't like that. Mr Chandler-Powell, Mr Westhall and his sister, and Miss Cressett didn't show their feelings, at least not in public. They must have feelings; everyone did. Kim knew she cried too easily, but surely they cried sometimes, although it seemed an indecent assumption even to imagine it. Sister Holland's eyes had been red and swollen. Perhaps she had cried. Was it because she had lost a patient? But didn't nurses get used to that? She wished she knew what was happening outside the kitchen which, despite its size, had become claustrophobic.

Dean had told her that Mr Chandler-Powell had spoken to everyone in the library. He had said that the patients' wing and the lift were out of bounds but that people should carry on normally as far as possible. The police would want to question everyone but in the meantime he stressed that they should avoid talking among themselves about Miss Gradwyn's death. But Kim knew that they would be discussing it, not in groups but in pairs: the Westhalls, who had returned to Stone Cottage, Miss Cressett with Mrs Frensham and surely Mr Chandler-Powell with Sister. Mog would probably keep silent – he could if it paid him – and she couldn't imagine anyone discussing Miss Gradwyn with Sharon. She and Dean certainly wouldn't if she came into the kitchen. But she and Dean had talked, quietly as if that could somehow make their words innocuous. And now Kim couldn't resist again going over the same ground.

'Suppose the police ask me exactly what happened when I took up Mrs Skeffington's tea, every single detail, must I tell them?'

Dean was trying to be patient. She heard it in his voice. 'Kim, we've settled that. Yes, you tell them. If they ask a direct question we have to answer and tell the truth otherwise we're in trouble. But what happened isn't important. You didn't see anyone or talk to anyone. It can't have anything to do with Miss Gradwyn's death. You could make mischief and for no good reason. Keep quiet until they ask.'

'And you're sure about the door?'

'I'm sure. But if the police start badgering me about it I'll probably end up being sure of nothing.'

Kim said, 'It's very quiet, isn't it? I thought someone would be here by now. Ought we to be here by ourselves?'

Dean said, 'We were told to get on with our work. The kitchen is where we work. And this is where you belong, here with me.'

He came over soundlessly and took her into his arms. They stood immobile for a minute, unspeaking, and she was comforted. Releasing her, he said, 'Anyway, we ought to think about lunch. It's already half past one. So far all anyone has been able to face is coffee and biscuits. They'll want something hot sooner or later and they won't fancy the casserole.'

The beef casserole had been made the previous day and was ready to reheat in the bottom oven of the Aga. Enough had been made for the whole household and for Mog when he came in from working in the garden. But now even the rich smell of it would make her sick.

Dean said, 'No, they won't want anything heavy. I could make pea soup. We've got that stock from the hambone, and then perhaps sandwiches, eggs, cheese . . .' His voice faded.

Kim said, 'But I don't think Mog has gone for the fresh bread. Mr Chandler-Powell said that we ought to stay here.'

'We could make some soda bread, that's always popular.'

'What about the police, will we have to feed them? You said you didn't feed Chief Inspector Whetstone when he arrived, except for coffee, but this new lot are coming from London. They'll have had a long drive.'

'I don't know. I'll have to ask Mr Chandler-Powell.'

And then Kim remembered. How odd, she thought, that she had forgotten. She said, 'It was today we were going to tell him about the baby, after Mrs Skeffington's operation. Now they know and they don't seem worried. Miss Cressett says there's plenty of room in the Manor for a baby.'

Kim thought she detected a small note of impatience, even of subdued satisfaction, in Dean's voice. He said, 'It's no good deciding whether we want to stay on here with the baby when we don't even know if the clinic can continue. Who'd want to come here now? Would you want to sleep in that room?'

Glancing at him, Kim saw his features momentarily harden as if in resolution. And then the door opened and they turned to face Mr Chandler-Powell.

5

Glancing at his watch, Chandler-Powell saw that it was one forty. Perhaps he should now have a word with the Bostocks who were closeted in the kitchen. He needed to check again that Kimberley had fully recovered and that they were giving thought to food. No one had yet eaten. The six hours since the murder was discovered had seemed an eternity in which small unrelated events were recalled with clarity in a waste of unrecorded time. Sealing the murder room as Chief Inspector Whetstone had instructed; finding the widest roll of Sellotape in the recesses of his desk; forgetting to seal the end so that it sprang back and the roll became unusable; Helena taking it from him and coping; at her suggestion, initialling the tape to ensure that it wasn't tampered with. He had no awareness of the growing of the light, of utter darkness becoming a grey winter morning, of the occasional gusts of the dying wind like erratic gunfire. Despite the blips of memory, the confusion of time, he was confident that he had done what was expected of him – coping with Mrs Skeffington's hysteria, examining Kimberley Bostock and giving directions for her care, trying to keep everyone calm during the interminable wait until the local police arrived.

The smell of hot coffee pervaded the house, seeming to intensify. Why had he ever found it comforting? He wondered if he would ever again smell it without a pang of remembered failure. Familiar faces had become those of strangers, carved faces like those of patients enduring unexpected pain, funereal faces seeming as unnaturally solemn as mourners composing themselves appropriately for the obsequies of someone little known, unregretted, but taking on in death a terrifying power. Flavia's bloated face, the swollen eyelids, eyes dulled by tears. Yet he hadn't actually seen her cry and the only words he could remember her speaking had struck him as irritatingly irrelevant.

'You did a beautiful job. Now she'll never see it, and she'd waited so long. All that time and skill wasted, just wasted.'

They had both lost a patient, the only death which had occurred in his clinic at the Manor. Were her tears the tears of frustration or failure? They could hardly, surely, be of grief.

And now he would have to deal with the Bostocks. He must face their demands for reassurance, comfort, decisions on matters which would seem irrelevant but which wouldn't be irrelevant to them. He had said all that was necessary at that meeting at eight fifteen in the library. There at least he had taken responsibility. He had set out to be brief and he had been brief. His voice had been calm, authoritative. They would all have learnt by now of the tragedy that would touch their lives. Miss Rhoda Gradwyn had been found dead in her room at seven thirty this morning. There was some evidence that the death had been unnatural. *Well*, he thought, *that was one way of putting it*. The police had been phoned and a chief inspector from the local constabulary was on his way. Naturally they would all co-operate with police enquiries. In the meantime they should stay calm, refrain from gossip or speculation and get on with their work. What work exactly, he wondered. Mrs Skeffington's operation had been cancelled. The anaesthetist and theatre staff had been telephoned; Flavia and Helena between them had coped with that. And after this brief speech, avoiding questions, he had left the library. But hadn't that exit, all eyes on him, been a histrionic gesture, a deliberate avoidance of responsibility? He remembered standing for a moment outside the door, like a stranger in the house wondering where to go.

And now, seated at the kitchen table with Dean and Kimberley, he was expected to concern himself with pea soup and soda bread. From the moment of entering a room which he seldom had need to visit he felt as inept as an intruder. What reassurance, what comfort were they expecting from him? The two faces confronting his were those of frightened children, seeking the answer to a question that had nothing to do with bread or soup.

Controlling his irritation at their obvious need for firm instructions, he was about to say, 'Just do what you think best', when he heard Helena's footsteps. She had come up quietly behind him. And now he heard her voice.

'Pea soup is an excellent idea, hot, nourishing and comforting. As you've got the stock it could be quickly made. Let's keep the food simple, shall we? We don't want it to look like a parish harvest festival. Serve the soda bread warm and with plenty of butter. A cheese board would be a good addition to the cold meats, people should have some protein, but don't overdo it. Make it look appetising as you always do. No one will be hungry but they'll need to eat. And it would be a good idea to put out Kimberley's excellent home-made lemon curd and apricot jam with the bread. People in shock often crave something sweet. And keep the coffee coming, plenty of coffee.'

Kimberley said, 'Will we need to feed the police, Miss Cressett?'

'I shouldn't think so. No doubt we'll learn that in time. As you know, Chief Inspector Whetstone won't be undertaking this investigation now. They're sending a special squad from the Metropolitan Police. I imagine they'll have fed on the road. You're being splendid, both of you, as you always are. Life is likely to be disturbed for all of us for some time but I know you'll cope. If you have any questions, come to me.'

Reassured, the Bostocks murmured their thanks. Chandler-Powell and Helena moved out together. He said, trying but without success to inject his voice with warmth, 'Thank you. I should have left the Bostocks to you. And what on earth is soda bread?'

'Made with wholemeal flour and without yeast. You've eaten it here often enough. You like it.'

'At least we've sorted out the next meal. I seem to have spent the morning on trivialities. I wish to God this Commander Dalgliesh and his squad would arrive and get on with the investigation. We've got a distinguished forensic pathologist lounging around until Dalgliesh deigns to arrive. Why can't she get on with her job?

And Whetstone's got something better to do than kicking his heels here.'

Helena said, 'And why the Met? The Dorset police are perfectly competent so why can't Chief Inspector Whetstone take on the investigation? It makes me wonder whether there might not be something secret and important about Rhoda Gradwyn, something we don't know.'

'There's always been something we don't know about Rhoda Gradwyn.'

They had passed into the front hall. There was the firm closing of car doors, the sound of voices.

Helena said, 'You best get to the front door. It sounds as if the squad from the Met has arrived.'

6

It was a good day for a drive into the country, a day on which Dalgliesh would usually take his time exploring byways and parking from time to time to enjoy gazing at the thrusting trunks of the great trees stripped for winter, the rising boughs and the dark intricacies of the high twigs patterned against a cloudless sky. Autumn had been prolonged but now he drove under the dazzling white ball of a winter sun, its frayed rim smudging a blue as clear as on a summer day. Its light would soon fade but, now, under its strong brightness, the fields, low hills and clusters of trees were sharp edged and shadowless.

Once free of the traffic of London, they made good time and two and a half hours later they were in east Dorset. Driving into a lay-by, they stopped briefly to eat their picnic lunch and Dalgliesh consulted his map. Fifteen minutes later they came to a crossroads directing them to Stoke Cheverell and about a mile past the village a signpost pointing to Cheverell Manor. They drew up in front of two wrought-iron gates and saw beyond them an avenue of beech trees. Inside the gates an elderly man wrapped in a long overcoat was sitting in what looked like a kitchen chair reading a newspaper. He folded it carefully, taking his time, then advanced to open the high gates. Dalgliesh wondered whether to get out to help him, but the gates swung open easily enough and he drove through, Kate and Benton following. The old man closed the gates behind them, then came up to the car.

He said, 'Miss Cressett don't like cars littering the drive. You'll 'ave to go round the back of the east wing.'

Dalgliesh said, 'We'll do that, but it can wait.'

The three of them pulled their murder bags out of the cars. Even the urgency of the moment, the knowledge that a group of people was awaiting him in various stages of anxiety or apprehension, didn't deter Dalgliesh from pausing for a few seconds to look at the house. He knew that it was regarded as one of the loveliest Tudor manor houses in England and now it was before him in its perfection of form, its confident reconciliation of grace and strength; a house built for certainties, for birth, death and rites of passage, by men who knew what they believed and what they were doing. A house grounded in history, enduring. There was no grass or garden and no statuary in front of the Manor. It presented itself unadorned, its dignity needing no embellishment. He was seeing it at its best. The white morning glare of wintry sunlight had softened, burnishing the trunks of the beech trees and bathing the stones of the manor in a silvery glow, so that for a moment in the stillness it seemed to quiver and become as insubstantial as a vision. The daylight would soon fade; it was the month of the winter solstice. Dusk would fall and night would follow quickly. He and the team would be investigating a deed of darkness in the blackness of midwinter. For someone who loved the light, this imposed a disadvantage which was as much psychological as practical.

As he and the team moved forward, the door of the great porch opened and a man came out to them. He seemed for a moment uncertain whether to salute, then held out his hand and said, 'Chief Inspector Keith Whetstone. You've made good time, sir. The Chief said you'd be wanting SOCOs. We've only got a couple available at present, but they should be here within forty minutes. The photographer's on his way.'

There could, thought Dalgliesh, be no doubt that Whetstone was a policeman, either that or a soldier. He was heavily built but held himself upright. He had a plain but agreeable face, ruddy cheeked, his eyes steady and watchful under hair the colour of old straw, cut *en brosse* and neatly shaped round over-large ears. He was dressed in country tweeds and wearing a greatcoat.

The introductions made, he said, 'Have you any knowledge why the Met are taking the case, sir?'

'None, I'm afraid. I take it you were surprised when the AC phoned.'

'I know the Chief Constable thought it a bit odd, but we're not looking for work. You'll have heard about those arrests on the coast. We've got the Customs and Excise boys crawling all over us. The Yard said you could do with a DC. I'm leaving Malcolm Warren. He's a bit on the quiet side but bright enough and he knows when to keep his mouth shut.'

Dalgliesh said, 'Quiet, reliable and discreet. I've no quarrel with that. Where is he now?'

'Outside the bedroom, guarding the body. The household – well, the six most important members, I suppose – are waiting in the great hall. That's Mr George Chandler-Powell who owns the place, his assistant Mr Marcus Westhall – he's a surgeon so they call him Mr – his sister Miss Candace Westhall, Flavia Holland, the sister in charge, Miss Helena Cressett, who's a kind of house-keeper, secretary and general administrator as far as I can make out, and Mrs Letitia Frensham who does the accounts.'

'An impressive feat of memory, Chief Inspector.'

'Not really, sir. Mr Chandler-Powell's a newcomer but most people hereabouts know who's at the Manor.'

'Has Dr Glenister arrived?'

'An hour ago, sir. She's had tea and done a tour of the garden, had a word with Mog – he's by way of being the gardener – to tell him he's over-pruned the viburnum. And now she's in the hall, unless she's gone for another walk. A lady very fond of outdoor exercise, I'd say. Well, it makes a change from the smell of corpses.'

Dalgliesh asked, 'When did you get here?'

'Twenty minutes after receiving the phone call from Mr Chandler-Powell. I was getting set to act as chief investigating offi-cer when the Chief Constable rang to tell me that the Yard were taking over.'

'Any thoughts, Inspector?'

Dalgliesh's question was partly prompted by courtesy. This wasn't his patch. Time might or might not disclose why the Home

Office had taken a hand, but Whetstone's apparent acceptance of the department's involvement didn't mean that he liked it.

'I'd say it's an inside job, sir. If it is, you've got a limited number of suspects, which in my experience doesn't make the case any easier to crack. Not if they've all got their wits about them, which I reckon most of these will have.'

They were approaching the porch. The door opened as if some-one had been watching to time exactly the moment of arrival. There could be no doubt about the identity of the man who moved to one side as they entered. He was grave faced and with the strained pallor of a man in shock, but had lost none of his author-ity. This was his house and he was in control both of it and of him-self. Without holding out a hand or gazing at Dalgliesh's subordinates, he said, 'George Chandler-Powell. The rest of the party are in the great hall.'

They followed him through the porch and to a door to the left of the square entrance hall. Surprisingly the heavy oak door was shut and Chandler-Powell opened it. Dalgliesh wondered whether he had intended this first sight of the hall to be so dramatic. He experienced an extraordinary moment in which architecture, colours, shape and sounds, the soaring roof, the great tapestry on the right-hand wall, the vase of winter foliage on an oak table to the left of the door, the row of portraits in their gilt frames, some objects clearly seen even in a first glance, others perhaps dredged from some childish memory or fantasy, seemed to fuse into a living picture which immediately impregnated his mind.

The five people who were waiting on each side of the fire, their faces turned towards him, looked like a tableau, cunningly arranged to give the room its identity and humanity. There was a minute, oddly embarrassing because it seemed an inappropriate formality, in which Dalgliesh and Chandler-Powell quickly made their introductions. Chandler-Powell's were hardly necessary. The only other male had to be Marcus Westhall, the pale-faced woman with the distinctive features Helena Cressett, the shorter dark woman and the only one whose face bore signs of possible tears, Sister Flavia Holland. The tall elderly woman standing on the fringe of the group seemed to have been overlooked by Chandler-Powell. Now she came quietly forward, shook Dalgliesh's hand and said, 'Letitia Frensham. I do the accounts.'

Chandler-Powell said, 'I understand you already know Dr Glenister.'

Dalgliesh went over to her chair and they shook hands. She was the only person still seated and it was apparent from the tea service on a table beside her that she had been served tea. She wore the same clothes as he remembered from their last meeting, trousers tucked into leather boots and a tweed jacket which looked too heavy for her diminutive frame. A wide-brimmed hat, which she invariably wore at a rakish angle, now rested on the arm of the chair. Without it, her head, the scalp half-visible through the short white hair, looked as vulnerable as a child's. Her features were delicate and her skin so pale that occasionally she looked like a woman gravely ill. But she was extraordinarily tough and her eyes, so dark they were almost black, were the eyes of a much younger woman. Dalgliesh would have preferred, as he always did, his long-standing colleague Dr Kynaston, but he was glad enough to see someone he liked and respected and with whom he had worked before. Dr Glenister was one of the most highly regarded forensic pathologists in Europe, an author of distinguished textbooks on the subject and a formidable expert witness in court. But her presence was an unwelcome reminder of Number Ten's interest. The distinguished Dr Glenister tended to be called in when the government was involved.

Getting to her feet with the ease of a young woman, she said, 'Commander Dalgliesh and I are old colleagues. Well, shall we get started? Mr Chandler-Powell, I'd like you to come up if Commander Dalgliesh has no objections.'

Dalgliesh said, 'None.'

He was probably the only police officer whom Dr Glenister would invite to concur in any decision of hers. He recognised the problem. There were medical details which only Chandler-Powell could provide, but there were things she and Dalgliesh might want to say which it would be unwise to discuss over the body with

Chandler-Powell present. Chandler-Powell had to be a suspect; Dr Glenister knew it – and so, no doubt, did Chandler-Powell.

They crossed the square entrance hall and climbed the staircase, Chandler-Powell and Dr Glenister leading. Their feet sounded unnaturally loud on the uncarpeted wood. The stairs led to a landing. The door to the right was open and Dalgliesh could glimpse a long low room with an intricate ceiling. Chandler-Powell said, 'The long gallery. Sir Walter Raleigh danced there when he visited the Manor. Apart from the furnishings it's still as it was then.'

No one commented. A second and shorter flight of stairs led to a door which opened on to a carpeted passage with rooms facing west and east.

Chandler-Powell said, 'The patients' accommodation is on this corridor. Suites with sitting room, bedroom and shower. Immediately underneath the long gallery has been furnished as a joint sitting room. Most patients prefer to stay in their suite or, occasionally, to use the library on the ground floor. Sister Holland's rooms are the first facing west, opposite the lift.'

There was no need to point out which room Rhoda Gradwyn had occupied. A uniformed police officer seated at the door sprang up smartly as they appeared and saluted.

Dalgliesh said, 'You're Detective Constable Warren?'

'Yes, sir.'

'How long have you been on guard?'

'Since Inspector Whetstone and I arrived, sir. That was at five past eight. The tape was already in place.'

Chandler-Powell said, 'I was instructed to seal the door by Inspector Whetstone.'

Dalgliesh peeled the adhesive tape away and he entered the sitting room with Kate and Benton following. There was a strong smell of vomit, strangely at odds with the formality of the room. The door to the bedroom was to the left. It was closed and Chandler-Powell pushed it gently open against the impediment of a fallen tray, the cups broken and the teapot, its lid detached, lying on its side. The bedroom was in darkness, lit only by the daylight streaming in from the sitting room. The dark stain of tea splattered the carpet.

Chandler-Powell said, 'I left things exactly as I found them. No one has entered this room since Sister and I left it. I suppose this mess can be cleared up once the body has been moved.'

Dalgliesh said, 'Not until the scene has been searched.'

The room was not unduly small but, with five people, it suddenly seemed crowded. It was a little smaller than the sitting room but furnished with an elegance which intensified the dark horror of what lay on the bed. With Kate and Benton at the rear they approached the body. Dalgliesh switched on the light at the door and then turned to the bedside lamp. He saw that the bulb was missing and that the cord with its red call button had been looped high above the bed. They stood by the body in silence, Chandler-Powell keeping a little distant, aware that he might be there under sufferance.

The bed faced the window, which was closed and with the curtains drawn. Rhoda Gradwyn was lying on her back, her two arms, the hands clenched, were raised awkwardly above her head as if in a gesture of theatrical surprise, the dark hair splayed over the pillow. The left side of her face was covered by a taped surgical dressing but what flesh could be seen was a bright cherry red. The right eye, filmed in death, was fully open, the left, partly obscured by the thick dressing, was half-closed, giving the body a bizarre and unnerving look of a corpse peering balefully from an eye not yet dead. The sheet covered her body up to the shoulders as if her killer were deliberately exposing his handiwork framed by the two narrow straps of her white linen nightdress. The cause of death was evident. She had been throttled by a human hand.

Dalgliesh knew that speculative gazes fixed on a corpse – his own among them – were different from the gazes fixed on living flesh. Even for a professional inured to the sight of violent death there would always be a vestige of pity, anger or horror. The best pathologists and police officers, standing where they stood now, never lost respect for the dead, a respect born of shared emotions, however temporary, the unspoken recognition of a common humanity, a common end. But all humanity, all personality was extinguished with the last breath. The body, already subject to the inexorable process of decay, had been demoted to an exhibit, to be treated with a serious professional concern, a focus for emotions it could no longer share, no more be troubled by. Now the only physical communication was with gloved exploring hands, probes, thermometers, scalpels, wielded on a body laid open like the carcase of an animal. This was not the most horrific corpse he had seen in his years as a detective, but now it seemed to hold a career's accumulation of pity, anger and impotence. He thought, *Perhaps I've had enough of murder.*

The room in which she lay, like the sitting room through which they had passed, despite its comfort was too carefully furnished, achieving an organised perfection which for him was unwelcoming and impersonal. The objects he had glimpsed as he passed through the sitting room to her bedside arranged themselves in his memory: the Georgian writing desk, the two modern easy chairs before a stone grate fitted with an electric heater, the mahogany bookcase and bureau arranged to their advantage. And yet they were rooms in which he would never have felt at home. They reminded him of a country-house hotel once – and only once – visited, where the overcharged guests were subtly made to feel socially inferior in their taste to that of the owners. No imperfections were allowed. He wondered who had arranged the rooms. Presumably Miss Cressett. If so, she was trying to convey that this part of the Manor was merely a short-stay hotel. Visitors were here to be impressed but not to take over even temporary possession. Rhoda Gradwyn may have felt differently, may even have been at home here. But the room, for her, had not been tainted by the noxious contamination of murder.

Turning to Chandler-Powell, Dr Glenister said, 'You had, of course, seen her the evening before.'

'Naturally.'

'And is this how you found her this morning?'

'Yes. When I saw her throat I knew that there was nothing I could do, that there was no possibility that this was a natural death. It hardly needs a consultant forensic pathologist to diagnose how she died. She's been throttled. What you see now is exactly what I saw when I first approached the bed.'

Dalgliesh asked, 'Were you alone?'

'I was alone at the bedside. Sister Holland was in the sitting room coping with Kimberley Bostock, the assistant cook who had brought up the early morning tea. When she saw the body, Sister pressed the red call button in the sitting room several times so I knew that there was some kind of emergency. As you'll see, the one by the bed has been looped out of reach. Very wisely, Sister Holland didn't touch it. She has assured me that it was lying as usual on the bedside table when she settled the patient for the night. I thought that probably the patient had panicked or was ill and I expected to find Sister here also responding to the call. We shut both doors and I carried Kimberley down to her own apartment. I called her husband to stay with her and immediately telephoned the local police. Chief Inspector Whetstone instructed me about sealing the room and was here in charge until you arrived. I had already arranged for this corridor and the lift to be out of bounds.'

Dr Glenister had been bending over the body but without touching it. Now she straightened herself and said, 'She was strangled by a right-handed grip, the hand probably in a smooth glove. There is bruising by the right-hand fingers and thumb but no nail scratches. I'll know more when I have her on the table.' She turned to Chandler-Powell. 'There's one question, please. Did you prescribe any sedatives for her yesterday night?'

'I offered her Temazepam but she said she didn't need it. She had come out of the anaesthetic well, had had a light supper and was now feeling drowsy. She thought she'd have no difficulty in sleeping. Sister Holland was the last person to see her – apart, of course, from her murderer – and all she asked for was a glass of hot milk laced with brandy. Sister Holland waited while she drank and then removed the glass. It has of course now been washed.'

Dr Glenister said, 'I think the lab will find it useful if they could have a list of all the sedatives that you keep in the dispensary here, or any drugs to which a patient could have had access or been given. Thank you, Mr Chandler-Powell.'

Dalgliesh said, 'It would be helpful to have a preliminary talk with you alone, perhaps in ten minutes' time. I need to get an idea of the layout here and the number and function of the staff, and how Miss Gradwyn came to be your patient.'

Chandler-Powell said, 'I'll be in the general office. It's inside the porch opposite the great hall. I'll look out a plan of the Manor for you.'

They waited until they heard his footsteps in the next room and the closing of the corridor door. Now Dr Glenister took her surgical gloves from the Gladstone bag and gently touched Gradwyn's face, then her neck and arms. The forensic pathologist had been a notable teacher and Dalgliesh knew from experience of working with her that she could seldom resist the opportunity to instruct the young.

She said to Benton, 'No doubt you know all about rigor mortis, Sergeant.'

'No ma'am. I know it begins in the eyelids about three hours after death, then spreads down through the face and neck to the thorax, and finally the trunk and lower extremities. The stiffening is generally complete in about twelve hours and begins to wear off in reverse order after about thirty-six hours.'

'And do you think that rigor mortis is a reliable assessment of the time of death?'

'Not entirely reliable, ma'am.'

'Not reliable at all. It can be complicated by the temperature of the room, the muscular condition of the subject, the cause of death, and by some conditions which may simulate rigor mortis but are different, that includes bodies exposed to great heat and a cadaveric spasm. You know what that is, Sergeant?'

'Yes ma'am. It can occur at the instant of death. The muscles of the hand tighten so that anything the dead person may have been clutching is difficult to extract.'

'The assessment of an accurate time of death is one of the most important responsibilities of a medical examiner, and one of the most difficult. One development is the analysis of the amount of potassium in the fluid of the eye. Here I shall know more precisely when I've taken the rectal temperature and done the post mortem. In the meantime, I can give a preliminary assessment based on the hypostasis – you know what that is, I'm sure.'

'Yes ma'am. Post-mortem lividity.'

'Which we see here probably at its height. Based on that and the present development of rigor mortis, my preliminary estimate would be that she died between eleven p.m. and twelve thirty a.m., probably closer to the first. I'm relieved, Sergeant, that you're not likely to become one of those investigative officers who expect the forensic pathologist to provide an accurate estimate within minutes of viewing the body.'

The words were a dismissal. It was then that the telephone on the bedside table rang. The bell was strident and unexpected, the insistent peal seeming a macabre invasion of the privacy of the dead. For a few seconds no one moved except Dr Glenister, who went calmly over to her Gladstone bag as if she were stone deaf.

Dalgliesh picked up the receiver. It was Whetstone's voice. 'The photographer has arrived and the two SOCOs are on their way, sir. If I could just hand over to one of your team I'll be on my way.'

Dalgliesh said, 'Thank you. I'll be down.'

He had seen all he needed to at the bedside. He wasn't sorry to be spared Dr Glenister's examination of the body. He said, 'The photographer has arrived. I can send him up if that's convenient for you.'

Dr Glenister said, 'I shan't need more than another ten minutes. Then yes, send him up. I'll phone for the mortuary van as soon as he's done. No doubt the people here will be glad to see the body leave. And then we can have a word before I go.'

Kate had been silent throughout. As they walked down the stairs, Dalgliesh said to Benton, 'Cope with the photographer and SOCOs will you, Benton. They can get started after the body has been removed. We'll take prints later but I'm not hopeful of getting anything significant. Probably any one of the staff here could legitimately have entered the room at some time or other. Kate, will you come with me to the general office. Chandler-Powell should have the name of Rhoda Gradwyn's next of kin, possibly also her solicitor. Someone will have to break the news and that will probably be best done by the local police, whoever they are. And we need to know a great deal more about this place, the layout, what staff Chandler-Powell has and when they're here.

Whoever throttled her could have been using surgical gloves. Most people know that you can get prints from the inside of latex gloves so they'll probably have been destroyed. And the SOCOs need to pay attention to the lift. And now, Kate, we'll see what Mr Chandler-Powell has to say to us.'

7

In the office Chandler-Powell was seated at the desk with two maps spread out before him, one of the house in relation to the village, and a plan of the Manor. He got up as they entered and moved round the desk. Together they bent over the plans.

He said, 'The patients' wing, which you've just visited, is here on the west, together with Sister Holland's bedroom and sitting room. The centre part of the house comprises the entrance hall, the great hall, the library and the dining room, and a flat for the cook and his wife, Dean and Kimberley Bostock, above the kitchen which overlooks the knot garden. The domestic helper, Sharon Bateman, has a bed-sitting room next to them. My rooms and the flat occupied by Miss Cressett are in the east wing, as is Mrs Frensham's sitting room and bedroom, and two guest rooms, now unoccupied. I've made a list of the non-resident staff. Apart from the staff you've met, I employ an anaesthetist and additional nursing staff for the theatre. Some come in by bus early on operating mornings, others drive. None stay here overnight. A part-time nurse, Ruth Frazer, shared responsibility with Sister Holland until nine thirty when she went off duty.'

Dalgliesh asked, 'The elderly man who opened the gate for us, is he here full time?'

'That's Tom Mogworthy. I inherited him after I bought the Manor. He'd worked as gardener here for thirty years. He comes from an old Dorset family and regards himself as an expert on the history, traditions and folklore of the county, the bloodier the better. Actually his father moved to London's East End before Mog was born and he was thirty before he returned to what he sees as his roots. In some ways he's more of a cockney than a countryman. As far as I know he's displayed no murderous tendencies and if one discounts headless horsemen, witches' curses and the ghostly armies of marching Royalists, he's truthful and reliable. He lives with his sister in the village. Marcus Westhall and his sister occupy Stone Cottage, which is part of the Manor estate.'

Dalgliesh said, 'And Rhoda Gradwyn. How did she come to be a patient?'

'I first saw her in Harley Street on the 21st of November. She wasn't referred by her GP as is general, but I had a word with him. She came for the removal of a deep scar on her left cheek. I saw her once at St Angela's Hospital where she underwent tests, and briefly when she arrived on Thursday afternoon. She was also here on the 27th of November for a preliminary visit and stayed for two nights, but we didn't meet on that occasion. I'd never met her before she came to Harley Street and have no idea why she chose the Manor. I assumed she had checked on the reputation of cosmetic surgeons and, given a choice of London or Dorset, chose the Manor because she wanted privacy. I know nothing about her except her reputation as a journalist and, of course, her medical history. At our first interview I found her very calm, very straightforward, very clear about what she wanted. One thing was interesting. I asked her why she had waited so long to get rid of the disfigurement and why now. She replied, "Because I no longer have need of it."'

There was a silence, then Dalgliesh said, 'I have to ask you this. Have you any idea who is responsible for Miss Gradwyn's death? If you have suspicions or if there is anything I should know, please tell me now.'

'So you're assuming that this is what you no doubt call an inside job?'

'I'm assuming nothing. But Rhoda Gradwyn was your patient, killed in your house.'

'But not by one of my staff. I don't employ homicidal maniacs.'

Dalgliesh said, 'I doubt very much whether this is the work of a maniac, nor am I assuming that a member of your staff was responsible.' He went on, 'Would Miss Gradwyn have been physically capable of leaving her room and taking the lift to the ground floor to unlock the door of the west wing?'

Chandler-Powell said, 'It would be perfectly possible after she had fully regained consciousness, but as she was constantly monitored while she was in the recovery room and initially visited every half-hour after she was wheeled back to her suite at four thirty, the only possibility would have been after ten o'clock when she had been settled for the night. Then in my view she would have been physically capable of leaving her suite, although there would, of course, have been a possibility that someone would have seen her. And she would have needed a set of keys. She couldn't have taken a set from the key cupboard in the office without setting off the alarm. This map of the Manor shows how the system works. The front door, the great hall, library, dining room and office are all protected but not the west wing where we rely on bolts and keys. I am responsible at night for setting the alarm, Miss Cressett when I'm not here. I bolt the west door at eleven unless I know someone is out. Last night I bolted it at eleven as usual.'

'Was Miss Gradwyn given a set of keys to the west door when she arrived for her preliminary visit?'

'Certainly. All patients are. Miss Gradwyn inadvertently took her keys with her when she left. It does happen. She returned them with apologies within two days.'

'And on this visit?'

'She arrived on Thursday after dark and said she had no wish to go into the garden. In the normal course of events she would have been given the keys this morning.'

'And you keep a check on them?'

'A reasonable check. There are six suites for patients and six numbered keys with two spares. I can't vouch for every set. Patients, particularly long-stay patients, have freedom to come and go. I'm not running a psychiatric hospital. The west door is the one they use. And, of course, all members of the household have keys to the front and west doors. These are all accounted for, as are the patients' keys. They're in the key cupboard.'

The keys were in a small mahogany cupboard fitted to the wall beside the fireplace. Dalgliesh checked that all six numbered sets were there with two spares.

Chandler-Powell didn't question what possible reason Rhoda Gradwyn could have had for arranging an assignation when post-operative, nor the many objections to any theory based on this unlikely hypothesis, and nor did Dalgliesh pursue the matter. But it had been important to ask the question.

Chandler-Powell said, 'From what Dr Glenister said at the scene and what I myself observed, no doubt you will be interested in the surgical gloves we keep here. The ones for use while operating are kept in the surgical supplies room in the operating suite, which is kept locked. Latex gloves are also used by nursing and household staff when necessary and this supply is in the housemaid's cupboard on the ground floor next to the kitchen. The gloves are bought by the box and one box is open, but none of the gloves, either there or in the operating suite, are checked. They're disposable items used as necessary and thrown away.'

Kate thought, *So anyone at the Manor would know that there were gloves in the housemaid's cupboard. But no outsider would unless told in advance.* There was no evidence at present that surgical gloves had been used, but they would be the obvious choice for anyone in the know.

Chandler-Powell began folding the map and the plan of the Manor. He said, 'I have Miss Gradwyn's personal file here. There is information which you may need and which I've already given to Chief Inspector Whetstone, the name and address of her mother whom she gave as next of kin and of her solicitor. And there's one other patient who spent the night here who I think may be helpful, Mrs Laura Skeffington. At her request I fitted her in for a minor procedure today, although I'm running down the clinic for the long Christmas break. She was in the room next to Miss Gradwyn and claims she saw lights in the grounds during the night. Not unnaturally she's anxious to leave, so it would be helpful if you or one of your team could see her first. She has already returned her keys.'

Dalgliesh was tempted to say that this information could well have been given earlier. He said, 'Where is Mrs Skeffington now?'

'In the library with Mrs Frensham. I thought it wise not to leave Mrs Skeffington alone. She's frightened and shocked, that's to be expected. Obviously she couldn't stay in her room. And I thought you wouldn't want anyone on the guest landing, so I put the corridor and lift out of bounds as soon as I was called to the body. Later, on Chief Inspector Whetstone's telephoned instructions, I sealed the room. Mrs Frensham has helped Mrs Skeffington to pack and she has her suitcases with her ready to leave. It can't be too soon for her – or indeed for us.'

Kate thought, *So, he took care to preserve the scene of crime as far as possible, even before he rang the local police. Thoughtful of him. Or is he demonstrating his willingness to co-operate? Either way, it was sensible to keep the landing and lift sacrosanct, but hardly crucial. People – patients and staff – must use them daily. If this is an inside job we shan't get much help from prints.*

The group passed into the great hall. Dalgliesh said, 'I should like to see everyone together, that is all those who had any contact with Miss Gradwyn from the time she arrived and who were in the house yesterday from four thirty when she was taken back to her room, including Mr Mogworthy. There will be individual interviews later in the Old Police Cottage. I shall try to interrupt people's routine as little as possible but some disruption is inevitable.'

Chandler-Powell said, 'You'll need a reasonably large room. When Mrs Skeffington has been interviewed and has left, the library will be free, if that will be convenient. The library can also be made available to you and your officers for any individual interviews.'

Dalgliesh said, 'Thank you. That will be convenient for both parties. But first I need to see Mrs Skeffington.'

As they left the office, Chandler-Powell said, 'I'm arranging for a team of private security men to ensure that we don't get bothered by the media or a crowd of rubber-necking locals. You have no objection to that, I presume.'

'None as long as they stay outside the gate and don't interfere with my investigation. It will be for me to decide whether or not they do.'

Chandler-Powell made no reply. Outside the door Benton joined them and they made their way to the library and Mrs Skeffington.

8

Passing through the great hall, Kate was again jolted into a vivid impression of light, space and colour, the leaping flames of the wood fire, the chandelier which transformed the dimness of the winter afternoon, the muted but clear colour of the tapestry, gilt frames, richly painted robes, and high above the dark beams of the soaring roof. Like the rest of the Manor, it seemed a place to be visited in wonder, never actually lived in. She could never be happy in such a house, imposing the obligations of the past, a publicly borne burden of responsibility, and thought with satisfaction of that light-filled, sparsely furnished flat high above the Thames. The door to the library, concealed in the oak linen-fold, was on the right-hand wall close to the fireplace. Kate doubted whether she would have noticed it if it hadn't been opened by Chandler-Powell.

In contrast to the great hall, the room they entered struck her as surprisingly small, comfortable and unpretentious, a book-lined sanctum guarding its silence as it did the shelves of leather-backed books so closely aligned in height that they looked as if none of them had ever been taken down. As always she assessed the room with a quick surreptitious glance. She had never forgotten a rebuke of AD's to a detective sergeant when she had first entered the Squad. 'We're here by consent but we're not welcome. It's still their home. Don't gawp at their belongings, Simon, as if you're assessing them for a car-boot sale.' The shelves, which lined all the walls except the one with the three tall windows, were in a lighter wood than the hall, the carvings simpler and more elegant.

Perhaps the library was a later addition. Above the shelves were ranged marble busts, dehumanised by their sightless eyes into mere icons. No doubt AD and Benton would know who they were, would know, too, the approximate date of the wood carving, would feel at home here. She thrust the thought out of her mind. Surely by now she had disciplined a tinge of intellectual inferiority which she knew was as unnecessary as it was tedious. No one she had ever worked with on the Squad had made her feel less intelligent than she knew herself to be, and after their case on Combe Island she thought she had put behind her for ever this demeaning half-paranoia.

Mrs Skeffington was sitting in a high-backed chair before the fire. She didn't rise but settled herself more elegantly, the thin legs held side by side. Her face was a pale oval, the skin taut over high cheekbones, the full mouth glossy with scarlet lipstick. Kate thought that if this unlined perfection was the result of Mr Chandler-Powell's expertise, he had served her well. But her neck, darker, creped and ringed with the creases of age, and the hands with their purple veins, were not those of a young woman. The hair, glossy black, rose from a peak at the forehead and fell in straight waves to her shoulders. Her hands were busy with it, twisting it and pushing it back behind her ears. Mrs Frensham, who had been sitting opposite, got up and stood, hands folded, while Chandler-Powell made the introductions. Kate watched with cynical amusement the expected reaction as Mrs Skeffington's eyes fixed on Benton, widened into a fleeting but intense look compounded of surprise, interest and calculation. But it was to Chandler-Powell that she spoke, her voice as resentful as a querulous child.

'I thought you'd never arrive. I've been sitting here for hours waiting for someone to come.'

'But you weren't left alone at any time, were you? I arranged that you shouldn't be.'

'It was as bad as being alone. Just the one person. Sister, who didn't stay for long, wouldn't talk about what happened. I suppose she was told not to. Nor did Miss Cressett when she took over.

And now Mrs Frensham is saying nothing. It's like being in a morgue or under supervision. The Rolls is outside. I saw it arrive from the window. Robert, our chauffeur, will need to get back, and I can't stay here. It's nothing to do with me. I want to go home.'

Then, recovering herself with surprising suddenness, she turned to Dalgliesh and held out her hand. 'I'm so glad you've come, Commander. Stuart said that you would. He told me not to worry, he'd get the best.'

There was a silence. Mrs Skeffington looked momentarily disconcerted and turned her eyes to George Chandler-Powell. *So that's why we're here,* thought Kate, *why the request for the Squad had come from Number Ten.* Without turning her head, she couldn't resist a glance at Dalgliesh. No one was better than her chief in concealing anger, but it was there for her to read in the momentary flush across the forehead, the coldness of his eyes, the face briefly hardening into a mask, the almost imperceptible tightening of the muscles. She told herself that Emma had never seen that look. There were still areas of Dalgliesh's life which she, Kate, shared which were closed to the woman he loved, and always would be. Emma knew the poet and the lover but not the detective, not the police officer. His job and hers were prohibited territory to anyone who had not taken the oath, been invested with their dangerous authority. It was she who was the comrade-in-arms, not the woman who had his heart. You couldn't understand the job of policing if you hadn't done it. She had taught herself not to feel jealousy, to try to rejoice in his triumph, but she couldn't help relishing from time to time this small ungenerous consolation.

Mrs Frensham murmured a goodbye and left, and Dalgliesh seated himself in the chair she had vacated. He said, 'I hope we won't have to detain you too long, Mrs Skeffington, but there is information I need to have from you. Can you tell us exactly what has happened to you since you arrived here yesterday afternoon.'

'You mean from the time I actually got here?' Dalgliesh didn't reply. Mrs Skeffington said, 'But that's ridiculous. I'm sorry, but there's nothing to tell. Nothing happened, well nothing out of the ordinary, not until last night, and I suppose I could have been mistaken. I came to have an operation set for tomorrow – I mean today. I just happened to be here. I don't suppose I'll ever come back. It's all been a terrible waste of time.'

Her voice trailed off. Dalgliesh said, 'If we could take it from the time you arrived. Did you drive from London?'

'I was driven. Robert brought me in the Rolls. I've told you, he's waiting to take me home. My husband sent him back as soon as I phoned.'

'And that was when?'

'As soon as they told me that a patient was dead. I suppose it was about eight o'clock. There was a great deal of coming and going, footsteps and voices, so I put my head out of the door and Mr Chandler-Powell came in and told me what had happened.'

'Did you know Rhoda Gradwyn was a patient in the room next door?'

'No, I didn't. I didn't know she was here at all. I didn't see her after I arrived and no one told me she was here.'

'Did you ever meet her before you came?'

'No, of course I didn't. I mean, why would I meet her? Isn't she a journalist or something? Stuart says to keep away from people like that. You tell them things and they always betray you. I mean, it's not as if we're in the same social circle.'

'But you knew that someone was in the room next to you?'

'Well, I knew that Kimberley had been in with some supper. I heard the trolley. Of course, I hadn't had anything to eat since a light lunch at home. I couldn't because of the anaesthetic next day. Only now, of course, it doesn't matter.'

Dalgliesh said, 'Can we get back to the time of your arrival. When was that?'

'Well, it was about five o'clock. I was met by Mr Westhall, Sister Holland and Miss Cressett in the hall and I had tea with them, but nothing to eat. It was too dark to walk in the garden so I said I'd spend the rest of the day in my suite. I had to be up fairly early because the anaesthetist would be here and he and Mr Chandler-Powell would want to check on me before my operation. So I went to my room and watched television until about ten o'clock, when I thought I'd go to bed.'

'And what happened in the night?'

'Well, I took some time getting to sleep, and it must have been after eleven before I did. But later on I woke needing to go to the bathroom.'

'What time was that?'

'I looked at my watch to check how long I'd been sleeping. It was about twenty to twelve. It was then I heard the lift. It's opposite Sister's suite – well, I expect you've seen it. I just heard the gentle clang of the doors and then a sort of purring sound as it went down. Before going back to bed I went to draw back the curtains. I always sleep with the window a little open and I thought I'd like some air. It was then I saw this light among the Cheverell Stones.'

'What kind of light, Mrs Skeffington?'

'A small light moving among the stones. It could have been a torch, I suppose. It flickered and then it disappeared. Perhaps whoever was there had switched it off, or pointed it down. I didn't see it again.' She paused.

Dalgliesh said, 'And then what did you do?'

'Well, I was frightened. I remembered about the witch who was burnt there and how the stones are said to be haunted. There was some light from the stars, but it was very dark and I had the sense that there was someone there. Well, there must have been or I wouldn't have seen the light. I don't believe in ghosts of course, but it was eerie. Horrible really. Suddenly I wanted company. I wanted someone to talk to, so I thought of the patient next door. But when I opened the door into the corridor I realised that I wasn't being – well, considerate I suppose. After all, it was nearly midnight. She was probably asleep. If I woke her she'd probably complain to Sister Holland. Sister can be quite strict if you do something she disapproves of.'

Kate said, 'So you knew it was a woman next door?'

Mrs Skeffington looked at her, Kate thought, as she might have turned her gaze on a recalcitrant housemaid. 'It usually is a woman, isn't it? I mean, this is a clinic for cosmetic surgery. Anyway, I didn't knock on the next door. I decided I'd ring Kimberley for some tea and read or listen to the radio until I felt tired.'

Dalgliesh asked, 'And when you looked out into the corridor, did you see anyone or hear anything?'

'No, of course I didn't. I would have said so before now. The corridor was empty and very quiet. Creepy really. Just the one low light outside the lift.'

Dalgliesh asked, 'When exactly did you open your door and look out? Can you remember?'

'I suppose about five to twelve. I couldn't have spent more than five minutes at the window. So I rang for tea and Kimberley brought it up.'

'Did you tell her about the light?'

'Yes I did. I said it was the light flickering in the stones that had frightened me and was keeping me awake. That's why I wanted the tea. And I wanted company. But Kimberley didn't stay long. I suppose she's not allowed to chatter to the patients.'

Chandler-Powell suddenly intervened. 'You didn't think of waking Sister Holland? You knew her room was on the corridor next to yours. That's why she sleeps on the patients' floor, to be available if a patient needs her.'

'She'd probably have thought I was being foolish. And I didn't think I was a patient, not until the operation. It wasn't as if I needed anything, medicine or sleeping pills.'

There was a silence. As if realising for the first time the importance of what she had been saying, Mrs Skeffington looked from Dalgliesh to Kate. 'Of course I could have been mistaken about the light. I mean, it was late at night and I could have been imagining things.'

Kate said, 'When you went into the corridor with the idea of visiting the patient next door, were you certain then that you'd seen a light?'

'Well, I must have been, mustn't I? I mean, otherwise I wouldn't have gone out like that. But that doesn't mean it really had been there. I hadn't been awake for long and I suppose looking out on the stones and thinking of the poor woman burnt alive I could have imagined I was seeing a ghost.'

Kate said, 'And earlier, when you heard the lift door clang and the lift descending, are you now saying that too could have been imagination?'

'Well, I don't suppose I could have imagined hearing the lift. I mean, someone must have been using it. But they easily could, couldn't they? I mean, anyone wanting to come up to the patients' corridor. Someone visiting Rhoda Gradwyn, for example.'

The silence which fell seemed to Kate to last for minutes. Then Dalgliesh said, 'Did you at any time last night see or hear anything next door, or anything in the corridor outside your room?'

'No, nothing, nothing. I only knew that there was anyone next door because I heard Sister going in. I mean, everyone is kept very confidential at the clinic.'

Chandler-Powell said, 'Surely Miss Cressett told you when she took you up to your room?'

'She did mention that there was only one other patient in residence but she didn't tell me where she was, or her name. Anyway, I don't see that it matters. And I could have been mistaken about the light. Only I wasn't about the lift. I don't think I could have been mistaken about hearing the lift going down. Perhaps that was what woke me up.' She turned to Dalgliesh, 'And now I want to go home. My husband said I wouldn't be bothered, that the best team in the Met would be put on the job and I'd be protected. I don't want to stay in a place where there's a murderer on the loose. And it could have been me. Perhaps it was me he wanted to kill. After all, my husband has enemies. Powerful men always have. And I was next door, alone, helpless. Suppose he'd gone to the wrong room and killed me by mistake? Patients come here because they believe it's safe. God knows it's expensive enough. And how did he get in? I've told you everything I know, but I don't think I could swear to it in court. I don't see why I should have to.'

Dalgliesh said, 'It may be necessary, Mrs Skeffington. I shall almost certainly want to speak to you again and if so, I can of course see you in London, either at your house or at New Scotland Yard.'

The prospect was clearly unwelcome but, glancing from Kate to Dalgliesh, Mrs Skeffington obviously decided it was wiser not to comment. Instead she smiled at Dalgliesh and assumed the voice of a wheedling child. 'And please may I go now? I've tried to be helpful, I really have. But it was late and I was alone and frightened and now it all seems like a terrible dream.'

But Dalgliesh hadn't yet finished with his witness. He asked, 'Were you given keys to the west door when you arrived, Mrs Skeffington?'

'Yes I was. By Sister. I'm always given two security keys. This time it was set number one. I gave them to Mrs Frensham when she helped me with my packing. Robert came up to carry the bags to the car. He wasn't allowed to use the lift so he had to lug them down the stairs. Mr Chandler-Powell ought to employ a manservant. Mog isn't really suitable to be in the Manor in any capacity.'

'Where did you put the keys during the night?'

'By my bed I suppose. No, it was on the table in front of the television. Anyway, I gave them to Mrs Frensham. If they're lost that's nothing to do with me.'

Dalgliesh said, 'No, they're not lost. Thank you for your help, Mrs Skeffington.'

Now that she was at last free to leave, Mrs Skeffington became gracious and bestowed vague thanks and insincere smiles indiscriminately on everyone present. Chandler-Powell escorted her out to the car. No doubt, Kate thought, he would take the opportunity to reassure or propitiate her but even he could hardly hope that she would hold her tongue. She wouldn't return, of course, and nor would others. Patients might enjoy a small frisson of vicarious terror at the thought of a seventeenth-century burning, but were unlikely to choose a clinic where a relatively helpless post-operative patient had been brutally done to death. If George Chandler-Powell depended on his income from the clinic to keep the Manor going, he was likely to be in trouble. There would be more than one victim of this murder.

They waited until they heard the sound of the departing Rolls-Royce and Chandler-Powell reappeared. Dalgliesh said, 'The incident room will be in the Old Police Cottage and my officers will be staying at Wisteria House. I would be grateful if the household could be assembled in the library in half an hour's time. Meanwhile the scene of crime officers will be busy in the west wing. I'm grateful to you for putting the library at my disposal for the next hour or so.'

9

By the time Dalgliesh with Kate had returned to the scene of crime Rhoda Gradwyn's body had been removed. The two mortuary attendants had with practised ease zipped her into a body bag and wheeled the stretcher into the lift. Benton was below to see the departure of the ambulance, which had arrived instead of a mortuary van to collect the corpse, and to await the arrival of the scene-of-crime officers. The photographer, a large nimble-footed man of few words, had completed his work and had already left. And now, before beginning the protracted routine of interviewing the suspects, Dalgliesh returned with Kate to the empty bedroom.

When the young Dalgliesh had first been promoted to the CID, it seemed to him that the air of a murder room always changed when the corpse had been removed, and more subtly than the physical absence of the victim. The air seemed easier to breathe, voices were louder, there was a shared relief as if an object with some mysterious power to threaten or contaminate had been robbed of its potency. Some vestige of this feeling remained. The disordered bed with the indent of the head still on the pillow looked as innocuous and normal as if the occupant had recently got up from sleep and would shortly return. It was the dropped tray of crockery just inside the door that, for Dalgliesh, imposed on the room a symbolism both dramatic and discomforting. The scene looked as if it had been set up to be photographed for the jacket of an upmarket thriller.

None of Miss Gradwyn's belongings had been touched and her briefcase was next door, still propped against the bureau in the sitting room. A large metallic suitcase on wheels stood beside the chest of drawers. Dalgliesh placed his murder bag – a description which persisted despite the fact that it was now a fitted attaché case – on the folding baggage stool. He opened it and he and Kate put on their search gloves.

Miss Gradwyn's handbag, made of green leather with a silver clasp and shaped like a Gladstone bag, was obviously a designer model. Inside was a set of keys, a small address book, a pocket engagement diary and a wallet with a set of credit cards attached to a purse containing four pounds in coins and sixty pounds in twenty- and ten-pound notes. There was also a handkerchief, her chequebook in a leather cover, a comb, a small bottle of perfume and a silver ballpoint pen. In the pocket designed for it they found her mobile phone.

Kate said, 'Normally you would expect this to be on the bedside table. It looks as if she didn't want any calls.'

The mobile was small and a new model. Flicking it open and switching it on, Dalgliesh checked the calls and messages. The old text messages had been deleted but there was one new one which was listed as received from 'Robin' and read: *Something very important has cropped up. I need to consult you. Please see me, please don't shut me out.*

Dalgliesh said: 'We'll need to identify the sender to see if this urgency involved his coming to the Manor. But that can wait. I just want to take a quick look at the other patients' rooms before we start the questioning. Dr Glenister said that the killer was wearing gloves. He or she would want to get rid of them as quickly as possible. If they were surgical gloves they could have been cut up and disposed of down one of the WCs. Anyway, it's worth a look. This oughtn't to wait for the SOCOs.'

They were lucky. In the bathroom of the suite at the far end of the corridor they found a minute fragment of latex, fragile as a piece of human skin, caught under the rim of the lavatory bowl. Dalgliesh carefully detached it with tweezers and placed it in an evidence bag, closed it, and he and Kate scribbled their initials over the seal.

Dalgliesh said, 'We'll let the SOCOs know about this find when they arrive. This is the suite they need to concentrate on, particularly the walk-in cupboard in the bedroom, the only bedroom which has one. One more pointer to this being an inside job. And now I'd better telephone Miss Gradwyn's mother.'

Kate said, 'Chief Inspector Whetstone told me that he arranged for a WPC to visit her. He did that soon after he arrived here. It won't be news to her. Do you want me to speak to her, sir?'

'No thank you, Kate. She has a right to hear from me. But if she's already been told there's no hurry. We'll get on with the group interviews. I'll see you and Benton in the library.'

10

The household was assembled and waiting with Kate and Benton when Dalgliesh entered the library with George Chandler-Powell. Benton was interested in how the group had arranged itself. Marcus Westhall had distanced himself from his sister, who was seated in an upright chair by the window, and had taken a chair next to Sister Flavia Holland, perhaps in medical solidarity. Helena Cressett had seated herself in one of the armchairs beside the fire but, perhaps sensing that an appearance of complete relaxation would be inappropriate, sat upright, hands resting loosely on the chair arms. Mogworthy, an incongruous Cerberus, had changed into a shiny blue suit and striped tie, which gave him the look of an ancient undertaker, and stood beside her, back to the fire, the only one on his feet. He turned to glare at Dalgliesh as they entered; the glare seemed to Benton more minatory than aggressive. Dean and Kimberley Bostock, seated rigidly side by side on the only sofa, made a slight movement as if uncertain whether they should rise then, slewing their eyes quickly round, subsided into the cushions and Kimberley surreptitiously slid her hand into her husband's.

Sharon Bateman also sat alone, bolt upright a few feet from Candace Westhall. Her hands were folded in her lap, her thin legs placed side by side, and the eyes which stared briefly into his showed more wariness than fear. She was wearing a cotton dress with a blue floral pattern under a denim jacket. The dress, more appropriate to summer than to a bleak December afternoon, was too large for her and Benton wondered if this hint of a Victorian charity child, obstinate and over-disciplined, had been contrived.

Mrs Frensham had taken a chair beside the window and from time to time glanced out as if to remind herself that there was a world, fresh and comfortingly normal, outside this air made sour by fear and tension. All were pale and, despite the warmth of the central heating and the blaze and crackle of the fire, looked pinched with cold.

Benton was interested to see that the rest of the company had taken time to dress appropriately for an occasion on which it would be more prudent to show respect and grief rather than apprehension. Shirts were crisply pressed, slacks and tweeds had taken the place of country corduroy or denim. Jumpers and cardigans looked as if they had been recently unfolded. Helena Cressett was elegant in slim-fitting trousers in a fine black and white check topped with a black turtleneck cashmere jumper. Her face was drained of colour so that even the soft lipstick she was wearing seemed an ostentatious mark of defiance. Trying not to fix his eyes on her, Benton thought, *That face is pure Plantagenet*, and was surprised to discover that he found her beautiful.

The three chairs at the mahogany eighteenth-century desk were empty and were obviously placed there for the police. They seated themselves and Chandler-Powell took his stance opposite, close to Miss Cressett. All their eyes turned to him, although Benton was aware that their thoughts were with the tall dark-haired man on his right. It was he who dominated the room. But they were there with the consent of Chandler-Powell; this was his house, his library, and subtly he made this plain.

He said, his voice calm and authoritative, 'Commander Dalgliesh has asked for the use of this room so that he and his officers can see and question us together. I think you've all met Mr Dalgliesh, Detective Inspector Miskin and Detective Sergeant Benton-Smith. I'm not here to make a speech. I just want to say that what happened here last night has appalled all of us. It is now our duty to co-operate fully with the police in their investigation. Obviously we can't hope that this tragedy will remain unknown outside the Manor. Answering the press and other media enquiries will be handled by experts, and I'm asking you all now not to speak to anyone outside these walls, at least for the present. Commander Dalgliesh, would you like to take over?'

Benton got out his notebook. He had early in his career devised a distinctive if eccentric method of shorthand which, although it owed something to Mr Pitman's ingenious system, was highly personal. His chief had almost perfect recall, but it was his job to watch, listen and record everything said or seen. He knew why AD had decided on this preliminary group interrogation. It was important to get an overall view of exactly what had taken place since Rhoda Gradwyn had entered the Manor on the afternoon of 13 December and this could be achieved more accurately if everyone concerned was present to add comments or make corrections. Most suspects were capable of lying with some conviction when questioned alone – some, indeed, were remarkably adept at it. Benton recalled a number of occasions when tearful, apparently heart-broken, lovers and relations appealed for help in solving a murder, even when they knew where they had hidden the body. But to sustain a lie in company was more difficult. A suspect might be adept at controlling his own facial expression but the responses of his hearers could be a revelation.

Dalgliesh said, 'The idea of calling you together is to get a group picture of exactly what happened to Rhoda Gradwyn from the moment she arrived here until the discovery of her body. I shall, of course, need to speak to you separately but I hope we shall be able to make some progress in the next half-hour or so.'

There was a silence broken by Helena Cressett, who said, 'The first person to see Miss Gradwyn was Mogworthy, who opened the gate for her. The reception party, consisting of Sister Holland, Mr Westhall and myself, was waiting in the great hall.'

Her voice was calm, the words direct and matter-of-fact. For Benton the message was clear. *If we have to go through this public charade, for God's sake let's get on with it.*

Mogworthy stared at Dalgliesh. 'That's right. She was on time, more or less. Miss Helena said to expect her after tea and before dinner, and I had my eyes open for her from four o'clock. At six forty-five she arrived. I opened the gate for her and she parked the car herself. And she said she'd cope with her own luggage – only one case and that on wheels. A very determined lady. I waited till she'd gone round to the front of the Manor and saw the door open and Miss Helena waiting for her. I reckoned there was no more for me to do so I went home.'

Dalgliesh said, 'You didn't go into the Manor, perhaps to carry her bag up to her room?'

'I did not. If she could wheel it from the car park I reckoned she could get it up to the patients' floor. If not, someone would do it for her. The last I saw of her was going through the front door.'

'Did you enter the Manor at any time after you saw Miss Gradwyn arrive?'

'Why would I do that?'

Dalgliesh said, 'I don't know, I'm asking if you did.'

'I did not. And since we're talking about me, I like to say things plain. No shilly-shallying. I know what you want to ask so I'll save you the trouble. I knew where she was sleeping – on the patients' floor, where else? And I've got keys to the garden door, but I never set eyes on her dead or alive after she went through the front door. I didn't kill her and I don't know who did. If I did know, like as not I'd tell you. I don't hold with murder.'

Miss Cressett said, 'Mog, no one is suspecting you.'

'You may not be, Miss Helena, others will. I know how the world wags. Just as well to speak plainly.'

Dalgliesh said, 'Thank you, Mr Mogworthy. You have spoken plainly and it has been helpful. Is there anything else you can think of that we ought to know, anything you saw or heard after you left? For example, did you see anyone near the Manor, a stranger perhaps, someone acting suspiciously?'

Mog said stoutly, 'Any stranger round the Manor after dark is suspicious to me. I never seen nobody last night. But there were a car parked in the lay-by by the stones. Not when I left; later.'

Catching Mog's quickly disciplined smirk of sly satisfaction, Benton suspected that the timing of the disclosure was less naïve than it sounded. The reception of his news was certainly gratifying. No one spoke but in the silence Benton detected a soft hiss like the intake of breath. This was news to them all, as no doubt Mogworthy had intended. Benton watched their faces as they glanced at each other. It was a moment of shared relief, quickly concealed but unmistakable.

Dalgliesh asked, 'Can you remember anything about the car? The make, colour?'

'Saloon car, darkish. Could be black or blue. The lights were out. Someone sitting in the driver's seat but I don't know whether anyone else was there.'

'You didn't note the registration number?'

'No I didn't. Why would I be noticing car numbers? I were just passing, cycling home from Mrs Ada Denton's cottage where I'd been having my Friday fish and chips, same as I always do. When I'm on the bike I keep my eyes on the road, not like some. All I know is there were a car there.'

'At what time?'

'Before midnight. Maybe five or ten minutes before. I always reckon to get home by midnight.'

Chandler-Powell said, 'This is important evidence, Mog. Why didn't you speak earlier?'

'For why? You said yourself that we weren't to gossip about Miss Gradwyn's death but wait until the police arrived. Well, the boss man is here now so I'm telling him what I saw.'

Before anyone could respond the door was flung open. All eyes turned towards it. A man burst in with DC Warren expostulating just behind him. His appearance was as extraordinary as his irruption was dramatic. Benton saw a pale, handsome, somewhat androgynous face, blazing blue eyes and fair hair plastered to his forehead like the marbled locks of a sculpted god. He was wearing a long black coat almost to the floor over pale blue jeans, and for a moment Benton thought he was in his pyjamas and dressing gown. If his sensational entrance had been planned, he could hardly have chosen a more propitious moment, but contrived histrionics seemed unlikely. The newcomer was shaking with poorly controlled emotions, grief perhaps, but also fear and anger. He stared from face to face, seemingly confused, and before he could speak Candace Westhall spoke calmly from her seat by the window.

'Our cousin, Robin Boyton. He's staying in the guest cottage. Robin, this is Commander Dalgliesh of New Scotland Yard, and his colleagues Inspector Miskin and Sergeant Benton-Smith.'

Robin ignored her and turned his blaze of anger on Marcus. 'You bastard! You cold black-hearted bastard! My friend, a dear close friend, is dead. Murdered. And you didn't even have the decency to tell me. And here you all are, cosying up to the police, deciding together to keep all this quiet. We mustn't upset Mr Chandler-Powell's valuable work, must we? And she's lying upstairs dead. You should have told me! Somebody should have told me. I need to see her. I want to say goodbye.'

And now he was openly weeping, his tears falling unrestrained. Dalgliesh didn't speak but Benton, glancing at him, saw that the dark eyes were watchful.

Candace Westhall half rose as if about to comfort her cousin, then subsided. It was her brother who spoke. 'I'm afraid that isn't possible, Robin. Miss Gradwyn's body has been taken to the mortuary. But I did attempt to tell you. I called at the cottage shortly before nine but you were obviously still asleep. The curtains were drawn and the front door locked. I think you did tell us at some time that you knew Rhoda Gradwyn, but not that you were a close friend.'

Dalgliesh spoke. 'Mr Boyton, at present I'm interviewing only those people who were in this house from the time Miss Gradwyn arrived on Thursday until the discovery of her death at seven thirty this morning. If you were among them then please stay. If not, I or one of my officers will see you as soon as possible.'

Boyton had controlled his rage. Through the gulps of indrawn breath his voice took on the tone of a petulant child.

'Of course I'm not among them. I haven't been inside until now. The policeman at the door wouldn't let me in.'

Dalgliesh said, 'That was on my orders.'

Chandler-Powell said, 'And earlier on mine. Miss Gradwyn asked for absolute privacy. I'm sorry you've been caused this distress, Mr Boyton, but I'm afraid I was so busy here with the police officers and the pathologist that I'd overlooked the fact that you were a guest in the cottage. Have you had lunch? Dean and Kimberley can get you something to eat.'

'Of course I haven't had lunch. When have you ever fed me when I've been in Rose Cottage? And I don't want your bloody food. Don't patronise me!'

He drew himself up and, stretching out a shaking arm, pointed his finger at Chandler-Powell, then realising perhaps that, dressed as he was, the histrionic stance made him look ridiculous, he dropped his arm and gazed round the company in mute misery.

Dalgliesh said, 'Mr Boyton, as you were a friend of Miss Gradwyn's, what you have to tell us will be helpful, but not now.'

The words, quietly spoken, were a command. Boyton turned away, his shoulders drooping. Then he swung back and spoke directly to Chandler-Powell. 'She came here to have that scar removed, to make a new life for herself. She trusted you and you killed her, you murdering bastard!'

Without waiting for a response, he was gone. DC Warren, who had stood inscrutably throughout, followed him out and closed the door firmly. There were five seconds of silence during which Benton sensed that the mood had changed. Someone at last had spoken that sonorous word. The unbelievable, the grotesque, the horrifying had at last been acknowledged.

Dalgliesh said, 'Shall we get on? Miss Cressett, you received Miss Gradwyn at the door, can we take it from there?'

For the next twenty minutes the recital proceeded smoothly and Benton concentrated on his hieroglyphics. Helena Cressett had welcomed the new patient to the Manor and had taken her directly to her room. As she was to have an anaesthetic next morning, no dinner was served and Miss Gradwyn had said she would like to be alone. The patient had insisted on wheeling her own case to the bedroom and was unpacking her books when Miss Cressett left. On Friday she knew, of course, that Miss Gradwyn had had her operation and been transferred in the early evening from the recovery room to her suite in the patients' wing. This was the usual procedure. She was not concerned with patient care, nor did she visit Miss Gradwyn in her suite. She had dinner in the dining room with Sister Holland, Miss Westhall and Mrs Frensham. She was told that Marcus Westhall was having dinner and staying the night with a consultant in London with whom he was hoping to work in Africa. She and Miss Westhall had worked together in the office until nearly seven o'clock, when pre-dinner drinks were served by Dean in the library. Afterwards she and Mrs Frensham had played chess and talked in her private sitting room. She had been in bed by midnight and had heard nothing during the night. On Saturday she had showered and dressed when Mr Chandler-Powell arrived to tell her that Rhoda Gradwyn was dead.

Miss Cressett's evidence was quietly confirmed by Mrs Frensham, who said that she had left Miss Cressett in her sitting room and had herself gone to her own apartment in the east wing at about eleven thirty and had seen and heard nothing during the night. She knew nothing about Miss Gradwyn's death until she came down to the dining room at quarter to eight and found no one there. Later Mr Chandler-Powell had arrived and had told her that Miss Gradwyn was dead.

Candace Westhall confirmed that she had worked with Miss Cressett in the office until dinner. After dinner she had returned to tidy away papers in the office and left the Manor shortly after ten by the front door. Mr Chandler-Powell was coming down the stairs and they said goodnight before she left. Next morning he rang from the office to say Miss Gradwyn had been found dead, and she and her brother came over to the Manor immediately. Marcus Westhall had returned from London in the early hours. She had heard his car arrive but had not got up, though he had knocked on her bedroom door and they had spoken briefly.

Sister Flavia Holland gave her evidence succinctly and calmly. Early in the morning of the operation the anaesthetist and additional medical and technical staff had arrived. Nurse Frazer, one of the temporary staff, had brought the patient down to the operating suite where she had been examined by the anaesthetist who had previously examined her at St Angela's in London. Mr Chandler-Powell had spent some time with her to greet and reassure her. He would have described exactly what he proposed to do when Miss Gradwyn had met him in his office in St Angela's. Miss Gradwyn had been very calm throughout and had shown no sign of fear, or indeed of particular anxiety. The anaesthetist and all the ancillary staff had left as soon as the operation was completed. They would have been returning the following morning for Mrs Skeffington's operation. She had arrived yesterday afternoon. After the operation Miss Gradwyn had been in the recovery room under the care of Mr Chandler-Powell and herself and at four thirty had been wheeled back to her room. By then the patient was able to walk and said she felt little pain. She then slept until seven thirty when she had been able to eat a light supper. She refused a sedative but asked for a glass of hot milk and brandy. Sister Holland was in the end room on the left and looked in to check on Miss Gradwyn every hour until she herself went to bed, which was perhaps as late as midnight. The eleven o'clock check was the last and the patient was asleep. She heard nothing during the night.

Mr Chandler-Powell's account agreed with hers. He emphasised that at no time had the patient shown fear, either of the operation or of anything else. She had specifically asked that no visitors be allowed during her period of a week's convalescence and that was why Robin Boyton had been refused entry. The operation had gone well but had been longer and more difficult than he had expected. He had, however, felt confident of an excellent result. Miss Gradwyn was a healthy woman who had stood the anaesthesia and operation well and he had no anxieties about her progress. He had visited her on the night she died at about ten o'clock and had been returning from that visit when he saw Miss Westhall leaving.

Sharon had been sitting very still with a look which, Kate thought, could only be described as sulky throughout the proceedings, but when asked where she had been and what she had done the previous day, had at first embarked on a tedious, sullenly expressed review of every detail of the morning and afternoon. Asked to confine herself to the time from four thirty onwards, she said that she had been busy in the kitchen and dining room helping Dean and Kimberley Bostock, had had her meal with them at eight forty-five and had then gone to her own room to watch television. She couldn't remember when she went to bed or what she had seen on television. She had been very tired and had slept soundly throughout the night. She knew nothing about Miss Gradwyn being dead until Sister Holland had come up to waken her, telling her to come on duty and help in the kitchen, which she thought had been at about nine o'clock. She liked Miss Gradwyn, who had asked her to show her round the garden on her previous visit. Asked by Kate what they had talked about, she said it was about her childhood and where she had gone to school, and her work at the old people's home.

There was no surprise until Dean and Kimberley Bostock gave their evidence. Kimberley said she was sometimes asked by Sister to take food to the patients but she hadn't visited Miss Gradwyn because she was fasting. Neither she nor her husband had seen the patient arriving and they had been particularly busy that evening preparing meals for the extra operating theatre staff who would arrive next day and always had lunch before leaving. She had been woken by the telephone just before midnight on the Friday evening by Mrs Skeffington, who had asked for tea. Her husband had helped her carry up the tray. He never went into the patients' rooms but had waited outside until she came out. Mrs Skeffington had appeared frightened and talked about seeing a light flickering among the stones, but Kimberley thought this was just imagination. She had asked Mrs Skeffington if she wanted her to call Sister Holland but she had said no, that Sister Holland would only be annoyed with her for waking her unnecessarily.

At this stage Sister Holland had broken in. 'Your instructions, Kimberley, are to call me if patients ask for anything in the night. Why didn't you? Mrs Skeffington was pre-operative.'

And now Benton, raising his head from his notebook, was alert. He could see that the question was deeply unwelcome. The girl flushed. She glanced at her husband and their hands tightened. She said, 'I'm sorry, Sister, I thought she wouldn't really be a patient until the next day so I didn't wake you. I did ask her if she wanted to see you or Mr Chandler-Powell.'

'Mrs Skeffington was a patient from the time she arrived at the

Manor, Kimberley. You knew how to contact me. You should have done so.'

Dalgliesh said, 'Did Mrs Skeffington mention anything about hearing the lift in the night?'

'No. She only spoke about the lights.'

'And did either of you hear or see anything unusual while you were on that floor?'

They looked at each other, then shook their heads vigorously. Dean said, 'We were only there a few minutes. Everything was quiet. A dimmed light was on in the corridor as it always is.'

'And the lift? Did you notice the lift?'

'Yes, sir. The lift was on the ground floor. We used it to take up the tea. We could have gone up the stairs, but the lift is quicker.'

'And is there anything else you need to tell me about that night?'

And now there was a silence. Again the two looked at each other. Dean seemed to be gathering resolve. He said, 'There's one thing, sir. When we got back to the ground floor I saw that the door to the garden wasn't bolted. We have to pass the door to get back to our flat. It's a heavy oak door on the right, sir, leading to the lime walk and the Cheverell Stones.'

Dalgliesh said, 'Are you sure about this?'

'Yes, sir, quite sure.'

'Did you draw your wife's attention to the unbolted door?'

'No, sir. Not until we were together in the kitchen next morning and then I mentioned it.'

'Did either or both of you go back to check?'

'No, sir.'

'And you noticed this on your return, not when you were helping your wife carry up the tea?'

'Just on our return.'

Sister Holland broke in. 'I don't know why you needed to help with the tea, Dean. The tray was hardly heavy. Couldn't Kimberley have managed on her own? She usually does. It's not as if there isn't a lift. And there's always a dim light on in the west wing.'

Dean said stoutly, 'Yes, she could, but I don't like her moving about the house on her own late at night.'

'What are you afraid of?'

Dean said miserably, 'It's not that. I just don't like it.'

Dalgliesh said quietly, 'Did you know that Mr Chandler-Powell normally bolts that door promptly at eleven o'clock?'

'Yes, sir, I knew it. Everyone does. But sometimes it's a little later if he takes a walk in the garden. I thought if I bolted it he might be out there and not able to get back in.'

Sister Holland said, 'Walking in the garden after midnight, in December? Is that likely, Dean?'

He looked not at her but at Dalgliesh, and said defensively, 'It wasn't my job to bolt it, sir. And it was locked. No one could have got in without a key.'

Dalgliesh turned to Chandler-Powell. 'And you're confident that you bolted the door at eleven?'

'I bolted it as usual at eleven and I found it bolted at six thirty this morning.'

'Did anyone here unbolt it for any purpose? You can all see the importance of this. We need to get this cleared up now.'

No one spoke. The silence lengthened. Dalgliesh said, 'Did anyone else notice that the door was either bolted or unbolted after eleven?'

Again a silence, this time finally broken by a low murmur of negatives. Benton noticed that they avoided each other's eyes.

Dalgliesh said, 'Then that will be enough for now. Thank you for your co-operation. I would like to see you all separately, either here or in the incident room in Old Police Cottage.'

Dalgliesh got to his feet and the rest of the room quietly and in turn also rose. Still no one spoke. They were crossing the hall when Chandler-Powell caught up with them. He said to Dalgliesh, 'I'd like a quick word now if you can spare the time.'

Dalgliesh and Kate followed him into the office and the door closed. Benton felt no resentment at an exclusion which had been subtly conveyed but not spoken. He knew there were moments in any investigation when two officers could elicit information and three inhibit it.

Chandler-Powell wasted no time. While the three of them stood, he said, 'There's something I ought to say. Obviously you saw

Kimberley's discomfort when she was asked why she hadn't woken Flavia Holland. I think it likely that she tried. The door to the suite wasn't locked and if she or Dean partly opened it they would have heard voices, mine and Flavia's. I was with her at midnight. I think the Bostocks may have felt some inhibition in telling you this, particularly with the others present.'

Kate said, 'But wouldn't you have heard the door opening?'

He looked at her calmly. 'Not necessarily. We were busy talking.'

Dalgliesh said, 'I'll confirm that with the Bostocks later. How long were you together?'

'After I finished setting the alarms and bolting the garden door I joined Flavia in her sitting room. I was there until about one o'clock. There were things we needed to discuss, some professional, some personal. Neither has any relevance to Rhoda Gradwyn's death. During that time neither of us heard or saw anything untoward.'

'And you didn't hear the lift?'

'We didn't hear it. Nor would I expect to. As you saw, it's by the stairs opposite Sister's sitting room, but it's modern and comparatively soundless. Sister Holland will, of course, confirm my story and I've no doubt that Kimberley, when questioned by someone experienced in extracting information from the vulnerable, will admit to hearing our voices now she knows that I've spoken to you. And don't give me too much credit for telling you what I hope will remain confidential. I'd have to be particularly naïve not to notice that, if Rhoda Gradwyn died at about midnight, Flavia and I have given each other an alibi. I may as well be frank. I've no wish to be treated differently from the others. But doctors do not commonly murder their patients and if I had it in mind to destroy this place and my reputation, I'd have done it before not after the operation. I hate having my work wasted.'

Looking at Chandler-Powell's face suddenly suffused with an anger and disgust which transformed him, Dalgliesh could believe that those last words, at least, were the truth.

Dalgliesh walked alone into the garden to telephone Rhoda Gradwyn's mother. It was a call he dreaded. To commiserate in person, as a local woman police officer had already done, was difficult enough. It was a duty no police officer welcomed, and he had done his share of it, hesitating before raising a hand to knock or ring at the door, a door that was invariably immediately opened, and meeting eyes, puzzled, beseeching, hopeful or anguished, with news that would change a life. Some of his colleagues, he knew, would have left this task to Kate. To convey sympathy to a bereaved parent by telephone struck him as maladroit, but he had always felt that the next of kin should know who was the investigating officer in charge of a murder case and should be kept in touch with the progress as far as the operation made this practicable.

A man's voice answered. It sounded both puzzled and apprehensive, as if the phone were some technically advanced instrument from which no good news could ever be expected. Without identifying himself, he said with obvious relief, 'The police, you said? Hold on, please. I'll fetch my wife.'

Dalgliesh again identified himself and expressed his sympathy as gently as possible, knowing that she had already received news which no gentleness could soften. He was met by an initial silence. And then, in a voice as insensate as if he had been conveying an unwelcome invitation to tea, she said, 'It's good of you to phone but we do know. The young lady from the local police has been to break the news. She said that someone from the Dorset police had phoned her. She left at ten o'clock. She was very kind. We had a cup of tea together but she didn't tell me much. Just that Rhoda had been found dead and that it wasn't a natural death. I still can't believe it. I mean, who would want to harm Rhoda? I asked what had happened and if the police knew who was responsible, but she said that she wasn't able to answer questions like that because another force was in charge and that you'd be in touch. She'd only come to break the news. Still, it was kind of her.'

Dalgliesh asked, 'Had your daughter any enemies you were aware of, Mrs Brown? Anyone who might have wished her harm?'

And now he could hear the clear note of resentment. 'Well she must've had, mustn't she, or she wouldn't have been murdered. She was in a private clinic. Rhoda didn't do things on the cheap. So why didn't they look after her? The clinic must have been very careless, letting a patient get murdered. She had so much to look forward to. Rhoda was very successful. She was always clever, just like her dad.'

'Did she tell you that she was having her scar removed at the Cheverell Manor clinic?'

'She told me she was planning to get rid of the scar but not where she was going or when. She was very private, Rhoda. She was like that as a child, keeping her secrets, not telling anyone what she thought. We didn't see much of each other after she left home, but she did come to my wedding down here in May and she told me then about getting rid of the scar. Of course she should have had something done about it years ago. She's had it for over thirty years. It was caused by knocking her face against the kitchen door when she was thirteen.'

'So you can't tell us very much about her friends, her private life?'

'I've told you. I've said she was private. I don't know anything about her friends or her private life. And I don't know what's going to happen about the funeral, whether it ought to be in London or here. I don't know whether there are things that I ought to do. There are usually forms to fill in. People have to be told. I don't want to bother my husband. He's very upset about it. He liked Rhoda when they met.'

Dalgliesh said, 'There will have to be a post mortem, of course, and then the coroner may release the body. Have you some friends who could help and advise you?'

'Well, I've got friends at the church. I'll speak to our vicar and perhaps he can help. Perhaps we could have the service down here, only of course she was quite well known in London. And she wasn't religious so perhaps she wouldn't want a service. I hope I'm not expected to go to this clinic, wherever it is.'

'It's in Dorset, Mrs Brown. In Stoke Cheverell.'

'Well, I can't leave Mr Brown to come to Dorset.'

'There's really no need unless later you particularly wish to attend the inquest. Why not have a word with your solicitor? I expect that your daughter's solicitor will be getting in touch with you. We found the name and address in her handbag. I'm sure he'll be helpful. I'm afraid I shall need to examine her possessions both here and in her London home. I may have to take some away for examination but they will all be carefully looked after and later returned to you. Have I your permission for that?'

'You can take what you like. I've never been to her London house. I suppose I'll have to sooner or later. There may be something valuable there. And there'll be books. She always had plenty of books. All that reading. She always had her head in a book. What good will they do? They won't bring her back. Has she had the operation?'

'Yes, yesterday, and I gather it was successful.'

'So all that money wasted for nothing. Poor Rhoda. She hasn't had much luck for all her success.'

And now her voice changed and Dalgliesh thought she might be trying to hold back tears. She said, 'I'll ring off now. Thank you for phoning. I don't think I can take in any more now. It's a shock. Rhoda murdered. It's the kind of thing you read about or see on television. You don't expect it to happen to someone you know. And she had so much to look forward to with that scar gone. It doesn't seem fair.'

Dalgliesh thought, *'Someone you know', not 'someone you love'.* He could hear now that she was crying and the line went dead.

He paused for a moment, gazing at the phone before making the next call to Miss Gradwyn's solicitor. Grief, that universal emotion, had no universal response, was manifested in different ways, some of them bizarre. He remembered his mother's death, how at the time, wanting to behave well in the face of his father's sorrow, he had managed to control his tears, even at the funeral. But grief revisited him down the years, briefly remembered scenes, snatches of conversation, a look, her apparently indestructible gardening gloves and, more vivid than all the small lasting regrets which still visited him, himself leaning out of the window of the slowly moving train which was taking him back to school and seeing her figure in the same coat she had worn year after year, carefully not turning back to wave because he had asked her not to.

He shook himself into the present. His next call, to the solicitor, was answered by a recorded message to say that the office was now closed until Monday at ten o'clock, but that urgent matters would be dealt with by the duty solicitor who could be reached at a given number. This number was answered promptly in a crisp impersonal voice and once Dalgliesh had identified himself and explained that he wished urgently to speak to Mr Newton Macklefield, his private number was given. Dalgliesh had given no explanation but his voice must have carried conviction.

Not surprisingly on a Saturday, Newton Macklefield was out of London with his family at his country house in Sussex. Their conversation was business-like, punctuated by children's voices and the barking of dogs. After expressions of shock and personal regret which sounded more formal than heartfelt, Macklefield said, 'Naturally I'll do all I can to assist the investigation. You say you'll be at Sanctuary Court tomorrow morning? You've got a key? Yes, of course, she would have had it with her. I've none of her private keys in the office. I could come up and join you at ten thirty, if that time is convenient. I'll call in at the office and bring the will with me, although you'll probably find a copy in the house. I'm afraid that there's little more I can do to help. As you'll know, Commander, a relationship between a solicitor and his client can be close, particularly if the solicitor has acted for the family, perhaps for some generations, and has come to be regarded as a confidant and friend. That wasn't the case here. Miss Gradwyn's relationship with me was one of mutual respect and trust and, certainly on my part, of liking. But it was purely professional. I knew the client but not the woman. I take it, by the way, that the next of kin has been informed.'

Dalgliesh said, 'Yes, there's only her mother. She described her daughter as a very private person. I told her I should want access to her daughter's house and she had no objection to that or my taking away anything that might be helpful.'

'Nor, as her solicitor, have I. So, I'll see you at her house at about ten thirty. Extraordinary business! Thank you, Commander, for getting in touch.'

Snapping shut his mobile, Dalgliesh reflected that murder, a unique crime for which no reparation is ever possible, imposes its own compulsions as well as its conventions. He doubted whether Macklefield would have interrupted his country weekend for a less sensational crime. As a young officer he too had been touched, even if unwillingly and temporarily, by the power of murder to attract even while it appalled and repelled. He had watched how people involved as innocent bystanders, provided they were unburdened by grief or suspicion, were engrossed by homicide, drawn inexorably to the place where the crime had occurred in fascinated disbelief. The crowd and the media who served them had not yet congregated outside the wrought-iron gates of the Manor. But they would come, and he doubted whether Chandler-Powell's private security team would be able to do more than inconvenience them.

12

The rest of the afternoon was occupied with the individual interviews, most of them taking place in the library. Helena Cressett was the last of the household to be seen and Dalgliesh had given the task to Kate and Benton. He sensed that Miss Cressett expected him to do the questioning and he needed her to know that he headed a team and that both his junior officers were competent. Surprisingly she invited Kate and Benton to join her in her private flat in the east wing. The room into which she led them was obviously her sitting room but in its elegance and richness was hardly the accommodation a housekeeper-administrator would expect to occupy. The furnishings and the placing of the pictures revealed a highly individual taste, and although the room wasn't exactly cluttered, there was a suggestion of valued objects being brought together more for the satisfaction of the owner than as part of a coherent decorative plan. It was, thought Benton, as if Helena Cressett had colonised part of the Manor for her private domain. Here was none of the dark solidity of Tudor furniture. Apart from the sofa, covered in cream linen and piped with red, which stood at right angles to the fireplace, most of the furniture was Georgian.

Nearly all the pictures on the panelled walls were family portraits and Miss Cressett's resemblance to them was unmistakable. None seemed to him particularly fine – perhaps those had been sold separately – but all had a striking individuality and were competently painted, some more than competently. Here a Victorian bishop in his lawn sleeves gazed at the painter with ecclesiastical hauteur belied by a suspicion of unease as if the book on which his palm rested was *The Origin of Species*. Next to him a seventeenth-century Cavalier, hand on sword, posed with unashamed arrogance while, over the mantelpiece, an early Victorian family was grouped in front of the house, the ringletted mother with her younger children gathered about her, the eldest boy mounted on a pony, the father at their side. And always there were the high arched brows above the eyes, the dominant cheekbones, the full curve of the upper lip.

Benton said, 'You're among your ancestors, Miss Cressett. The resemblance is striking.'

Neither Dalgliesh nor Kate would have said that; it was maladroit and could be unwise to begin an interview with a personal comment and, although Kate was silent, Benton felt her surprise. But he quickly justified to himself a remark which had been spontaneous by reflecting that it would probably prove useful. They needed to know the woman they were dealing with and, more precisely, her status at the Manor, how far she was in control and how strong her influence on Chandler-Powell and the other residents. Her response to what she might see as a minor impertinence could be revealing.

Looking him full in the face, she said coolly, '*The years-heired feature that can/ In curve and voice and eye/ Despise the human span/ Of durance – that is I;/ The eternal thing in Man/ That heeds no call to die.* It doesn't take a professional detective to detect that. Do you enjoy Thomas Hardy, Sergeant?'

'As a poet more than a novelist.'

'I agree. I find depressing his determination to make his characters suffer even when a little common sense on both his part and theirs could avoid it. Tess is one of the most irritating young women in Victorian fiction. Won't you both sit down?'

And here was the hostess, recalling duty but unable or unwilling to control the note of condescending reluctance. She indicated the sofa and seated herself in an armchair facing it. Kate and Benton sat.

Without preliminaries, Kate took over. 'Mr Chandler-Powell described you as the administrator here. What exactly does the job entail?'

'My job here? It's difficult to describe. I'm a manager, administrator, housekeeper, secretary and part-time accountant. I suppose general manager covers it all. But Mr Chandler-Powell usually describes me as the administrator when speaking to patients.'

'And you've been here how long?'

'It will be six years next month.'

Kate said, 'It can't have been easy for you.'

'Not easy in what way, Inspector?'

Miss Cressett's tone was one of detached interest but Benton didn't miss the note of suppressed resentment. He had encountered this reaction before, a suspect, usually one with some authority, more used to putting questions than answering them, unwilling to antagonise the chief investigating officer but venting their resentment on a subordinate. Kate wasn't intimidated.

She said, 'To return to a house so beautiful which your family has owned for generations and to see someone else in occupation. Not everyone could cope with that.'

'Not everyone is required to. Perhaps I should explain. My family owned and lived in the Manor for more than four hundred years but everything comes to an end. Mr Chandler-Powell is fond of the house and it is better in his care than in the care of the others who viewed and wanted to buy it. I didn't murder one of his patients in order to shut down the clinic and pay him back for buying my family home or for getting it cheap. Forgive my frankness, Inspector, but isn't that what you came to find out?'

It was never wise to rebut an allegation which hadn't yet been made, particularly with such brutal frankness, and it was obvious that she realised her mistake as soon as the words were out of her mouth. So the resentment was there. But against whom or what, Benton wondered. The police, Chandler-Powell's desecration of the west wing, or Rhoda Gradwyn who so inconveniently and embarrassingly had brought the vulgarity of a criminal investigation into her ancestral halls?

Kate asked, 'How did you come to get the job?'

'I applied for it. Isn't that usually how one gets a job? It was advertised and I thought it would be interesting to return to the Manor and see what changes had been made, apart from the building of the clinic. My own profession, if you can call it that, is of an art historian, but I could hardly combine that with living here. I hadn't intended to stay long but I find the work interesting and I'm in no hurry at present to move on. I expect that's what you wanted to know. But is my personal history really relevant to Rhoda Gradwyn's death?'

Kate said, 'We can't tell what is or what is not relevant without asking questions which may seem an intrusion. Often they are. We can only hope for co-operation and understanding. A murder investigation isn't a social occasion.'

'Then let's not treat it as one, Inspector.'

A flush flowed quickly over her pale and remarkable face like a dying rash. The temporary loss of composure made her more human and, surprisingly, more attractive. She held her emotions under control but they were there. She was not, thought Benton, a passionless woman, only one who had learnt the wisdom of keeping her passions under control.

He said, 'How much contact did you have with Miss Gradwyn either on her first visit or subsequently?'

'Practically none, except on both occasions to be part of the reception committee and to show her to her room. We hardly spoke. My job has nothing to do with the patients. Their treatment and comfort is the responsibility of the two surgeons and Sister Holland.'

'But you recruit and control the domestic staff?'

'I find them when there's a vacancy. I have been used to running this house. And, yes, they come under my general authority, although that word is too strong for the kind of control I exercise. But when, as occasionally happens, they have anything to do with the patients, then that's Sister Holland's responsibility. I suppose there's a certain overlapping of duties since I'm responsible for the kitchen staff and Sister for the kind of food the patients receive, but it seems to work quite well.'

'Did you appoint Sharon Bateman?'

'I placed the advertisement in a number of papers and she applied. She was working at the time in a home for the elderly and presented very good references. I didn't actually interview her. I was at my London flat at the time so Mrs Frensham, Miss Westhall and Sister Holland saw her and took her on. I don't think anyone has regretted it.'

'Did you know, or did you ever meet Rhoda Gradwyn before she arrived here?'

'I never met her, but of course I'd heard of her. I suppose everyone has who reads a broadsheet. I knew her to be a successful and influential journalist. I had no reason to think kindly of her but a personal resentment, which was really no more than discomfort on hearing her name, didn't make me wish her dead. My father was the last male Cressett and he lost almost all the family money in the Lloyd's disaster. He was forced to sell the Manor and Mr Chandler-Powell bought it. Shortly after the sale, Rhoda Gradwyn wrote a short article in a financial paper critical of the Lloyd's Names, and in particular naming my father, among others. There was a suggestion that those who were unfortunate had got what they deserved. She gave a brief description of the Manor and something of its history in the article, but that must have been taken from a guidebook since, as far as any of us knew, she'd never actually been here. Some of my father's friends thought it was the article that killed him, but I've never believed that and nor, I think, did they. It was an overdramatic response to comments which were unkind but hardly libellous. My father had long-standing heart problems and knew that his life was fragile. It may have been selling the Manor that was the final blow, but I very much doubt whether anything Rhoda Gradwyn could write or say would have troubled him. After all, what was she? An ambitious woman who made money out of the pain of others. Someone hated her enough to put his hands round her throat, but it wasn't anyone who slept here last night. And now, if you'll excuse me, I'd like you to leave. I shall, of course, be here tomorrow whenever you wish to see me, but I've had enough excitement for today.'

It was not a request they could refuse. The interview had lasted less than half an hour. As they heard the door close firmly behind them, Benton reflected, and with some regret, that a preference for Thomas Hardy's poetry over his novels was probably the only thing the two of them had in common, or were ever likely to have.

13

Perhaps because the group interrogation in the library was a fresh and unpleasant memory, the suspects, as if by unspoken agreement, avoided open discussion of the murder, but Lettie knew that they spoke of it privately – herself and Helena, the Bostocks in the kitchen which they had always regarded as their home but now saw as a refuge and, she assumed, the Westhalls in Stone Cottage. Only Flavia and Sharon seemed to distance themselves from the others and kept their silence, Flavia busying herself with unspecified jobs in the operating suite, Sharon seeming to regress to a moody monosyllabic teenager. Mog moved between them distributing pieces of gossip and theory like alms into outstretched hands. Without any formal meeting or agreed strategy, it seemed to Lettie that a common theory was emerging which only the most sceptical found unconvincing, and they were holding their peace.

Obviously the murder was an outside job and Rhoda Gradwyn herself had let her killer into the Manor, the date and time probably by prior agreement before she left London. That was why she had been so adamant that no visitors should be admitted. She was, after all, a notorious investigative journalist. She must have made enemies. The car seen by Mog was probably the killer's, and the light glimpsed at the stones by Mrs Skeffington was his waving torch. The bolted door next morning was a difficulty, but the murderer could have bolted the door himself after the deed and then hidden himself in the Manor until the door was unbolted next morning by Chandler-Powell. There had, after all, been only a superficial search of the Manor before the police arrived. Had anyone, for example, searched the four empty suites in the west wing?

And there were plenty of cupboards in the Manor large enough to contain a man. It was perfectly possible for an intruder to be undetected. He could have made his exit unnoticed by the west door and escaped down the lime walk to the field while the whole household was immured in the north-facing library being interrogated by Commander Dalgliesh. If the police hadn't been so anxious to concentrate on the household the killer might have been caught by now.

Lettie couldn't remember who first named Robin Boyton as an alternative chief suspect, but when raised the idea spread by a kind of osmosis. After all, he had come to Stoke Cheverell to visit Rhoda Gradwyn, had apparently been desperate to see her and had been rebuffed. Probably the killing hadn't been premeditated. Miss Gradwyn had been perfectly able to walk after the operation. She had let him in, there had been a quarrel and he had lost his temper. Admittedly he wasn't the owner of the car parked near the stones, but that might well have had nothing to do with the murder. The police would be trying to trace the owner. No one said what they all thought: that it would be convenient if they failed. Even if the motorist proved to be an over-tired traveller prudently stopping for a short sleep, the theory of an outside intruder held good.

By dinner time Lettie sensed that the speculation was dying down. It had been a long and traumatic day and what they all craved now was a period of peace. They seemed also to need solitude. Chandler-Powell and Flavia told Dean that they would have dinner served in their rooms. The Westhalls departed for Stone Cottage and Helena invited Lettie to share a meal of a herb omelette and salad which she would cook in her small private kitchen. After the meal, they washed up together, then settled down before the wood fire to listen to a concert on Radio Three in the subdued light of a single lamp. Neither mentioned Rhoda Gradwyn's death.

By eleven the fire was dying. A fragile blue flame licked at the last log as it disintegrated into grey ash. Helena turned off the radio and they sat in silence. Then she said, 'Why did you leave the

Manor when I was thirteen? Was it to do with Father? I've always thought it was, that you were lovers.'

Lettie replied quietly. 'You were always too sophisticated for your age. We were getting too fond of each other, too interdependent. It was right for me to go. And you needed to be with other girls, to have a wider education.'

'I suppose so. That dreadful school. Were you lovers? Did you have sex? Awful expression, but all alternatives are even cruder.'

'Once. That's why I knew it had to end.'

'Because of Mummy?'

'Because of all of us.'

'So it was *Brief Encounter* without the railway station?'

'Something like that.'

'Poor Mummy. Years of doctors and nurses. After a time her failing lungs hardly seemed like an illness, just part of what she was. And when she died I hardly missed her. She hadn't really been there. I remember being sent for from school, but too late. I think I was glad not to be there in time. But that empty bedroom, that was horrible. I still hate that room.'

Lettie said, 'A question in return. Why did you marry Guy Haverland?'

'Because he was funny, clever, charming and very rich. Even at eighteen I knew from the first it wouldn't last. That's why we got married in London in a registry office. The promises seemed less onerous than in a church. Guy couldn't resist any good-looking woman and he wasn't going to change. But we had three wonderful years and he taught me so much. I'll never regret them.'

Lettie got up. She said, 'Time for bed. Thanks for the dinner, and goodnight, my dear.' And she was gone.

Helena moved over to the west-facing window and drew back the curtains. The west wing was in darkness, no more than a long shape lit by the moon. Was it, she wondered, violent death that had released the impulse to confide, to ask questions which had remained unspoken for years? She wondered about Lettie and her marriage. There had been no children and she suspected that this had been a grief. Was that priest she had married one who still

thought of sex as somehow indecent and saw his wife and all virtuous women as Madonnas? And were that night's revelations a
substitute for the question which was in both their minds and
which neither had dared to ask?

14

Until seven thirty Dalgliesh had had little opportunity to examine and settle into his temporary home. The local police had been helpful and busy, phone lines had been checked, a computer installed and a large corkboard attached to the wall in case Dalgliesh should need to display visual images. Thought had also been given to his comfort, and although the stone cottage had the faint musty smell of a house unoccupied for some months, a wood fire had been set and was blazing in the hearth. The bed had been made up and an electric fire provided upstairs. The shower, although not modern, delivered very hot water when he tested it and the refrigerator had been stocked with sufficient provisions to keep him going for at least three days, including a casserole of obviously home-made lamb stew. There were also cans of beer and two bottles each of very drinkable red and white wine.

By nine o'clock he had showered and changed and had heated up and eaten the lamb stew. A note found under the casserole dish explained that it had been cooked by Mrs Warren, a discovery which reinforced Dalgliesh's view that her husband's temporary assignment to the Squad was fortunate. He opened a bottle of the red wine and placed it with three glasses on a low table before the fire. With the cheerfully patterned curtains drawn against the night, he found himself, as he sometimes did on a case, comfortably ensconced in a period of solitude. To spend at least some part of the day totally alone was something which from childhood had been as necessary to him as food and light. Now, the brief respite over, he took out his small personal notebook and began his review of the day's interviews. From the time when he was a detective sergeant he had put down in an unofficial notebook a few salient words and phrases which could immediately bring to mind a person, an unwise admission, a snatch of dialogue, an exchange of glances. With this aid he had almost complete recall. This private review done, he would phone Kate and ask her and Benton to join him, when the day's progress would be discussed and he would set out the programme for tomorrow.

The interviews had produced no fundamental changes in the evidence they had already given. Admittedly Kimberley, despite having been assured by Mr Chandler-Powell that she had acted correctly, was obviously unhappy, seeking to persuade herself that she might after all have been mistaken. Alone in the library with Dalgliesh and Kate, she kept stealing glances at the door as if hoping to see her husband or fearing the arrival of Mr Chandler-Powell. Dalgliesh and Kate were patient with her. Asked if she had been sure at the time that the voices she had heard were those of Mr Chandler-Powell and Sister Holland, she had squeezed her face into a parody of agonised thought.

'I did think it was Mr Chandler-Powell and Sister, but I would, wouldn't I? I mean, I wouldn't expect it to be anyone else. It did sound like them or I wouldn't have thought that it was them, would I? But I can't remember what they were saying. I thought they sounded as if they were quarrelling. I opened the sitting-room door just a little and they weren't there, so perhaps they were in the bedroom. But, of course, they might have been in the sitting room and I didn't see them. And I did hear loud voices, but perhaps they were just talking together. It was very late . . .'

Her voice had faltered. Kimberley, like Mrs Skeffington, if called for the prosecution, would be a gift for the defence. Asked what had happened next, Kimberley said that she had returned to where Dean was waiting outside Mrs Skeffington's sitting room and had told him.

'Had told him what?'

'That I thought I heard Sister arguing with Mr Chandler-Powell.'

'And that's why you didn't call out to them and tell Sister that you had taken tea to Mrs Skeffington?'

'It's like I said in the library, sir. We both thought Sister wouldn't like to be disturbed and that it wouldn't really matter because Mrs Skeffington hadn't had her operation. Anyway, Mrs Skeffington was all right. She hadn't asked for Sister and, if she'd wanted her, she could have rung her bell.'

Kimberley's evidence had been later corroborated by Dean. He looked if anything more distressed than Kimberley. He hadn't noticed whether the door to the lime avenue was unbolted when he and Kimberley took up the tea tray, but was adamant that it was unbolted when they returned. He had noticed it when passing the door. He repeated that he hadn't bolted it because it was possible that someone was taking a particularly late walk and in any case it wasn't his job. He and Kimberley were the first to rise and had early morning tea together in the kitchen at six o'clock. He then went to look at the door and saw that it was bolted. He had not thought that surprising; Mr Chandler-Powell seldom unbolted it before nine o'clock in the winter months. He hadn't told Kimberley about the door being unbolted at the time in case she became nervous. He wasn't himself worried because there were the two security locks. He couldn't explain why he hadn't returned later to check both the locks and the bolt except to say that security wasn't his responsibility.

Chandler-Powell had remained as calm as he had been when the team first arrived. Dalgliesh admired the stoicism with which he must be contemplating the destruction of his clinic, possibly of the greater part of his private practice. At the end of the interview in his study, which produced nothing new, Kate said, 'No one here, with the exception of Mr Boyton, says that they knew Miss Gradwyn before she came to the Manor. But in a sense she isn't the only victim. Her death must inevitably affect the success of your work here. Is there anyone who might have an interest in harming you?'

Chandler-Powell had said, 'All I can say is that I have every confidence in everyone who works here. And it seems to me extremely far-fetched to suggest that Rhoda Gradwyn was murdered to inconvenience me. The idea is bizarre.'

Dalgliesh had resisted the obvious retort: Miss Gradwyn's death had been bizarre. Chandler-Powell confirmed that he had been with Sister Holland in her apartment from just after eleven until one o'clock. Neither of them had seen or heard anything unusual. There were medical matters he needed to discuss with Sister Holland but they were confidential and had nothing to do with Miss Gradwyn. His evidence had been confirmed by Sister Holland and it was obvious that neither had any intention at present of saying more. Medical confidentiality was an easy excuse for silence but it was a valid one.

He and Kate had interviewed the Westhalls together in Stone Cottage. Dalgliesh had seen little family resemblance and the differences were emphasised by Marcus Westhall's youthful, if conventional, good looks and his air of vulnerability compared with the strong sturdy body, dominant features and anxiety-lined face of his sister. He had said little except to confirm that he had had dinner at the Chelsea house of a surgeon, Matthew Greenfield, who would be including him in his team to spend a year in Africa. He had been invited to stay the night and proposed to do some Christmas shopping the next day in London, but his car had been causing trouble and he had thought it wiser to leave promptly after an early dinner at eight fifteen so that he could take it in next morning to the local garage. He hadn't yet done so because the murder had put everything else out of mind. The traffic had been light but he had driven slowly and it had been about twelve thirty when he got back. He had seen no one in the road and there were no lights on in the Manor. Stone Cottage was also in darkness and he thought that his sister was asleep, but as he parked the car her light went on so he knocked at her door, looked in and said goodnight before going to his own room. His sister had seemed perfectly normal but sleepy and had said that they would talk about the dinner party and his plans for the African trip in the morning. The alibi would be difficult to challenge unless Robin Boyton, when questioned, had heard the car arriving next door and could confirm the time. The car could be checked but even if it were now running well, Westhall could allege that he was unhappy with the noises it was making and felt it safer not to risk being stuck in London.

Candace Westhall said that she had indeed been woken by the car and had spoken to her brother, but couldn't say precisely when he returned as she hadn't looked at her bedside clock. She had gone to sleep immediately. Dalgliesh had no difficulty in remembering what she had said at the end of the interview. He had always had almost complete recall of a conversation and a glance at his notes brought her words clearly to mind.

'I'm probably the only member of the household who expressed dislike of Rhoda Gradwyn. I made it plain to Mr Chandler-Powell that I thought it undesirable for a journalist of her reputation to be treated at the Manor. People who come here expect not only privacy but absolute discretion. Women like Gradwyn are always on the lookout for stories, preferably scandal, and I have no doubt she would have used her experience here in some way, perhaps to inveigh against private medicine or the waste of a brilliant surgeon on purely cosmetic procedures. With a woman like that no experience goes unused. She probably expected to recoup the cost of her treatment. I doubt whether the inconsistency that she herself was a private patient would have troubled her. I suppose I was influenced by my disgust at much that appears in our popular press and transferred that revulsion to Gradwyn. However, I didn't kill her and I have no idea who did. I would hardly have expressed my dislike of all she stood for so plainly if I'd had murder in mind. I can't grieve for her; it would be ridiculous to pretend that I could. She was, after all, a stranger. But I do feel a strong resentment against the killer for the harm he will do to the work here. I suppose Gradwyn's death justifies my warning. It was an ill day for everyone at the Manor when she came here as a patient.'

Mogworthy, whose voice and demeanour had been pitched one degree short of what could reasonably be described as dumb insolence, confirmed his sighting of the car but was unable to remember anything more about the vehicle or its occupants but, when called on by Benton and DC Warren, Mrs Ada Denton, a plump, comely and unexpectedly young woman, had said that Mr Mogworthy had indeed shared a supper of haddock and chips as he did most Friday nights, but had left just after half past eleven to cycle home. She did think it was a sad business that a respectable woman couldn't share a fish-and-chip supper with her gentleman friend without the police coming round to bother her, a comment which DC Warren thought was intended for Mogworthy's later benefit rather than out of rancour. Her final smile at Benton as they left had made it plain that he was exonerated from criticism.

It was time to summon Kate and Benton. He arranged more logs on the fire and picked up his mobile.

15

By nine thirty Kate and Benton were back in Wisteria House and had showered, changed and eaten the supper served by Mrs Shepherd in the dining room. Both liked to get out of their working clothes before joining Dalgliesh at the end of the day when he would review the state of the investigation and set out the programme for the next twenty-four hours. It was a familiar routine to which both looked forward, Kate with more confidence than Benton. He knew that AD was satisfied with him – he wouldn't otherwise still be part of the team – but he recognised that he could be over-enthusiastic in putting forward opinions which more thought would have modified, and his anxiety to curb this tendency to over-enthusiasm inhibited spontaneity, so that the evening review, although an exhilarating and important part of the investigation, was never without anxiety.

Since their arrival at Wisteria House, Kate and he had seen little of their hosts. There had been time only for brief introductions before they had left their bags in the hall and returned to the Manor. A white visiting card, with the address and the names Claude and Caroline Shepherd, had been handed to them, on which the initials EMO signified, as Mrs Shepherd explained, that the evening meal was optional and that dinner could and would be provided. This had set off a fascinating chain of more esoteric initials in Benton's mind: HBO – Hot Baths Optional, or Hard Beds Optional, HWBO – Hot Water Bottles Optional. Kate had spent only a minute in reiterating the warning already given by Chief Inspector Whetstone that their arrival should be kept private. She did it with tact. Both she and Benton had needed no more than a glance at the Shepherds' intelligent and serious faces to know that they didn't need and wouldn't welcome any reminder of an assurance already given.

Mr Shepherd had said, 'We've no temptation to be indiscreet, Inspector. The village people are polite and not unfriendly, but they are a little suspicious of incomers. We've only been here for nine years, which makes us recent arrivals in their eyes, so we don't see much of each other. We never drink in the Cressett Arms and we aren't church-goers.' He made the last statement with the self-satisfaction of one who has resisted the temptation to fall into a dangerous habit.

The Shepherds were, Kate thought, unlikely proprietors of a B & B. In her occasional experience of these useful stopping places she had recognised a number of characteristics the proprietors held in common. She found them friendly, sometimes gregarious, fond of meeting new people, house-proud, ready with helpful information about the area and its attractions, and – in defiance of contemporary warnings about cholesterol – providers in chief of the full English breakfast at its best. And surely their hosts were older than most people who coped with the hard work of catering for a succession of visitors. They were both tall, Mrs Shepherd the taller, and perhaps looked older than their years. Their mild but wary eyes were unclouded, their handshakes firm, and they moved with none of the stiffness of old age. Mr Shepherd, with his thick white hair cut in a fringe above steel-rimmed spectacles, looked like a benign edition of the self-portrait of Stanley Spencer. His wife's hair, less thick and now steel grey, was twisted into a long thin plait and secured at the top of her head by two combs. Their voices were remarkably similar, an unselfconscious distinctive upper-class accent which can so irritate those not in possession of it, and which, Kate told herself, would effectively have banned them from any hope of a job at the BBC or even a career in politics, had either unlikely option appealed to them.

Kate's bedroom held everything necessary for a comfortable night and nothing superfluous. She guessed that Benton's room next door was probably identical. Two single beds side by side were covered with immaculate white counterpanes, the bedside lamps were modern to facilitate reading and there was a two-drawer chest and a small wardrobe provided with wooden hangers. The bathroom had no bath but a shower which a preliminary turn of the taps showed to be efficient. The soap was unscented but expensive, and on opening the bathroom cabinet she saw that it was equipped with the necessary items which some visitors might have neglected to pack: toothbrush in a cellophane cover, toothpaste, shampoo and shower gel. As an early riser Kate regretted the absence of a kettle and other facilities for brewing morning tea, but a small notice on the chest of drawers informed her that tea could be brought up at any time between six and nine on request, although newspapers wouldn't be delivered until eight thirty.

She exchanged her shirt for one freshly laundered, drew on a cashmere pullover and, picking up her jacket, joined Benton in the hall.

At first they stepped out into an impenetrable and disorientating blackness. Benton's torch, its beam strong as a miniature headlight, transformed the paving stones and the path into disconcerting hazards and distorted the shape of bushes and trees. As Kate's eyes became accustomed to the night, one by one the stars became visible against the curdle of black and grey clouds through which a half moon gracefully slipped and reappeared, bleaching the narrow road and making the darkness mysteriously iridescent. They walked without speaking, their shoes sounding hobnailed on the tarmac like resolute and threatening invaders, alien creatures disturbing the peace of the night. Except, Kate thought, that it wasn't peace. Even in the stillness she could hear the faint shuffles in the grasses and from time to time a distant, almost human cry. The inexorable succession of kill and be killed was being played out under cover of darkness. Rhoda Gradwyn wasn't the only living creature that had died on that Friday night.

Some fifty yards on they passed the Westhalls' cottage with one light in an upstairs window and two shining from the windows of the ground floor. Within yards to the left was the parking space, the black shed and, beyond, a glimpse of the Cheverell circle, the stones no more than half-imagined shapes until the clouds parted under the moon and they stood, pale and insubstantial, seeming to float, moon-bleached, above the black unfriendly fields.

And now they were at the Old Police Cottage, with its light shining from the two ground-floor windows. As they approached Dalgliesh opened the door, looking for a second unfamiliar in slacks, a checked open-necked shirt and pullover. There was a wood fire burning, scenting the air, and a faint savoury aroma. Dalgliesh had pulled three comfortable low chairs before the fire with an oak coffee table between them. On it stood an open bottle of red wine, three glasses and a plan of the Manor. Kate felt an uplifting of her heart. This routine at the end of the day was like coming home. When the time came to accept promotion with the inevitable change of job, these were the moments she would miss. The talk would be of death and murder, sometimes in its most horrific form, but in memory these sessions at the end of the day would hold the warmth and security, the sense of being valued, which in childhood she had never known. There was a desk before the window holding Dalgliesh's laptop, a telephone and a thick file of papers beside it, and a bulging briefcase propped against the table leg. He had brought some of his other work with him. She thought, *He looks tired. It isn't good enough, he's been overworking for weeks*, and felt a surge of an emotion which she knew she could never express.

They settled themselves round the table. Looking at Kate, Dalgliesh asked, 'Are you comfortable at the B & B? You've had a meal?'

'Very comfortable, thank you, sir. Mrs Shepherd did us well. Home-made soup, fish pie and – what was that sweet, Sergeant? You know about food.'

'Queen of puddings, ma'am.'

Dalgliesh said, 'Chief Inspector Whetstone has arranged with the Shepherds that they take no other visitors while you are there. They ought to be compensated for any loss, but no doubt this has been arranged. The local force has been extraordinarily co-operative. It can't have been easy.'

Benton broke in. 'I don't think the Shepherds will be bothered about other visitors, sir. Mrs Shepherd said they haven't any bookings and don't expect any. They've only got the two rooms anyway. They're busy in the spring and summer, but mostly with regular visitors. And they're choosy. If people arrive they don't like the look of, they immediately put the *No Vacancies* sign in the window.'

Kate said, 'So who don't they like the look of?'

'People with large expensive cars and the kind who ask to see the rooms before booking. They never refuse women arriving alone or people without cars who are obviously desperate at the end of the day. They have their grandson staying for the weekend, but he's in an annexe at the bottom of the garden. Chief Inspector Whetstone knows about him. And he'll keep his mouth shut. They love their grandson but not his motorbike.'

Kate said, 'Who told you all this?'

'Mrs Shepherd when she showed me to my room.'

Kate didn't comment on Benton's formidable ability to extract information without asking for it. Obviously Mrs Shepherd was as susceptible to a handsome and deferential young man as most of her sex.

Dalgliesh poured the wine then spread the plan of the Manor on the table. He said, 'Let's be absolutely plain about the layout of the house. As you see, it's H-shaped, south facing and with western and eastern wings. The entrance hall, great hall, dining room and library are in the main part of the house, as is also the kitchen. The Bostocks occupy two rooms above the kitchen and Sharon Bateman's room is next to them. The west wing at the rear has been adapted as accommodation for the patients. The ground floor comprises the operating suite, which includes the theatre, adjacent room for anaesthetics, the recovery suite, the nurses' station, storeroom and showers and cloakroom at the end. The lift, large enough for wheelchairs but not for a stretcher, goes up to the second floor, where there is Sister Holland's sitting room, bedroom and bathroom, then the patients' rooms, the first suite occupied by Mrs Skeffington, then Rhoda Gradwyn's, and the spare suite at the end, all with sitting rooms and bathrooms. The windows from the bedrooms look out over the lime avenue to the Cheverell Stones, and those in the east-facing rooms over the knot garden. Mr Chandler-Powell is on the first floor of the east wing, Miss Cressett and Mrs Frensham on the ground floor. The rooms at the top are spare bedrooms, occasionally used for ancillary medical and nursing staff who may need to stay the night.'

He paused, then looked at Kate who took over.

'Our problem is that we have a group of seven people in the Manor, any of whom could have killed Miss Gradwyn. All knew where she was sleeping, knew that the suite beyond was unoccupied providing a possible hiding place, knew where the surgical gloves were kept, and all either had or could have obtained keys to the west door. And although the Westhalls are non-resident, they knew Gradwyn's room and have keys to the front door and the one leading to the lime walk. If Marcus Westhall didn't return to Stone Cottage until twelve thirty he's probably in the clear, but he hasn't been able to provide a witness. He could very well have got back earlier. And his explanation of why he decided to return here last night is odd. If he feared the car might be unreliable wouldn't it have been safer to stay in London and get it fixed rather than risk a breakdown on the motorway? And then there's Robin Boyton. It's doubtful whether he knew where Miss Gradwyn was sleeping and he wouldn't have been given a house key, but he is the only one to have known the victim personally and he admits he booked into Rose Cottage because she was here. Mr Chandler-Powell is insistent that he bolted the door to the lime walk promptly at eleven o'clock. If the murderer came from outside and was a stranger to the Manor, he would have had to be let in by one of the household, told where to find his victim, provided with gloves and eventually let out again, the door bolted behind him. The strong possibility is that this was an inside job, which makes motive of prime importance.'

Dalgliesh said, 'It's usually unwise to concentrate too early or too strongly on motive. People kill for a variety of reasons, some unacknowledged even by the killer. And we must bear in mind that

Rhoda Gradwyn might not have been the sole victim. Was this directed against Chandler-Powell, for example? Did the murderer want to destroy the clinic or had he a double motive, to get rid of Gradwyn and ruin Chandler-Powell? It's difficult to imagine a more effective deterrent than the brutal and unexplained murder of a patient. Chandler-Powell calls the motive bizarre but it has to be kept in mind.'

Benton said, 'Mrs Skeffington for one won't be back, sir. It may be unwise to concentrate too much and too early on motive, but I can't imagine Chandler-Powell or Sister Holland killing a patient. Mr Chandler-Powell apparently made a good job of repairing that scar. It's his job. Would a rational man destroy his own handiwork? And I can't see the Bostocks as murderers. He and Kimberley seem to have a very comfortable billet here. Is Dean Bostock going to throw up a good job? That leaves us with Candace Westhall, Mogworthy, Miss Cressett, Mrs Frensham, Sharon Bateman and Robin Boyton. And, as far as we know, none has a motive for murdering Gradwyn.'

Benton stopped and looked round, Kate thought in some embarrassment at going down a path which Dalgliesh might not have wanted to open up.

Without commenting Dalgliesh said, 'Well, let's be clear what we've learnt so far. We'll leave motive for the moment. Benton, will you begin?'

Kate knew that her chief always asked the most junior member of the team to initiate the discussion. Benton's silence on their walk suggested that he had already spent some time deciding how best to proceed. Dalgliesh hadn't made it clear whether Benton was meant to review the facts or to comment on them or both, but invariably, if he didn't, Kate would, and she suspected that this interchange, often lively, was what Dalgliesh had in mind.

Benton took a gulp of his wine. He had given thought to what he would say on the walk to the Old Police Cottage. Now he was succinct. He gave an account of Rhoda Gradwyn's involvement with Chandler-Powell and the Cheverell Manor clinic from her appointment with him in his Harley Street consulting room on 21

November until the time of her death. She had had a choice of a private bed in St Angela's in London or Cheverell Manor. She chose the Manor, at least provisionally, and came for a preliminary visit on 27 November, when the member of staff who saw most of her was Sharon, who showed her the garden. This was a little surprising since contact with the patients was usually with more senior members of staff or with the two surgeons and Sister Holland.

'On Thursday the 13th of December she went straight to her suite after being received on arrival by Mr Chandler-Powell, Sister Holland and Mrs Frensham. All say she was perfectly calm, apparently unworried and not very communicative. One of the temporary non-resident staff, Nurse Frazer, took her down to the operating theatre next morning where she was examined by the anaesthetist and then underwent the operation. Mr Chandler-Powell says it was complicated but successful. She was in the recovery room until four thirty, when she was returned to her suite on the patients' wing. She ate a light supper and was seen by Sister Holland on several occasions, and by Chandler-Powell and Sister Holland at ten o'clock, when Miss Gradwyn said she was ready to sleep. She refused a sedative. Sister Holland said that the last time she looked in on her was at eleven, when she found Miss Gradwyn asleep. She was murdered by manual strangulation, Dr Glenister estimates between eleven and twelve thirty.'

Dalgliesh and Kate listened in silence. Benton was seized by the fear that he was taking too much time on the obvious. He glanced at Kate but, getting no response, went on. 'We've been told of several significant things that happened that night. The only other patient present, Mrs Skeffington, was wakeful and went to the bathroom. She could have been woken by the sound of the lift which, she says, she heard at eleven forty. From the bedroom window she claims she saw a light flickering among the Cheverell Stones. This was just before midnight. It frightened her and she rang the assistant cook, Kimberley Bostock, and asked for a pot of tea. Probably she wanted company, however briefly, but didn't like to wake up Sister Holland who was in the suite next door.'

Kate said, 'Didn't she admit as much when Kimberley and Dean brought up the tea?'

Benton said, 'She certainly seemed to prefer Kimberley Bostock to Sister Holland. Seems reasonable to me, sir. Mrs Bostock wondered whether she should have the tea as she was having an operation the next morning. She knew she ought to check with Sister Holland. Leaving Dean standing outside Mrs Skeffington's suite, she knocked on Sister's door and peered in.'

Kate said, 'She said she heard quarrelling. Chandler-Powell said talking. Whichever it was, Chandler-Powell obviously feels his admission provides an alibi for both him and Sister Holland. Of course, that depends on the actual time of death. He claims to be unsure exactly when he went to Sister Holland's suite, and she too is surprisingly vague. By leaving the time so uncertain they avoided the mistake of claiming an alibi for the actual time of death, which is always suspicious, or leaving themselves with no alibi. It's possible that by the time they were together, one or both of them had killed Rhoda Gradwyn.'

Benton said, 'Can't we be a little more precise about the time of death? Mrs Skeffington says she heard the lift descending when she first woke up and before she rang for tea. She put that at about eleven forty. The lift is opposite Sister Holland's suite at the end of the corridor and it's modern and comparatively quiet. But we've checked and it's perfectly possible to hear it if there's no other noise.'

Kate said, 'But there was. Apparently the wind gusted quite strongly last night. But if she heard it, why didn't Sister Holland? Unless, of course, she and Chandler-Powell were in the bedroom and too busy quarrelling to hear. Or having sex, which doesn't exclude quarrelling. Either way, there's no hope of expecting Kimberley to stand firm on her evidence.'

Benton went on without commenting. 'If they'd been in the sitting room, one of them would surely have heard Kimberley when she knocked on the door or seen her when she half opened it. No one admits to using the lift that night at any time except the Bostocks when they brought up the tea. If Mrs Skeffington's evidence is accurate, it seems reasonable to place the time of death at about eleven thirty.'

Glancing at Dalgliesh, Benton paused and Kate took over. 'It's a pity she can't be more accurate about the time when she heard the lift and saw the lights. If there's a significant difference between them – longer, for example, than it would take to walk from the bottom of the lift to the stones – then there must be two people involved. The murderer can't be descending in the lift and shining a torch at the stones at the same time. Two people, maybe two different enterprises. And if there was collusion, the two obvious suspects are the Westhalls. The other significant evidence is Dean Bostock's statement about the unbolted back door leading to the lime walk. The door has two security locks, but Chandler-Powell is adamant he bolts it every night at eleven o'clock unless he knows a member of the household is still out. He's absolutely sure he bolted the door as usual, and found it bolted in the morning. The first thing he did after getting up at six thirty was to turn off the alarm system and check the west door to the lime walk.'

Benton broke in. 'And Dean Bostock checked the bolt when he got up at six. Is there a chance we may get a print from the bolt?'

Kate said, 'Not a chance, I'd say. Chandler-Powell unlocked the door when he and Marcus Westhall went out to search the grounds and the stone circle. And remember that fragment of glove? This killer wasn't about to leave prints.'

Dalgliesh said, 'If we assume that neither Chandler-Powell nor Bostock was lying – and I don't think Bostock was – then someone in the house unbolted that door after eleven o'clock, either to leave the Manor or to let someone in. Or, of course, both. That leads us to Mogworthy's alleged sighting of a car parked near the stones shortly before midnight. Miss Gradwyn was killed either by some-one who was already in the Manor that night – a member of staff or someone else who had gained access – or by someone from out-side. And even if that person had the two security keys, he or she couldn't gain access until the door was unbolted. But we can't go on talking about he or she. The murderer needs a name.'

The murderer was always given a name by the team since

Dalgliesh strongly disliked the usual soubriquets, and usually it was Benton who supplied it. Now he said, 'We usually make it a he, sir, so why not a woman for a change? Or an androgynous name which would do for either sex. The murderer came by night. How about Noctis – by or from the night?'

Dalgliesh said, 'That seems appropriate. Noctis it is, but let's keep him male for the present.'

Kate said, 'We're still back with the problem of motive. We know that Candace Westhall tried to persuade Chandler-Powell not to let Rhoda Gradwyn come to the Manor. If Westhall had murder in mind, why discourage Chandler-Powell from admitting her? Unless, of course, it was a double bluff. And isn't it possible that this was an unpremeditated death, that Noctis hadn't got murder in mind when he went to that room?'

Dalgliesh said, 'Against that, of course, is the use of gloves and their destruction afterwards.'

Benton said, 'But if it was premeditated, why now? With only one other patient and all the non-resident staff absent the circle of suspects is bound to be smaller.'

Kate was impatient. 'It had to be now. She wasn't planning to return. She was killed because she was here in the Manor and relatively helpless. It's just a question of whether the murderer took advantage of that fortunate fact or actually connived to ensure that Gradwyn chose not only this particular surgeon, but the Manor instead of a bed in London, which on the face of it would have been more convenient for her. London was her city. Her life was London-based. Why here? And that leads us on to why her so-called friend, Robin Boyton, booked in at the same time. We haven't interviewed him yet but he's certainly got some questions to answer. What exactly is their relationship? And then there's his urgent message on Gradwyn's mobile. He was obviously pretty desperate to see her. He seemed genuinely upset at her death, but how much of that was play-acting? He's a cousin of the Westhalls and apparently he stays at the visitors' cottage fairly regularly. He could have got access to keys and had them copied on one of his previous visits. Or he may have been given them by Rhoda

Gradwyn. She could have deliberately taken the keys home with her on her first visit with the intention of having them copied. And how do we know he didn't get access to the Manor earlier that day and hide himself in the suite at the end of the patients' corridor? We know from the scrap of latex that Noctis was there. It could have been before as well as after the murder. Who was likely to look in there?'

Benton said, 'Whoever killed her, I doubt whether she'll be much missed, here or anywhere. She seems to have caused a lot of damage in her lifetime. The archetypical investigative journalist – get your exclusive story, take the cash, never mind the pain.'

Dalgliesh said, 'Our job is to decide who killed her, not to make moral judgements. Don't go down that path, Sergeant.'

Benton said, 'But don't we always make moral judgements, sir, even if we don't voice them? Isn't it important to know as much as we can about the victim, good or ill? People die because of who they are and what they are. Isn't that part of the evidence? I'd feel differently about the death of a child, a young person, the innocent.'

Dalgliesh said, 'Innocent? So you feel confident to make the distinction between the victims who deserve death and those who don't? You haven't yet been part of an investigation into the murder of a child, have you?'

'No, sir.' Benton thought, *You knew that already, you didn't need to ask.*

'If and when you are, the pain you'll have to witness will confront you with more questions, emotional and theological, even than the one you'll be there to answer: who did this? Moral outrage is natural. Without it we're hardly human. But for a detective faced with the dead body of a child, the young, the innocent, making an arrest can become a personal campaign, and that's dangerous. It can corrupt judgement. Every victim deserves the same commitment.'

Benton wanted to say, *I know that, sir. I'll try to give it.* But the unspoken words struck him as pretentious, the response of a guilty schoolboy to criticism. He said nothing.

Kate broke the silence. 'And for all our probing, how much in the end do we ever really know? The victim, the suspects, the killer? Why, I wonder, did Rhoda Gradwyn come here.'

Benton said, 'To get rid of that scar.'

Dalgliesh said, 'A scar she had had for thirty-four years. Why now? Why this place? Why did she need to keep it and why now to get rid of it? If we knew that, we might get closer to knowing something about the woman. And you're quite right, Benton, she died because of who and what she was.'

Benton instead of Sergeant – well that was something. He thought, *I wish I knew who you are*. But that was part of the fascination of this job. He served a boss who remained an enigma to him, and always would.

Kate said, 'Isn't Sister Holland's behaviour this morning a bit odd? When Kim phoned to say that Miss Gradwyn hadn't rung for her tea, wouldn't it be more natural for Sister Holland to check at once if her patient was all right rather than asking Kim to bring up the tea? I'm wondering whether she was taking care to ensure that there was a witness with her when she found the body. Did she already know that Miss Gradwyn was dead?'

Benton said, 'Chandler-Powell says that he left Sister Holland's room at one o'clock. Wouldn't it be a natural thing for her to check then on her patient? She might well have done so and known that Gradwyn was dead when she asked Kimberley to bring up the tea. It's always advisable to have a witness when you find the body. But that doesn't mean that she killed her. As I said earlier, I can't see either Chandler-Powell or Sister Holland throttling the life out of a patient, particularly one they had just operated on.'

Kate looked as if she was ready to argue but said nothing. It was late and Dalgliesh knew that they were all tired. It was time to set out the programme for the next day. He and Kate would drive to London to see what evidence could be obtained from Rhoda Gradwyn's house in the City. Benton and DC Warren would remain at the Manor. Dalgliesh had deferred seeing Robin Boyton in the hope that, by tomorrow, he would have calmed down and be ready to co-operate. The priorities were for Benton with DC Warren to interview Boyton, if possible to trace the car seen parked near the Cheverell Stones, to liaise with the scene-of-crime officers who were expected to finish their work by midday, and to maintain a police presence at the Manor and ensure that the security guards employed by Mr Chandler-Powell kept clear of the scene. Dr Glenister's report on the post mortem was expected by midday and Benton would ring Dalgliesh as soon as this had been received. Apart from these tasks, he would of course use his initiative in deciding whether any of the suspects should be questioned again.

It was nearly midnight before Benton carried the three wineglasses into the kitchen to wash, and he and Kate set out to make their way back through the sweet-smelling rain-washed darkness to Wisteria House.

BOOK THREE

16–18 December
London, Dorset, Midlands, Dorset

Dalgliesh and Kate left Stoke Cheverell before six o'clock, an early start planned partly because of Dalgliesh's strong dislike of getting tangled in the heavy morning traffic, but also because he needed the extra time in London. There were papers on which he had been working to be delivered to the Yard, a confidential draft report requiring his comments to be collected, and a note to be left on his secretary's desk. This done, he and Kate drove in silence through the almost empty streets.

For Dalgliesh, as for many, the early hours of Sunday morning in the City held a particular appeal. For five weekdays the air pulsates with energy so that one can believe that its great wealth is being physically hammered out with sweat and exhaustion in some underground engine room. By Friday afternoon the wheels slowly stop spinning, and to watch the City toilers swarm in their thousands over the Thames bridges to their railway termini is to see this mass exodus less as a matter of will than of obedience to some centuries-old compulsion. By early Sunday morning the City, so far from settling itself for a deeper sleep, lies silently expectant, awaiting the visitation of a ghostly army, summoned by bells to worship old gods in their carefully preserved shrines and to walk down quiet remembered streets. Even the river seems to flow more slowly.

They found a parking space some hundred yards from Absolution Alley and Dalgliesh gave a final glance at the map, took his murder bag from the car and they set off eastwards. The narrow cobbled entrance under a stone arch, discordantly ornate for such a narrow opening, would have been easy to miss. The paved courtyard, lit by two wall-mounted lamps, which merely illumined a Dickensian gloom, was small with a centre plinth supporting an age-crumbled statue, possibly of antiquated religious significance but now no more than a shapeless mass of stone. Number eight was on the eastern side, the door painted a green so dark that it looked almost black and with an iron knocker in the shape of an owl. Next to number eight was a shop which sold old prints, with a wooden display tray outside, now empty. A second building was obviously a select employment agency but gave no sign of the type of workers it hoped to attract. Other doors bore small polished plaques with unfamiliar names. The silence was absolute.

The door had been fitted with two security locks but there was no problem in selecting the right keys from Miss Gradwyn's bunch and the door opened easily. Dalgliesh put out his hand and found the light switch. They entered a small room, oak panelled and with an ornate plaster ceiling incorporating the date: 1684. A mullioned window at the rear gave a view of a paved patio with room for little more than a leaf-denuded tree in an immense terracotta pot. There was a row of coat hooks to the right with a shelf beneath for shoes, and on the left a rectangular oak table. It held four envelopes, clearly either bills or catalogues, which Dalgliesh thought had probably arrived before Miss Gradwyn left on Thursday for the Manor and which she had judged could well await her return. The only picture was a small oil painting of a seventeenth-century man with a long sensitive face which hung above the stone fireplace and which Dalgliesh, on first scrutiny, thought was a copy of the well-known portrait of John Donne. He switched on the strip of lighting fixed to shine on the portrait and studied it for a moment in silence. Hanging alone in a room which was a place of passage, it acquired an iconic power, perhaps as the presiding genius of the home. Switching off the light, Dalgliesh wondered if that was how Rhoda Gradwyn had seen it.

A wooden uncarpeted stair led to the first floor. Here at the front was the kitchen with a small dining room at the back. The kitchen was extraordinarily well arranged and equipped, the room of a woman who knew how to cook, although neither it nor the dining room showed any signs of recent use. They mounted the second flight. There was a guest bedroom with two single beds, the identical counterpanes tightly stretched and, overlooking the courtyard, a shower and lavatory. Again neither room bore any signs of occupation. The room above was almost a replica, but the bedroom here, with one single bed only, was obviously Miss Gradwyn's. A bedside table held a modern anglepoise lamp, a carriage clock whose ticking sounded unnaturally loud in the silence, and three books: Claire Tomalin's biography of Pepys, a volume of Charles Causley's verse and a collection of modern short stories. The bathroom shelf held very few pots and jars, and Kate, stretching out her hand in feminine curiosity, drew back. Neither Dalgliesh nor she entered the private world of the victim without an awareness that their presence, although necessary, was a violation of privacy. Kate, he knew, had always drawn a distinction between the objects they needed to examine and take away and a natural curiosity about a life which had escaped for ever from any human power either to hurt or embarrass. She merely said, 'It doesn't look as if she tried to camouflage the scar.'

Finally, they moved to the top storey and entered a room which ran the length of the house with windows to both east and west giving a panorama of the City. Only here did Dalgliesh begin to feel strongly that he was in mental touch with the owner. In this room she had lived, worked, rested, watched television, listened to music, needing no one and nothing that was not within those four walls. One was almost completely covered with an elegantly carved bookcase with adjustable shelves. He saw that it had been important to her, as it was to him, that books should neatly fit the height of the shelves. Her mahogany desk was to the left of the bookcase and looked Edwardian. It was practical rather than decorative with drawers on each side, the right ones locked. Above was a shelf holding a rack of box files. On the opposite side of the room was a comfortable sofa with cushions, an easy chair facing the television with a small footstool, and to the right of the black Victorian grate, a high-backed armchair. The stereo equipment was modern but unobtrusive. To the left of the window there was a small refrigerator with a tray on top holding an electric percolator, a coffee grinder and a single mug. Here, with a tap in the bathroom one storey below, she could make herself a drink without having to go down three flights to the kitchen. Not an easy house to live in, but it was one in which he too could have felt at home. He and Kate moved about the room without speaking. He saw that the east-facing window gave access to a small wrought-iron balcony with iron steps leading upwards to the roof. He opened the window to the cold freshness of the morning and climbed up. Kate didn't follow.

His own flat, high above the Thames at Queenhithe, was within walking distance and he turned his eyes towards the river. Even if he had time or needed to go there, he knew he wouldn't find Emma. Although she had a key she never visited the flat when she was in London unless he was there. It was, he knew, part of her unspoken and careful distancing of herself from his job, a wish that amounted almost to an obsession not to invade his privacy, a privacy which she respected because she understood and shared it. A lover was not an acquisition or a trophy to be possessed. There was always some part of the personality which remained inviolate. When they first fell in love she would fall asleep at night in his arms, and he would stir in the small hours, reaching for her but knowing she was no longer there. It was to the guest room that he took her early morning tea. This happened less often now. At first the separation had worried him. Inhibited from asking her, partly because he feared to know the answer, he had arrived at his own conclusions. Because he didn't, or perhaps wouldn't speak openly about the reality of his job, she needed to separate the lover from the detective. They could talk about her Cambridge job and frequently did, sometimes happily arguing, because they shared a passion for literature. His offered no common ground. She wasn't a fool or over-sensitive, she recognised the importance of his work, but he knew that it still lay between them like unexplored scrubland dangerously mined.

He had been on the roof for less than a minute. From this high and private place Rhoda Gradwyn would have watched the dawn touching the City spires and towers and painting them with light. Now, climbing down, he joined Kate.

He said, 'We'd better get started on the files.'

They seated themselves side by side at the desk. All the boxes were neatly labelled. The one named Sanctuary Court contained her copy of the complicated lease – now, he saw, with sixty-seven years outstanding – correspondence with her solicitor, details and quotations relating to redecoration and maintenance. Her agent and solicitor both had named files. In another, under Finance, were her bank statements and regular reports from her private bankers on the state of her investments. Looking through them, Dalgliesh was surprised how well she was doing. She was worth nearly two million pounds, the portfolio clearly balanced between equities and government securities.

Kate said, 'You would expect to see these reports in one of the locked drawers. She didn't seem worried that an intruder might find out exactly what she was worth, probably because she thought the house secure. Or perhaps she didn't greatly care. She didn't live like a rich woman.'

'We can hope to learn who is going to benefit from this largesse when Newton Macklefield gets here with the will.'

They turned their attention to the rank of files containing copies of all her press and magazine articles. Each box, labelled with the years covered, contained the articles in date order, some in plastic covers. They took a file each and settled down to work.

Dalgliesh said, 'Note anything she wrote that relates, however indirectly, to Cheverell Manor or any of the people there.'

For almost an hour they worked in silence, then Kate slid a bunch of press cuttings across the desk. She said, 'This is interesting, sir. It's a long article in the *Paternoster Review* about plagiarism, published in the spring number in 2002. It seems to have attracted notice. There's a number of newspaper cuttings attached, including a report of an inquest and another of a burial with a photograph.' She passed it across. 'One of the people at the graveside looks very like Miss Westhall.'

Dalgliesh took a magnifying glass from his murder bag and studied the picture. The woman was hatless and standing a little apart from the group of mourners. Only her head was visible and the face was partly obscured but Dalgliesh, after a minute's scrutiny, had little trouble with the identification. He handed the magnifying glass to Kate and said, 'Yes, it's Candace Westhall.'

He turned his attention to the article. He was a fast reader and it was easy to get the gist. The article was intelligent, well written and meticulously researched and he read it with genuine interest and growing respect. It dealt with cases of plagiarism dispassionately and he thought fairly, some from the distant past, others more recent, some notorious, many new to him. Rhoda Gradwyn was interesting about apparently unconscious copying of phrases and ideas and the occasional curious coincidences in literature when a strong idea enters simultaneously into two minds as if its time has come, and examined the subtle ways in which the greatest writers had influenced succeeding generations, as had Bach and Beethoven in music and the major painters of the world on those who followed. But the main contemporary case covered was undoubtedly one of blatant plagiarism, which Gradwyn claimed she had by chance discovered. The case was fascinating because, on the face of it, the filching by a talented young writer of obvious originality had been unnecessary. A young female novelist still at university, Annabel Skelton, had produced a first novel, widely praised and shortlisted for a major British literary prize, in which some phrases and paragraphs of dialogue and powerful descriptions were taken word for word from a work of fiction published in 1927 by a long-forgotten woman writer of whom Dalgliesh had never heard. The case was unanswerable, not least because of the quality of Gradwyn's prose and the fairness of the article. It had appeared when the tabloids were short of news and journalists had made the most of the scandal. There had been vociferous demands that Annabel Skelton's novel should be removed from the shortlist. The result had been tragedy: three days after the article appeared the girl had killed herself. If Candace Westhall had been intimate with the dead girl – lover, friend, teacher, admirer –

here was a motive which for some people might be strong enough for murder.

It was then that the telephone rang. Benton was speaking, and Dalgliesh switched his mobile to speakerphone so that Kate could hear. Carefully controlling his excitement, Benton said, 'We've traced the car, sir. It's a Ford Focus, W341 UDG.'

'That was quick, Sergeant. Congratulations.'

'Undeserved, I'm afraid, sir. We struck lucky. The Shepherds' grandson arrived late on Friday night to spend a weekend with them. He was away all yesterday visiting a girlfriend so we didn't see him until this morning. He was behind the car on his motorbike for some miles and saw it draw in to park at the stones. This was at about eleven thirty-five on Friday. There was only one person in the car and the driver switched off the lights when he parked. I asked him why he noticed the registration and he said it was because 341 is a brilliant number.'

'I'm glad it caught his interest. Brilliant in what way? Did he explain the fascination?'

'Apparently it's a mathematical term, sir: 341 is described as a brilliant number because it has two prime factors, 11 and 31. Multiply them and you get 341. Numbers with two prime factors of equal length are known as brilliant numbers and are used in cryptography. Apparently it's also the sum of the squares of the divisors of 16, but I think he was more impressed by the two prime factors. He had no trouble with UDG. It stands in his mind for U Done Good – seems appropriate, sir.'

Dalgliesh said, 'The maths means nothing to me, but we must hope he's right. I suppose we can find someone to confirm it.'

'I don't think we need bother, sir. He's just got a first in Mathematics at Oxford. He said he can never get stuck behind another vehicle without mentally playing about with the registration number.'

'And the car owner?'

'A bit surprising on the face of it. It's a clergyman. The Reverend Michael Curtis. Lives in Droughton Cross. St John's Church Vicarage, 2 Balaclava Gardens. It's a suburb of Droughton.'

The Midlands industrial city could be reached in little over two hours on the motorway. Dalgliesh said, 'Thank you, Sergeant. We'll go on to Droughton Cross as soon as we've finished here. The driver may have nothing to do with the murder but we need to know why that car was parked by the stones and what, if anything, he saw. Is there anything else, Sergeant?'

'One find by the SOCOs, sir, before they left. It's more odd than significant, I'd say. It's a bundle of eight old postcards, all of foreign views and all dated 1993. They've been cut in two with the address on the right-hand side missing, so there's no way of knowing who the recipient was, but they read as if written to a child. They were wrapped tightly in silver paper inside a plastic bag and buried by one of the Cheverell Stones. The SOCO concerned was pretty sharp eyed and he saw some evidence that the grass had been disturbed, although not recently. It's difficult to say what connection they could have with Miss Gradwyn's death. We know someone was at the stones with a light that night, but if they were looking for the cards they didn't find them.'

'Have you asked anyone about the ownership?'

'Yes, sir. It seemed most likely that they belonged to Sharon Bateman, so I asked her to come to the Old Police Cottage. She admitted they were hers and said they'd been sent to her by her father after he'd left home. She's an odd girl, sir. When I first laid the cards out she went so white that DC Warren and I thought she was going to faint. I made her sit down, but I think it was anger, sir. I could see she wanted to snatch them from the table but was managing to control herself. After that she was perfectly calm. She said they were the most precious things she had and that she had buried them near the stone when she first came to the Manor because that was a very special place and they would be safe there. I was worried about her for a moment, sir, so I said I'd need to show them to you but that we'd take great care of them and I could see no reason why she couldn't have them back. I'm not sure I did right, sir. It might have been better to wait until you were back and let Inspector Miskin speak to her.'

Dalgliesh said, 'Possibly, but I shouldn't worry about it, if you're satisfied that she's happier now. Keep a careful eye on her. We'll discuss it tonight. Has Dr Glenister's report on the PM arrived?'

'Not yet, sir. She rang to say we should get it by the evening unless she needs a toxicology report.'

'It's unlikely to surprise us. Is that all, Sergeant?'

'Yes, sir. I don't think there's anything else to report. I'm seeing Robin Boyton in half an hour.'

'Right. Find out, if you can, whether he has any expectations from Miss Gradwyn's will. You're having an eventful day. Well done. There's an interesting development here but we'll discuss that later. I'll ring you from Droughton Cross.'

The call was over. Kate said, 'Poor girl. If she's speaking the truth I can see why the cards are important to her. But why cut off the address, and why bother to hide them? They can't be of value to anyone else and if she did go to the stones on Friday night to check on them or retrieve them, why did she need to, and why late at night? But Benton said that the package was undisturbed. It looks, sir, as if the cards are nothing to do with the murder.'

Events were moving fast. Before Dalgliesh could reply the doorbell rang. Kate said, 'That'll be Mr Macklefield,' and went down to let him in.

There was a clatter of feet on the wooden stairs but no voices. Newton Macklefield came in first, evinced no curiosity about the room and, unsmiling, held out his hand. He said, 'I hope I'm not inconveniently early. The traffic on a Sunday morning is light.'

He was younger than Dalgliesh had expected from his voice on the telephone, probably no more than early forties, and was conventionally good looking – tall, fair haired and clear skinned. He brought with him the confidence of assured metropolitan success which was so in contrast to his corduroy trousers, checked open-necked shirt and well-worn tweed jacket, that the clothes, appropriate for a weekend in the country, had a contrived air of fancy dress. His features were regular, the mouth well shaped and firm, the eyes wary, a face, Dalgliesh thought, disciplined to reveal only appropriate emotions. The appropriate one now was of regret and shock, gravely but not emotionally expressed and, to Dalgliesh's ears, not without a note of displeasure. An eminent City firm of solicitors did not expect to lose a client in so notorious a manner.

He refused the chair which Kate had pulled out from the desk without looking at it, but used it to hold his briefcase. Opening it, he said, 'I've brought a copy of the will. I doubt if there is anything in its provisions to help your enquiry but it is, of course, right that you should have it.'

Dalgliesh said, 'I expect my colleague has introduced herself. Detective Inspector Kate Miskin.'

'Yes. We met at the door.'

Kate received a handshake so brief that their fingers barely touched. No one sat down.

Macklefield said, 'Miss Gradwyn's death will distress and hor-rify all the partners in the firm. As I explained when we spoke, I knew her as a client, not as a friend, but she was much respected and will be greatly missed. Her bank and my firm are joint execu-tors of the will, so we shall take responsibility eventually for the funeral arrangements.'

Dalgliesh said, 'I think that her mother, now Mrs Brown, will find that a relief. I've already spoken to her. She seemed anxious to dissociate herself as far as possible from the aftermath of her daughter's death, including the inquest. It seems not to have been a close relationship and there may be family matters which she doesn't want to disclose or even think about.'

Macklefield said, 'Well, her daughter was pretty good at disclosing other people's secrets. Still, the family's non-involvement probably suits you better than being landed with a tearful publicity-avid mother milking the tragedy for all it's worth and demanding a progress report on the investigation. I'll probably have more prob-lems with her than you. Anyway, whatever her relationship with her daughter, she'll get the money. The amount will probably surprise her. Of course you'll have seen the bank statements and the portfolio.'

Dalgliesh said, 'And it all goes to the mother?'

'All but twenty thousand pounds of it. That goes to a Robin Boyton, whose relationship with the deceased is unknown as far as I'm concerned. I remember when Miss Gradwyn came to discuss the will with me. She showed a singular lack of interest in disposing of her capital. People usually mention a charity or two, their old university or school. None of that. It was as if with her death she wanted her private life to remain anonymous. I'll phone Mrs Brown on Monday and arrange a meeting. Obviously we'll help in any way we can. No doubt you'll keep us in touch, but I don't think there's anything more I can tell you. Have you been able to make progress with your investigation?'

Dalgliesh said, 'As much as has been possible in the one day since her death. I shall know the date of the inquest on Tuesday. At this stage it's likely to be adjourned.'

'We may send someone. A formality, but it's as well to be there if there's going to be publicity as, inevitably, there will be once the news breaks.'

Taking the will, Dalgliesh thanked him. It was obvious that Macklefield was ready to go. Closing the briefcase, he said, 'Forgive me if I leave now, unless there's anything else you need. I promised my wife I would be back in time for lunch. My son has brought some school friends for the weekend. A houseful of Etonians and four dogs can be a riotous mixture to keep in hand.'

He shook hands with Dalgliesh and Kate preceded him down the stairs. Returning, she said, 'He'd hardly be likely to mention his son from Bogside Comprehensive,' and then regretted the comment. Dalgliesh had responded to Macklefield's remark with a wry, briefly contemptuous smile, but this momentary revelation of an unattractive quirk of character hadn't irritated him. It would have amused but not irritated Benton.

Taking out the bunch of keys, Dalgliesh said, 'And now for the drawers. But first I feel the need for coffee. Perhaps we should have offered some to Macklefield but I wasn't anxious to prolong the visit. Mrs Brown said that we could take what we wanted from the house, so she won't grudge milk and coffee. That's if there is milk in the fridge.'

There wasn't. Kate said, 'It's not surprising, sir. The fridge is empty. A carton of milk, even unopened, could have been out of date by the time she returned.'

She took the percolator down one flight to add water. Returning with a toothbrush holder which she rinsed to use as a second mug, she felt a moment of disquiet as if this small act, which hardly ranked as a violation of Miss Gradwyn's privacy, was an impertinence. Rhoda Gradwyn had been particular about her coffee, and on the tray with the coffee grinder was a tin of beans. Kate, still burdened with an irrational guilt that they should be taking from the dead, switched on the grinder. The noise was incredibly loud and seemed interminable. Later, when the percolator had stopped dripping, she filled the two mugs and carried them over to the desk.

Waiting for the coffee to cool, he said, 'If there's anything else interesting, this is where we'll probably find it,' and unlocked the drawer.

Inside there was nothing but a beige manila folder, the inside pocket stuffed with papers. The coffee for the moment forgotten, they pushed the mugs to one side and Kate pulled in a chair beside Dalgliesh. The papers were almost entirely copies of press cuttings, at the top an article from a Sunday broadsheet dated February 1995. The heading was stark: *Killed Because She Was Too Pretty.* Underneath, taking half the page, was a photograph of a young girl. It looked like a school photograph. The fair hair had been carefully brushed and tied with a bow to one side, and the white cotton blouse, looking pristine clean, was open at the neck and worn with a dark blue tunic. The child had indeed been pretty. Even simply posed and with no particular skill in lighting, the stark photograph conveyed something of the frank confidence, the openness to life and the vulnerability of childhood. As Kate stared at it, the image seemed to disintegrate into dust and became a meaningless blur, then refocused again.

Beneath the image the reporter, eschewing the worst of hyperbole or outrage, had been content to let the story speak for itself. *Today in the Crown Court, Shirley Beale, aged twelve years and eight months, pleaded guilty to the murder of her nine-year-old sister, Lucy. She strangled Lucy with her school tie, then bashed in the face she hated until it was unrecognisable. All she has said, either at the time of the arrest or since, is that she did it because Lucy was too pretty. Beale will be sent to a secure children's unit until she can be transferred at seventeen to a young offenders' institution. Silford Green, a quiet East London suburb, has become a place of horror. Full report on page five. Sophie Langton writes on page 12 – 'What Makes Children Kill?'*

Dalgliesh turned over the cutting. Beneath it, clipped to a plain sheet of paper, was a photograph. The same uniform, the same white blouse, only this time with a school tie, the face turned to the camera with a look Kate remembered from her own school photographs, resentful, a little nervous, participating in a small annual rite of passage, unwillingly but resigned. It was an oddly adult face, and it was one they knew.

Dalgliesh took up his magnifying glass again, studied the picture, then handed the glass to Kate. The distinctive features were there, the high forehead, the slightly protuberant eyes, the small precise mouth with the full upper lip, an unremarkable face which it was now impossible to see as innocent or childish. The eyes stared into the camera as inexpressive as the dots which formed the image, the lower lip seeming fuller now in adulthood but with the same suggestion of a petulant obstinacy. As Kate stared, her mind superimposed a very different picture: a child's face smashed into blood and broken bone, fair hair caked in blood. It hadn't been a case for the Met and with a guilty plea there had been no trial, but the murder stirred old memories for her and, she thought, for Dalgliesh.

Dalgliesh said, 'Sharon Bateman. I wonder how Gradwyn managed to get hold of this. It's odd they were able to publish it. Restrictions must have been lifted.'

It wasn't the only thing Rhoda had managed to get hold of. Her research had obviously started since her first visit to the Manor, and it had been thorough. The first cutting was followed by others. Former neighbours had been voluble, both in expressing horror and spilling out information about the family. There were pictures of the small terraced house in which the children had lived with their mother and grandmother. At the time of the murder the parents were divorced, their father having walked out two years previously. Neighbours still living in the street reported that the marriage had been turbulent but there had been no trouble with the children, no police or social workers round or anything like that. Lucy was the pretty one, no doubt about it, but the girls had seemed to get on all right. Shirley was the quiet one, a bit surly, not exactly a friendly child. Their memories, obviously influenced by the horror of what had happened, suggested the child had always been the odd one out. They reported sounds of quarrels, shouting and occasional blows before the parents parted but the children had always seemed properly cared for. The grandmother saw to that. There had been a succession of lodgers after the father left – some obviously boyfriends of the mother, although this was reported with tact – and one or two students looking for cheap accommodation, none of whom stayed long.

Rhoda Gradwyn had somehow or other got hold of the post-mortem report. Death had been by strangulation and the injuries to the face, which had destroyed the eyes and broken the nose, were inflicted after death. Gradwyn had also traced and interviewed one of the police officers concerned with the case. There had been no mystery. Death had occurred at about three thirty on a Saturday afternoon when the grandmother, then aged sixty-nine, had gone to a local hall to play bingo. It was not unusual for the children to be left alone. The murder had been discovered when the grandmother returned home at six o'clock. Lucy's body was on the floor of the kitchen in which the family mostly lived, and Shirley was upstairs asleep in her bed. She had made no attempt to wash her sister's blood from her hands and arms. Her fingerprints were on the weapon, an old flat iron which was used as a doorstop, and she had admitted killing her sister with no more emotion than if she had confessed to leaving her briefly alone.

Kate and Dalgliesh sat for a moment in silence. Kate knew that their thoughts ran in parallel. This discovery was a complication which would influence both their perception of Sharon as a suspect – how could it fail to? – and the conduct of the investigation. She saw it now as fraught with procedural pitfalls. Both victims had been strangled; that fact might prove irrelevant, but it was still a fact. Sharon Bateman – and they would continue to use that name – wouldn't be living in the community if the authorities hadn't seen her as no longer a threat. To that extent, wasn't she entitled to be regarded as one of the suspects, no more likely to be guilty than any of the others? And who else knew? Had Chandler-Powell been told? Had Sharon confided in anyone at the Manor and, if so, in whom? Had Rhoda Gradwyn suspected Sharon's identity from the first and was that why she had stayed on? Had she threatened exposure and, if so, had Sharon, or perhaps someone else who knew the truth, taken steps to stop her? And if they arrested some-one else, wouldn't the very presence of a convicted murderer at the Manor influence the Crown Prosecution Service in deciding whether the case would stand up in court? The thoughts seemed to tumble in her mind but she didn't voice them. With Dalgliesh she was always careful not to state the obvious.

Now Dalgliesh said, 'This year we've had the separation of functions in the Home Office but I think I've got the changes more or less clear in my mind. Since May the new Ministry of Justice became responsible for the National Offender Management Service and the probation officers who undertake the supervision are now called offender managers. Sharon will certainly have one. I'll have to check that I've got the facts right, but my understand-ing is that an offender has to spend at least four trouble-free years in the community before the supervision is lifted but the licence remains in force for life so that a lifer is eligible to be recalled at any point.'

Kate said, 'But surely Sharon has a legal obligation to inform her PO that she's become involved, even if innocent, in a case of murder?'

'Certainly she should have done, but if she hasn't, the National Offender Management Service will learn about it tomorrow when the news breaks. Sharon should also have told them about her change of job. Whether or not she has been in touch with her supervisor, it's certainly my responsibility to inform the probation service and theirs to provide a report for the Ministry of Justice.

It's the probation service not the police who must handle the information and make decisions on a need-to-know basis.'

Kate said, 'So we say and do nothing until Sharon's supervisor takes over? But don't we need to interview her again? This alters her status in the investigation.'

'Obviously it's important for the supervising officer to be present when we do question Sharon, and I'd like that to be tomorrow if possible. Sunday isn't the best day to get this set up, but I can probably get in touch with the supervising officer through the duty officer at the Ministry of Justice. I'll phone Benton. I need to have Sharon watched but it has to be done with complete discretion. While I get this set up, could you continue looking through the files here? I'll phone from the dining room downstairs. It may take some time.'

Left alone, Kate settled again to the files. She knew that Dalgliesh had left her so that she could be undisturbed and it would indeed have been difficult to sort conscientiously through the remaining boxes without listening to what he was saying.

Half an hour later she heard Dalgliesh's foot on the stairs. Coming in, he said, 'That was rather quicker than I feared. There were the general hoops to be jumped through but I got the supervising probation officer in the end. A Mrs Madeleine Rayner. Fortunately she lives in London and I caught her just as she was leaving for a family lunch. She'll come to Wareham tomorrow by an early train and I'll arrange for Benton to meet her and bring her straight to the Old Police Cottage. If possible I want her visit to be unnoticed. She seems convinced that Sharon needs no particular supervision and isn't a danger, but the sooner she leaves the Manor the better.'

Kate asked, 'Are you thinking of going back to Dorset now, sir?'

'No. There's nothing to be done about Sharon until Mrs Rayner arrives tomorrow. We'll go on to Droughton and clear up the matter of the car. We'll take the copy of the will, the file about Sharon and the article on plagiarism, but I think that's all, unless you've found anything else relevant.'

Kate said, 'Nothing that's new to us, sir. There's an article about the huge losses suffered by the Lloyd's Names in the early 1990s. Miss Cressett told us that Sir Nicholas was among them and was forced to sell Cheverell Manor. The best pictures were apparently sold separately. There's a picture of the Manor and one of Sir Nicholas. The article isn't particularly kind to the Names but I can't see it as a possible motive for murder. We know that Helena Cressett wasn't especially anxious to have Miss Gradwyn under her roof. Shall I put this article with the rest of the papers?'

'Yes, I think we should have anything she wrote which relates to the Manor. But I agree. The article on the Names is hardly a credible motive for anything more dangerous than a cool reception when Miss Gradwyn arrived. I've been looking through the box of correspondence with her agent. It seems she was thinking of cutting down on the journalism and writing a biography. It might be helpful to see her agent, but that can wait. Anyway, add any relevant letters, will you, Kate, and we'll need to write a list for Macklefield of what we've taken, but that can be done later.'

He took a large exhibit bag from his case and got the papers together while Kate went to the kitchen and washed up the mug and toothbrush holder, quickly checking that anything she had disturbed was now back in its place. Rejoining Dalgliesh, she sensed that he had liked the house, that he had been tempted to revisit the rooftop, that it was in this unencumbered seclusion that he, too, could happily live and work. But it was with relief that she stood again in Absolution Alley and watched in silence as he closed and double locked the door.

2

Benton thought it unlikely that Robin Boyton would be an early riser and it was after ten before he and DC Warren set off to walk to Rose Cottage. The cottage, like the adjoining one occupied by the Westhalls, was stone walled under a slate roof. There was a garage to the left with standing for a car, and in front a small garden, mostly of low shrubs, cut by a narrow strip of crazy paving. The porch was covered with strong intertwined boughs, and a few tight and browning buds and a single pink rose in full bloom explained the name of the cottage. DC Warren pressed the brightly polished bell to the right of the door but it was a full minute before Benton detected footfalls followed by the rasp of bolts being drawn and the click of the raised latch. The door was opened wide and Robin Boyton stood before them, unmoving and seeming deliberately to block their entrance. There was a moment of uneasy silence before he stood aside and said, 'You'd better come in. I'm in the kitchen.'

They entered a small square hall, unfurnished except for an oak bench next to uncarpeted wooden stairs. The door to the left was open and the glimpse of easy chairs, a sofa, a polished circular table and what looked like a range of watercolours on the far wall suggested that this was the sitting room. They followed Boyton through the open door to the right. The room stretched the length of the cottage and was full of light. At the garden end was the kitchen with a double sink, a green Aga, a central working surface, and a dining area with an oak rectangular table and six chairs. Against the wall facing the door a large dresser with cupboards held a miscellany of jugs, mugs and plates while the space under the front window had been furnished with a coffee table and four low chairs, all old and none matching.

Taking control, Benton introduced DC Warren and himself, then moved towards the table. He said, 'Shall we sit here?' and seated himself with his back to the garden. He said, 'Perhaps you would sit opposite, Mr Boyton,' leaving Boyton no choice but to take the facing chair with the light from the windows full on his face.

He was still under some strong emotion, whether grief, fear or perhaps a mixture of both, and looked as if he hadn't slept. His skin was drab, the forehead beaded with sweat, and the blue eyes darkly shrouded. But he had recently shaved and Benton detected a confusion of smells – soap, aftershave and, when Boyton spoke, a trace of alcohol on his breath. He had managed in the short time since his arrival to make the room look untidy and dirty. The draining board was piled with food-encrusted plates and smeared glasses and the sink held a couple of saucepans, while his long black coat hanging over the back of a chair, a pair of muddy trainers near the French window and open newspapers strewn on the coffee table completed the air of general dishevelment, a room temporarily occupied but without pleasure.

Looking at Boyton, Benton thought that his was a face that would always be memorable; the strong waves of yellow hair falling without artifice over the forehead, the remarkable eyes, the strong perfect curve of the lips. But it wasn't beauty which could withstand tiredness, sickness or fear. Already there were signs of incipient decadence in a draining of vitality, the pouches under the eyes, a slackness of the muscles round the mouth. But, if he had fortified himself for the ordeal, when he spoke it was without slurring.

Now, turning, he gestured towards the stove and said, 'Coffee? Tea? I haven't had breakfast. In fact, I can't remember when I last ate, but I mustn't waste police time. Or would a mug of coffee count as bribery and corruption?'

Benton said, 'Are you saying you aren't fit to be questioned?'

'I'm as fit as I'm likely to be, given the circumstances. I expect you take murder in your stride, Sergeant – it was Sergeant, wasn't it?'

'Detective Sergeant Benton-Smith and Detective Constable Warren.'

'The rest of us find murder distressing, especially when the victim is a friend, but of course you're only doing your job, an excuse these days for practically anything. I expect you want to take down my particulars – that sounds indecent – my full name and address, if the Westhalls haven't already provided it. I had a flat but I had to give it up – a little difficulty with the landlord about the rent – so I'm lodging with my business partner in his house in Maida Vale.'

He gave his address and watched while Constable Warren wrote it down, his huge hand moving with deliberation over the notebook.

Benton asked, 'And what job do you do, Mr Boyton?'

'You can put me down as an actor. I have an Equity card and from time to time, given the opportunity, I act. I'm also what you might call an entrepreneur. I get ideas. Some of them work and some of them don't. When I'm not acting and have no bright ideas, I get help from my friends. And if that fails, I look to a benevolent government for what is laughingly called the job-seeker's allowance.'

Benton asked, 'What are you doing here?'

'What do you mean? I've rented the cottage. I've paid for it. I'm on holiday. That's what I'm doing here.'

'But why at this time? December can't be the most propitious month for a holiday.'

The blue eyes fixed on Benton's. 'I could ask you what you're doing here. I look more at home than you do, Sergeant. The voice so very English, the face so very – well – Indian. Still, it must have helped you to get taken on. It can't be easy, the job you've chosen – not easy for your colleagues, I mean. One disrespectful or disobliging word about your colour and they'd find themselves sacked or hauled up before one of those race-relations tribunals. Hardly part of the police-canteen culture, are you? Not one of the boys. Can't be easy to cope with.'

Malcolm Warren looked up and gave an almost imperceptible

shake of the head as if deploring one more example of the propensity of people in a hole to go on digging, then returned to his notebook, his hand again moving slowly across the page.

Benton said calmly, 'Will you answer my question, please? I'll put it differently. Why are you here at this particular time?'

'Because Miss Gradwyn asked me to come. She booked in for an operation which would be life-changing for her, and she wanted to have a friend here to join her for her week's convalescence. I come to this cottage fairly regularly, as no doubt my cousins have told you. It was probably because the assistant surgeon, Marcus, is my cousin and I recommended the Manor that Rhoda came here. Anyway, she said she needed me, so I came. Does that answer your question?'

'Not entirely, Mr Boyton. If she was so anxious to have you here, why did she make it plain to Mr Chandler-Powell that she didn't want any visitors? That's what he says. Are you accusing him of lying?'

'Don't put words into my mouth, Sergeant. She may have changed her mind, although I don't think it likely. She may not have wanted me to see her until the bandages were off and the scar healed, or the great George might have thought it medically unwise for her to have visitors and put a stop to it. How should I know what happened? I only know she asked me to come and I was going to stay here until she left.'

'But you sent her a text message, didn't you? We found it on her mobile. *Something very important has cropped up. I need to consult you. Please see me, please don't shut me out.* What was this very important matter?'

There was no reply. Boyton covered his face with his hands. The gesture might, Benton thought, be an attempt to conceal a wave of emotion, but it was also a convenient way of marshalling his thoughts. After a few moments' silence Benton said, 'And did you see her to discuss this important matter at any time after she arrived here?'

Boyton spoke through his hands. 'How could I? You know I didn't. They wouldn't let me into the Manor before or after the operation. And by Saturday morning she was dead.'

'I have to ask you again, Mr Boyton, what was this important matter?'

And now Boyton was looking at Benton, his voice controlled. 'It wasn't really important. I tried to make it sound as if it was. It was about money. My partner and I need another house for our business and a suitable one has come on the market. It would be a really good investment for Rhoda and I hoped she'd help. With the scar gone and a new life before her, she might have been interested.'

'And I suppose your partner can confirm this?'

'About the house? Yes, he could, but I don't see why you should ask him. I didn't tell him I was going to approach Rhoda. None of this is your business.'

Benton said, 'We're investigating a murder, Mr Boyton. Everything is our business, and if you cared for Miss Gradwyn and want to see her killer caught, you can help best by answering our questions fully and truthfully. No doubt you'll be anxious now to get back to London and your entrepreneurial activities?'

'No, I booked for a week and I'm staying for a week. That's what I said I'd do and I owe it to Rhoda. I want to find out what's going on here.'

The answer surprised Benton. Most suspects, unless they actively enjoy involvement with violent death, are anxious to put as much distance between themselves and the crime as possible. It was convenient to have Boyton here in the cottage, but he had expected his suspect to protest that they couldn't legally hold him and that he needed to get back to London.

He asked, 'How long have you known Rhoda Gradwyn and how did you meet?'

'We met about six years ago after a not very successful fringe theatre production of Waiting for Godot. I'd just left drama school. We met at a drinks party afterwards. A gruesome occasion, but a lucky one for me. We talked. I asked her to have dinner the following week and to my surprise she agreed. After that we met from time to time, not frequently, but always with pleasure, at least as far as I'm concerned. I've told you, she was my friend, a dear friend, and one of those who helped me when there was no acting job and I had no lucrative ideas. Not often and not much. She always paid for dinner when we met. I can't make you understand and I don't see why I should try. It's not your business. I loved her. I don't mean I was in love with her, I mean I loved her. I depended on seeing her. I liked to think she was in my life. I don't think she loved me, but she usually saw me when I asked. I could talk to her. It wasn't maternal and it wasn't about sex, but it was love. And now one of those bastards at the Manor has killed her and I'm not leaving here until I know who. And I'm not answering any more questions about her. What we felt, we felt. It's nothing to do with why or how she died. And if I could explain, you wouldn't understand. You'd only laugh.' He was beginning to cry, making no attempt to stem the flow of tears.

Benton said, 'Why should we laugh about love?' and thought, *Oh God, it sounds like some ghastly ditty. Why should we laugh about love? Why, oh why, should we laugh about love?* He could almost hear a cheerfully banal tune insinuating itself into his brain. It might do well at the Eurovision Song Contest. Looking across at Boyton's disintegrating face, he thought, *The emotion is real enough, but what exactly is it?*

He asked more gently, 'Can you tell us what you did from the moment you arrived at Stoke Cheverell? When was that?'

Boyton managed to control himself, and more quickly than Benton had expected. Looking at Boyton's face he wondered whether this swift alteration was the actor demonstrating his range of emotions. 'On Thursday night at about ten o'clock. I drove down from London.'

'So Miss Gradwyn didn't ask you to drive her down?'

'No, she didn't, and I didn't expect her to. She likes driving, not being driven. Anyway, she needed to be here early for examinations and so on, and I couldn't get away until the evening. I brought some food with me for breakfast on Friday, but otherwise I thought I'd shop locally for what I needed. I rang the Manor to say I'd arrived and to enquire after Rhoda and was told she was sleeping. I asked when I could see her and I was told by Sister

Holland that she had specifically asked for no visitors, so I let it rest. I did consider calling in on my cousins – they're next door in Stone Cottage and the lights were on – but I didn't think they'd exactly welcome me, particularly after ten at night. I watched TV for an hour and went to bed. On Friday I'm afraid I slept in, so it's no good asking me about anything before eleven, then I phoned the Manor again and was told that the operation had gone well and Rhoda was recovering. They repeated that she didn't want visitors. I had lunch at about two in the village pub and afterwards went for a drive and did some shopping. Then I came back here and was in all evening. On Saturday I found out about Rhoda's murder when I saw the police cars arriving and tried to get into the Manor. In the end I managed to push past PC Plod on the door and broke into the cosy little set-up your boss had arranged. But you know all about that.'

Benton asked, 'Did you at any time enter the Manor before you forced your way in on Saturday afternoon?'

'No. I thought I'd made that plain.'

'What were your movements from four thirty on Friday afternoon until Saturday afternoon when you learnt about the murder? I'm asking in particular if you went out at any time during Friday night. It's very important. You might have seen something or someone.'

'I told you, I didn't go out, and as I didn't go out, I saw nothing and nobody. I was in bed by eleven.'

'No cars? No one arriving late at night or early Saturday morning?'

'Arriving where? I've told you. I was in bed by eleven. I was drunk if you must know. I suppose if a tank had crashed through the front door I might have heard it, but I doubt I could have made it downstairs.'

'But then there's Friday afternoon after you'd had a drink and lunch at the Cressett Arms. Didn't you visit a cottage near the junction with the main road, the one set back from the road with a long front garden? It's called Rosemary Cottage?'

'Yes, I did. There was no one there. The cottage was empty with a "For Sale" board on the gate. I hoped the owners might have the address of someone I knew who used to live there. It was a small private unimportant matter. I want to send her a Christmas card – as simple as that. It's got nothing to do with the murder. Mog was cycling past, no doubt to visit his girlfriend for a bit of anything on offer, and I suppose he handed you that titbit of gossip. Some people in this bloody village can't keep their mouths shut. I'm telling you, it had nothing to do with Rhoda.'

'We're not suggesting it had, Mr Boyton. But you were asked for an account of what you did since arriving here. Why leave that out?'

'Because I'd forgotten it. It wasn't important. OK, I went to the village pub for lunch. I saw nobody and nothing happened. I can't remember every single detail. I'm upset, confused. If you're going to keep on badgering me I'll have to send for a lawyer.'

'You could certainly do that if you think it's necessary. And if you seriously believe you're being badgered, no doubt you'll make a formal complaint. We may wish to question you again, either before you leave or in London. In the meantime I suggest that, if there's any other fact, however unimportant, that you have omitted to mention, you let us know as soon as possible.'

They rose to go. It was then that Benton remembered that he hadn't asked about Miss Gradwyn's will. To have forgotten such an instruction from AD would have been a bad mistake. Angry with himself, he spoke almost without thinking.

'You say you were Miss Gradwyn's dear friend. Did she ever confide in you about her will, hint that you might be a beneficiary? At your last meeting, perhaps. When was that?'

'On November the 21st, at the Ivy. She never mentioned her will. Why should she? Wills are about death. She wasn't expecting to die. The operation wasn't life-threatening. Why would we talk about her will? Are you saying you've seen it?'

And now, unmistakable under his tone of outrage was the half-shameful curiosity and spark of hope.

Benton said casually, 'No, we haven't seen it. It was just a thought.'

Boyton didn't come to the door and they left him sitting at the table, head in hands. Closing the garden gate behind them, they set out to return to the Old Police Cottage.

Benton said, 'Well, what did you think of him?'

'Not much, Sarge. Not bright is he? And spiteful with it. But I can't see him as a killer. If he'd wanted to murder Miss Gradwyn, why follow her down here? He'd have more opportunity in London. But I don't see how he could have done it without an accomplice.'

Benton said, 'Perhaps Gradwyn herself, letting him in for what she thought would be a confidential chat. But on the day of her operation? Unusual surely. He's frightened, that's obvious, but he's also excited. And why is he staying on? I have a feeling he was lying about the important matter that he wanted to discuss with Rhoda Gradwyn. I agree it's hard to see him as a murderer, but then that goes for everyone here. And I think he was lying about the will.'

They walked on in silence. Benton wondered whether he had confided too much. It must, he thought, be difficult for DC Warren, part of the team and yet a member of another force. Only members of the special unit took part in the evening discussions, but DC Warren would probably feel more relieved than aggrieved at being excluded. He had told Benton that by seven, unless specifically needed, he drove back to Wareham to his wife and four children. Altogether he was proving his worth and Benton liked him and felt at ease with the six-foot-two of solid muscle pacing by his side. Benton had a strong interest in helping to ensure that Warren's home life wasn't greatly disturbed: his wife was Cornish and that morning Warren had arrived with six Cornish pasties of remarkable flavour and succulence.

3

Dalgliesh spoke little on the journey north. This wasn't unusual and Kate didn't find his taciturnity uncomfortable; to journey with Dalgliesh in companionable silence had always been a rare and private pleasure. As they approached the outskirts of Droughton Cross, she concentrated on giving precise instructions well in advance of a turning, and on contemplating the interview ahead. Dalgliesh hadn't phoned to give the Reverend Curtis warning of their arrival. It was hardly necessary as clergymen could usually be found on a Sunday, if not in their vicarages or churches, then somewhere in the parish. And there was also advantage in a surprise visit.

The address they were seeking was 2 Balaclava Gardens, the fifth turning off Marland Way, a wide road running to the centre of the city. Here was no Sunday calm. The traffic was heavy, cars, delivery vans and a succession of buses bunching on the glistening road. The grinding roar was a constant discordant descant to the continually repeated blare of 'Rudolph the Red Nosed Reindeer' interposed with the first verses of the better-known carols. No doubt in the city centre the 'Winterfest' was being appropriately celebrated by the official municipal decorations, but in this less-privileged highway the individual and uncoordinated efforts of the local shopkeepers and café owners, the rain-soaked lanterns and faded bunting, the swinging lights blinking from red to green to yellow, and the occasional meanly decorated Christmas tree seemed less a celebration than a desperate defence against despair. The faces of the shoppers seen through the rain-besmirched side windows of the car had the melting insubstantial look of disintegrating wraiths.

Peering through the blur of the rain which had persisted throughout their journey, they could have been driving through any thoroughfare in an unprosperous inner-city suburb, not so much featureless as an amorphous mixture of the old and new, the neglected and the renovated. Terraces of small shops were broken by a series of high-rise flats set well back behind railings, and a short terrace of well-maintained and obviously eighteenth-century houses was an unexpected and incongruous contrast to the takeaway cafés, the betting shops and the garish shop signs. The people, heads hunched against the driving rain, seemed to move with no apparent purpose, or stood under the shelter of shop awnings surveying the traffic. Only the mothers pushing their baby buggies, the hoods shrouded in plastic, showed a desperate and purposeful energy.

Kate fought off the depression tinged with guilt which always descended on her at the sight of high-rise flats. In such a grimy oblong container, monument to local authority aspiration and human desperation, had she been born and bred. From childhood her one compulsion had been to escape, to break free from the pervading smell of urine on the stairs, a lift that was always broken down, the graffiti, the vandalism, the raucous voices. And she had escaped. She told herself that life in a high-rise was probably better now, even in a city centre, but she couldn't drive past without feeling that in her personal liberation something that was inalienably part of her had not been so much rejected as betrayed.

No one could miss St John's church. It stood on the left of the road, a huge Victorian building with a dominant spire on the junction with Balaclava Gardens. Kate wondered how a local congregation could possibly support this grimed architectural aberration. Apparently it was with difficulty. A tall billboard outside the gate bore a painted thermometer-like structure which proclaimed that three hundred and fifty thousand pounds remained to be raised, and underneath the words, *Please help save our tower.* An arrow pointing to a hundred and twenty-three thousand looked as if it had remained stationary for some time.

Dalgliesh drew up outside the church and went over quickly to look at the notice board. Sliding back into his seat, he said, 'Low

Mass at seven, High Mass at ten thirty, Evensong and Vespers at six, confessions five to seven Mondays, Wednesday and Saturdays. With luck we'll find him at home.'

Kate was grateful that she and Benton weren't facing this interview together. Years of experience in interrogation of a variety of suspects had taught her the accepted techniques and, where necessary, modification in the face of widely differing personalities. She knew when softness and sensitivity were necessary and when they were seen as weakness. She had learnt never to raise her voice or avert her gaze. But this suspect, if that's what he proved to be, was one she wouldn't find it easy to question. Admittedly it was difficult to see a clergyman as a suspect for murder, but there might be an embarrassing if less horrific reason for his stopping at that remote and lonely spot so late at night. And what exactly was one supposed to call him? Was he a vicar, rector, clergyman, minister, parson or priest? Should she call him father? She had heard all used at different times, but the subtleties, and indeed the orthodox belief, of the national religion were alien to her. The morning assembly at her inner-city comprehensive had been determinedly multi-faith with occasional reference to Christianity. What little she knew about the country's established Church had been unconsciously learnt from architecture and literature and from the pictures in the major galleries. She knew herself to be intelligent with an interest in life and people, but the job she loved had largely satisfied her intellectual curiosity. Her personal creed of honesty, kindness, courage and truth in human relationships had no mystical basis and no need of one. The grandmother who grudgingly had brought her up had given her only one piece of advice on religion which, even at the age of eight, she had found unhelpful.

She had asked, 'Gran, do you believe in God?'

'What a daft question. You don't want to start wondering about God at your age. Only one thing to remember about God. When you're dying, call in a priest. He'll see you're all right.'

'But suppose I don't know I'm dying?'

'Folk usually do. Time enough then to start bothering your head with God.'

Well, at this moment she didn't need to bother her head. AD was the son of a priest and had interviewed parsons before. Who better to cope with the Reverend Michael Curtis?

They turned into Balaclava Gardens. If there had ever been gardens all that remained now were occasional trees. Many of the original Victorian terraced houses still stood, but number two, and four or five houses beyond, were square modern red-brick dwellings. Number two was the largest with a garage to the left, and a small front lawn with a central bed. The garage door was open and inside was a dark blue Ford Focus with the registration W341 UDG.

Kate rang the bell. Before there was any response she caught the sound of a woman's voice calling and the high shout of a child. After some delay there was the sound of keys being turned and the door opened. They saw a young woman, pretty and very fair. She was wearing trousers with a smock and was carrying a child on her right hip while two toddlers, obviously twins, pulled at both sides of her trousers. They were miniatures of their mother, each with the same round face, corn-coloured hair cut in a fringe and wide eyes which now stared at the newcomers in unblinking judgement.

Dalgliesh took out his warrant card. 'Mrs Curtis? I'm Commander Dalgliesh from the Metropolitan Police, and this is Detective Inspector Miskin. We're here to see your husband.'

She looked surprised. 'The Metropolitan Police? That's something new. We do get the local police round from time to time. Some of the youths from the high-rises cause trouble occasionally. They're a good crowd – the local police I mean. Anyway, please come in. Sorry I kept you waiting but we've got these double security locks. It's awful I know, but Michael has been attacked twice in the last year. That's why we had to take down the sign saying that this is the vicarage.' She called in a voice totally devoid of anxiety, 'Michael, darling. Someone from the Met Police is here.'

The Reverend Michael Curtis was wearing a cassock with what looked like an old college scarf wound round his neck. Kate was glad when Mrs Curtis shut the front door behind them. The house struck her as cold. He came forward and rather absent-mindedly shook hands. He was older than his wife, but perhaps not so much older as he seemed, his thin rather stooped frame in contrast to her buxom comeliness. His brown hair, cut in a monk-like fringe, was beginning to grey, but the kindly eyes were watchful and shrewd and when he grasped Kate's hand his grip was confident. Bestowing on his wife and children a look of puzzled love, he indicated a door behind him.

'Perhaps in the study?'

It was a larger room than Kate had expected, its French windows looking out on a small garden. Obviously no attempt at cultivating the beds or mowing the lawn had been made. The small space had been given over to the children, with a climbing frame, a sandpit and a swing. Various toys were strewn across the grass. The study itself smelled of books and, she thought, faintly of incense. There was a crowded desk, a table piled with books and magazines set against the wall, a modern gas fire, at present lit with only one bar, and to the right of the desk, a crucifix with a stool for kneeling before it. There were two rather battered armchairs in front of the fire.

Mr Curtis said, 'I think you'll find these two chairs reasonably comfortable.'

Seating himself at the desk, he edged round the swivel chair to face them, hands on knees. He looked a little puzzled but completely unworried.

Dalgliesh said, 'We wanted to ask you about your car.'

'My old Ford? I don't think it can have been taken and used in the commission of a crime. It's very reliable for its age, but it doesn't go very fast. I can't believe anyone has taken it with evil intent. As you probably saw, it's in the garage. It's perfectly all right.'

Dalgliesh said, 'It was seen parked late on Friday night close to the scene of a serious crime. I'm hoping that whoever was driving might have seen something that would help our enquiries. Perhaps another parked car or someone acting suspiciously. Were you in Dorset on Friday night, Father?'

'Dorset? No, I was here with the Parochial Church Council on

Friday from five o'clock. As it happens, I wasn't driving the car myself that evening. I'd lent it to a friend. He'd taken his in for servicing and its MOT, but I gather there were things that needed to be done. He had an urgent appointment he was very anxious to keep so he asked if he could borrow mine. I said I could use my wife's bike if I were called out. I'm sure he'll be happy to help in any way he can.'

'When did he return the car?'

'It must have been very early yesterday morning, before we got up. I remember that it was back when I went out to seven o'clock Mass. He left a thank-you note on the dashboard and he'd filled it with petrol. I thought he would; he's always considerate. Dorset, you say? That was a long journey. I think if he'd seen anything suspicious or had witnessed an incident he would have phoned and told me. Actually, we haven't spoken since he returned.'

Dalgliesh said, 'Anyone near the scene could have useful information without realising its significance. It might not have seemed unusual or suspicious at the time. May we have his name and address? If he lives locally it would save time if we could see him now.'

'He's the head of our local comprehensive, Droughton Cross school. Stephen Collinsby. You might catch him now at the school. He usually goes in on Sunday afternoons to prepare in peace for the week ahead. I'll write the address down for you. It's quite close. You could walk there if you want to leave your car here. It should be safe in our drive.'

Swivelling round, he pulled open the left-hand drawer and, after rummaging for a time, found a blank sheet of paper and began writing. Folding it neatly and handing it to Dalgliesh, he said, 'Collinsby's our local hero. Well, he's become something of a national hero now. Perhaps you read something in the papers or saw that television programme on education in which he appeared? He's a brilliant man. He's completely turned round Droughton Cross Comprehensive. It was all done by principles which I suppose most people would support but which others don't seem to be able to put into effect. He believes that every child has a talent, skill or intellectual ability which can enhance his whole life and that it's the job of the school to discover and nurture it. Of course he needs help and he's got the whole community involved, particularly the parents. I'm a school governor so I do what I can. I give Latin lessons here to two boys and two girls once a fortnight, helped by the organist's wife who augments my deficiencies. Latin isn't on the syllabus. They come because they want to learn the language and they're wonderfully rewarding to teach. And one of our churchwardens runs the chess club with his wife. They have boys in that club who have a rare talent for the game and huge enthusiasm, boys who no one thought would ever achieve anything. And if you become school champion with a hope of playing for the county you don't have to earn respect by carrying a knife. Forgive me for nattering on like this, but since I've known Stephen and become a school governor I've got very interested in education. And it's heartening when good things happen against the odds. If you have time to talk to Stephen about the school I think you'll be fascinated by his ideas.'

Now they were rising together. He said, 'Oh dear, I'm afraid I've been very remiss. Won't you stay for tea, or perhaps coffee?' He looked round vaguely as if expecting the beverage to materialise from the air. 'My wife could . . .' He made for the door and was about to call.

Dalgliesh said, 'Thank you, Father, but we must be away. I think we'd better take the car. We may have to leave in a hurry. Thank you for seeing us and for your help.'

In the car, their seatbelts buckled, Dalgliesh opened the paper and passed it to Kate. Father Curtis had drawn a meticulous little diagram with arrows pointing to the school. She knew why Dalgliesh had decided not to walk. Whatever the coming interview revealed, it would be prudent not to return and risk questions from Father Curtis.

After a moment's silence, sensing Dalgliesh's mood, she asked, knowing that he would understand, 'Do you think this is going to be bad, sir?' She meant bad for Stephen Collinsby, not for them.

'Yes, Kate, I think it may be.'

4

They had turned into the noise and heavy traffic of Marland Way. The journey wasn't easy and Kate didn't speak except to give Dalgliesh directions until he had taken a right turn at the second set of traffic lights and they found themselves in a quieter road.

'Sir, do you think that Father Curtis will have phoned to say we're on our way?'

'Yes, he's an intelligent man. By the time we left he'll have put several puzzling facts together, the involvement of the Met, our rank – why a commander and a detective inspector if this is a routine enquiry? – the early return of his car and his friend's silence.'

'But he obviously doesn't know yet about the murder.'

'He will when he reads tomorrow's broadsheets or listens to the news. Even then I doubt whether he'll be suspecting Collinsby, but he knows that his friend may be in trouble. That's why he was determined to get in all that information about how he's transformed the school. It was an impressive testimonial.'

Kate hesitated before the next question. She knew that Dalgliesh respected her and thought that he was fond of her. Over the years she had learnt to discipline her emotions; but though the core of what she had always known was a hopeless love remained and always would, it didn't give her the freehold of his mind. There were questions better not asked, but was this one?

After a silence in which she kept her eyes on Father Curtis's instructions, she said, 'You knew he'd warn his friend but you didn't tell him not to.'

'He'll have a bad five minutes of spiritual struggle without me making it worse for him. Our man isn't going to run away.'

Another turn. Father Curtis had been optimistic in describing the school as 'quite close'. Or was it the turnings, her companion's reticence or the apprehension about the coming interview which made the journey seem long?

Now a billboard. Someone had painted in streaks of black paint, *The Devil is in the Internet.* Beneath it, more precisely written, *There is no Devil and no God.* Then the next panel, this time in red paint. *God lives. See Book of Job.* This led to the final exhortation: *Fuck off.*

Dalgliesh said, 'A not uncommon ending to theological dispute but rarely so crudely expressed. I think this must be the school.'

She saw a Victorian building of patterned brick faced with stone standing back in a large asphalt playground surrounded by tall railings. To her surprise the gate to the playground was unlocked. A smaller and more ornate version of the main building, obviously by the same architect, was linked to it by a newer-looking corridor. Here an attempt had been made to compensate for size by ornamentation. Rows of windows and four carved stone steps led to an intimidating door which was opened to their ring so quickly that Kate suspected the headmaster had been waiting for them. She saw a spectacled man in early middle age, almost as tall as Dalgliesh, wearing a pair of old slacks and a jumper with patches of leather on the elbows.

He said, 'If you'll just wait a moment, I'll lock the playground gate. There's no bell there so I hoped you'd find your way in.' Within a minute he was back with them.

He waited while Dalgliesh showed his warrant card and introduced Kate, then said briefly, 'I've been expecting you. We'll speak in my study.'

Following him through the sparsely furnished entrance hall and down the terrazzo-floored corridor, Kate was back in her comprehensive school; here was the faint, almost illusory smell of paper, bodies, paint and cleaning materials. There was no smell of chalk. Did teachers ever use it now? Blackboards had largely given way to computers, even in primary schools. But gazing through the few open doors she saw no classrooms. Perhaps the formal headmaster's house was now largely devoted to his study and to seminar rooms or administration. It was obvious that he didn't live on the premises.

He stood aside to let them enter a room at the end of the corridor. It was a mixture of conference room, study and sitting room. There was a rectangular table set in front of the window with six chairs, bookshelves almost to the ceiling on the left-hand wall and the head-master's desk, with his own chair and two before it, to the right. One wall was covered with school photographs: the chess club, a row of smiling faces with the board set up in front of them, the captain hold-ing the small silver trophy; the football and swimming teams; the orchestra; the cast of the Christmas pantomime and a scene from what looked like *Macbeth* – wasn't it always *Macbeth*: short, suitably bloody, not too difficult to learn? An open door gave a glimpse of what was obviously a small kitchen. There was a smell of coffee.

Collinsby pulled out two chairs at the table and said, 'I take it that this is a formal visit. Shall we sit here?'

He seated himself at the top of the table with Dalgliesh on his right, Kate on his left. And now she could look at him fleetingly but more closely. She saw a good face, sensitive and firm jawed, a face one saw on television advertisements chosen to inspire confi-dence in the actor's spiel about the bank's superiority over its com-petition, or to persuade the viewers that that unaffordable car could provoke envy among the neighbours. He looked younger than Kate had expected, perhaps because of the informality of his weekend clothes, and might, she thought, have shown some of the confident insouciance of youth if he hadn't looked so tired. The grey eyes, which briefly met hers and then turned to Dalgliesh, were dulled with exhaustion. But when he spoke his voice was sur-prisingly youthful.

Dalgliesh said, 'We're making enquiries into the suspicious death of a woman at a house in Stoke Cheverell in Dorset. A Ford Focus with the number plate w341 UDG was seen parked close to the house between eleven thirty-five and eleven forty on the night she died. That was last Friday, December the 14th. We are told that you had borrowed the car on that date. Were you driving and were you there?'

'Yes. I was there.'

'Under what circumstances, Mr Collinsby?'

And now Collinsby roused himself. Speaking to Dalgliesh, he said, 'I want to make a statement. Not an official statement at present, although I realise that will have to come. I want to explain to you why I was there, and to do it now just as events come into my mind, without even worrying how they sound or what the effect of them might be. I know you'll have questions and I'll try to answer them, but it would be helpful if I could first just tell the truth without interruption. I was going to say, tell what happened in my own words, but what other words have I?'

Dalgliesh said, 'Perhaps that would be the best way to start.'

'I'll try not to make it too long. The story has become complicated, but basically it's very simple. I won't go into details about my early life, my parents, my upbringing. I'll just say that I knew from childhood that I wanted to teach. I got a scholarship to a grammar school and later a major county award to Oxford. I read History. After my degree I gained a place at London University to take a teacher-training course leading to a Diploma in Education. This took a year. Once I'd qualified I decided to take a year off before applying for a job. I felt I had been breathing academic air for too long and needed to travel, to experience something of the world, to meet people from other walks of life before I began teaching. I'm sorry, I've got ahead of myself. We need to return to the time when I gained my place at London University.

'My parents had always been poor – not distressingly poor but every pound counted – and any money I needed had to be saved either from my grant or from working in the holidays. So when I went to London I needed to find somewhere cheap to live. The city centre was obviously too expensive and I had to look further afield. A friend who had gained a place the year before was lodging in Gidea Park, an Essex suburb, and suggested I tried there. It was when I was visiting him that I saw an advertisement outside a tobacconist's shop for a room suitable for a student in Silford Green, only two further stations on the East London line. There was a phone number so I rang and went to the house. It was semi-detached, occupied by a docker, Stanley Beale, his wife and their two daughters, Shirley, who was eleven, and her younger sister Lucy, aged eight. Their maternal grandmother also lived in the house. There wasn't really room for a lodger. The grandmother shared the largest bedroom with the two girls and Mr and Mrs Beale had the second bedroom at the back. I had the third and smallest bedroom, also at the back. But it was cheap, close to the station, the journey was quick and easy and I was desperate. The first week fulfilled my worst fears. The husband and wife were on shouting terms, the grandmother, a sour, disagreeable old woman, was obviously resentful that she was basically a childminder, and whenever we met was full of complaints about her pension, the local council, her daughter's frequent absences, her son-in-law's mean insistence that she contribute towards her keep. As I was in London most days and often worked late in the University library, I avoided the worst of the family disputes. Within a week of my arrival, after a quarrel of house-shaking ferocity, Beale finally walked out. I could have done the same but what kept me there was the younger daughter, Lucy.'

He paused. The silence lengthened and no one interrupted him. He raised his head to look at Dalgliesh, and Kate could hardly bear to watch the anguish she saw.

He said, 'How can I describe her to you? How can I make you understand? She was an enchanting child. She was beautiful, but it was more than that. She had grace, gentleness, a fine intelligence. I began getting home early so that I could study in my room and Lucy would join me before she went to bed. She used to knock on my door and come in to sit quietly and read while I was working. I would bring home books, and when I stopped writing to make coffee for myself and a milk drink for her, we would talk. I tried to answer her questions. We spoke about the book she'd been reading. I can see her now. Her clothes looked as if her mother had found them in a jumble sale, long summer dresses in winter under a shapeless cardigan, short socks and sandals. If she was cold she never said so. Some weekends I would ask her mother if I could take her up to London to a museum or gallery. There was never any problem; she was glad to have her out of the way, particularly when she was bringing her men home. I knew what was going on, of course, but it wasn't my responsibility. I wouldn't have stayed except for Lucy. I loved her.'

Again there was a silence, then he said, 'I know what you're going to ask. Was this a sexual relationship? I can only say that even the thought would have been a blasphemy for me. I never touched her in that way. But it was love. And isn't love always to some extent physical? Not sexual but physical? A delight in the beauty and grace of the one who is loved? You see, I'm a schoolmaster. I know all the questions I shall be asked. "Were any of your actions inappropriate?" How can one answer that in an age when even to put your arm round the shoulders of a weeping child is regarded as inappropriate? No, it was never inappropriate, but who is ever going to believe me?'

There was a prolonged silence. After a minute Dalgliesh asked, 'At this time, was Shirley Beale, now Sharon Bateman, living in the house?'

'Yes. She was the older sister, a difficult, morose, uncommunicative child. It was hard to believe that they were sisters. She had a disconcerting habit of staring at people, not speaking, just looking, an accusatory look, more adult than childish. I suppose I should have realised that she was unhappy – well I must have realised it – but it wasn't something I felt I could help. I did once suggest to Lucy, when I'd planned to take her to London to see Westminster Abbey, that Shirley might like to come too. Lucy said, "Yes, you ask her," and I did. I can't remember what response I got; something about not wanting to go to boring London to see the boring Abbey with boring me. But I know I was relieved that I'd brought myself to ask and she'd refused. After that, I needn't bother again. I suppose I should have realised what she was feeling – the neglect, the rejection – but I was twenty-two and I hadn't the sensitivity to recognise her pain or to deal with it.'

And now Kate interposed. She said, 'Was it your responsibility to deal with it? You weren't her father. If things were going wrong in the family it was for them to deal with the problems.'

He turned to her almost, it seemed, with relief. 'That's what I tell myself now. I'm not sure I believe it. It wasn't a comfortable house for me or for any of them. If it hadn't been for Lucy I would have looked elsewhere. Because of her I stayed until the end of my year. After I qualified as a teacher I decided to start on the planned journey. I'd never been abroad except for a school trip to Paris, and I went first to the obvious places: Rome, Madrid, Vienna, Siena, Verona, and then on to India and Sri Lanka. At first I sent postcards to Lucy, sometimes two a week.'

Dalgliesh said, 'It's probable Lucy never received your cards. We think they were intercepted by Shirley. They've been found cut in half and buried beside one of the Cheverell Stones.'

He didn't explain what the stones were. But then, thought Kate, did he need to?

'After a time I stopped sending them, thinking that Lucy had either forgotten me or was busy with her school life; that I had been an important influence for a time, but not a lasting one. And the awful thing is this: in a way, I was relieved. I had a career to carve out for myself and perhaps Lucy would have been a responsibility as well as a joy. And I was looking for adult love – aren't we all in our youth? I learnt of the murder when I was in Sri Lanka. For a moment I was physically sick with shock and horror and, of course, I grieved for the child I had loved. But later, when I remembered that year with Lucy, it was like a dream and the grief was an unfocused sorrow for all ill-treated and murdered children and for the death of innocence. Perhaps that was because I now had a child. I didn't write to the mother or grandmother to commiserate. I never mentioned to anyone that I had known the family. I felt absolutely no responsibility for her death. I had none. I did feel some shame and regret that I'd not continued trying to keep in touch, but that passed. Even when I returned home the police didn't contact me to question me. Why should they? Shirley had confessed and the evidence was overwhelming. The only explanation anyone ever received was that she had killed Lucy because her sister was too pretty.'

There was a momentary silence, then Dalgliesh spoke. 'When did Shirley Beale get in touch with you?'

'On the 30th of November I received a letter from her. Apparently she had seen a television programme on secondary education in which I had appeared. She recognised me and noted the name of the school where I was working – still work. The letter simply said that she remembered me, that she still loved me and she needed to see me. She told me she was working at Cheverell Manor and how to find my way there, and suggested that we meet. The letter horrified me. I couldn't imagine what she meant by still loving me. She had never loved me or shown the slightest sign of affection for me, nor I to her. I acted weakly and unwisely. I burnt the letter and tried to forget I'd ever seen it. It was hopeless, of course. Ten days later she wrote again. This time there was a threat. She said she had to see me and if I didn't come she had found someone who would tell the world how I had rejected her. I still don't know what the proper response would have been. Probably to tell my wife, even to inform the police. But could I make them believe the truth about my relationship with Lucy or with Shirley? I decided that the best plan, at least at first, would be to see her and to try to reason her out of her delusions. She had told me to meet her at a parking place by the side of the road near the Cheverell Stones at midnight. She even sent a little map, carefully drawn. The letter ended, "It's so wonderful to have found you. We must never let each other go again."'

Dalgliesh asked, 'Have you got the letter?'

'No. Again I acted stupidly. I took it with me on the journey and when I got to the parking space I used the car lighter to burn it. I suppose I was in denial from the moment her first letter arrived.'

'And did you meet her?'

'Yes we met, and at the stones as she had arranged. I didn't touch her even to shake hands, nor did she seem to expect that. She repelled me. I suggested we return to the car where we would be more comfortable and we sat side by side. She said that even when I had been infatuated with Lucy – that was the word she used – she had loved me. She had killed Lucy because she was jealous, but now she had served her sentence. That meant she was free to love me. She wanted to marry me and have my children. It was all said very calmly, almost without emotion, but with a terrible will. She stared ahead and I don't think she even looked at me as she spoke. I explained as gently as I could that I was married, that I had a child, and that there could never be anything between us. I didn't offer her even friendship; how could I? My only wish was never to see her again. It was bizarre, a horror. When I told her I was married she said that needn't stop us from being together. I could get a divorce. We would have children together and she would look after the son I had.'

He had been looking down as he spoke, his hands clasped on the table. Now he lifted his face to Dalgliesh and he and Kate could see the horror and desperation in his eyes.

'To look after my child! The thought of even having her in the house, close to my family, appalled me. I suppose I failed again in imagination. I should have sensed her need, but all I felt was horror, the compulsion to get away from her, to buy time. I did that by lying. I said I would talk to my wife but that she mustn't hope because there was none. I did at least make that clear. And then she said goodbye, again without touching me, and left. I sat watching as she disappeared into the darkness, following a small pinprick of light.'

Dalgliesh said, 'Did you at any time enter the Manor?'

'No.'

'Did she ask you to do so?'

'No.'

'Did you, while you were parked, see or hear anyone else?'

'No one. I drove away the minute Shirley got out of the car. I saw no one.'

'That night one of the patients there was murdered. Did Shirley Beale say anything which leads you to believe that she might be responsible?'

'Nothing.'

'The patient's name was Rhoda Gradwyn. Did Shirley Beale mention that name to you, speak about her, tell you anything about the Manor?'

'Nothing, except that she worked there.'

'And was this the first time you've heard of the Manor?'

'Yes, the first time. There hasn't been anything on the news, surely, and certainly not in the Sunday papers. I wouldn't have missed it.'

'Nothing yet, but there probably will be tomorrow morning. Have you spoken to your wife about Shirley Beale?'

'No, not yet. I think I've been in denial, hoping but without real hope that I might hear nothing more from Shirley, that I'd convinced her that we had no future together. The whole incident was fantastic, unreal, a nightmare. As you know, I borrowed Michael Curtis's car for the journey and I'd decided that, if Shirley wrote again, I'd confide in him. I had a desperate need to tell someone and I knew that he would be wise and kind and sensible, and at least would advise me what I should do. Only then would I speak to my wife. I realise, of course, that if Shirley did make the past public it could destroy my career.'

And now Kate spoke again. She said, 'But surely not if the truth were accepted. You showed kindness and affection to an obviously lonely and needy child. You were only twenty-two at the time. You couldn't possibly know that your friendship with Lucy would lead to her death. You aren't responsible for that death. No one is but Shirley Beale. She was lonely and needy too, but you weren't responsible for her unhappiness.'

'But I was responsible. Indirectly and without malice. If Lucy hadn't met me she'd be alive today.'

Kate's voice was urgent, compelling. 'Would she? Wouldn't there have been another cause for jealousy? Particularly when they became adolescents and it was Lucy who had the boyfriends, the attention, the love? You can't possibly tell what might have happened. We can't be held morally responsible for the long-term results of all our actions.'

She stopped, her face flushed, and looked across at Dalgliesh. He knew what she was thinking. She had spoken from pity and outrage but in betraying those emotions she had acted unprofessionally. No suspect in a murder case should be led to believe that the investigating officers are on his side.

Now Dalgliesh spoke directly to Collinsby. 'I'd like you to make a statement setting out the facts as you have described them. We shall almost certainly need to talk again when we have interviewed Sharon Bateman. So far she has told us nothing, not even her true identity. And if she has spent less than four years living in the community after her release from custody she will still be under supervision. Please put your private address on the statement, we shall need to know how to reach you at home.' Reaching for his briefcase, he took out an official form and handed it over.

Collinsby said, 'I'll take this over to the desk, the light's better there,' and sat with his back to them. Then he turned and said, 'I'm sorry, I haven't offered you coffee or tea. If Inspector Miskin would like to make it, everything necessary is next door. This may take some time.'

Dalgliesh said, 'I'll see to it,' and went into the adjoining room leaving the door open. There was a chink of china, the sound of a kettle being filled. Kate waited a couple of minutes, then went to join him, searching in a small refrigerator for the milk. Dalgliesh carried in the tray with three cups and saucers and placed one with the sugar bowl and milk jug beside Collinsby, who continued writing, and then, without looking at them, stretched out a hand and drew the cup towards him. He took neither milk nor sugar and Kate moved them over to the table where she and Dalgliesh sat in silence. She felt extraordinarily tired but resisted the temptation to lean back in the chair.

Thirty minutes later Collinsby turned and handed the pages to Dalgliesh. He said, 'It's finished now. I tried to keep it factual. I haven't attempted any justification, but there is none. Do you need to watch me signing it?'

Dalgliesh went over and the paper was signed. He and Kate picked up their coats and were ready to go. As if they were parents who had come to discuss the progress of their children, Collinsby said formally, 'It was good of you to come to the school. I'll see you to the door. When you need to speak to me again, no doubt you'll be in touch.'

He unlocked the front door and went with them to the gate. The last they saw of him was his pale taut face staring at them from behind the bars like a man incarcerated. Then he closed the gate, turned and, walking with firm steps to the school door, entered without looking back.

In the car, Dalgliesh switched on the reading light and took up the map. He said, 'The best route seems to be to take the M1 south, then the M25 and the M3. You must be hungry. We both need to eat, and this doesn't look a particularly promising place.'

Kate found herself desperate to get away from the school, from the town, from the memory of the last hour. She said, 'Couldn't we stop somewhere on the motorway? I don't mean for a meal, but we could pick up a sandwich.'

The rain had stopped now except for a few heavy drops which fell, viscous as oil, on the bonnet. When they were at last on the motorway Kate said, 'I'm sorry I said what I did to Mr Collinsby. I know it's unprofessional to sympathise with a suspect.' She wanted to go on, but her voice was choked and she simply said again, 'I'm sorry, sir.'

Dalgliesh didn't glance at her. He said, 'You spoke out of compassion. To feel compassion strongly can be dangerous in a murder investigation, but not as dangerous as losing the capacity to feel it at all. No harm was done.'

But the tears still came and he let her quietly weep, keeping his eyes on the road. The motorway unwound before them in a phantasmagoria of light, the procession of dipped headlights on their right, the moving pattern of the southward traffic, the blotting out of black hedges and trees by the huge shapes of trucks, the roar and grind of a world of unknowable travellers caught up in the same extraordinary compulsion. When he saw a sign saying *Services*, Dalgliesh moved into the left-hand lane, and then pulled off onto the slip road. He found a space on the edge of the car park and switched off the engine.

They moved into a building ablaze with light and colour. Every café and shop was hung with Christmas decorations and in a corner a small amateur choir, largely disregarded, was singing carols and collecting for charity. They made their way to the washrooms, then picked up sandwiches and two large plastic beakers of coffee and returned with them to the car. While they ate, Dalgliesh phoned Benton to put him in the picture and within twenty minutes they were on their way.

Glancing at Kate's face, strained with stoical determination not to betray her tiredness, he said, 'It's been a long day and it isn't over yet. Why not put the seat back and have a sleep?'

'I'm all right, sir.'

'There's no need for both of us to stay awake. There's a rug on the back seat, if you can reach it. I'll wake you up in good time.'

He resisted tiredness when driving by keeping the heating low. If she slept she would need the rug. She jerked back her seat and settled herself, the rug huddled close to her neck, her face turned towards him. Almost at once she was asleep. She slept so quietly that he could hardly hear her gently drawn breath, except that from time to time she made a small contented grunt like a sleeping child and snuggled deeper into the rug. Glancing at her face, all anxiety smoothed away by the benison of life's little semblance of death, he thought what a good face it was – not beautiful, certainly not conventionally pretty, but a good face, honest, open, pleasant to look at, a face that would last. For years, when on a case, she had worn her light brown hair in a single thick plait; now she had had it cut and it lay softly on her cheeks. He knew that what she needed from him was more than he could give, but what he did give he knew that she valued – friendship, trust, respect and affection. But she deserved much more. About six months ago he had thought that she had found it. Now he was not so sure.

Soon, he knew, the Special Investigation Squad would fold or be absorbed into another department. He would make his own decision about his future. Kate would gain her overdue promotion to detective chief inspector. But what then for her? He had sensed of late that she was tired of travelling alone. At the next service station he pulled in and cut off the engine. She didn't stir. He tucked the rug close round her sleeping body and settled himself for a short break. Ten minutes later he slid back into the stream of traffic and drove south-westward through the night.

5

Despite the exhaustion and trauma of the previous day, Kate woke early and refreshed. On Dalgliesh's and her late return from Droughton, the team's usual review of progress had been intensive but brief, an exchange of information not a prolonged discussion of its implications. The result of the autopsy on Rhoda Gradwyn's body had been received in the late afternoon. Dr Glenister's reports were always comprehensive but this was uncomplicated and unsurprising. Miss Gradwyn had been a healthy woman with all that implied of hope and fulfilment. It had been her two fatal decisions – to have the scar removed and the operation performed at Cheverell Manor – which had led to those seven stark decisive words: *Death by asphyxia caused by manual strangulation.* Reading the report with Dalgliesh and Benton, Kate was seized by the familiar impotent surge of anger and pity at the wanton destructiveness of murder.

Now she dressed quickly and found that she was hungry for the breakfast of bacon and egg, sausages and tomatoes served to her and Benton by Mrs Shepherd. Dalgliesh had decided that she, not himself or Benton, should meet Mrs Rayner at Wareham. The supervising officer had telephoned late the previous night to say that she would take the five-past-eight train from Waterloo and hoped to arrive at Wareham at ten thirty.

The train was on time and Kate had no difficulty in identifying Mrs Rayner among the small number of alighting passengers. She looked intently into Kate's eyes and shook hands with a brief pumping action, as if this formal meeting of flesh was a validation of some pre-arranged contract. She was shorter than Kate, stout bodied with a square clear-skinned face given strength by the firmness of the mouth and chin. Her dark brown hair, greying in streaks, had been well and – as Kate knew – expensively cut. She was without the usual symbol of bureaucracy, a briefcase, and carried instead a large linen bag with a drawstring and straps slung over her shoulder. For Kate everything about her spoke of authority quietly and confidently exercised. She reminded Kate of one of her schoolteachers, Mrs Butler, who had transformed the dreaded Fourth into acting like comparatively civilised beings by the simple expedient of believing that when she was present they could do no other.

Kate made the customary enquiry about the journey. Mrs Rayner said, 'I had a window seat with no children or obsessive squawkers on their mobiles. The bacon sandwich from the refreshment car was fresh and I enjoyed the scenery. That for me is a good journey.'

They didn't speak of Shirley, now Sharon, on the drive, although Mrs Rayner asked about the Manor and the people who worked there, perhaps to put herself in the picture. Kate guessed that she was saving the essentials until she was with Dalgliesh; there was no point, and there might be misunderstanding, in saying things twice.

In the Old Police Cottage Mrs Rayner, welcomed by Dalgliesh, declined the offer of coffee and asked for tea, which Kate made. Benton had arrived and the four of them sat round the low table in front of the fire. Dalgliesh, who had Rhoda Gradwyn's file in front of him, briefly explained how the team had come to know of Sharon's real identity. He handed the file to Mrs Rayner, who examined the picture of Lucy's battered face without comment. After a few minutes' scrutiny she closed the file and handed it back to Dalgliesh.

She said, 'It would be interesting to find out how Rhoda Gradwyn managed to get hold of some of this material, but as she's dead there seems little point in instituting an enquiry. Anyway, that won't be for me to do. Certainly we've had no instances of anything about Sharon being published and there was a legal prohibition when she was a minor.'

Dalgliesh asked, 'She didn't notify you of her change of job and address?'

'No. She should have done, of course, and I should have been in touch before now with the retirement home. I last met her by arrangement ten months ago when she was still there. She must have already decided to move. Her excuse will probably be that she didn't want to tell me and saw no need. My excuse, less valid, is the usual one: a too-heavy workload and the reorganisation following the splitting of Home Office responsibilities. In common parlance, Sharon fell through the net.'

Falling Through the Net, thought Dalgliesh, would be a perfect title for a contemporary novel. He said, 'You had no particular anxiety about her?'

'None in the sense of seeing her as a public danger. She wouldn't have been released if the Parole Board hadn't been satisfied that she wasn't a danger to herself or others. She was no trouble when she was in Moorfield House, and has been none since release. If I had anxiety – indeed, still have – it's about finding a satisfying and suitable job for her, helping her to make a life for herself. She has always resisted taking any form of training. The job at the retirement home wasn't a long-term solution. She should be with people of her own age. But I'm not here to discuss Sharon's future. I can see that she presents a problem for your investigation. Wherever she goes we'll ensure she's available if you wish to question her. Has she been co-operating so far?'

Dalgliesh said, 'She hasn't been a problem. At present we have no prime suspect.'

'Well, obviously she can't stay here. I'll make arrangements for her to go to a hostel until we can arrange something more permanent. I hope to be able to send someone for her in three days' time. Of course I'll keep in touch.'

Kate asked, 'Has she ever expressed remorse for what she did?'

'No, and that has been a problem. She only repeats that she wasn't sorry at the time and what was the point of being sorry afterwards just because you've been found out.'

Dalgliesh said, 'There's a certain honesty in that. Shall we see her now? Kate, would you find her please and bring her here.'

They were kept waiting for Kate to return with Sharon and when, after fifteen minutes, they arrived, the reason for the delay was apparent. Sharon had taken trouble over her appearance. A skirt and jumper had been substituted for her working overall, her hair had been brushed to shininess and she was wearing lipstick. There was an immense gilt earring in each ear. She came in belligerently but with a certain wariness and took a seat opposite Dalgliesh. Mrs Rayner took a chair beside her, an indication, Kate thought, of where her professional concern and loyalty lay. She herself sat beside Dalgliesh, and Benton, notebook open, sat close to the door.

On entering the room Sharon had shown no surprise at seeing Mrs Rayner. Now, fixing her eyes on her, she said without apparent resentment, 'I thought you'd be along sooner or later.'

'It would have been sooner, Sharon, if you'd told me about your change of job and Miss Gradwyn's death – as, of course, you should have.'

'Well I was going to, but fat chance with the cops all over the house and everyone watching me. If they saw me phone they'd ask why. Anyway, she was only killed on Friday night.'

'Well, I'm here now and there are a number of things we need to talk about in private, but first of all Commander Dalgliesh has some questions and I want you to promise to answer them truthfully and in full. This is important, Sharon.'

Dalgliesh said, 'You have the right, Miss Bateman, to ask for a solicitor to be present if you think it necessary.'

She stared at him. 'Why would I want a solicitor? I haven't done anything wrong. Anyway, Mrs Rayner's here. She'll see there's no funny business. And I told you everything I know when we were in the library on Saturday.'

Dalgliesh said, 'Not all. You didn't say then that you left the Manor on Friday night. We now know that you did. You went out to meet someone at about midnight, and we know who it was. We've spoken to Mr Collinsby.'

And now there was a change. Sharon started from her chair,

then sat back and clasped the edge of the table. Her face flushed and the deceptively mild eyes widened and seemed to Kate to darken into pools of anger.

'You can't pin it on Stephen! He never killed that woman. He wouldn't kill anyone. He's good and he's kind – and I love him! We're going to get married.'

Mrs Rayner said, her voice gentle, 'That isn't possible, Sharon, and you know it isn't. Mr Collinsby is already married and has a child. I think in asking him to come back into your life you were acting out a fantasy, a dream. Now we have to face reality.'

Sharon looked at Dalgliesh, who said, 'How did you discover where Mr Collinsby was?'

'Saw him on TV, didn't I? I was watching it in my room after dinner. I just turned it on and I saw him. That's why I kept on watching. It was a boring programme about education but I saw Stephen and I heard his voice, and he was just the same, only older. The programme said how he'd changed this school, so I wrote down the name and that's where I sent the letter. He never replied to the first one, so I sent another and told him he'd better meet me. It was important.'

Dalgliesh said, 'Did you make threats – either he met you or you'd tell someone that he'd lodged with your family and had known both you and your sister? Had he harmed either of you?'

'He didn't do any harm to Lucy. He's not one of them paedophiles, if that's what you're thinking. He loved her. They were always reading together up in his room or going out for treats. She liked being with him, but she didn't care about him. She just liked the treats. And she only went up to his room because that was better than staying in the kitchen with me and Gran. Gran was always picking on us. Lucy said she was bored with Stephen but I cared about him. I loved him. I've always loved him. I never thought I'd see him again but now he's back in my life. I want to be with him. I know I can make him happy.'

Kate wondered if either Dalgliesh or Mrs Rayner would mention Lucy's murder. Neither did. Instead Dalgliesh asked, 'So you arranged for Mr Collinsby to meet you at the parking space for the stones. I want you to tell me exactly what happened and what passed between you.'

'You said you'd seen him. He must've told you what happened. I don't see why I should have to go over it all again. Nothing happened. He said he was married but he was going to talk to his wife and ask for a divorce. And then I went back into the house and he drove away.'

Dalgliesh asked, 'And that was all?'

'Well, we weren't going to sit in the car all night, were we? I just sat there beside him for a bit but we never kissed or anything like that. You don't have to kiss when you're really in love. I knew he was speaking the truth. I knew he loved me. So after a time I got out and went back to the house.'

'Did he go back with you?'

'No, he didn't. Why would he? I knew my way, didn't I? Anyway, he wanted to be off, I could tell that.'

'Did he at any time mention Rhoda Gradwyn?'

'Of course he didn't. Why would he talk about her? He never met her.'

'Did you give him keys to the Manor?'

And now she was suddenly angry again. 'No, no, no! He never asked for the keys. Why would he want them? He never went near the place. You're trying to pin murder on him because you're protecting all the others – Mr Chandler-Powell, Sister Holland, Miss Cressett – all of them. You're trying to pin it all on Stephen and me.'

Dalgliesh said quietly, 'We're not here to pin this crime on the innocent. Our job is to find out who's guilty. The innocent have nothing to fear. But Mr Collinsby may well be in trouble if the story about you becomes known. I think you understand what I mean. We don't live in a kind world and people might very easily misinterpret the friendship between him and your sister.'

'Well, she's dead, isn't she? What can they prove now?'

Mrs Rayner broke her silence. She said, 'They can't prove anything, Sharon, but gossip and rumour don't rely on truth. I think when Mr Dalgliesh has finished questioning you we'd better have a talk about your future after this terrible experience. You've done very well so far, Sharon, but I think it may be time to move on.' She turned to Dalgliesh. 'Could I have the use of a room here for a time, if you've finished?'

'Of course. It's straight across the hall.'

Sharon said, 'All right. I'm sick of the cops anyway. Sick of their questions, sick of their stupid faces. Sick of this place. I don't see why I can't leave right away. I could come with you now.'

Mrs Rayner had already got up. 'I don't think that will be possible immediately, Sharon, but we'll certainly work on it.' She turned to Dalgliesh. 'Thank you for the use of the room. I don't think Sharon and I will need it for long.'

They didn't, but the forty-five minutes or so which passed before they reappeared seemed long to Kate. Sharon, who was no longer truculent, said goodbye to Mrs Rayner and meekly enough returned to the Manor with Benton. As the gates were unlocked by the security guard, Benton said, 'Mrs Rayner seemed a very nice person.'

'Oh she's all right. I'd have been in touch with her earlier if you lot hadn't been watching me like a cat with a mouse. She's going to find a place for me so I'll be out of here soon. In the meantime, you lay off Stephen. I wish I'd never called him to this bloody place.'

In the interview room Mrs Rayner put on her jacket and took up her bag. She said, 'It's unfortunate that this is happening. She was doing very well at the geriatric unit, but it was reasonable for her to want a job with younger people. The old patients liked her, though. They spoilt her a bit, I imagine. But it's time she got some proper training and settled into something with a future. I hope to find a place for her fairly soon where I think she'll be happy to spend a few weeks until we can settle the next move. And she may need psychiatric help. Obviously she's in denial about Stephen Collinsby. But if you're asking me whether she killed Rhoda Gradwyn – which of course you aren't – I'd say it's extremely unlikely. I would say impossible, except that one can never use that word about anyone.'

Dalgliesh said, 'The fact that she's here, and with her record, is a complication.'

'I can see that. Unless you get a confession it will be difficult to justify arresting anyone else. But like most murderers, hers was that one act.'

Kate said, 'She's managed to do some appalling harm in her short life. A child murdered and a good man's job and future at risk. It's hard to look at her without seeing an image of that smashed face superimposed on hers.'

Mrs Rayner said, 'The anger of a child can be terrible. If an out-of-control four-year-old had a gun and the strength to use it, how many families would be left standing?'

Dalgliesh said, 'Lucy was apparently a lovely endearing little girl.'

'Possibly to other people. Not perhaps to Sharon.'

Within minutes she was ready to leave and Kate drove her to Wareham station. On the way they spoke from time to time about Dorset and the countryside through which they were passing. But Mrs Rayner didn't mention Sharon's name, and nor did Kate. Kate had decided that it would be both polite and sensible to wait with Mrs Rayner until the train had arrived and she was safely on her way. It wasn't until it was approaching the platform that her companion spoke.

She said, 'Don't worry about Stephen Collinsby. Sharon will be looked after and given the help she needs, and he won't be harmed.'

6

Candace Westhall came into the front room of the Old Police Cottage in a jacket and scarf and wearing her gardening gloves. She seated herself, then took off her gloves and placed them, large and mud caked, on the table between herself and Dalgliesh like an allegorical challenge. The meaning, if crude, was plain. She had been called from a necessary job once again to answer unnecessary questions.

Her antagonism was palpable and he knew that it was shared, if less openly, by most of his suspects. This he expected and in part understood. At first he and his team were awaited and greeted with relief. Action would be taken, the case cleared up, the horror which was also an embarrassment would be salved, the innocent vindicated, the guilty – probably a stranger whose fate could cause no distress – would be arrested and dealt with. Law, reason and order would replace the contaminating disorder of murder. But there had been no arrest and no sign of one. It was still early days, but for the small company at the Manor there was no foreseeable end to his presence or to his questioning. He understood their growing resentment because he had once experienced it when he had discovered the murdered body of a young woman on a Suffolk beach. The crime was not on his patch and another investigating officer had taken over. There had been no question of his being regarded as a serious suspect, but the police questioning had been detailed, repetitive and, it seemed to him, unnecessarily intrusive. An interrogation was uncomfortably like a mental violation.

He said, 'In 2002 Rhoda Gradwyn wrote an article for the *Paternoster Review* dealing with plagiarism in which she attacked a young writer, Annabel Skelton, who subsequently took her own life. What was your relationship with Annabel Skelton?'

She met his eyes, hers cold with dislike and, he thought, contempt. There was a brief silence in which the antagonism crackled from her like an electric current. Without altering her gaze, she said, 'Annabel Skelton was a dear friend. I would say I loved her except that you would misinterpret a relationship which I doubt I can make you understand. All friendships seem to be defined now in terms of sexuality. She was my pupil but her talent was for writing, not Classics. I encouraged her to complete her first novel and to submit it for publication.'

'Did you know at the time that parts of it had been plagiarised from an earlier work?'

'Are you asking me, Commander, whether she told me?'

'No, Miss Westhall, I'm asking whether you knew.'

'I didn't, not until I read Gradwyn's article.'

Kate intervened. 'It must have surprised and distressed you.'

'Yes, Inspector, both of those things.'

Dalgliesh asked, 'Did you take any action – see Rhoda Gradwyn, write to protest either to her or to the *Paternoster Review*?'

'I saw Gradwyn. We met briefly in her agent's office at her request. It was a mistake. She was, of course, totally unrepentant. I prefer not to discuss the details of that encounter. I didn't know at the time that Annabel was already dead. She hanged herself three days after the *Paternoster Review* appeared.'

'So you didn't have an opportunity to see her, ask for an explanation? I'm sorry if this is painful for you.'

'Surely not too sorry, Commander. Let there be honesty between us. Like Rhoda Gradwyn, you're merely doing your distasteful job. I tried to get in touch but Annabel wouldn't see me, the door locked, the phone unplugged. I'd wasted time with Gradwyn when I might have succeeded in seeing her. The day after her death I received a postcard. There were only eight words and no signature. *I'm sorry. Please forgive me. I love you.*'

There was a silence, then she said, 'The plagiarism was the least

264

important part of a novel which showed extraordinary promise. But I think Annabel realised that she would never write another and for her that was death. And there was the humiliation. That, too, was more than she could bear.'

'Did you hold Rhoda Gradwyn responsible?'

'She was responsible. She murdered my friend. As I suppose that wasn't her intention there would be no hope of legal redress. But I didn't take private revenge after five years. Hatred doesn't die but it loses some of its power. It's like an infection in the blood, never completely lost, liable to flare up unexpectedly but its fever becoming less debilitating, less acutely painful with the passing years. I'm left with regret and a lasting sadness. I didn't kill Rhoda Gradwyn but I can't feel even a minute's regret that she's dead. Does that satisfy the question you were about to ask, Commander?'

'You say, Miss Westhall, that you didn't kill Rhoda Gradwyn. Do you know who did?'

'I do not. And if I did, Commander, I think it unlikely that I would tell you.'

She rose from the table to go. Neither Dalgliesh nor Kate made a move to stop her.

7

In the three days following Rhoda Gradwyn's murder, Lettie was struck by how briefly death is allowed to interfere with life. The dead, however they die, are tidied away with decent speed to their designated place, a tray in a hospital mortuary, the undertaker's embalming room, the pathologist's table. The doctor may not come when called; the undertaker always does. Meals, however sparse or unconventional, are prepared and eaten, post arrives, telephones ring, bills have to be paid, official forms filled in. Those who mourn, as she in her time had mourned, move like automata into a shadow world in which nothing is real or familiar or seemingly ever will be again. But even they speak, attempt to sleep, raise untasting food to their mouths, continue as if by rote to play their destined part in a drama in which all the other characters seem familiar with their roles.

At the Manor no one pretended to mourn Rhoda Gradwyn. Her death was a shock made more terrible by mystery and fear, but the routine of the Manor went on. Dean continued to cook his excellent meals, although a certain simplicity in the menus suggested that he was paying a perhaps unconscious tribute to death. Kim continued to serve them, although appetite and frank enjoyment seemed a gross insensitivity, inhibiting conversation. Only the coming and going of the police and the presence of the cars of the security team and the caravan in which they ate and slept parked outside the main entrance were an ever-constant reminder that nothing was normal. There had been a spurt of interest and half-shameful hope when Sharon was called for by Inspector Miskin and taken for questioning at the Old Police Cottage. She had returned to say briefly that

Commander Dalgliesh was preparing for her to leave the Manor and a friend would be calling for her in three days. In the meantime she didn't intend to do any more work. As far as she was concerned the job was over and they knew where they could shove it. She was tired and upset and couldn't fucking well wait to get away from the fucking Manor. Now she was going to her room. Sharon had never been heard to utter an obscenity and the word was as shocking as if it had come from Lettie's mouth.

Commander Dalgliesh had then been closeted with George Chandler-Powell for half an hour and after he left George had summoned them to the library. They had gathered silently with a shared anticipation that something of significance was about to be told. Sharon had not been arrested, so much was obvious, but there might have been developments and even unwelcome news was preferable to this continuing uncertainty. For all of them, and sometimes they confided as much, life was on hold. Even the simplest decisions – which clothes to put on in the morning, what orders to give Dean and Kimberley – required an effort of will. Chandler-Powell did not keep them waiting but it seemed to Lettie that he was unusually ill at ease. Entering the library he seemed uncertain whether to stand or sit, but after a moment's hesitation, positioned himself beside the fire. He must know himself to be a suspect, as were they all, but now, with their eyes fixed expectantly on him, he seemed more a surrogate of Commander Dalgliesh, a role which he neither wanted nor felt comfortable with.

He said, 'I'm sorry to interrupt what you're doing but Commander Dalgliesh has asked me to speak to you and it seemed sensible to get you together to hear what he had to say. As you know, Sharon will be leaving us in a few days' time. There was an incident in her past which makes her progress and her welfare a matter for the probation service and it's thought best that she should leave the Manor. I understand that Sharon will be co-operating with the arrangements made for her. That's all I have been told and it's all anyone has a right to know. I must ask you all not to discuss Sharon among yourselves or to speak to her about her past or her future, neither of which is our concern.'

Marcus asked, 'Does this mean that Sharon is no longer regarded as a suspect, if she ever was?'

'Presumably.'

Flavia's face was flushed, her voice uncertain. 'Could we know precisely what her status here is? She's told us that she doesn't intend to do any more work. I take it that, as the Manor seems to be regarded as a crime scene, we can't call in any of the village cleaners. With the Manor empty of patients there's not a lot of work, but someone has to do it.'

Dean said, 'Kim and I could help. But what about her food? Usually she eats with us in the kitchen. Suppose she stays upstairs? Is Kim expected to carry up trays and wait on her?' His voice made it plain that this would not be acceptable.

Helena glanced at Chandler-Powell. It was obvious his patience was wearing thin. She said, 'Of course not. Sharon knows the time of the meals. If she's hungry she'll appear. It will only be for a day or two. If there's any trouble, tell me and I'll speak to Commander Dalgliesh. Meanwhile we carry on as normally as possible.'

Candace spoke for the first time. 'As I was one of those who interviewed her I suppose I ought to take some responsibility for Sharon. It might be a help if she moved into Stone Cottage with Marcus and me, if Commander Dalgliesh is happy about it. We have the room. And she can give me a hand with Father's books. It's not good for her to have nothing to do. And it's time someone tried to discourage her obsession with Mary Keyte. Last summer she took to laying wild flowers on the centre stone. It's morbid and unhealthy. I'll go up to her now and see if she's calmed down.'

Chandler-Powell said, 'By all means have a try. As a teacher you're probably more experienced than the rest of us in dealing with the recalcitrant young. Commander Dalgliesh has assured me that Sharon doesn't require supervision. If she does, it's for the police or the probation service to provide it, not us. I've cancelled my American trip. I have to be back in London by Thursday and I'll need Marcus with me. I'm sorry if that sounds like desertion but I have to catch up on some of the NHS patients I should have operated on this week. Obviously I had to cancel all those operations.

The security team will be here and I shall arrange for two of them to sleep in.'

Marcus asked, 'And the police? Did Dalgliesh say when they expect to leave?'

'No, and I hadn't the temerity to ask. They've only been here three days so unless they make an arrest I imagine we'll have to tolerate some police presence for quite a time.'

Flavia said, 'You mean we'll have to tolerate it. You'll be safely out of it in London. Are the police happy about your leaving?'

Chandler-Powell looked at her coldly. 'What legal power do you suppose Commander Dalgliesh has to detain me?'

And then he was gone, leaving the little group with the impression that somehow they had all behaved unreasonably. They looked at each other in an uneasy silence. It was broken by Candace. 'Well, I'd better tackle Sharon. And perhaps, Helena, you'd have a private word with George. I know I'm in the cottage and it hardly affects me as it does the rest of you, but I do work here and I'd rather the security team slept outside the Manor. It's bad enough seeing their caravan parked outside the gate and them wandering round the grounds without having them in the house.'

And then she, too, was gone. Mog, who had seated himself in one of the most impressive chairs, had gazed impassively at Chandler-Powell throughout but had remained silent. Now he heaved himself up and left. The rest of the group waited for Candace's return, but after half an hour during which Chandler-Powell's injunction not to discuss Sharon inhibited conversation, they dispersed and Helena closed the library door firmly behind them.

8

The three days of the week when no patients were operated on and George Chandler-Powell was in London gave Candace and Lettie time to work on the accounts, deal with any financial problems with the temporary staff and settle the bills for the additional food necessary to feed the influx of non-resident nursing staff, the technicians and anaesthetist. The change in the atmosphere of the Manor between the beginning and end of the week was as dramatic as it was welcome to the two women. Despite the surface calm of operating days, the mere presence of George Chandler-Powell and his team seemed to permeate the whole atmosphere. But the days before he left for London were periods of almost total calm. The Chandler-Powell who was a distinguished and overworked surgeon became Chandler-Powell the country squire, content with a domestic routine which he never criticised or attempted to influence, a man breathing in solitude like reviving air.

But now, on Tuesday morning, the fourth day after the murder, he was still at the Manor, his London list postponed and he himself obviously torn between his responsibility to his St Angela's patients and the need to support the remaining staff at the Manor. But by Thursday both he and Marcus would have gone. Admittedly they would be back by Sunday morning, but reaction to even a temporary absence was mixed. People already slept behind locked doors, although Candace and Helena had succeeded in dissuading Chandler-Powell from instituting nightly patrols by the police or security team. Most of the residents had convinced themselves that an intruder, probably the owner of the parked car, had killed Miss Gradwyn and it seemed unlikely that he had any interest in another victim. But presumably he still possessed the keys to the west door – a frightening thought. Mr Chandler-Powell wasn't a guarantee of safety but he was the owner of the Manor, their go-between with the police, a reassuring authoritative presence. On the other hand, he was obviously irked at time wasted and impatient to be getting on with his job. The Manor would be more peaceful without his restless footsteps, the occasional spats of ill humour. The police were still silent about the progress, if any, of the investigation. The news of Miss Gradwyn's death had, of course, broken in the media, but to everyone's relief the reports had been surprisingly short and ambiguous, helped by the competition of a political scandal and a pop star's particularly acrimonious divorce. Lettie wondered whether some influence on the media had been exerted. But the restraint wouldn't last for long and, if an arrest were made, the dam would burst and the polluted waters sweep over them.

And now, with no part-time domestic staff, the patients' section sealed, the telephone frequently on the answerphone and the police presence a daily reminder of that departed presence which was still, in imagination, locked in the silence of death behind that sealed door, it was a comfort to Lettie and, she suspected, to Candace, that there was always work to be done. On Tuesday morning both were at their desks shortly after nine, Lettie sorting through a collection of grocer's and butcher's bills, and Candace at the computer. The telephone was on the table before her and now it rang.

Candace said, 'Don't answer it.'

It was too late. Lettie had already lifted the receiver. She handed it over. 'It's a man. I didn't catch his name but he sounds agitated. He's asking for you.'

Candace took the receiver, was silent for a minute, then said, 'We're busy in the office here and, frankly, we haven't time to chase after Robin Boyton. I know he's our cousin, but that doesn't make us his keepers. How long have you been trying to reach him . . .? All right, someone will go round to the guest cottage and if we've got any news we'll tell him to ring you . . . Yes, I'll ring back if we've no luck. What's your number?'

She reached for a sheet of paper, took down the number then replaced the receiver and turned to Lettie. 'That's Robin's business partner, Jeremy Coxon. Apparently one of his teachers has let him down and he wants Robin back urgently. He phoned late last night but got no reply so left a message, and he's been repeatedly trying again this morning. Robin's mobile rings, but no answer.'

Lettie said, 'Robin may have come here to get away from phone calls and the demands of their business. But then why not turn off his mobile? I suppose someone had better take a look.'

Candace said, 'When I left Stone Cottage this morning his car was there and the curtains were drawn. He could be still asleep and has left his mobile where he can't hear it. Dean could run over if he's not busy. He'll be quicker than Mog.'

Lettie got to her feet. 'I'll go. I could do with a breath of fresh air.'

'Then you'd better take the spare key. If he's still sleeping off a hangover he might not hear the bell. It's a nuisance that he's still here at all. Dalgliesh can't detain him without cause and you'd think he'd be only too glad to get back to London, if only for the fun of spreading the gossip.'

Lettie was tidying the papers on which she was working. 'You dislike him, don't you? He seems harmless enough but even Helena sighs when she books him in.'

'He's a hanger-on with a grievance. A perfectly legitimate one, probably. His mother got herself pregnant and subsequently married an obvious fortune hunter, to old grandfather Theodore's disgust. Anyway, she was cast off, more, I suspect, for stupidity and naïvety than for the pregnancy. Robin likes to turn up from time to time to remind us of what he sees as unfair discrimination and frankly we find his persistence boring. We do hand out the odd subvention from time to time. He takes the money but I think he finds it humiliating. Actually it's humiliating for both parties.'

This frank disclosure of family affairs surprised Lettie. It was so unlike the reticent Candace she knew – or, she told herself, thought she knew.

She took her jacket from the back of her chair. Departing, she said, 'Wouldn't he be less of a nuisance if you gave him a moderate sum from your father's estate and put an end to his opportunism? That is if you feel he has a genuine grievance.'

'It did cross my mind. The difficulty with Robin is he'd always want more. I doubt whether we'd agree on what constitutes a moderate sum.'

Lettie left, closing the door behind her, and Candace turned her attention again to the computer and brought up the figures for November. The west wing was again in profit, but only just. The fees paid covered the general upkeep of the house and gardens as well as the surgical and medical costs, but the income fluctuated and costs were rising. It was certain that the next month's figures would be disastrous. Chandler-Powell had said nothing but his face, taut with anxiety and a kind of desperate resolve, told her all. How many patients would care to occupy a room in the west wing with their minds filled with images of death and – worse – the death of a patient? The clinic, so far from being a money-spinner, was now a financial liability. She gave it less than a month.

Fifteen minutes later Lettie returned. 'He's not there. There's no sign of him in the cottage or the garden. I found his mobile on the kitchen table among the remains of what could be his lunch or supper, a plate with congealed tomato sauce and a few strands of spaghetti and a plastic packet which had held two chocolate eclairs. The mobile rang as I was unlocking the door. It was Jeremy Coxon again. I told him we were looking. The bed looked as if it hasn't been slept in and, as you said, the car's outside so he obviously hasn't driven off. He can't have gone far. He doesn't sound like someone who goes in for long country walks.'

'No, he isn't. I suppose we'd better instigate a general search, but God knows where we'll start. He could be anywhere including, I suppose, comfortably over-sleeping in someone else's bed, in which case he's hardly likely to welcome a general search. We could give it another hour or so.'

Lettie said, 'Is that wise? It looks as if he's been gone for some time.'

Candace considered. 'He's an adult and entitled to go where and with whom he chooses. But it is odd. Jeremy Coxon seemed worried as well as irritated. Perhaps we should at least ensure that he's not here in the Manor or anywhere in the grounds. I suppose it's possible that he's ill or has had an accident, although it seems unlikely. And I'd better check Stone Cottage. I'm not very conscientious about locking the side door, and he may have sneaked in after I left to see if there's anything there to find. And you're right. If he's not in the cottages or here we'd better tell the police. If there's a serious search, I suppose it will be by the local force. See if you can find Sergeant Benton-Smith or DC Warren. I'll take Sharon with me. She seems to be hanging about doing nothing most of the time.'

Lettie, still standing, thought for a moment then said, 'I don't think we need to involve Sharon. She's been in an odd mood since Commander Dalgliesh sent for her yesterday, sulky and withdrawn some of the time and looking pleased with herself, almost triumphant, at others. And if Robin really is missing, best keep her out of it. If you want to extend the search, I'll come. Frankly, if he's not here or in either cottage, I don't see where else we can look. Better pass it on to the police.'

Candace took down her jacket from the peg on the door. 'You're probably right about Sharon. She wouldn't leave the Manor and come to Stone Cottage and, frankly, it was a relief, not one of my most sensible ideas. But she agreed to help me for a couple of hours a day with Father's books, probably because she wants an excuse to get out of the kitchen. She and the Bostocks have never hit it off. She seemed to enjoy handling the books. I've lent her one or two she seemed interested in.'

Again Lettie was surprised. Lending books to Sharon was a kindness which she hadn't expected from Candace, whose attitude to the girl had been one of grudging tolerance rather than benevolent interest. But Candace was after all a teacher. Perhaps this was a resurgence of her pedagogic vocation. And it was surely a natural impulse in any lover of reading to lend a book to a young person who showed an interest in it. She would have done the same herself. Walking beside Candace, she felt a small stab of pity. They worked together amicably, as both of them did with Helena, but they had never been close and were colleagues rather than friends. But she was useful at the Manor. The three days Candace had spent visiting Toronto a couple of weeks ago had proved that. Perhaps it was because Candace and Marcus lived in Stone Cottage that they sometimes seemed emotionally as well as physically distanced from the life of the Manor. She could only imagine what the last two years had been like for an intelligent woman, her job in jeopardy, and now – so it was rumoured – no longer available, her nights and days spent ministering to a domineering and querulous old man, her brother desperate to get away. Well there should be no difficulty about that now. The clinic could hardly continue after Miss Gradwyn's murder. Only patients with a pathologically morbid fascination with death and horror would book in at the Manor now.

It was a drab and sunless morning. There had been heavy showers during the night and now from the rain-drenched earth there rose a pungent miasma of rotting leaves and sodden grass. Autumn had come early this year but already its mellow refulgence had faded into the bleak almost odourless breath of the dying year. They walked through the damp mist which struck cold on Lettie's face and brought with it the first chill touch of unease. Earlier she had entered Rose Cottage without apprehension, half expecting to find Robin Boyton returned, or at least some evidence of where he had gone. Now, as they walked between the winter-scarred rose bushes to the front door, she felt she was being inexorably drawn towards something which was none of her business, which she had no wish to get involved in and which boded ill. The front door was unlocked, as she had found it, but, entering the kitchen, it seemed to her that the air was now more rancid than the smell of unwashed plates.

Candace approached the table and regarded the debris of the meal with a moue of distaste. She said, 'Certainly it looks more like yesterday's lunch or supper than breakfast, but with Robin who can tell? You said you'd checked upstairs?'

'Yes. The bed wasn't properly made, just the bedclothes pulled together, but it didn't look as if he'd slept there last night.'

Candace said, 'I suppose we'd better check the whole cottage, and then the garden and next door. Meanwhile I'll get rid of this mess. The place stinks.'

She picked up the soiled plate and moved towards the sink. Lettie's voice seemed as sharp as a command, 'No Candace, no!' halting Candace in her tracks. She went on, 'I'm sorry, I didn't mean to shout, but hadn't we better leave things as they are? If Robin has had an accident, if something's happened to him, timing might be important.'

Candace returned to the table and replaced the plate. 'I suppose you're right, but all this tells us is that he ate a meal, probably lunch or dinner, before setting off.'

They went upstairs. There were only two bedrooms, both a good size and each with a bathroom and shower. The slightly smaller one at the back was obviously unused, the bed made up with clean sheets covered with a patchwork counterpane.

Candace opened the door of the fitted wardrobe, then closed it and said defensively, 'God knows why I thought he could be in here, but if we've come to search, we might as well be thorough.'

They moved to the front bedroom. It was simply and comfortably furnished but now looked as if it had been ransacked. A towelling dressing gown was lying on the bed with a crumpled T-shirt and a Terry Pratchett paperback. Two pairs of shoes had been flung into a corner and the low padded chair was heaped with a jumble of woollen sweaters and trousers. Boyton had at least come prepared for the worst of December weather. The wardrobe door was open to reveal three shirts, a suede jacket and a dark suit. Was the suit, Lettie wondered, brought to be worn when he was at last admitted to see Rhoda Gradwyn?

Candace said, 'This looks ominously like either a fight or a hasty departure, but taken with the state of the kitchen I think all we can safely assume is that Robin is exceptionally untidy, and that I knew already. Anyway, he isn't in the cottage.'

Lettie said, 'No, he isn't here,' and turned towards the door.

But in one sense, she thought, he was there. The half-minute in which she and Candace had surveyed the bedroom had intensified her sense of foreboding. Now it had deepened into an emotion which was a puzzling mixture of dread and pity. Robin Boyton was absent but paradoxically he seemed more fully present than he had been three days ago when he erupted into the library. He was here in the jumble of youthful clothes, in the shoes, one pair with worn-down heels, in the carelessly discarded book, the crumpled T-shirt.

They moved into the garden, Candace striding out ahead. Lettie, although usually as energetic as her companion, felt as if she were being dragged behind like a dilatory encumbrance. They searched both cottage gardens and the wooden sheds at the end of each. The one at Rose Cottage held a miscellany of dirty tools, implements, some rusty, broken flowerpots and swathes of raffia thrown together on a shelf with no attempt at organisation, while the door was partly jammed with an old lawnmower and a net sack of wood kindling. Candace closed the door without comment. In contrast the shed at Stone Cottage was a model of logical and impressive tidiness. Spades, forks and hoses, their metal gleaming, were ranged on one wall, while the shelves held flowerpots arranged in order and the lawnmower was clean of any trace of its function. There was a comfortable wicker chair with a checked cushion, obviously well used. The contrast between the state of the two sheds was reflected in the gardens. Mog was responsible for the garden at Rose Cottage but his interest was in the Manor gardens, particularly the knot garden of which he was jealously proud and which he trimmed with obsessive care. He did little more at Rose Cottage than was necessary to avoid criticism. The Stone Cottage garden showed evidence of expert and regular attention. Dead leaves had been swept up and added to the wooden box which held the compost heap, shrubs pruned, the earth dug and tender plants shrouded against frost. Remembering the wicker chair with its indented cushion, Lettie felt a surge of pity and irritation. So this hermetic shack, the air of which felt warm even in winter, was a refuge as well as a utilitarian garden shed. Here

Candace could hope to snatch an occasional half-hour of peace from the antiseptic odour of the sickroom, could escape to the garden in short periods of freedom when it would have been more difficult to find time for her other known passion, swimming from one of her favourite coves or beaches.

Candace closed the door on the smell of warm wood and earth without comment and they made their way to Stone Cottage. Although it was not yet noon, the day was gloomy and dark and Candace switched on a light. Lettie had been in Stone Cottage several times since Professor Westhall's death, always on the business of the Manor and never with pleasure. She was not superstitious. Her faith, maverick and undogmatic as she knew it to be, had no place for disembodied souls revisiting the rooms in which they had unfinished business or had last drawn breath. But she was sensitive to atmosphere and Stone Cottage still provoked in her an unease, a lowering of the spirit as if accumulated unhappiness had infected the air.

They were in the stone-paved room referred to as the old pantry. A narrow conservatory led into the garden, but the room was virtually unused and seemed to have no function except as a repository for unwanted furniture including a small wooden table and two chairs, a decrepit-looking freezer and an old dresser holding a miscellany of mugs and jugs. They passed through a small kitchen into the sitting room, which was also used for dining. The grate was empty and a clock on the otherwise bare mantelpiece ticked the present into the past with irritating insistence. The room was comfortless except for a wooden settle with cushions to the right of the fireplace. One wall was covered with bookshelves to the ceiling but most of the shelves were empty and the remaining volumes fell against each other in disorder. A dozen tightly packed cardboard boxes of books were ranged against the opposite wall where oblongs of unfaded paper showed where pictures had once hung. The whole cottage, although very clean, struck Lettie as almost deliberately cheerless and unwelcoming as if, after their father's death, Candace and Marcus had wanted to emphasise that, for them, Stone Cottage could never be a home.

Upstairs Candace, with Lettie following, moved with deliberate strides through the three bedrooms, giving a cursory glance inside the cupboards and wardrobes, then almost slamming them shut as if the search were a tedious routine chore. There was a fleeting but pungent aroma of mothballs, a tweedy country smell of old clothes, and in Candace's wardrobe Lettie glimpsed the scarlet of a doctor's gown. The front room had been her father's. Here everything had been cleared away apart from the narrow bed to the right of the window. This had been stripped bare except for a single sheet stretched taut and pristine over the mattress, the universal domestic acknowledgement of the finality of death. Neither spoke. The search was nearly over. They went downstairs, their feet sounding unnaturally loud on the uncarpeted staircase.

The sitting room had no cupboards and they passed again into the old pantry. Candace, suddenly realising for the first time what Lettie had been feeling throughout, said, 'What on earth do we think we're doing? We're acting as if searching for a child or a lost animal. Let the police take over if they're worried.'

Lettie said, 'But we're nearly through and at least we've been thorough. He's not anywhere in either cottage or in the sheds.'

Candace had moved into the large walk-in larder. Her voice was muffled. 'It's time I cleared out this place. While Father was ill I became obsessive about making marmalade. God knows why. He liked home-made preserves but not that much. I'd forgotten the jars were still here. I'll get Dean to collect them. He'll find a use for them if he condescends to take them. My marmalade is hardly up to his standard.'

She reappeared. Lettie, turning to follow her to the door, paused, then unlatched and lifted the lid of the freezer. The action was instinctive and without thought. Time stopped. For a couple of seconds, which in retrospect would stretch to minutes, she stared down at what lay below.

The lid fell out of her hands with a soft clang and she slumped over the freezer, shaking uncontrollably. Her heart was pounding and something had happened to her voice. She gasped and tried to form words, but no sound came. At last, struggling, she found a voice. It didn't sound like her voice, or anyone's she knew. She croaked, 'Candace, don't look, don't look! Don't come!'

But Candace was pushing her aside, forcing the lid wide open against the weight of Lettie's body.

He was lying curled on his back, both legs raised stiffly in the air. His feet must have been pressed against the lid of the freezer. His two hands, curved like claws, lay pale and delicate, the hands of a child. In his desperation he had beaten his hands against the lid, his knuckles were bruised and there were threads of dried blood on his fingers. His face was a mask of terror, the blue eyes wide and lifeless as a doll's, the lips drawn back. He must have bitten his tongue in the final spasm and two trickles of blood had dried on his chin. He was wearing blue jeans and a blue and fawn checked open-necked shirt. The smell, familiar and revolting, rose up like gas.

Somehow Lettie found the strength to stagger to one of the kitchen chairs and collapsed into it. And now, no longer standing, her strength began to return and her heartbeats became slower, more regular. She heard the sound of the lid being closed, but quietly, almost gently, as if Candace were afraid of waking the dead.

She looked across. Candace was standing motionless against the freezer. Then suddenly she began retching and, running to the stone sink, was violently sick, clutching the sink sides for support. The retching continued long after there was nothing to bring up, loud whooping cries which must have torn her throat. Lettie watched, wanting to help but knowing Candace wouldn't want to be touched. Now Candace turned the tap to full power and was splashing water over her face as if the skin were on fire. Streams of water ran down over her jacket and her hair lay in sodden strands against her cheeks. Without speaking she stretched out a hand and found a tea towel hanging by the sink on a nail, then wrung it out under the still flowing tap and began again to wash her face. At last Lettie felt able to get to her feet and, placing an arm round Candace's waist, led her to the second chair.

Candace said, 'I'm sorry, it's the stink. I never could stand that particular smell.'

With the horror of that lonely death still seared on her mind,

Lettie felt a sharp defensive pity. 'It isn't the smell of death, Candace. He couldn't help it. He had an accident, perhaps out of terror. It happens.'

She thought, but didn't say, *And that must mean that he went into the freezer alive. Or does it? The forensic pathologist will know.* Now that her physical strength had returned her mind felt preternaturally clear. She said, 'We must ring the police. Commander Dalgliesh gave us a number. Do you remember it?' Candace shook her head. 'Nor do I. It never occurred to me that we'd need it. He and that other policeman were always about the place. I'll fetch him.'

But now Candace, her head stretched back, her face so white that it looked as if cleansed of all emotion, all that made her uniquely herself, no more than a mask of flesh and bone, said, 'No! Don't go. I'm all right but I think we ought to stay together. My mobile's in my pocket. Use it to get someone at the Manor. Try the office first and then George. Tell him to call Dalgliesh. He mustn't come himself. None of them should. I couldn't stand a crowd, questions, curiosity, pity. We'll get all that, but not now.'

Lettie was ringing the office. There was no reply and she tried George's number. Listening and waiting for a response, she said, 'He shouldn't come here anyway. He'll know that. The cottage will be a crime scene.'

Candace's voice was sharp. 'What crime?'

There was still no reply from George's phone. Lettie said, 'It could be suicide. Isn't suicide a crime?'

'Does it look like suicide? Does it? Does it?'

Lettie, appalled, thought, *What are we arguing about?* But she said calmly, 'You're right. We know nothing. But Commander Dalgliesh won't want a crowd. We'll stay here and wait.'

And now at last the mobile was answered and Lettie heard George's voice. She said, 'I'm phoning from Stone Cottage. Candace is here with me. We've found Robin Boyton's body in the disused freezer. Could you get Commander Dalgliesh as soon as possible? Better say nothing to anyone else until he's arrived. And don't come over. Don't let anyone come.'

George's voice was sharp. 'Boyton's body? You sure that he's dead?'

'Quite sure. George, I can't explain now. Just get Dalgliesh. Yes, we're all right. Shocked but all right.'

'I'll get Dalgliesh.' And the call was ended.

Neither of them spoke. In the silence Lettie was aware only of their deeply drawn breath. They sat on the two kitchen chairs, not speaking. Time passed, endless unmeasured time. Then there were faces passing the opposite window. The police had arrived. Lettie had expected them to walk in but there was a knock on the door and, glancing at Candace's rigid face, she went to open it. Commander Dalgliesh came in followed by Inspector Miskin and Sergeant Benton-Smith. To her surprise Dalgliesh didn't immediately go to the freezer but concerned himself with the two women. Taking two mugs from the dresser he filled them at the tap and brought them over. Candace left her mug on the table but Lettie found herself desperate for water and drained hers. She was aware of Commander Dalgliesh watching them closely.

He said, 'I need to ask some questions. You've both had a terrible shock. Are you well enough to talk?'

Regarding him steadily Candace said, 'Yes, perfectly, thank you.'

Lettie murmured her consent.

'Then perhaps we had better go next door. I'll be with you in a minute.'

Inspector Miskin followed them into the sitting room. Lettie thought, *So he's not going to leave us alone until he's heard our story*, then wondered if she was being perspicacious or unreasonably suspicious. If Candace and she had wanted to concoct an agreed account of their actions there had been time enough before the police arrived.

They seated themselves on the oak settle and Inspector Miskin drew up two chairs from the table to face them. Without sitting, she said, 'Can I get you anything? Tea, coffee – if Miss Westhall will tell me where to find things.'

Candace's voice was uncompromisingly harsh. 'Nothing, thank you. All I want is to get out of here.'

'Commander Dalgliesh won't be long.'

Nor was he. Hardly had she spoken than he appeared and took one of the chairs directly opposite them. Inspector Miskin took the other. Dalgliesh's face, only feet from theirs, was as pale as Candace's but it was impossible to guess what was going on behind that carved enigmatic mask. When he spoke his voice was gentle, almost sympathetic, but Lettie had no doubt that the ideas his mind was busily processing had little to do with compassion. He asked, 'How did you both come to be in Stone Cottage this morning?'

It was Candace who replied. 'We were looking for Robin. His business partner rang the office at about nine forty to say that he hadn't been able to contact Robin since yesterday morning and was worried. Mrs Frensham came over first and found the remains of a meal on the kitchen table, his car in the driveway and his bed apparently not slept in. So we came back to make a more thorough search.'

'Did either of you know or suspect that you would find Robin Boyton in the freezer?'

He made no apology for the question, which was almost brutally explicit. Lettie hoped that Candace would keep her temper. She confined herself to a quiet 'No' and, looking into Dalgliesh's eyes, thought that she had been believed.

Candace was silent for a moment while Dalgliesh waited. 'Obviously not or we would have looked into the freezer immediately. We were looking for a living man, not a dead body. Personally I thought that Robin would turn up soon enough, but his absence was puzzling since he isn't given to country walks and I suppose we were looking for a clue to explain where he might have gone.'

'Which of you opened the freezer?'

Lettie said, 'I did. The old pantry, the room next door, was the last place we searched. Candace had gone into the walk-in larder and I lifted the freezer lid on impulse, almost without thinking. We'd looked in all the cupboards in Rose Cottage and in here and in the garden sheds and I suppose looking in the freezer seemed a natural action.'

Dalgliesh didn't speak. Lettie thought, *Is he going to point out that a search which included cupboards and a freezer was hardly a search for a living man?* But she had given her explanation. She wasn't sure that it sounded convincing even to her own ears, but it was the truth and she had nothing to add. It was Candace who attempted to explain.

'It never occurred to me that Robin might be dead and neither of us ever mentioned that possibility. I took the initiative and once we'd begun to peer in cupboards and were making a thorough search I suppose, as Lettie has said, it seemed natural to carry on. I may have had the possibility of an accident at the back of my mind but the word wasn't mentioned between us.'

Dalgliesh and Inspector Miskin got to their feet. Dalgliesh said, 'Thank you both. You need to get out of here. I won't trouble you any further for now.' He turned to Candace. 'I'm afraid for the present, and probably for some days, Stone Cottage will have to be closed.'

Candace said, 'As a crime scene?'

'As a scene of an unexplained death. Mr Chandler-Powell tells me that there are rooms for you and your brother at the Manor. I'm sorry for the inconvenience but I'm sure you'll understand the necessity. There will also be a forensic pathologist and technical officers coming here but care will be taken not to cause damage.'

Candace said, 'You can pull the place apart for all I care. I've finished with it.'

He went on as if he hadn't heard. 'Inspector Miskin will go with you to collect what you need to take to the Manor.'

Lettie thought, so they were under escort. What did he fear? That they might make a run for it? But she told herself that she was being unfair. He had been polite and courteous, scrupulously so. But then what did he gain by being otherwise?

Candace got to her feet. 'I can collect what I need. My brother can pack for himself, no doubt under supervision. I've no intention of rummaging through his room.'

Dalgliesh said calmly, 'I'll let you know when it will be possible for him to collect what he needs. Inspector Miskin will help you now.'

The three of them, led by Candace, climbed the stairs, Lettie glad of an excuse for getting away from the old pantry. In her bedroom Candace dragged a suitcase from the wardrobe, but it was Inspector Miskin who lifted it onto the bed. Candace began taking clothes from her drawers and wardrobe, folding them quickly and packing them expertly into the case: warm jumpers, trousers, shirts, underwear, nightclothes and shoes. She went into the bathroom and returned with her toilet bag. Without a backward glance they were ready to go.

Commander Dalgliesh and Sergeant Benton-Smith were in the old pantry, obviously waiting for them to leave. The lid of the freezer was closed. Candace handed over the house keys. Sergeant Benton-Smith scribbled a receipt and the cottage door was closed behind them. Lettie, listening, thought she heard the turning of the key.

Silently, with Inspector Miskin walking between them, they took deep cleansing breaths of the sweet damp morning air and in silence made their slow measured way back to the Manor.

9

As they approached the front door of the Manor, Inspector Miskin stood back and tactfully turned away as if anxious to demonstrate that they hadn't returned under police escort. It gave Candace time for a quick whisper as Lettie opened the door. 'Don't discuss what's happened. Just give them the facts.'

Lettie was tempted to say that she had no intention of doing more, but had time only to murmur, 'Of course.'

She noticed that Candace immediately put herself out of risk of discussing anything by saying that she wanted to see where she would be sleeping. Helena came forward at once and the two of them disappeared into the east wing which, with Flavia already sleeping there since the patients' corridor was barred, was likely soon to become uncomfortably crowded. Marcus, after phoning for Dalgliesh's consent, went to Stone Cottage to collect the clothes and books he needed, then joined his sister in the east wing. Everyone was quietly solicitous. No inconvenient questions were asked but as the morning dragged on the air seemed to be humming with unspoken comments, chief among them why exactly had Lettie lifted the freezer lid. Since in the end someone would surely voice it, Lettie increasingly felt that she should break her silence despite what she and Candace had agreed.

As one o'clock approached there was still no news from Commander Dalgliesh or his team. Only four of the household sat down in the dining room for lunch, Mr Chandler-Powell, Helena, Flavia and Lettie. Candace had asked that a tray for herself and Marcus should be sent up to her room. On operating days Chandler-Powell ate lunch later with his team, if he ate a formal meal at all, but at other times, as today, he joined the party in the dining room. Lettie sometimes felt uneasily that the small household should eat together, but Dean, she knew, would have considered it demeaning to his status as chef to be expected to lunch or dine with those he served. He and Kim with Sharon ate later in their own apartment.

The meal was simple, a first course of minestrone followed by a pork and duck terrine, baked potatoes and a winter salad. When Flavia, helping herself to salad, asked whether anyone knew when they could expect the police to appear, Lettie broke in with what seemed to her an unnatural nonchalance.

'They didn't say when we were at Stone Cottage. I expect they're busy examining the freezer. Perhaps they'll take it away. I can't explain why I lifted the lid. We were on our way out and it was an impulsive gesture, perhaps no more than curiosity.'

Flavia said, 'It's just as well you did. He could have been there for days while the police were searching the countryside. After all, unless they suspected they were looking for a body, why would they open the freezer? Why would anybody?'

Mr Chandler-Powell frowned but didn't comment. There was a silence broken by the entrance of Sharon to remove the soup bowls. A period of unaccustomed idleness had proved boring and she had condescended to undertake a limited number of household tasks. At the door she turned and said with, for her, unexpected brightness, 'Perhaps there's a serial murderer loose in the village picking us all off one by one. I read a book by Agatha Christie which deals with that. They were all cut off on this island and the serial killer was among them. In the end only one was left alive.'

Flavia's voice was sharp. 'Don't be ridiculous, Sharon. Miss Gradwyn's death, did that look like the work of a serial murderer? They kill to a pattern. And why should a mass murderer put a body in a freezer? But perhaps your serial killer has an obsession with freezers and is even now looking for one to accommodate his next victim.'

Sharon opened her mouth to retort, caught a glance from Chandler-Powell and thought better of it, then kicked the door closed after her. No one spoke. Lettie sensed the general feeling that, if Sharon's comment had been ill judged, Flavia's hadn't improved on it. Murder was a contaminating crime, subtly changing relationships which, even if not close, had been easy and without strain, hers with Candace and now with Flavia. It wasn't a question of active suspicion, more the spread of an atmosphere of unease, a growing awareness that other people, other minds, were unknowable. But she felt a concern for Flavia. With her sitting room in the west wing barred to her she had taken to walking alone in the garden or down the lime walk to the stones, returning with eyes more red and swollen than could be caused by a keen wind or sudden shower. Perhaps, thought Lettie, it wasn't surprising that Flavia seemed more affected by Miss Gradwyn's death than were the others. She and Chandler-Powell had lost a patient. For both of them it was a professional disaster. And then there were the rumours about the relationship with George. When they were together at the Manor it was always one of surgeon and theatre sister, sometimes seeming almost unnecessarily professional. Certainly if they had been sleeping together at the Manor someone would have known. But Lettie wondered if Flavia's changing moods, the new waspishness, the solitary walks had a cause other than the death of a patient.

As the day wore on it became apparent to Lettie that this death was creating more covert interest than either fear or anxiety. Robin Boyton was hardly known except to his cousins, and not particularly liked by those who did know him. And at least he had had the decency to die outside the Manor. None would have expressed the thought with such callous insensitivity, but the hundred yards or so between the house and Stone Cottage was a psychological as well as a physical separation from a corpse imagined but by the majority not witnessed. They felt more like onlookers than participants in a drama, isolated from the action, beginning indeed to feel unreasonably excluded by Dalgliesh and his team, who asked for information and gave so little in return. Mog, who by virtue of his job in the garden and throughout the grounds had an excuse to loiter at the gate, had fed them nuggets of information.

He reported on the return of the scene-of-crime officers, the arrival of the photographer and Dr Glenister, and finally the lumpy body bag being stretchered down the cottage path to the sinister mortuary van. With that news the company at the Manor braced themselves for the return of Dalgliesh and his team.

10

Dalgliesh, who was occupied at Stone Cottage, left the initial questioning to Kate and Benton. It was three thirty before they arrived to begin their enquiries and, again with the consent of Mr Chandler-Powell, used the library for the majority of their interviews. For the first few hours the results were disappointing. Dr Glenister couldn't be expected to give a precise assessment of the time of death until after the post mortem, but given the accuracy of her preliminary estimations they could work on the assumption that Boyton had died the previous day sometime between two o'clock and six. The fact that he hadn't had time to wash his plates after a meal that was clearly more likely to be lunch than breakfast was less helpful than it seemed since there were in the sink unwashed crockery and two saucepans which looked as if they had been there from the night before.

Kate decided to ask people where they were the previous day from one o'clock until dinner, which was served at eight. Nearly everyone could provide an alibi for part of the time, but none for the whole seven hours. The afternoon was a time when people were generally free to follow their own interests or inclinations, and most had been alone for some of the time, either in the Manor or in the garden. Marcus Westhall had driven into Bournemouth to do some Christmas shopping, leaving shortly after lunch, and had not returned until seven thirty. Kate sensed that the rest of the household thought that it was a little odd that, whenever there was a dead body to be explained, Marcus Westhall had the good fortune to be absent. His sister had worked with Lettie in the office in the morning and after lunch had returned to Stone Cottage to garden. She had been sweeping leaves, building up the compost heap and cutting away the dead branches of the bushes until the light began to fail. She had then returned to the cottage to make tea, entering by the door into the conservatory, which she had left open. She had seen Boyton's car parked outside but had seen and heard nothing of him the whole afternoon.

George Chandler-Powell, Flavia and Helena had occupied themselves in the Manor, either in their own apartments or in the office, but were only able to provide firm alibis for the time when, with the others, they were eating lunch, having afternoon tea in the library and dinner at eight o'clock. Kate sensed their resentment, shared by the others, at having to be so specific about time. It had, after all, been for them an ordinary day. Mog claimed that he had been busy for most of the previous afternoon in the rose garden and planting tulip bulbs in the large urns in the formal gardens. No one remembered seeing him, but he was able to produce a bucket with a few bulbs waiting to be planted and the torn packets which had contained the others. Neither Kate nor Benton felt inclined to entertain him by digging into the urns to see if the bulbs were there, but no doubt this could be done if it proved expedient.

Sharon had been persuaded to spend some time in the afternoon dusting and polishing furniture and vacuum-cleaning the rugs in the great hall, entrance hall and library. Certainly the noise of the vacuum had from time to time been an irritant to others in the Manor, but no one could be specific when exactly it was heard. Benton pointed out that it was possible for a vacuum to be left on without anyone using it, a suggestion which Kate found difficult to take seriously. Sharon had also spent time in the kitchen helping Dean and Kimberley. She gave her evidence willingly enough but took an unconscionable time before answering questions and stared throughout at Kate with a speculative interest and a hint of pity which Kate found more disconcerting than the expected undisguised hostility.

Altogether by late afternoon they felt that little had so far been achieved. It was perfectly possible for any of the residents of the Manor, including Marcus on his way to Bournemouth, to have called at Stone Cottage, but how could anyone other than a Westhall have enticed Robin into the cottage, managed to kill him and returned undetected to the Manor avoiding the security guards? Obviously the prime suspect had to be Candace Westhall, who certainly had the strength to shove Boyton into the freezer, but it was premature to decide on a prime suspect when at present they had no convincing evidence that the death had been murder.

It was nearly five o'clock before they got round to seeing the Bostocks. The interview took place in the kitchen where Kate and Benton were comfortably ensconced in low chairs beside the window while the Bostocks drew up a couple of upright chairs from the table. Before seating themselves they made tea for the four of them and set up with some ceremony a low table in front of the visitors, inviting them to sample Kim's biscuits, newly baked and hot from the Aga. An irresistible smell, rich and spicy, wafted from the open oven door. The biscuits, almost too hot to handle, thin and crisp, were delicious. Kim, with the face of a happy child, smiled on them as they ate and pressed them not to hold back – there were plenty more. Dean poured the tea; the atmosphere became domestic, almost cosy. Outside the rain-saturated air pressed against the windows like a fog and the deepening darkness obscured all but the geometry of the knot garden while the high beech hedge became a distant blur. Inside all was light, colour and warmth, and the comforting aroma of tea and food.

The Bostocks were able to provide an alibi for each other, having spent almost all the previous twenty-four hours together, mostly in the kitchen or when, taking advantage of Mog's temporary absence, they had together visited the kitchen garden to select vegetables for dinner. Mog tended to resent every gap in his carefully planted rows. Kim on her return had served the main meals and later cleared the table, but usually there had been someone present, Miss Cressett or Mrs Frensham.

Both Bostocks looked shocked but less distressed or frightened than Kate and Benton had expected, partly, Kate thought, because Boyton had been only an occasional visitor for whom they had no responsibility and whose rare appearances, so far from adding to the gaiety of the community, were regarded, particularly by Dean, as a potential source of irritation and extra work. Boyton had made his mark – a young man with his looks could hardly fail – but Kimberley, happily in love with her husband, was impervious to classic handsomeness and Dean, uxorious, was largely concerned to guard his kitchen against unwarranted intrusions. Neither seemed particularly frightened, perhaps because it became apparent that they had managed to convince themselves that Boyton's death had been an accident.

Conscious of their own uninvolvement, interested, a little excited and ungrieving, they chatted on and Kate let the talk flow. The Bostocks, like the rest of the household, had been told only that Boyton's body had been found, and where. What else at present was there to tell? And there had been no point in leaving anyone in ignorance. It might with luck be possible to keep this present death out of the press, and for a while from the village if Mog held his tongue, but it was hardly feasible or necessary to keep it from anyone at the Manor.

It was nearly six o'clock when the breakthrough came. Kim roused herself from a minute's silent reverie and said, 'Poor man. He must have climbed into the freezer and then the lid fell down on him. Why would he do that? Perhaps he was playing a silly game, a sort of private dare like kids do. My mum had a big wicker basket at home, more like a trunk really, and we kids used to hide in it. But why didn't he push up the lid?'

Dean was already clearing the table. He said, 'He couldn't, not if the catch fell down. But he's not a kid. Daft thing to do. Not a nice way to go, suffocation. Or maybe he had a heart attack.' Looking at Kim's face, creasing in distress, he added firmly, 'That's probably what it was, a heart attack. He got into the freezer out of curiosity, panicked when he couldn't open the lid and died. Nice and quick. He wouldn't have felt a thing.'

Kate said, 'That's possible. We'll know more after the autopsy. Had he ever complained to you about his heart, said he had to be careful, anything like that?'

Dean looked at Kim, who shook her head. 'Not to us. Well, he wouldn't, would he? He wasn't here often and we didn't usually see him. The Westhalls may know. They're cousins and his story was that he came here to see them. Mrs Frensham makes him pay something but Mog says he doesn't think it's the full visitors' rent. He says Mr Boyton was just after a cheap holiday.'

Kim said, 'I don't think Miss Candace would know anything about his health. Mr Marcus might, being a doctor, but I don't think they were close. I've heard Miss Candace say to Mrs Frensham that Robin Boyton never bothered to tell them when he was renting the cottage, and if you ask me they weren't all that pleased to see him. Mog says that there was some kind of family feud but he doesn't know what about.'

Kate said, 'This time, of course, Mr Boyton said he was here to see Miss Gradwyn.'

'But he didn't see her did he? Not this time or when she was here a couple of weeks ago. Mr Chandler-Powell and Sister Holland saw to that. I don't believe they were friends, Mr Boyton and Miss Gradwyn. That was probably him trying to make himself look important. But it's odd about the freezer. It isn't even in his cottage but he seemed sort of fascinated with it. Do you remember, Dean, all those questions he asked when he was last here and came to borrow some butter? He never paid it back.'

Concealing her interest and taking care to avoid Benton's eyes, Kate said, 'When was that?'

Dean glanced at his wife. 'The night Miss Gradwyn first arrived. Tuesday the twenty-seventh, wasn't it? Guests are expected to bring their own food and then they either shop locally or eat out. I always leave milk in the fridge, and tea, coffee and sugar, but that's all unless they order provisions in advance and then Mog shops for them. Mr Boyton rang to say that he had forgotten to bring butter and could I let him have a packet. He said he'd come over for it but I wasn't keen to have him poking about the kitchen so I said I'd take it. It was six thirty and the cottage looked as if he'd just arrived. His gear was dumped on the kitchen floor. He asked if Miss Gradwyn had arrived and when could he see her, but I said I couldn't discuss anything to do with a patient and he'd better speak to Sister or Mr Chandler-Powell. And then, casual like, he began asking about the freezer – how long had it been next door, was it still working, did Miss Westhall use it? I told him that it was old and useless and no one used it. I said Miss Westhall had asked Mog to get rid of it but he said it wasn't his job. It was for the council to take it away and Miss Cressett or Miss Westhall had better ring them. I don't think anyone did. Then he stopped asking questions. He offered me a beer but I didn't want to drink with him – I haven't the time anyway – so I left and came back to the Manor.'

Kate said, 'But the freezer was next door in Stone Cottage. How did he know about it? It must have been dark by the time he arrived.'

'I suppose he'd seen it on a previous visit. He must have been in Stone Cottage at some time, at least after the old man died. He used to make a lot of the Westhalls being cousins. Or he could have snooped round when Miss Westhall wasn't there. People round here don't bother much about locking their doors.'

Kim said, 'And there's a door from the old pantry through the lean-to conservatory to the garden. That could have been open. Or he could have seen the freezer from the window. Funny though, him taking an interest like that. It's only an old freezer. It isn't even working. It broke in August. D'you remember, Dean? You wanted to use it to store that haunch of venison over the bank holiday and you found it wasn't working.'

At last something had been achieved. Benton glanced quickly at Kate. Her face was expressionless but he knew that their thoughts marched in step. She asked, 'When was it last used as a freezer?'

Dean said, 'I can't remember. No one ever reported that it wasn't working. We didn't need it except for bank holidays and when Mr Chandler-Powell had guests, when it could come in useful. The freezer here is usually plenty big enough.'

Kate and Benton were rising to go. Kate said, 'Have you told anyone here about Mr Boyton's interest in the freezer?' The Bostocks looked at each other, then vigorously shook their heads. 'Then please keep this strictly to yourselves. Don't discuss the freezer with anyone at the Manor.'

Kimberley, wide eyed, asked, 'Is it important?'

'Probably not but we don't yet know what is or could be important. That's why I want you to say nothing.'

Kim said, 'We won't. Cross my heart and hope to die. Anyway, Mr Chandler-Powell doesn't like us to gossip and we never do.'

Kate and Benton had hardly got to their feet and were thanking Dean and Kimberley for the tea and biscuits when Kate's mobile rang. She listened, acknowledged the call, and said nothing until they were outside. Then she said, 'That was AD. We're to go at once to the Old Police Cottage. Candace Westhall wants to make a statement. She'll be there in fifteen minutes. It looks as if we may be getting somewhere at last.'

11

They reached the Old Police Cottage just before Candace left the gates of the Manor and from the window Kate could see her stalwart figure pausing to look both ways at the edge of the road, then walking confidently across, the strong shoulders swinging. Dalgliesh greeted her at the door and led her to a seat at the table and, with Kate, sat opposite. Benton took the fourth chair and, notebook in hand, positioned himself to the right of the door. In her country tweeds and brogues Candace, he thought, had the assurance of a rural vicar's wife visiting a backsliding parishioner. But from his seat he could glimpse the only sign of nervousness, a momentary tightening of the hands clasped in her lap. Whatever she had come to tell them she had taken her time over it, but he had no doubt that she knew precisely what she was prepared to say and how she would phrase it. Without waiting for Dalgliesh to speak, she began her story.

'I have an explanation for what could have happened, what seems to me possible, even probable. It doesn't reflect well on me but I think you should know of it even if you decide to discount it as fantasy. Robin could have been experimenting with or rehearsing some ludicrous joke and it went disastrously wrong. I need to explain, but it will involve disclosing family affairs which can't in themselves be relevant to Rhoda Gradwyn's murder. I take it that what I tell you will be treated as confidential if you're satisfied that it has no direct bearing on her death.'

Dalgliesh's words were unemphatic, a statement not a warning, but they were direct. 'It will be for me to decide what is relevant and how far family secrets can be protected. I can't give any assurances in advance, you must know that.'

'So in this, as in other matters, we have to trust the police. Forgive me, but that doesn't come easily in an age when newsworthy information is money.'

Dalgliesh said quietly, 'My officers do not sell information to newspapers. Miss Westhall, aren't we wasting time? You have a responsibility to assist my investigation by disclosing any information you have which could be relevant. We have no wish to cause unnecessary distress and have enough problems in processing relevant information without wasting time on matters that are not relevant. If you know how Robin Boyton's body got into the freezer, or have any information which could help to answer that question, hadn't we better get on with it?'

If the rebuke stung her she betrayed no sign of it. She said, 'Some of it may already be known to you if Robin has spoken to you about his relationship with the family.'

As Dalgliesh didn't reply, she went on. 'He is, as he's fond of proclaiming, Marcus's and my first cousin. His mother, Sophie, was our father's only sister. For at least the past two generations the Westhall men have undervalued and occasionally despised their daughters. The birth of a son was a cause for celebration, the birth of a daughter a misfortune. This prejudice isn't totally uncommon even today, but with my father and grandfather it amounted almost to a family obsession. I'm not saying there was any physical neglect or cruelty. There wasn't. But I've no doubt Robin's mother suffered emotional neglect and acquired a weight of inferiority and self-distrust. She wasn't clever or pretty, or indeed particularly likable, and was, not unnaturally, something of a problem from childhood. She left home as soon as she could and had some satisfaction in disobliging her parents by living a fairly rackety life in the hectic world on the fringes of the pop-music scene. She was just twenty-one when she married Keith Boyton and she could hardly have made a worse choice. I only met him once but I found him repellent. She was pregnant when they married but that was hardly an excuse and I'm surprised she went ahead with the pregnancy. Motherhood was a new sensation, I suppose. Keith had a certain superficial charm but I have never met anyone more obviously on the make. He was a designer, or claimed to be, and found work occasionally. In between he did odd jobs to bring in some income, at one time, I believe, selling double glazing by telephone. Nothing lasted. My aunt, who worked as a secretary, was the main wage-earner. Somehow the marriage lasted, largely because he depended on her. Maybe she loved him. Anyway, according to Robin, she died of cancer when he was seven and Keith found himself another woman and emigrated to Australia. No one has heard from him since.'

Dalgliesh asked, 'When did Robin Boyton make regular contact with you?'

'When Marcus took the job here with Chandler-Powell, and when we moved Father into Stone Cottage. He started having brief holidays here in the guest cottage, obviously hoping that he could kindle some cousinly interest in Marcus or myself. Frankly, it wasn't there. But I did have a slight conscience about him. I still have. From time to time I'd help him out with small sums, two-fifty here, five hundred there, when he asked, claiming desperation. But then I decided that this was unwise. It seemed too like assuming a responsibility which frankly I didn't accept. And then, about a month ago, he got an extraordinary idea into his head. My father's death followed my grandfather's by only thirty-five days. If it had been less than twenty-eight days there would have been a difficulty about the will, which has a clause stating that a beneficiary must outlive the testator by twenty-eight days to inherit. Obviously if my father hadn't benefited from our grandfather's will there would have been no fortune to pass down to us. Robin obtained a copy of Grandfather's will and conceived the bizarre idea that our father had died some time before the twenty-eight days were up and that Marcus and I together – or one or other of us – had concealed his body in the freezer in Stone Cottage, thawed him out after a couple of weeks or so and then called in old Dr Stenhouse to write the death certificate. The freezer finally broke down last summer but at that time, although seldom used, it was working.'

Dalgliesh said, 'When did he first put forward this idea to you?'

'During the three days when Rhoda Gradwyn was here for her preliminary visit. He arrived the morning after she did and I think had some idea of seeing her, but she was adamant that she didn't want visitors and as far as I know he was never admitted to the Manor. She may have been behind the whole idea. I've no doubt the two were in collusion – in fact he more or less admitted it. Why otherwise did Gradwyn choose the Manor, and why was it so important for Robin to be here with her? The scheme may have been mischief on her part, she could hardly have taken it seriously, but with him it was deadly serious.'

'How did he raise the matter with you?'

'By giving me an old paperback. Cyril Hare's *Untimely Death*. It's a detective story in which the time of death is falsified. He brought it in to me as soon as he arrived, saying he thought I would find it interesting. Actually I'd read it many years ago and as far as I know it's now out of print. I simply told Robin that I wasn't interested in reading it again and handed it back. I knew then what he was up to.'

Dalgliesh said, 'But surely the idea was fantastic, appropriate to an ingenious novel but not to the situation here. Can he possibly have believed there was truth in it?'

'Oh he believed all right. In fact, there were a number of circumstances which could be said to add credibility to the fantasy. The idea wasn't as ridiculous as it sounds. I don't think we could have kept the deception going for long, but for a few days or a week, maybe two, it would have been perfectly possible. My father was an extremely difficult patient who hated illness, resisted sympathy and was adamant that he wanted no visitors. I looked after him with the help of a retired nurse, who is now living in Canada, and an elderly maid who died just over a year ago. The day after Robin left I had a phone call from Dr Stenhouse, the GP who looked after my father. Robin had visited him with some specious excuse and tried to find out how long my father had been dead before the doctor was called in. The doctor was never a patient man and in retirement even less tolerant of fools than he was when in practice, and I can well imagine the response

Robin got for his impertinence. Dr Stenhouse said that he answered no questions about patients when they were alive, nor did he when they were dead. I imagine Robin came away convinced that the old doctor, if not senile when he signed the death certificate, had been either duped or was complicit. He probably assumed that we'd bribed the two helpers, Grace Holmes, the elderly nurse who emigrated to Canada, and the maid, Elizabeth Barnes, who's since died.

'There was, however, one fact he didn't know. On the night before he died my father asked to see the parish priest, the Reverend Clement Matheson – he's still the parish priest in the village. Of course he came at once, driven by his elder sister Marjorie who keeps house for him and can be said to personify the church militant. Neither will have forgotten that evening. Father Clement arrived equipped to give the last rites and no doubt to solace a penitent soul. Instead my father found the strength to inveigh for the last time against all religious belief, Christianity in particular, with scathing reference to Father Clement's own brand of churchmanship. This wasn't information that Robin could pick up in the bar of the Cressett Arms. I doubt whether Father Clement or Marjorie have ever spoken of it except to Marcus and myself. It had been an unpleasant and humiliating experience. Happily, both are still alive. But I have a second witness. I paid a short visit to Toronto ten days ago to see Grace Holmes. She was one of the very few people my father would tolerate but was left nothing in his will and, now that probate has been granted, I wanted to give her a lump sum to compensate for that last terrible year. She gave me a letter which I have passed to my solicitor stating that she was with my father on the day he died.'

Kate said quietly, 'Armed with this information, didn't you immediately confront Robin Boyton and disillusion him?'

'Probably I should have done, but it amused me to keep quiet and let him embroil himself further. If I look at my conduct with as much honesty as is possible when we are trying to justify ourselves, I think I was glad that he had revealed something of his true nature. I'd always felt some guilt that his mother had been so neglected. But now I didn't feel any necessity to pay him anything. By this one attempt at blackmail he had relieved me from any future obligation. I rather looked forward to my moment of triumph, however petty, and to his disappointment.'

Dalgliesh asked, 'Did he ever demand money?'

'No, he didn't get to that point. If he had I could have reported him to the police for attempted blackmail, but I doubt I should have gone down that road. But he hinted pretty clearly what he had in mind. He seemed content when I said I would consult my brother and be in touch. I made, of course, no admission.'

Kate asked, 'Does your brother know anything of this?'

'Nothing. He's been particularly anxious recently about leaving the job here and going to work in Africa and I saw no reason to burden him with what was essentially nonsense. And, of course, he would have had no sympathy with my plan to bide my time and devise the maximum humiliation for Robin. His is a more admirable character than is mine. I think that Robin was working himself up to a final accusation, possibly a suggestion that I should hand over a specific sum in exchange for his silence. I believe that's why he stayed on here after Rhoda Gradwyn's death. After all, I take it that you couldn't legally detain him unless he was charged, and most people would be only too glad to get away from the scene of crime. Since her death, he's prowled around Rose Cottage and the village, obviously unsettled and, I think, frightened. But he needed to bring the matter to a head. I don't know why he climbed into the freezer. It could have been to see how feasible it was for my father's body to be placed there. He was, after all, considerably taller than Robin, even when shrunken by his illness. Robin might have had an idea of summoning me to the utility room and then slowly opening the freezer, terrifying me into an admission. That's exactly the kind of dramatic gesture that might appeal.'

Kate said, 'If he was frightened, could it be because he feared you personally? It might have occurred to him that you could have killed Miss Gradwyn because of her involvement in the plot and that he, too, might be at risk.'

Candace Westhall turned her eyes to Kate. And now the dislike and contempt were unmistakable. 'I don't suppose that even Robin Boyton's fevered imagination could seriously conceive that I would see murder as a rational way out of any dilemma. Still, I suppose it's possible. And now, if you haven't any more questions, I would like to get back to the Manor.'

Dalgliesh said, 'Only two. Did you put Robin Boyton into the freezer dead or alive?'

'I did not.'

'Did you kill Robin Boyton?'

'No.'

She hesitated, and for a moment Dalgliesh thought she had something to add. But she got up without speaking and left without another word or a backward glance.

12

By eight o'clock that evening Dalgliesh had showered, changed and was beginning to decide on his supper when he heard the car. It came up the lane almost silently. The first he knew of it was the lightening of the windows behind the drawn curtains. Opening the front door, he saw a Jaguar being driven onto the opposite verge and the lights switched off. A few seconds later Emma was crossing the road towards him. She was wearing a thick jersey and a sheepskin jerkin, her head bare. As she came in without speaking, instinctively he put his arms round her but her body was unyielding. She seemed almost unaware of his presence and the cheek which momentarily brushed his was icy cold. He was full of dread. Something appalling had happened, an accident, even a tragedy. She wouldn't otherwise have arrived like this without a warning. When he was on a case Emma never even telephoned, not by his wishes but her own. Never before had she impinged on an investigation. To do so in person could only mean disaster.

He took off her jerkin and led her to a seat by the fire, waiting for her to speak. As she sat silently he went into the kitchen and switched on the electricity under the flask of coffee. It was already hot and it took only a few seconds to pour it into a mug, add the milk and bring it to her. Taking off her gloves, she wrapped her fingers round its warmth.

She said, 'I'm sorry I didn't phone. I had to come. I had to see you.'

'Darling, what is it?'

'Annie. She's been attacked and raped. Yesterday evening. She was on her way home from teaching English to two immigrants.

It's one of the things she does. She's in hospital and they think she'll recover. By that I suppose they mean she won't die. I don't see how she can recover, not completely. She's lost a lot of blood and one of the knife wounds pierced a lung. It only just missed her heart. Someone at the hospital said she was lucky. Lucky! What an odd word to use.'

He had nearly asked *How is Clara?*, but before the words were framed he knew that the question was as ridiculous as it was insensitive. And now she looked at him full in the face for the first time. Her eyes were full of pain. She was in a torment of anger and grief.

'I couldn't help Clara. I was useless to her. I took her in my arms but mine weren't the arms she wanted. There was only one thing she wanted from me – to get you to take over the case. That's why I'm here. She trusts you. She can talk to you. And she knows you're the best.'

Of course that was why she was here. She didn't come for his comfort or out of need to see him and share her grief. She wanted something from him, and it was something he couldn't give. He sat down opposite her and said gently, 'Emma, that isn't possible.'

She put her coffee mug on the hearth and he could see her hands were shaking. He wanted to reach out and take them but was afraid that she would withdraw. Anything would be better than that.

She said, 'I thought that was what you'd say. I tried to explain to Clara that it might be outside the rules, but she doesn't understand, not fully. I'm not sure I do. She knows that the victim here, the dead woman, is more important than Annie. That's what your special squad is all about, isn't it, solving crimes when people are important. But Annie is important to her. To her and to Annie rape is more awful than death. If you were investigating she'd know that the man who did this would be caught.'

He said, 'Emma, the Squad isn't primarily to do with the importance of the victim. To the police, murder is murder, unique, never put permanently on one side, the investigation never recorded as failure, only as at present unsolved. No murder victim is ever unimportant. No suspect, however powerful, can buy immunity from the enquiry. But there are cases which are best tackled by a small designated team, cases where it's in the interest of justice to get a quick result.'

'Clara doesn't believe in justice, not now. She thinks you could take over if you wanted to, that if you asked you would get your own way, rules or no rules.'

It felt wrong to be sitting so far distanced. He longed to take her in his arms but that would be too easy a comfort – almost, he felt, an insult to her grief. And what if she drew away, if she made it obvious by a shudder of distaste that he wasn't a comfort but a contribution to her anguish? What did he represent to her now? Death, rape, mutilation and decay? Hadn't his job been ring-fenced with an invisible sign, *Keep out*? And this wasn't a problem that could be solved with kisses and murmured reassurance, not for them. It couldn't even be solved by rational discussion, but this was their only way. Hadn't he prided himself, he thought bitterly, that they could always talk. But not now, not about everything.

He asked, 'Who is the chief investigating officer? Have you spoken to him?'

'He's Detective Inspector A. L. Howard. I've got a card some-where. He's spoken to Clara, of course, and he saw Annie in hospital. He said a woman DS needed to ask some questions before Annie went under the anaesthetic, I suppose in case she died. She was too weak to say more than a few words but appar-ently they were important.'

He said, 'Andy Howard is a good detective with a sound team. This isn't a case which can be solved by anything but conscientious police work, much of it laborious plodding routine. But they'll get there.'

'Clara didn't find him sympathetic, not really. I suppose it was because he wasn't you. And the woman sergeant – Clara almost hit her. She asked whether Annie had recently had sex with a man before she was raped.'

'Emma, that was a question she had to ask. It could mean that they may have DNA, and if they have, that's a huge advantage. But I can't take over another officer's investigation – apart from the fact that I'm in the middle of one myself – and it wouldn't help solve the rape even if I could. At this stage it could even hinder it. I'm sorry I can't go back with you to try to explain to Clara.'

She said sadly, 'Oh, I expect she'll understand eventually. All she wants now is someone she can trust, not strangers. I suppose I did know what you'd say, and I should have been able to explain it to her myself. I'm sorry I came. It was a wrong decision.'

She had got to her feet and, rising, he came towards her. He said, 'I can't be sorry for any decision you make which brings you to me.'

And now she was in his arms and shaking with the force of her weeping. The face that was pressed against his was wet with tears. He held her without speaking until she relaxed, then said, 'My darling, must you go back tonight? It's a long drive. I can sleep perfectly well in this chair.'

As he had once before, he remembered, at St Anselm's College after they had first met. She had been staying next door, but after the murder he had settled himself in an armchair in his sitting room so that she could feel safe in his bed while she tried to sleep. He wondered if she too was remembering.

She said, 'I'll drive carefully. We're getting married in five months. I'm not going to risk killing myself before then.'

'Whose is the Jaguar?'

'Giles's. He's in London attending a conference for a week and he rang to make contact. He's getting married and I expect he wanted to tell me about it. When he heard about Annie and that I was driving here he lent me his car. Clara needs hers to visit Annie and mine is in Cambridge.'

Dalgliesh was shaken by the sudden spurt of jealousy, as powerful as it was unwelcome. She had finished with Giles before they had met. He had proposed and been rejected. That was all he knew. He had never felt threatened by anything in her past, nor had she in his. So why this sudden primitive response to what after all had been a thoughtful and generous gesture? He didn't want to think of Giles as either of these things, and the man now had his Chair at some northern university, safely out of the way. So why the hell couldn't he stay there? He found himself thinking bitterly that Emma might point out that she was comfortable driving a Jag; after all, it wouldn't be for the first time. She drove his.

Mastering himself, he said, 'There's some soup and some ham, so I'll make us sandwiches. Stay by the fire and I'll bring it in.'

And even now, in the depth of distress, weary and heavy eyed, she was beautiful. That the thought in its egotism, its stirring of sex, should come so quickly to mind appalled him. She had come to him for comfort, and the only comfort she craved he couldn't give. And wasn't this onrush of anger and frustration at his powerlessness only the atavistic male arrogance which said that the world is a dangerous and cruel place but now you have my love and I can shield you? Wasn't his reticence about his job less a response to her own reluctance to be involved than a wish to shield her from the worst realities of a violent world? But even her world, academic and seeming so cloistered, had its brutalities. The hallowed peace of Trinity Great Court was an illusion. He thought, *We are violently propelled into the world with blood and pain and few of us will die with the dignity for which we hope and for which some pray. Whether we choose to think of life as an impending happiness broken only by inevitable grief and disappointments, or as the proverbial vale of tears with brief interludes of joy, the pain will come, except to those few whose deadened sensibilities make them apparently impervious to either joy or sorrow.*

They ate together almost in silence. The ham was tender and he heaped it generously on the bread. He drank the soup almost without tasting it, only vaguely knowing that it was good. She did manage to eat and within twenty minutes was ready to leave.

Helping her on with the jerkin, he said, 'You will phone me when you get back to Putney? I won't be a nuisance but I do need to know you got home safely. And I'll have a word with DI Howard.'

She said, 'I'll ring.'

He kissed her on the cheek almost formally and went across to see her into the car, then stood watching until it disappeared down the lane.

Returning to the fireplace, he stood looking down at the flames. Ought he to have insisted on her staying the night? But insist wasn't a word that would ever be used between them. And stay where? There was his bedroom, but would she want to sleep there, distanced by the complicated emotions and unexpressed inhibitions which kept them apart when he was on a case? Would she wish to confront Kate and Benton tomorrow morning if not tonight? But he was worried about her safety. She was a good driver and would rest if she became tired, but the thought of her in a lay-by, even with the precaution of a locked car, gave him no comfort.

He stirred himself. There were things to do before he summoned Kate and Benton. Firstly, he must get in touch with Detective Inspector Andy Howard and get the latest report. Howard was an experienced and reasonable officer. He wouldn't see the call either as an unwelcome distraction or, worse, as an attempt to influence. Then he must phone or write to Clara with a message for Annie. But to telephone was almost as inappropriate as to fax or e-mail. Some things had to be conveyed by a handwritten letter and by words which cost something in time and careful thought, indelible phrases which might have some hope of giving comfort. But there was only one thing Clara wanted from him and that he couldn't give. To phone now, for her to hear the bad news from him, would be intolerable for them both. The letter had better wait until tomorrow and in the meantime Emma would be back with Clara.

It took some time to reach DI Andy Howard. Howard said, 'Annie Townsend is doing well but it will be a long road, poor girl. I met Dr Lavenham at the hospital and she told me you had an interest in the case. I meant to get in touch earlier to have a word.'

Dalgliesh said, 'Speaking to me had to have a low priority. It still has. I won't keep you now, but I was anxious to have a more up-to-date report than Emma could give me.'

'Well, there is good news, if anything about this can be good. We've got his DNA. With luck he'll be on the database. I can't believe that he hasn't got form. It was a violent attack but the rape wasn't completed. Probably too drunk. She fought back with extraordinary courage for so slight a woman. I'll ring you as soon as I have anything to report. And, of course, we're keeping closely in touch with Miss Beckwith. He's most probably local. He certainly knew where to drag her. We've already started a house-to-house. The sooner the better, DNA or no DNA. Things going well with you, sir?'

'Not particularly. No clear line at present.' He didn't mention the new death.

Howard said, 'Well, it's early days, sir.'

Dalgliesh agreed that it was early days, and after thanking Howard, rang off.

He carried the plates and mugs into the kitchen, washed and dried them, then rang Kate. 'Have you had a meal?'

'Yes, sir, we've just finished.'

'Then come over now, please.'

13

By the time Kate and Benton arrived the three glasses were on the table, the wine uncorked, but for Dalgliesh it was a less successful, at times almost acrimonious meeting. He said nothing about the visit of Emma but he wondered whether his subordinates were aware of it. They must have heard the Jaguar passing Wisteria House and been curious about any car arriving at night on the road to the Manor, but neither of them spoke of it.

The discussion was probably unsatisfactory because, with Boyton's death, they were in danger of theorising in advance of the facts. There was little new to be said about Miss Gradwyn's murder. The post-mortem report had been received with Dr Glenister's expected conclusion that the cause of death was throttling by a right-handed killer wearing smooth gloves. This last was hardly necessary information in view of the fragment in the WC in one of the empty suites. She confirmed her final assessment of the time of death. Miss Gradwyn had been killed between eleven o'clock and twelve thirty.

Kate had had a tactful word with the Reverend Matheson and his sister. Both had found strange her questions about the vicar's one and only visit to Professor Westhall but confirmed that they had indeed visited Stone Cottage and that the priest had seen the patient. Benton had telephoned Dr Stenhouse who confirmed that Boyton had questioned him about the time of death, an impertinence to which he had given no response. The date on the death certificate had been correct, as had his diagnosis. He had shown no curiosity about why the questions were being put so long after the event, probably, Benton thought, because Candace Westhall had been in touch with him.

Members of the security team had been co-operative but not helpful. Their leader had pointed out that they were concentrating on strangers, particularly members of the press arriving at the Manor, not on individuals with a right to be there. Only one of the four men had been in the caravan outside the gates at the relevant time and he couldn't remember seeing any member of the household leave the Manor. The other three members of the team had concentrated on patrolling the boundary separating the Manor grounds from the stones and the field in which they stood in case this offered a convenient access. Dalgliesh made no attempt to press them. They were, after all, responsible to Chandler-Powell who was paying them, not to him.

For most of the evening Dalgliesh let Kate and Benton take over the discussion.

Benton said, 'Miss Westhall says she told no one about Boyton's suspicions that they faked the date of her father's death. It seems unlikely that she would. But Boyton himself may have confided in someone, either at the Manor or in London. And if so, that person might use the knowledge to kill him and then tell much the same story as Miss Westhall.'

Kate's voice was dismissive. 'I can't see an outsider killing Boyton, Londoner or not. At least not in this way. Think of the practicalities. He'd have to arrange a rendezvous with his victim in Stone Cottage when he could be sure that the Westhalls weren't there and the door would be open. And what reason could he give for enticing Boyton into a neighbour's cottage? And why kill him here anyway? London would be simpler and safer. The same complications would apply to anyone at the Manor. Anyway, there's no point in theorising until we get the autopsy report. On the face of it misadventure seems a more likely explanation than murder, particularly in view of the Bostocks' evidence about Boyton's fascination with the freezer, which gives some credence to Miss Westhall's explanation – provided, of course, that they're not lying.'

Benton broke in. 'But you were there, ma'am. I'm sure they weren't lying. I don't think Kim in particular has the wit to make up a story like that and tell it so convincingly. I was absolutely convinced.'

'So at the time was I, but we have to keep an open mind. And if this is murder, not misadventure, then it has to be tied up with Rhoda Gradwyn's death. Two killers in the same house at the same time beggars belief.'

Benton said quietly, 'But it has been known, ma'am.'

Kate said, 'If we look at the facts and ignore motive for the present, the obvious suspects are Miss Westhall and Mrs Frensham. What were they really doing at the two cottages, opening cupboards and then the freezer? It's as if they knew that Boyton was dead. And why did it take two of them to search?'

Dalgliesh said, 'Whatever they were up to they weren't moving the body. The evidence shows he died where he was found. I don't find their actions quite as odd as you do, Kate. People do behave irrationally under stress, and both women have been under stress since Saturday. Perhaps subconsciously they were fearing a second death. On the other hand, one of them might have needed to ensure that the freezer was opened. That would be a more natural action if the search so far had been thorough.'

Benton said, 'Murder or no murder, we won't get much help from prints. They both opened the freezer. One of them may have been taking good care that she did. Would there have been prints anyway? Noctis will have worn gloves.'

Kate was getting impatient. 'Not if he was tipping Boyton alive into the freezer. Wouldn't you find that a bit odd if you'd been Boyton? And isn't it premature to start using the word Noctis? We don't know whether this was murder.'

The three of them were getting tired. The fire was beginning to die and Dalgliesh decided it was time to end the discussion. Looking back, he felt he was living through a day which would never end.

He said, 'It's time for a relatively early night. There's a lot to do tomorrow. I'll be here but I want you, Kate, with Benton, to interview Boyton's partner. According to Boyton he was lodging at Maida Vale so his papers and belongings should be there. We're not going to get anywhere until we know what sort of man he was and, if possible, why he was here. Have you been able to get an appointment yet?'

Kate said, 'He can see us at eleven o'clock, sir. I didn't say who was coming. He said the sooner the better.'

'Right. Eleven o'clock in Maida Vale then. And we'll talk before you leave.'

At last the door was locked behind them. He placed the guard in front of the dying fire, stood for a moment gazing into the last flickers, then wearily climbed the stairs to bed.

BOOK FOUR

19–21 December
London, Dorset

Jeremy Coxon's house in Maìda Vale was one of a row of pretty Edwardian villas with gardens leading down to the canal, a neat domestic toy house grown to adult size. The front garden, which even in its winter aridity showed signs of careful planting and the hope of spring, was bisected by a stone path leading to a glossily painted front door. It wasn't at first sight a house which Benton associated with what he knew of Robin Boyton or expected of his friend. There was a certain feminine elegance about the façade and he recalled reading that it was in this part of London that Victorian and Edwardian gentlemen provided houses for their mistresses. Remembering Holman Hunt's painting *The Awakening Conscience*, he brought to mind a cluttered sitting room, a young woman starting up, bright eyed, from the piano, her lounging lover, one hand on the keys, reaching out to her. In recent years he had surprised in himself a fondness for Victorian genre painting but that hectic and, for him, unconvincing depiction of remorse was not one of his favourites.

As they unlatched the gate, the door opened and a young couple were gently but firmly propelled out. They were followed by an elderly man, neat as a manikin, with a bouffant of white hair and a tan which no winter sun could have produced. He was wearing a suit with a waistcoat, the exaggerated stripes of which diminished his meagre frame still further. He appeared not to notice the newcomers, but his fluting voice came clearly to them down the path.

'You don't ring. It's supposed to be a restaurant not a private house. Use your imagination. And Wayne, dear boy, get it right this time. You give your name and the booking details to the reception, someone will take your coats, then you follow the person greeting you to your table. The lady goes first. Don't bang on ahead and pull out your guest's chair as if you're afraid someone will grab it. Let the man do his job. He'll see to it that she's comfortably seated. So let's do it again. And try, dear boy, to look confident. You'll be paying the bill, for God's sake. Your job is to see that your guest has a meal which makes at least a pretence at being worth what you'll be paying for it, and a happy evening. She won't if you don't know what you're doing. All right, perhaps you'd better come in and we'll practise the knives-and-forks bit.'

The couple disappeared inside and it was then he deigned to turn his attention to Kate and Benton. They walked up to him and Kate flipped open her wallet. 'Detective Inspector Miskin and Detective Sergeant Benton-Smith. We're here to see Mr Jeremy Coxon.'

'I'm sorry I kept you waiting. I'm afraid you arrived at an inopportune moment. It'll be a long time before those two are ready for Claridge's. Yes, Jeremy said something about expecting the police. You'd better come in. He's upstairs in the office.'

They passed into the hall. Benton saw through the open door to the left that a small table for two had been set with four glasses in each place and a plethora of knives and forks. The couple were already seated, staring at each other disconsolately.

'I'm Alvin Brent. If you'll just wait, I'll pop up and see if Jeremy's ready. You will be very considerate with him, won't you? He's terribly upset. He's lost a dear, dear friend. But, of course, you'll know all about that, that's why you're here.'

He was about to walk up the stairs but at that moment a figure appeared at the top. He was tall and very thin with sleek black hair drawn back from a taut, pale face. He was expensively dressed with a careful casualness, which with his dramatic stance gave him the appearance of a male model posed for a camera shoot. His close-fitting black trousers looked immaculate. His tan jacket, unbuttoned, was a design Benton recognised and wished he could afford. His starched shirt was open necked and he wore a cravat.

His face had been furrowed with anxiety but now the features smoothed with relief.

Coming down to meet them, he said, 'Thank God you've come. Sorry about the reception. I've been frantic. I've been told nothing, absolutely nothing, except that Robin's been found dead. And of course he'd rung to tell me about Rhoda Gradwyn's death. And now Robin. You wouldn't be here if it was death by natural causes. I have to know – was it suicide? Did he leave a note?'

They were following him up the stairs and, standing aside, he indicated a room to the left. It was overcrowded and obviously both sitting room and study. A large trestle table before the window held a computer, fax machine and a rack of filing trays. Three smaller mahogany tables, one with a printer precariously balanced, were crowded with porcelain ornaments, brochures and reference books. There was a large sofa against one wall, but hardly usable since it was covered with box files. But despite the clobber an attempt at order and tidiness had been made. There was only one chair behind the desk and a small armchair. Jeremy Coxon looked round as if expecting a third to materialise, then went across the hall and came back with a cane-bottomed chair which he placed before the desk. They seated themselves.

Kate said, 'There was no note. Would you be surprised if it were suicide?'

'God yes! Robin had his difficulties but he wouldn't take that way out. He loved life and he had friends, people who would help him out in an emergency. Of course he had his moments of depression, don't we all? But with Robin they never lasted long. I only asked about the note because any alternative is even less believable. He had no enemies.'

Benton said, 'And there were no particular difficulties at present? Nothing you know which could have driven him to despair?'

'Nothing. Obviously he was devastated by Rhoda's death, but despair isn't a word I'd have used about Robin. He was a Micawber, always hoping something would turn up, and usually it did. And things were going rather well for us here. Capital was a problem, of course. It always is when you start up a business. But he said he had plans, that he was expecting money, big money. He wouldn't say where from but he was excited, happier than I had seen him for years. Rather different from when he came back from Stoke Cheverell three weeks ago. Then he seemed depressed. No, you can rule out suicide. But as I said, nobody's told me anything except that Robin's dead and to expect a visit from the police. If he's made a will, he's probably named me as an executor and he always put me down as next of kin. I don't know anyone else who will take responsibility for his stuff here, or for the funeral. So why the secrecy? Isn't it time you came clean and told me how he died?'

Kate said, 'We don't know for certain, Mr Coxon. We may know more when we get the results of the autopsy, which should be later today.'

'Well, where was he found?'

Kate said, 'His body was in a disused freezer in the cottage next to the guest cottage where he was staying.'

'A freezer? You mean one of those rectangular chest freezers for long-term storage?'

'Yes. A disused freezer.'

'Was the lid open?'

'The lid was shut. We don't yet know how your friend came to be in there. It could have been an accident.'

And now Coxon was looking at them in stark amazement, which even as they watched turned to horror. There was a pause, then he said, 'Let's get this clear. You're telling me that Robin's body was found shut in a freezer?'

Kate said patiently, 'Yes, Mr Coxon, but we don't yet know how it got there or the cause of death.'

He shifted his gaze, wide eyed, from Kate to Benton as if testing which, if either, could be believed. When he spoke his voice was emphatic, the note of hysteria barely suppressed. 'Then I'll tell you one thing. This was no accident. Robin was seriously claustrophobic. He never travelled by air or on the underground. He couldn't enjoy a restaurant meal if he wasn't seated close to the door. He was fighting it, but not successfully. Nothing and no one would ever have persuaded him to climb inside a freezer.'

Benton said, 'Not even if the lid was propped wide open?'

'He'd never believe that it wouldn't fall and trap him inside. What you're investigating is murder.'

Kate could have said that it was possible Boyton had died either by accident or natural causes and that someone, for reasons unknown, had placed his body in the freezer, but she had no intention of swapping theories with Coxon. Instead she asked, 'Was it generally known among his friends that he was claustrophobic?'

Coxon was calmer now, still gazing from Kate to Benton, willing them to believe. 'Some may have known or guessed, I suppose, but I never heard it mentioned. It's something he was rather ashamed of, particularly not being able to fly. That was why we didn't have foreign holidays unless we went by train. I couldn't get him onto a plane even if I tanked him up at the bar. It was a hell of an inconvenience. If he told anyone it would have been Rhoda, and Rhoda's dead. Look, I can't give you any proof. But you have to believe me about one thing. Robin would never have got into a freezer alive.'

Benton asked, 'Do his cousins or anyone at Cheverell Manor know that he was claustrophobic?'

'How the hell do I know? I've never met any of them and I've never been there. You'll have to ask them.'

His composure had cracked. He sounded close to tears. He muttered, 'Sorry, sorry,' and fell silent. After a minute in which he stood still taking deep regular breaths as if they were an exercise in regaining control, he said, 'Robin had taken to going to the Manor more frequently. I suppose it could have come up in conversation, if they were talking about holidays or the hell of London tube trains at rush hour.'

Kate said, 'When did you hear about Rhoda Gradwyn's death?'

'On Saturday afternoon. Robin phoned about five o'clock.'

'How did he sound when he gave you the news?'

'How would you expect him to sound, Inspector? He wasn't exactly ringing to enquire after my health. Oh God! I didn't mean that, I'm trying to be helpful. It's just that I'm still trying to take it in. How did he sound? He was almost incoherent at first. It took me some minutes to calm him down. After that – well, you can take your pick of the adjectives – shocked, horrified, surprised, frightened. Mostly shocked and frightened. A natural reaction. He'd just been told that a close friend had been murdered.'

'Did he use that word, murdered?'

'Yes, he did. A reasonable assumption I'd say, when the police were there and he'd been told they'd be coming to interview him. And not the local CID either. Scotland Yard. He didn't need telling that this wasn't a natural death.'

'Did he say anything about how Miss Gradwyn died?'

'He didn't know. He was pretty bitter that no one at the Manor had bothered to come and break the news to him. He only found out that something had happened when the police cars arrived. I still don't know how she died and I don't suppose you're about to tell me.'

Kate said, 'What we need from you, Mr Coxon, is anything you can tell us about Robin's relationship with Rhoda Gradwyn and, of course, with you. We now have two suspicious deaths which could be linked. How long have you known Robin?'

'About seven years. We met at the party after a drama-school production in which he had a not particularly distinguished part. I went with a friend who teaches fencing and Robin caught my eye. Well, that's what he does, he catches people's eyes. We didn't speak then, but the party lingered on and my friend, who had another date, had left by the time the last bottle was finished. It was a foul night, the rain pelting down, and I could see Robin, somewhat inadequately clad, waiting for a bus. So I hailed a cab and asked if I could drop him. That's how the acquaintanceship began.'

Benton said, 'And you became friends?'

'We became friends and later business partners. Nothing formal, but we worked together. He had the ideas and I had the practical experience and at least the hope of raising money. I'll answer the question you're thinking of a tactful way to ask. We were friends. Not lovers, not fellow-conspirators, not buddies, not drinking companions, friends. I liked him and I suppose we were useful to each other. I told him I'd inherited just over a million from a maiden aunt who'd recently died. The aunt was genuine enough, but the old dear hadn't a penny to leave. Actually I was lucky in the Lottery. I don't quite know why I'm bothering to tell you this except you'll no doubt find out sooner or later when you start wondering whether I have any financial interest in Robin's death. I haven't. I doubt whether he's left anything but debts and the jumble of things – mostly clothes – that he's dumped here.'

'Did you ever tell him about the Lottery win?'

'No I didn't. I never think it's wise to tell people if you have a big win. They simply take the view that, since you've done nothing to deserve your luck, you have an obligation to share it with the equally undeserving. Robin fell for the rich-auntie story. I invested over a million on this house and it was his idea that we started etiquette courses for the newly rich or social aspirants who don't want to be embarrassed every time they entertain the boss or take a girl out to dinner at a decent restaurant.'

Benton said, 'I thought the very rich didn't care one way or another. Don't they make their own rules?'

'We don't expect to attract billionaires, but most people care, believe me. This is an upwardly mobile society. No one likes to be socially insecure. And we're doing well. We've got twenty-eight clients already and they pay five hundred and fifty pounds for a four-week course. Part-time, that is. Cheap at the price. It's the only one of Robin's schemes that ever showed any promise of making money. He got chucked out of his flat a couple of weeks ago so he's been living here in one room at the back. He isn't – he wasn't – exactly a considerate house guest, but basically it suited us both. He kept an eye on the house and he was here when it was his turn to take a class. It might be hard to believe but he was a good teacher and he knew his stuff. The clients liked him. The problem with Robin is that he is – was – unreliable and volatile. Madly enthusiastic one minute and chasing off after some new hare-brained scheme the next. He could be maddening, but I never wanted to cast him off. It just never occurred to me. If you can explain the chemistry which keeps disparate people together, I'd be interested to hear it.'

'And what about his relationship with Rhoda Gradwyn?'

'Ah, that's more difficult. He didn't talk much about her, but he obviously liked having her as a friend. It gave him kudos in his own eyes, which is what matters after all.'

Kate said, 'Was it sex?'

'Oh hardly. I fancy that the lady swam with bigger fish than Robin. And I doubt whether she fancied him. People don't. Too beautiful perhaps, a bit asexual. Rather like making love to a statue. Sex wasn't important to him but she was. I think she represented a stabilising authority. He did once say that he could talk to her and be told the truth, or what passes for it. I used to wonder if she reminded him of someone who had influenced him that way, a schoolteacher, perhaps. And he lost his mother when he was seven. Some kids never get over that. He could've been looking for a substitute. Psychobabble, I know, but there could be something in it.'

Benton reflected that maternal wasn't a word he'd have used of Rhoda Gradwyn, but then, what did they really know about her? Wasn't that part of the fascination of his job, the unknowingness of other people? He asked, 'Did Robin tell you that Miss Gradwyn was having a scar removed and where it was being done?'

'No, and I'm not surprised. I mean I'm not surprised he didn't tell me. She probably asked him to keep it secret. Robin could keep a secret if he thought it was worth his while. All he said was that he was having a few days in the guest cottage at Stoke Cheverell. He never mentioned that Rhoda would be there.'

Kate asked, 'What was his mood? Did he seem excited or did you get the impression that this was just a routine visit?'

'Like I said, he was depressed when he got back after the first visit but excited when he set off last Thursday night. I've seldom seen him happier. He said something about having good news for me when he got back but I didn't take that seriously. Robin's good news usually turned out to be bad news or no news at all.'

'Apart from that first call, did he speak to you again from Stoke Cheverell?'

'Yes, he did. He gave me a ring after you'd interviewed him. He said you were pretty rough with him, not particularly considerate to a man grieving for a friend.'

Kate said, 'I'm sorry he felt that. He made no formal complaint of his treatment.'

'Would you in his place? Only fools or the very powerful antagonise the police. After all, you didn't exactly set about him with truncheons. Anyway, he did ring me again after you'd interviewed him in the cottage and I told him to come to me and let the police grill him here, where I'd arrange for my solicitor to be present if necessary. It wasn't entirely disinterested. We're busy and I needed him here. He said he was determined to stay on for the week he'd booked. He talked about not deserting her in death. A bit histrionic, but that was Robin. Of course, he knew more about it by then, and told me that she'd been found dead at seven thirty on the Saturday morning and that it looked like an inside job. After that I rang him again several times on his mobile, but couldn't get a reply. I left messages asking him to ring back, but he never did.'

Benton said, 'When he first rang you said he sounded frightened. Didn't it strike you as odd that he was preparing to stay on with a murderer on the loose?'

'Yes, it did. I pressed him and he said he had unfinished business.'

There was a silence. Kate's voice was deliberately incurious. 'Unfinished business? Did he give you any clue what he meant?'

'No, and I didn't ask. As I've said, Robin could be histrionic. Perhaps he thought of lending a hand in the investigation. He'd been reading a detective story which you'll probably find in his room. You'll want to see the room, I suppose?'

'Yes,' said Kate, 'as soon as we've finished speaking to you. There's one other thing. Where were you between the hours of four thirty last Friday afternoon and seven thirty the next morning?'

Coxon was unworried. 'I thought you'd get round to that. I was teaching here from three thirty until seven thirty, three couples with gaps in between. I then made myself spaghetti bolognese, watched TV until ten o'clock and went to the pub. Thanks to a benign government which allows us to drink until the early hours, that's what I did. The landlord was serving and he can confirm that I was there until about one fifteen. And if you care to tell me when Robin died, I daresay I could produce an equally valid alibi.'

'We don't know yet, Mr Coxon, exactly when he did die, but it was on Monday, probably between the hours of one o'clock and eight.'

'Look, it seems ludicrous to be supplying an alibi for Robin's death, but I suppose you have to ask. Luckily for me there's no problem. I lunched here at half past one with one of our temporary teachers, Alvin Brent – you met him at the door. At three o'clock I had an afternoon session with two new clients. I can give you their names and addresses and Alvin will confirm the lunch.'

Kate asked, 'At what time did the afternoon lesson end?'

'Well they were supposed to get an hour but I had no immediate engagements so I let it over-run a bit. It was half past four by the time they left. Then I worked here in the office until six when I went to the pub – the Leaping Hare, a new gastropub in Napier Road. I met a pal – I can give you his name and address – and was there with him until about eleven when I walked home. I'll have to look in my address book for the addresses and phone numbers, but I'll do that now if you can wait.'

They waited while he went to the desk and, within a few minutes of riffling through his address book, found a piece of paper in his desk drawer, copied the information and handed over the paper. He said, 'If you have to check I'd be glad if you'd make it plain that I'm not a suspect. It's bad enough trying to come to terms with the loss of Robin – it hasn't hit me yet, perhaps because I still can't believe it, but believe me it will – and I don't fancy being seen as his murderer.'

Benton said, 'If what you've told us is confirmed, I don't think there'll be any risk of that, sir.'

Nor would there. If the facts were accurate the only time when Jeremy was alone was the hour and a half between the end of his lesson and his arrival at the pub, and that wouldn't have given him time even to get to Stoke Cheverell.

Kate said, 'We'd like now to have a look at Mr Boyton's room. I suppose it hasn't been locked since his death?'

Coxon said, 'It couldn't be, there isn't a lock. Anyway, it never occurred to me that it needed to be locked. If you expected that, surely you'd have phoned me. As I keep saying, I haven't been told anything until your arrival today.'

Kate said, 'I don't expect it's important. I take it no one's been in the room since his death?'

'No one. Not even me. The place depressed me when he was alive. I can't face it now.'

The room was down the landing at the back. It was large and well proportioned with two windows looking out over the lawn with its central flowerbed and, beyond it, the canal.

Without entering the room, Coxon said, 'I'm sorry it's in such a mess. Robin only moved in two weeks ago and everything he owns has been dumped here except the stuff he gave away to Oxfam or sold at the pub, and I don't suppose there were many takers.'

The room was certainly uninviting. There was a single divan to the left of the door piled high with unwashed clothes. The doors of a mahogany wardrobe stood open revealing shirts, jackets and trousers crammed on metal hangers. There were half a dozen large square boxes stamped with the name of a removal firm and three bulging black plastic bags on top. In the corner to the right of the door were piles of books and a cardboard carton filled with magazines. Between the two windows a pedestal desk with drawers and a cupboard on each side held a laptop and an adjustable reading lamp. The room smelled unpleasantly of unwashed clothes.

Coxon said, 'The laptop is new, bought by me. Robin was supposed to help with some of the correspondence but he didn't get down to it. I imagine that's the only thing in the room worth anything. He's always been appallingly untidy. We had a bit of a row just before he left for Dorset. I complained that he could at least have got his clothes cleaned before he moved. Of course, now I feel a mean-spirited bastard. I suppose I always shall. It's irrational, but there it is. Anyway, all he possesses, as far as I know, is in this room and as far as I'm concerned you're welcome to rummage through it. He hasn't any relations to object. At least, he did mention a father, but I gather they haven't been in touch since he was a boy. You'll find the two drawers in the desk are locked but I don't have a key.'

Benton said, 'I don't see why you should feel guilty. The room is a mess. He could at least have gone to the launderette before he moved in. You were only speaking the truth.'

'But being untidy isn't exactly high moral delinquency. And what the hell did it matter? Not worth shouting about. And I knew what he was like. Some licence is surely due to a friend.'

Benton said, 'But we can't watch our words just because a friend might die before we have a chance to put things right.'

Kate thought it was time to move on. Benton seemed inclined to elaborate. Given the chance, he would probably initiate a quasi-philosophical discussion about the relative obligations of friendship and truth. She said, 'We've got his key ring. The key to the drawers is probably there. If there's a lot of paper we may need a bag to carry it away. I'll give you a receipt.'

'You can carry it all away, Inspector. Shove it in a police van. Hire a skip. Burn it. It depresses me profoundly. Give me a call when you're ready to go.'

His voice broke and he sounded close to tears. Without another word he disappeared. Benton walked over to the window and opened it wide. The fresh air flowed in. Benton said, 'Is this too much for you, ma'am?'

'No Benton, leave it open. How on earth can anybody live like this? It looks as if he didn't make the slightest effort to keep the room habitable. Let's hope we've got the desk key.'

It wasn't difficult to identify the one they needed. It was by far the smallest of the bunch and it fitted easily into the lock of both drawers. They tackled the left-hand one first, but Kate had to tug it open against a wedge of paper jammed at the back. As she jerked it open, old bills, postcards, an out-of-date diary, some unused Christmas cards and a collection of letters sprang from it and littered the floor. Benton opened the cupboard and that, too, was crammed with bulging files, old theatre programmes, scripts and publicity photographs, a wash bag which, when opened, revealed old stage make-up.

Kate said, 'We won't bother to go through all this mess now. Let's see if we get more joy from the other drawer.'

This yielded more easily to her pull. It contained a manila folder and a book. The book was an old paperback, *Untimely Death* by Cyril Hare, and the folder contained only one sheet of paper with writing on both sides. It was a copy of a will, headed *The Last Will and Testament of Peregrine Richard Westhall* and dated in letters on the last page: *Witness my hand this seventh day of July, two thousand and five.* With the will was a receipt for five pounds from the Holborn Probate Office. The whole document was handwritten, a black upright hand, strong in places but becoming more shaky in the last paragraph. The first paragraph appointed his son Marcus St John Westhall, his daughter Candace Dorothea Westhall and his solicitors, Kershaw & Price-Nesbitt as executors. The second paragraph expressed his wish for a private cremation with no one present other than immediate family, no religious observances and no later memorial service. The third paragraph – the writing here rather larger, stated: *I give and bequeath all my books to Winchester College. Any which the College does not wish to have to be sold or otherwise disposed of as my son, Marcus St John Westhall, shall decide. I give all else that I possess in money and chattels in equal measure to my two children, Marcus St John Westhall and Candace Dorothea Westhall.*

The will was signed and the signature witnessed by Elizabeth Barnes, describing herself as a domestic servant and giving the address as Stone Cottage, Stoke Cheverell, and Grace Holmes, a nurse, of Rosemary Cottage, Stoke Cheverell.

Kate said, 'Nothing on the face of it to interest Robin Boyton, but he obviously took the trouble to get this copy. I suppose the book had better be read. How quick a reader are you, Benton?'

'Pretty quick, ma'am. It's not particularly long.'

'Then you'd better start tackling it in the car and I'll drive. We'll get a bag from Coxon and get this stuff to the Old Police Cottage. I don't suppose there's anything in the other cupboard to interest us, but we better go through it.'

Benton said, 'Even if we find that he has more than one friend with a grievance, I can't somehow envisage an enemy going down to Stoke Cheverell to kill him, getting access to the Westhalls' cottage and sticking the body in their freezer. But obviously a copy of the will must mean something, unless he just wanted to confirm that the old man had left him nothing. I wonder why it was handwritten. Obviously Grace Holmes isn't still living in Rosemary Cottage. The place is for sale. But why was Boyton trying to contact her? And what's happened to Elizabeth Barnes? She isn't working for the Westhalls now. The date of the will is interesting though, isn't it?'

Kate said slowly, 'Not only the date. Let's get out of this mess. The sooner we get this to AD the better. But we've been told to see Miss Gradwyn's agent. I've a feeling that it shouldn't take long. Remind me who and where she is, Benton.'

'Eliza Melbury, ma'am. Our appointment's for three fifteen. The office is in Camden.'

'Damn! It's out of our way. I'll check with AD that there's nothing else he wants done in London while we're here. There's usually something he needs picking up at the Yard. Then we'll find somewhere for a quick lunch and be on our way to see what, if anything, Eliza Melbury has to tell us. But at least this morning hasn't been wasted.'

2

With their car enmeshed in London traffic, the journey to Eliza Melbury's address in Camden was tedious and time-consuming. Benton hoped that the information gained from her would justify the time and trouble taken to reach her. Her office was over a greengrocer's shop and the smell of fruit and vegetables followed them as they climbed the narrow stairs to the first floor and passed into what was obviously the general office. Three young women were seated at their computers while an elderly man was busy rearranging the books, all in their bright jackets, on a shelf which ran the whole length of one wall. Three pairs of eyes looked up and, when Kate showed her warrant card, one young woman got up and knocked on the door at the front of the building and called cheerily, 'The police are here, Eliza. You said you were expecting them.'

Eliza Melbury had been finishing a telephone call. Now she replaced the handset, smiled at them and indicated two chairs opposite the desk. She was a large handsome woman with a flaring bush of dark crimped hair to her shoulders, plump cheeked and wearing a bright caftan festooned with beads.

She said, 'You're here, of course, to talk about Rhoda Gradwyn. All I've been told is that you're investigating what was described as a suspicious death, which I take to mean murder. If so, it's deeply shocking, but I'm not sure there's anything I can tell you which will help. She came to me twenty years ago when I first split from the Dawkins-Bower agency and set up on my own, and she's been with me ever since.'

Kate asked, 'How well did you know her?'

'As a writer, I suppose very well. That means I could identify any piece of prose as being by her, knew how she liked to deal with her publishers and could anticipate what her response would be to any proposals I put forward. I respected her and liked her and was glad to have her on my list. We lunched together once every six months, usually to discuss literary concerns. Beyond that I can't say I knew her.'

Kate said, 'She's been described to us as a very private person.'

'Yes, she was. Thinking about her – as, of course, I have been since I got the news – it seems that she was like someone burdened with a secret which she needed to keep and which inhibited her from intimacy. I knew her little better after twenty years than I did when she first came to me.'

Benton, who had been taking a lively interest in the furnishing of the office, particularly the photographs of writers ranged on one wall, said, 'Isn't that unusual between an agent and a writer? I've always imagined that the relationship must be particularly close to succeed.'

'Not necessarily. There has to be liking and trust, and a common agreement about what is important. People differ. Some of my authors have become close friends. A number need a very high degree of personal involvement. One can be required to be mother confessor, financial adviser, marriage counsellor, editor, literary executor, occasionally even childminder. Rhoda needed none of these services.'

Kate said, 'And as far as you know, she had no enemies?'

'She was an investigative journalist. There were a number of people she may have offended. She never suggested to me that she ever felt in any physical danger from them. None as far as I know threatened physical harm. One or two threatened legal proceedings, but my advice to her then was that she say and do nothing and, as I expected, no one had recourse to law. Rhoda wasn't a woman to write anything which could be proved to be untrue or libellous.'

Kate said, 'Not even an article in the *Paternoster Review* accusing Annabel Skelton of plagiarism?'

'Some people used that article as a weapon to castigate modern journalism generally, but most recognised it as a serious piece on an interesting subject. Rhoda and I did have a visit from one of the aggrieved people, a Candace Westhall, but she took no action. Nor could she. The paragraphs which offended her were expressed in moderate language and their truth was undeniable. All that was about five years ago.'

Benton asked, 'Did you know that Miss Gradwyn had decided to have her scar removed?'

'No, she didn't tell me. We never spoke of her scar.'

'And her present plans? Was she proposing to make a change of career?'

'I'm afraid I can't discuss that. In any case nothing was settled and I think her plans were still being formed. She wouldn't wish me to discuss them with anyone other than herself when she was alive, and you'll understand that I can't talk about them now. I can assure you that they can have no possible relevance to her death.'

There was nothing else to be said and Ms Melbury was already making it clear that she had work to do.

Leaving the office, Kate said, 'Why that question about future plans?'

'Just that I wondered if she was thinking perhaps of a biography. If the subject were someone living, he or she might have a motive for stopping it before Gradwyn even got started.'

'Possibly. But unless you're suggesting this hypothetical person managed to find out what Ms Melbury herself didn't know – that Miss Gradwyn would be at the Manor – and managed to persuade the victim or someone else to let him in, whatever Miss Gradwyn had in mind for her future isn't going to help us.'

As they clipped on their seatbelts Benton said, 'I rather liked her.'

'Then when you write your first novel, which, given your range of interests you undoubtedly will, you'll know who to contact.'

Benton laughed. 'It's been quite a day, ma'am. But at least we're not going back empty-handed.'

3

The journey back to Dorset proved a nightmare. It took them over an hour to get from Camden to the M3 and they were then caught in the procession of cars almost bumper to bumper leaving London at the end of the working day. After junction 5 the slow procession drew to a halt because a coach had broken down, blocking one of the lanes, and they were stationary for nearly an hour before the road was cleared. As Kate was unwilling after that to stop for food, they didn't arrive at Wisteria House until nine o'clock, tired and hungry. Kate rang the Old Police Cottage and Dalgliesh asked them to come along as soon as they had fed. The meal to which they had increasingly looked forward was eaten in a hurry, and Mrs Shepherd's steak-and-kidney pudding hadn't improved with the long wait.

It was half past ten before they sat down with Dalgliesh to report on the day.

Dalgliesh said, 'So you've learnt nothing from the agent other than what we already know, that Rhoda Gradwyn was a very private woman. Eliza Melbury obviously respects that in death as she did in life. Let's look at what you've brought back from Jeremy Coxon. We'll start with the least important item, this paperback novel. You've read it, Benton?'

'Skimmed it quickly in the car, sir. It ends with a legal complication which I didn't manage to grasp. A lawyer would, and the novel was written by a judge. But the plot does deal with a fraudulent attempt to conceal the time of death. I can see that it could have given Boyton his idea.'

'So it's one more piece of evidence to confirm that Boyton did

334

indeed come to Stoke Cheverell with the idea of extracting money from the Westhalls, an idea which, according to Candace Westhall, he originally got from Rhoda Gradwyn who told him about the novel. Let's get on to a more important piece of information, what Coxon told you about Boyton's change of mood. He says that Boyton returned home despondent after his first visit on the 27th of November. Why despondent if Candace Westhall had promised to settle? Could it be because his suspicions about freezing the body had been shown to be nonsense? Do we really believe that Candace Westhall had decided to string him along while planning some more dramatic exposure? Would any sensible woman act like that? Then, before returning here on Thursday last when Rhoda Gradwyn was admitted for her operation, Coxon says that Boyton's mood had changed, that he was excited and optimistic and talking about the prospect of money. He sends his text message imploring Miss Gradwyn to see him, telling her that the matter is urgent. So what happened between his first and second visits to change the whole situation? He went to Holborn Probate Office and obtained a copy of Peregrine Westhall's will. Why, and why then? He must have known that he wasn't a beneficiary. Isn't it possible that, when Candace had demolished his allegation about freezing the body, she did offer him financial help, or in some way made him suspect that she wanted any argument about her father's will to end?'

Kate said, 'You're thinking of forgery, sir?'

'It's a possibility. It's time to take a look at the will.'

Dalgliesh spread out the will and they studied it in silence. He said, 'The whole will is in holograph with the date written in full, the seventh day of July, two thousand and five. The day of the London bombings. If one were forging the date, not a sensible one to choose. Most people remember what they were doing on 7/7 as we remember what we were doing on 9/11. Let's assume then that both the date and the will itself are in Professor Westhall's handwriting. The writing is distinctive and a forgery at such length would almost certainly be detected. But what about the three signatures? Today I telephoned a member of the firm of Professor

Westhall's solicitors with questions about the will. One signatory, Elizabeth Barnes, an elderly maid with long service at the Manor, is now dead. The other is Grace Holmes, who was something of a recluse in the village and emigrated to Toronto to live with a niece.'

Benton said, 'Boyton arrives last Thursday and tries to discover Grace Holmes's address in Toronto by calling at Rosemary Cottage. And it's after his first visit that Candace Westhall knew that, however ridiculous his first suspicions, he was now focusing his attention on the will. It was Mog who told us about Boyton's visit to Rosemary Cottage. Did he also pass on that piece of gossip to Candace? She flies to Toronto ostensibly to give Miss Holmes a contribution from Professor Westhall's bequest, something that could easily have been arranged by letter, telephone or e-mail. And why wait until now to reward her for her services? And why was it so important to see Grace Holmes in person?'

Kate said, 'If we're thinking of forgery, it's a strong motive all right. I suppose minor defects in a will can be put right. Can't bequests be changed if all the executors consent? But forgery is a criminal act. Candace Westhall couldn't risk jeopardising her brother's reputation as well as his inheritance. But if Grace Holmes accepted money from Candace Westhall in return for her silence, I doubt whether anyone will get the truth out of her now. Why should she speak? Perhaps the Prof was always writing wills then changing his mind. All she has to do is to say that she signed several holograph wills and can't remember specific ones. She helped to nurse the old professor. Those years couldn't have been easy for the Westhalls. She'd probably think it morally right that brother and sister should inherit the money.' She looked at Dalgliesh. 'Do we know, sir, what the previous will stipulated?'

'I did ask that when I spoke to the solicitors. The whole estate was divided into two parts. Robin Boyton was to receive half in recognition that his parents and he had been unfairly treated by the family; the remaining half to be divided equally between Marcus and Candace.'

'And he knew that, sir?'

'I very much doubt it. I hope to learn more on Friday. I've made an appointment with Philip Kershaw, the lawyer who dealt with both that will and the most recent. He's a sick man and lives in a retirement nursing home outside Bournemouth, but he's agreed to see me.'

Kate said, 'It's a strong motive, sir. Are you thinking of arresting her?'

'No, Kate. Tomorrow I propose to question her under caution and the interview will be recorded. Even so, this is going to be tricky. It will be unwise, and perhaps even futile, to reveal these new suspicions without more cogent evidence than we have. There's only Coxon's statement that Boyton was depressed after his first visit and exhilarated before the next. And his text message to Rhoda Gradwyn could mean anything. He was apparently a somewhat volatile young man. Well, we saw that ourselves.'

Benton said, 'We're getting somewhere, sir.'

'But without one piece of hard physical evidence either about the possible forgery or the deaths of Rhoda Gradwyn and Robin Boyton. And to complicate matters we have a convicted murderer in the Manor. We won't get further tonight and we're all tired so I think we'll call it a day.'

It was just before midnight but Dalgliesh continued to feed the fire. It would be useless to go to bed while his brain was so active. Candace Westhall had the opportunity and means to commit both murders, was indeed the only person who could confidently entice Boyton into the old pantry when she could be sure of being alone. She had the necessary strength to force him into the freezer, she had ensured that her fingerprints on the lid could be explained and she had made certain that someone was with her when the body was found and had remained with her until the police arrived. But none of this amounted to more than circumstantial evidence and she was intelligent enough to know this. He could do no more at present than question her under caution.

It was then that an idea came into his mind and he acted on it before a second thought could question its wisdom. Jeremy Coxon was apparently a late drinker in his local. His mobile might still be switched on. If not, he would try again in the morning.

Jeremy Coxon was in the pub. The background noise made coherent speech impossible and when he knew it was Dalgliesh who was phoning, he said, 'Hold on a minute and I'll go outside. I can't hear you properly in here.' And a minute later, 'Is there any news?'

Dalgliesh said, 'None at present. We shall be in touch with you if there are any developments. I'm sorry to call so late. I'm ringing about something different but important. Do you remember what you were doing on 7/7?'

There was a silence, then Coxon asked, 'You mean the day of the London bombings?'

'Yes, the 7th of July 2005.'

Again there was a pause in which Dalgliesh thought Coxon was resisting the temptation to ask what 7/7 had to do with Robin's death. Then he said, 'Who doesn't? It's like 9/11 and the day Kennedy died. One remembers.'

'Robin Boyton was your friend at that time, wasn't he? Do you recall what he did on 7/7?'

'I can remember what he told me he did. He was in central London. He turned up at the Hampstead flat where I was living then just before eleven at night and bored me into the small hours with the recital of his narrow escape and long walk to Hampstead. He'd been in Tottenham Court Road, close to the bomb that blew up that bus. He was clutched by some old biddy who was pretty shocked and had to spend time quietening her down. She told him that she lived in Stoke Cheverell and that she'd come to London the previous day to stay with a friend to do some shopping. She planned to return home the following day. Robin was afraid he was going to get stuck with her, but he managed to find a solitary cab outside Heal's, gave her twenty quid for the fare and she went off calmly enough. That was typical of Robin. He said he'd rather part with twenty quid than be landed with the old dear for the rest of the day.'

'Did he tell you her name?'

'No, he didn't. I don't know the name of the lady or the address of her friend – or, for that matter, the number of the cab. It wasn't a big deal, but it happened.'

'And that's all you remember, Mr Coxon?'

'That's all I was told. There is one more detail. I think he did mention she was a retired servant who was helping his cousins to look after some old relative they'd been landed with. Sorry I can't be more helpful.'

Dalgliesh thanked him and snapped shut his mobile. If what Coxon had told him was accurate and if the maid was Elizabeth Barnes, there was no way she could have signed the will on 7 July 2005. But was she Elizabeth Barnes? She could have been any village woman who was helping at Stone Cottage. With Robin Boyton's help they might have traced her. But Boyton was dead.

It was after three o'clock. Dalgliesh was still awake and restless. Coxon's memory of 7/7 was hearsay and now that both Boyton and Elizabeth Barnes were dead, what chance was there of tracing the friend with whom she had stayed or the cab that had taken her there? The whole of his theory about the forgery was based on circumstantial evidence. He had a strong dislike of making an arrest which was not followed by a charge of murder. If the case foundered, the accused was left under a pall of suspicion and the investigating officer could get a reputation for unwise and premature action. Was this going to be one of those deeply unsatisfying cases, and they were not rare, when the identity of a killer was known but the evidence inadequate to make an arrest?

Accepting at last that he had no hope of sleep, he got out of bed, pulled on trousers and a thick sweater, and wound a scarf round his neck. Perhaps a brisk walk down the lane would tire him sufficiently to make it worthwhile going back to bed.

At midnight there had been a brief but heavy shower and the air was sweet-smelling and fresh, but not bitterly cold. He strode out under a sky freckled with high stars, hearing nothing but his own footsteps. Then he felt, like a premonition, the breath of the rising wind. The night became alive as it hissed through the bleak hedgerows and set creaking the high branches of the trees, only to die after the brief tumult as quickly as it had arisen. And then, approaching the Manor, he saw distant tongues of flame. Who would be making a bonfire at three in the morning? Something was burning in the circle of stones. Taking his mobile from his pocket, he called for Kate and Benton as he raced, heart pounding, towards the fire.

4

She didn't set the alarm clock for two thirty, afraid that, however quickly she silenced its rattle, someone would hear it and be roused from sleep. But she didn't need an alarm. For years she had been able to wake by act of will, just as she could feign sleep so convincingly that her breathing became shallow and she herself hardly knew whether she was awake or asleep. Two thirty was a good time. Midnight was the witching hour, the potent hour of mystery and secret ceremony. But the world no longer slept at midnight. If Mr Chandler-Powell were restless he might well walk into the night at twelve, but he wouldn't be abroad at two thirty, and nor would the earliest risers. Mary Keyte's burning had been at three in the afternoon on 20 December, but the afternoon wasn't possible for her act of vicarious expiation, the final ceremony of identification which would silence Mary Keyte's troubled voice for ever and give her peace. Three o'clock in the morning would have to do. And Mary Keyte would understand. What was important was to pay this final tribute, to re-enact as closely as she dared those appalling final minutes. December the 20th was both the right day and perhaps her last chance. It might well be that Mrs Rayner would call for her tomorrow. She was ready to go, tired of being ordered about as if she were the least important person at the Manor when, if they knew, she was the most powerful. But soon all servitude would be over. She would be rich and people would be paid to look after her. But first there was this final goodbye to be said, the last time she would speak to Mary Keyte.

It was as well that she had made her plans so far in advance. Following on Robin Boyton's death the two cottages had been sealed by the police. It would be risky even to visit the cottages after dark and impossible at any time to leave the Manor without the security team seeing her. But she had acted as soon as Miss Cressett told her that a guest would be arriving at Rose Cottage on the same day as Miss Gradwyn had been booked in for her surgery. It was her job to vacuum or wash the floors, dust and polish and make up the bed before a guest arrived. Everything had come together. Everything had been meant. She even had the wicker basket on wheels to hold the clean linen and to bring back the soiled bed linen and towels for washing, the soap for the shower and washbasin and the plastic bag with her cleaning materials. She could use the basket to bring back two of the bags of kindling from the Rose Cottage shed, a length of old washing line which had been dumped there, and two cans of paraffin wrapped in the old newspapers which she always carried to spread over newly washed floors. Paraffin, even safely carried, smelled powerfully. But where could she hide them in the Manor? She decided to put the cans in two plastic bags and after dark to stow them away under the leaves and grasses of the ditch by the hedge. The ditch was deep enough to prevent the cans being seen and the plastic would keep the tins dry. The firewood and rope she could safely lock away in her one large suitcase under her bed. No one would find them there. She was responsible for cleaning her own room and making her own bed and everyone at the Manor was punctilious about privacy.

When her watch showed two forty she was ready to leave. She put on her darkest coat, a large box of matches already in the pocket, and tied a scarf over her head. Opening the door slowly, she stood for a moment hardly daring to breathe. The house was silent. Now that there was no risk of one of the security team patrolling at night she could move without fear that watchful eyes and keen ears were on the alert. Only the Bostocks slept in the central block of the Manor and she had no need to pass their door. Carrying the bags of kindling and the curled washing line slung over her shoulder, she moved quietly, step by careful step, along the corridor, down the side stairs to the ground floor, to the west door. As before, she had to stand on tiptoe to ease back the bolt and took her time, careful that no rasp of metal should disturb the silence. Then carefully she turned the key, went out into the night and locked the door behind her.

It was a cold night, the stars high, the air faintly luminous, and a few wispy clouds moved over the bright segment of the moon. And now the wind was rising, not steadily but in short gusts like an expelled breath. She moved like a ghost down the lime walk, flitting from trunk to concealing trunk. But she had no real fear of being seen. The west wing was in darkness and no other windows overlooked the lime walk. As she reached the stone wall and the moon-blanched stones were fully in sight, a blast of wind rippled along the dark hedgerow, setting the bare twigs creaking and the long grasses beyond the circle whispering and swaying. She was sorry that the wind was so erratic. She knew that it would help the fire, but its very unpredictability would be dangerous. This was to be a memorial, not a second sacrifice. She must take care that the fire never got too close. She sucked a finger and held it up, trying to decide the way the wind was blowing, then moved among the stones as quietly as if she feared that someone was lurking behind them, and set the bags of faggots beside the central stone. Then she made her way to the ditch.

It took a few minutes to find the plastic bags with the paraffin cans; for some reason she thought she had left them closer to the stones and the travelling moon, the brief periods of light and dark, was disorientating. She crept along the ditch, crouching low, but her hands encountered only weeds and grasses and the cold slime of the sludge. At last she found what she sought and carried the cans over to the kindling. She should have brought a knife. The first string bag was tougher than she had expected and it took a few minutes of her tugging before it burst open and the wood spilled out.

And now she began to construct a circle of wood inside the stones. It couldn't be too distanced or the ring of fire would be incomplete, or too near in case it caught her. Bending and working methodically, she at last completed the circle to her satisfaction, then, unscrewing the cap and holding the first paraffin can with great care, she bent double and made her way around the circle of kindling, anointing each stick. She found she had poured the paraffin too lavishly and, with the second can, was more careful. Anxious to start the fire and satisfied that the faggots were well doused, she used only half the paraffin.

Taking the washing line, she bound herself to the central stone. This was trickier than she had expected, but at last she discovered that the best plan was to circle the stone twice with the rope, then step into it, raise it along her body and tighten it. It helped that the centre stone, her altar, was taller but smoother and narrower than the others. This done, she tied the rope at the front of her waist, letting the long ends dangle. Taking the matches from her pocket, she stood rigid for a moment, her eyes closed. The wind gusted and then was calm. She said to Mary Keyte, 'This is for you. This is in memory of you. This is to tell you I know you were innocent. They're taking me away from you. This is the last time I can visit you. Speak to me.' But tonight there was no answering voice.

She struck a match and threw it towards the circle of wood, but the wind blew out the flame almost as soon as it had been lit. She tried again and again with shaking hands. She was close to sobbing. It wasn't going to work. She would have to get closer to the circle and then run back to the sacrificial stone and tie herself again. But suppose the fire didn't take even then? And as she stared up the avenue, the great trunks of the limes grew and closed in together; their top branches merged and tangled, fracturing the moon. The path narrowed to a cavern and the west wing, which had been a dark distant shape, dissolved into the greater darkness.

And now she could hear the crowd of villagers arriving. They were jostling down the narrowed lime walk, their distant voices rising to a shout which pounded at her ears. *Burn the witch! Burn the witch! She killed our cattle. She poisoned our babies. She murdered Lucy Beale. Burn her! Burn her!* And now they were at the wall. But they didn't climb over. They jostled against it, the crowd growing, gasping mouths like a row of death heads, screaming hatred at her.

344

And suddenly the shouting stopped. A figure detached itself, came over the wall and moved up to her. A voice she knew said gently and with a note of reproach, 'How could you think I would let you do this alone? I knew you wouldn't fail her. It won't work the way you're doing it. I'll help. I've come as the Executioner.'

She hadn't planned it like this. It was to be her act and hers alone. But perhaps it would be good to have a witness, and after all this was a special witness, this was the one who understood, the one she could trust. Now she had someone else's secret, one which gave her power and would make her rich. Perhaps it was right that they should be together. The Executioner selected a slender faggot, brought it over and, shielding it from the wind, lit it and held it high, then moving over to the circle, thrust it among the kindling. Immediately there was a rush of flame and the fire ran like a living creature, spluttering, crackling and sending out sparks. The night came alive, and now the voices on the other side of the wall rose in crescendo and she experienced a moment of extraordinary triumph, as if the past, hers and Mary Keyte's, were burning away.

The Executioner moved closer to her. Why, she wondered, were the hands so pinkly pale, so translucent? Why the surgical gloves? And then the hands took hold of the end of the washing line and, with one swift movement, curled it round her neck. There was a vicious tug as it tightened. She felt a cold splash on her face. Something was being thrown over her body. The reek of paraffin intensified, its fumes choking her. The Executioner's breath was hot on her face and the eyes which looked into hers were like veined marbles. The irises seemed to grow so that there was no face, nothing but dark pools in which she saw only a reflection of her own despair. She tried to cry out, but she had no breath, no voice. She fumbled at the knots which bound her, but her hands had no strength.

Barely conscious, she slumped against the rope and waited for death: Mary Keyte's death. And then she heard what sounded like a sob followed by a great cry. It couldn't be her voice; she had no voice. And then the can of paraffin was lifted and flung towards the hedge. She saw an arc of fire and the hedge exploded into flame.

And now she was alone. Half-fainting, she began pulling at the cord round her neck, but there was no strength to lift her arms. The crowd had gone now. The fire was beginning to die. She slumped against her bonds, her legs buckling, and knew nothing more.

Suddenly there were voices, a blaze of torches dazzling her eyes. Someone was vaulting over the stone wall, running to get her, leaping over the dying fire. There were arms round her, a man's arms, and she heard his voice.

'You're all right. You're safe. Sharon, can you understand me? You're safe.'

5

They had heard the sound of the departing car even before they reached the stones. There was no point in making a desperate dash to follow. Sharon had been the top priority. Now Dalgliesh said to Kate, 'Look after things here, will you? Get a statement as soon as Chandler-Powell says she's fit. Benton and I will go after Miss Westhall.'

The four security men, alerted by the flames, were coping with the blazing hedge, which, dampened by the earlier rain, was quickly subdued into charred twigs and acrid smoke. Now low cloud slid from the face of the moon and the night became numinous. The stones, silvered in the moon's aberrant light, shone like spectral tombs and the figures, which Dalgliesh knew were Helena, Lettie and the Bostocks, became discarnate shapes disappearing into the darkness. He watched while Chandler-Powell, hieratic in his long dressing gown, with Flavia at his side, carried Sharon over the wall and then they, too, disappeared into the lime walk. He was aware of someone who remained and now, suddenly in the moonlight, Marcus Westhall's face seemed a disembodied floating image, the face of a dead man.

Moving up to him, Dalgliesh said, 'Where is she likely to go? We have to know. Nothing is served by delay.'

Marcus's voice, when it came, was hoarse. 'She'll go to the sea. She loves the sea. She'll go where she likes to swim. Kimmeridge Bay.'

Benton had rapidly pulled on trousers and had struggled into a thick jersey as he ran towards the fire. Now Dalgliesh called out to him. 'Do you remember the number of Candace Westhall's car?'

'Yes, sir.'

'Get on to the local traffic division. They'll start the search. Suggest they try Kimmeridge. We'll use the Jag.'

'Right, sir.' Benton was off, running strongly.

But now Marcus had found his voice. He stumbled after Dalgliesh, clumsy as an old man, shouting hoarsely, 'I'm coming with you. Wait for me! Wait for me!'

'There's no point. In the end she will be found.'

'I have to come. I need to be there when you find her.'

Dalgliesh wasted no time in argument. Marcus Westhall had a right to be with them and could be helpful in identifying the right stretch of beach. He said, 'Get a warm coat, but hurry.'

His car was the fastest, but speed was hardly important, nor was it possible on the winding country road. It could be too late now to get to the sea before she walked to her death, if drowning was what she had in mind. It was impossible to know if her brother was speaking the truth but, remembering his anguished face, Dalgliesh thought that he probably was. Benton took only minutes fetching the Jaguar from the Old Police Cottage and was waiting as Dalgliesh and Westhall reached the road. Without speaking he opened the back door for Westhall to get in, then followed him. Apparently this passenger was too unpredictable to be left alone in the back of a car.

Benton took out his torch and gave directions for their route. The smell of paraffin from Dalgliesh's clothes and hands filled the car. He lowered the window and the night air, cold and sweet, filled his lungs. The narrow country roads, rising and falling, uncurled before them. On either side Dorset stretched away, its valleys and hills, the small villages, the stone cottages. There was little traffic in this, the dead of night. All the houses were in darkness.

And now he could smell a change in the air, a freshness which was more a sensation than a smell but to him unmistakable: the salt tang of the sea. The lane narrowed as they descended through the silent village and then on to the quayside at Kimmeridge Bay. Before them the sea shimmered under the stars and the moon. Whenever Dalgliesh was in reach of the sea he felt himself drawn to it like an animal to a pool of water. Here, down the centuries since man first stood upright on a shore, its immemorial plangency, unfailing, unseeing, uncaring, caught at so many emotions, not least, as now, the awareness of the transience of human life. They moved eastward to the beach under the looming blackness of the shale cliff, rising dark as coal and tufted at its base with grass and bushes. The slabs of black shale ran out to sea in a pathway of sea-splashed rocks. The waves slid over them, hissing their retreat. In the moonlight they glistened like polished ebony.

They crunched on by the light of their torches, sweeping them over the beach and the causeway of black shale. Marcus Westhall, who had been silent on the journey, seemed now re-vitalised and plunged on through the pebbled fringe of shoreline as if tireless. They rounded a promontory and were faced by another narrow beach, another stretch of black fissured rocks. They found nothing.

And now they could go no further. The beach ended and the cliffs, sloping to the sea, barred their way.

Dalgliesh said, 'She's not here. We could try the other beach.'

Westhall's voice, raised against the rhythmic boom of the sea, was a hoarse cry. 'She doesn't swim there. It's here she'd come. She's out there somewhere.'

Dalgliesh said calmly, 'We'll renew the search in daylight. I think this is where we call a halt.'

But Westhall was again making his way over the rocks, precari-ously balancing, until he was on the edge of the breaking tide. And there he stood, outlined against the horizon. Glancing at each other, Dalgliesh and Benton leaped carefully over the tide-swept slabs towards him. Westhall didn't turn. The sea, under a mottled sky in which low clouds were dulling the brightness of starlight and the moon, looked to Dalgliesh like an unending cauldron of dirty bathwater, heaving with soapsuds which drifted into the crevices in the rocks like scum. The tide was running strongly and he could see that Westhall's trousers were soaking and, as he reached his side, a sudden full-bellied wave broke over the legs of the rigid figure, nearly knocking them both from the rock. Dalgliesh grasped his arm, steadying him. He said quietly, 'Come away now. She isn't here. There's nothing you can do.'

Without a word, Westhall allowed himself to be helped across the treacherous stretch of shale and gently urged into the car.

They were halfway to the Manor when the radio crackled. It was DC Warren. 'We've found the car, sir. She didn't go further than Baggot's Wood, less than half a mile from the Manor. We're searching the wood now.'

'Was the car open?'

'No, sir, locked. And there's no sign of anything inside.'

'Right. Go ahead and I'll join you.'

It was not a search to which he looked forward. As she had parked the car and hadn't used the exhaust to kill herself the chances were that this was a hanging. Hanging had always horrified him, and not only because it had been for so long the British method of execution. However mercifully carried out there was something peculiarly degrading in the inhuman stringing up of another human being. He had little doubt now that Candace Westhall had killed herself but, please God, not that way.

Without turning his head, he said to Westhall, 'The local police have found your sister's car. She isn't there. I'll take you back to the Manor now. You need to get dry and changed. Now you must wait. There's absolutely no point in doing anything else.'

There was no reply, but when the gates were opened for them and they drew up at the front door, Westhall allowed himself to be led in by Benton and handed over to the waiting Lettie Frensham. He followed her like an obedient child into the library. There was a pile of blankets and a rug warming before a roaring fire and brandy and whisky on the table beside a fireside chair.

She said, 'I think you'd be better with some of Dean's soup. He has it ready. But now take off your jacket and trousers and wrap these blankets round you. I'll fetch your slippers and dressing gown.'

He said dully, 'They're somewhere in the bedroom.'

'I'll find them.'

Docile as a child he did as he was told. The trousers, like a pile of rags, steamed before the leaping flames. He sank back into the chair. He felt like a man coming out of an anaesthetic, surprised to find that he could move, reconciling himself to being alive, wishing that he could relapse into unconsciousness because that way the pain would stop. But he must have slept in the armchair for a few minutes. Opening his eyes he saw Lettie beside him. She helped him into his dressing gown and slippers. Soup in a mug appeared before him, hot and strong tasting, and he found that he could drink it, although he noticed only the taste of sherry.

After a time, during which she sat beside him in silence, he said, 'There's something I have to tell you. I shall have to tell Dalgliesh but I need to say it now. I need to tell you.'

He looked into her face and saw the tension in her eyes, the dawning anxiety over what she might be about to hear.

He said, 'I know nothing of Rhoda Gradwyn's or Robin's murders. It isn't that. But I lied to the police. It wasn't because the car was causing problems that I didn't stay with the Greenfields that night. I left to see a friend, Eric. He has a flat close to St Angela's Hospital where he works. I wanted to break the news that I was going to Africa. I knew it would distress him but I had to try to make him understand.'

She said quietly, 'And did he?'

'No, not really. I messed that up as I do everything.'

Lettie touched his hand. 'I shouldn't worry the police with that unless you need to or they ask. It won't be important to them now.'

'It is to me.'

There was a silence, then he said, 'Please leave me now. I'm all right. I promise I'm all right. I need to be alone. Just let me know when they find her.'

He could be sure that Lettie was the one woman who would understand his need to be left in peace and wouldn't argue. She said, 'I'll turn the lights low.' She placed a cushion on a stool. 'Lie back and put your feet up. I'll be back in an hour. Try to sleep.'

And then she was gone. But he had no intention of sleeping. Sleep had to be fought off. There was only one place where he needed to be if he was to stop himself from going mad. He had to think. He had to try to understand. He had to accept what his mind told him was true. He had to be where he found a greater peace and a surer wisdom than he could find here among these dead books and the empty eyes of the busts.

He made his way quietly out of the room, closing the door behind him, through the great hall, now in darkness, and to the back of the house, past the kitchen and through the side door into the garden. He neither felt the strength of the wind nor the cold. He passed the old stables then through the formal garden to the stone chapel.

As he approached through the dawning light, he saw that there was a dark shape on the stones outside the door. Something had been spilled, something which shouldn't be there. Confused, he knelt down and touched its stickiness with trembling fingers. And then he could smell it and, raising his hands, saw that they were covered with blood. He struggled forward on his knees and, willing himself to stand, managed to raise the latch. The door was bolted. And then he knew. He beat against it, sobbing, calling her name until his strength gave out and he sank slowly to his knees, his red palms pressed against the unyielding wood.

And it was there, still kneeling in her blood, that the searchers found him twenty minutes later.

6

Both Kate and Benton had been on duty for over fourteen hours and when the body had finally been removed, Dalgliesh had ordered them to rest for two hours, eat an early supper and join him in the Old Police Cottage at eight o'clock. Neither spent those two hours in sleep. In his darkening room, the window open to the fading light, Benton lay as rigidly as if nerves and muscles were tensed, ready at any moment to spring into action. The hours since the moment when, answering Dalgliesh's call, they had first glimpsed the fire and heard Sharon's screams seemed an eternity in which the longueurs of waiting for the pathologist, the photographer, the mortuary van, were interposed with moments so vividly recalled that he felt they were being clicked onto his brain like slides on a screen: the gentleness of Chandler-Powell and Sister Holland, half-carrying Sharon over the stone wall and supporting her down the lime avenue; Marcus standing alone on the slab of black shale, looking out over the grey pulsating sea; the photographer carefully mincing his way round the body to avoid the blood; the crack of the finger joints as Dr Glenister broke them one by one and forced the tape from Candace's grip. He lay there, unaware of tiredness but feeling still the pain of his bruised upper arm and shoulder from that final lunge at the chapel door.

He and Dalgliesh together had strained their shoulders against the oak but the bolt hadn't yielded. Dalgliesh had said 'We're getting in each other's way. Take a run at it, Benton.'

He had taken his time over it, choosing a line which would avoid the blood, walking back some fifteen yards. The first assault had shaken the door. At the third attempt it had burst open against the body. Then he had stood back while Dalgliesh and Kate entered first.

She had been lying, curled like a sleeping child, the knife beside her right hand. There was only one cut in her wrist but it was deep, gaping like an open mouth. Grasped in her left hand was a cassette.

The image was shattered by the clatter of his alarm and Kate's loud knock on the door. He sprang into action. Within minutes both of them were dressed and downstairs. Mrs Shepherd placed sizzling pork sausages, baked beans and mashed potato on the table and distanced herself in the kitchen. It wasn't a meal she usually served but she seemed to know that what they craved was hot comfort food. They were surprised to find themselves so hungry and ate avidly, mostly in silence, then set out together for the Old Police Cottage.

Passing the Manor, Benton saw that the security team's caravan and cars were no longer parked outside. The windows blazed with light as if for a celebration. It was not a word any of the household would have used but Benton knew that a great weight had been lifted from all of them, a final loosening of fear, suspicion and the deepening anxiety that the truth might never be known. The arrest of one of them would have been preferable to that, but an arrest would have meant prolonging the suspense, the prospect of a national trial, the public show of the witness box, the damaging publicity. A confession followed by suicide was the rational and – they would be able to tell themselves – the most merciful solution for Candace. It was not a thought they would voice but Benton, when he returned to the Manor with Marcus, had seen it in their faces. Now they would be able to wake in the morning without the descending cloud of fear of what that day might bring, could sleep behind unlocked bedroom doors, need not measure their words. Tomorrow or the day after they would see the end of the police presence. Dalgliesh and his team would have to return to Dorset for the inquest, but there was nothing left for the team to do now at the Manor. They would not be missed.

Three copies of the suicide tape had been made and authenticated and the original was in the custody of the Dorset police to be submitted as an exhibit at the inquest. Now they would listen again as a team.

It was apparent to Kate that Dalgliesh had not slept. The fire had been stacked with logs, the flames leaping, and as usual there was a smell of burning wood and freshly made coffee, but no wine. They sat at the table and he placed the tape in the machine and turned it on. Candace Westhall's voice was expected, but it was so clear and confident that for a moment Kate could believe she was in the room with them.

'I am speaking to Commander Adam Dalgliesh in the knowledge that this tape will be passed on to the coroner and anyone else with a legitimate interest in the truth. What I am speaking now is the truth, and I don't think it will come as a surprise to you. I have known for over twenty-four hours that you were going to arrest me. My plan to burn Sharon at the witch's stone was my last desperate attempt to save myself from a trial and life sentence, and all that would involve for those I care about. And if I had been able to kill Sharon I would have been safe, even if you had suspected the truth. Her burning would have looked like the suicide of a neurotic and obsessed murderer, a suicide which I hadn't arrived in time to prevent. And how could you have charged me with Gradwyn's murder with any hope of a conviction while Sharon, with her history, was among the suspects?

'Oh yes, I knew. I was there when she was interviewed for a job at the Manor. Flavia Holland was with me but she early saw that Sharon wouldn't be suitable for any work with the patients, and left me to decide whether there was a place for her with the domestic staff. And we were desperately short at the time. We needed her. Of course I was curious. A twenty-five-year-old woman with no husband, no lover, no family, apparently no history, no ambition to be more than the lowest in the domestic pecking order? There had to be some explanation. That mixture of irritating desire to please interposed with a silent withdrawal, a sense that she was at home in an institution, that she had been used to being watched, that she was in some way under surveillance. There was only one crime for which all this was appropriate. In the end I knew because she told me.

'And there was another reason why she had to die. She saw me as I was leaving the Manor after I had killed Rhoda Gradwyn. And now she, who had always had a secret to keep, knew another's secret. I could sense her triumph, her satisfaction. And she told me what she planned to do at the stones, her final tribute to Mary Keyte, a memorial and a farewell. Why wouldn't she tell me? We had both killed, bound together by that terrible iconoclastic crime. And then in the end, after I had wound the rope round her neck and poured paraffin over her, I couldn't strike the match. I realised in that moment what I had become.

'There's little to tell you about the death of Rhoda Gradwyn. The simple explanation is that I killed her to avenge the death of a dear friend, Annabel Skelton, but simple explanations never tell the whole truth. Did I go to her room that night with the intention of killing her? I had, after all, done all I could to dissuade Chandler-Powell from admitting her to the Manor. Afterwards I thought not, that I meant only to terrify her, to tell her the truth about herself, to let her know that she had destroyed a young life and a great talent, and that if Annabel plagiarised about four pages of dialogue and description, the rest of the novel was uniquely and beautifully hers. And when I lifted my hand from her neck and knew that there would be no communication between us ever again, I felt a release, a liberation which was as much physical as mental. It seemed by this one act I had washed away all the guilt, frustration and regret of the past years. In one exhilarating moment it had all passed away. And I still feel some remnant of that release.

'I believe now that I went to her bedroom knowing that I meant to kill. Why else would I have worn those surgical gloves which I later cut up in the bathroom of one of the empty suites? It was in that suite that I had hidden myself, leaving the Manor by the front door as usual, re-entering later at the back door with my key before Chandler-Powell locked up for the night, and taking the lift up to the patients' floor. There was no real risk of discovery. Who would think of searching a vacant room for an intruder? Afterwards I went down by the lift expecting to have to unbolt the door, but the door wasn't bolted. Sharon had left before me.

'What I said after the death of Robin Boyton was essentially true. He had devised this extraordinary idea that we had concealed my father's time of death by freezing his body. I doubt that this was his idea. This too came from Rhoda Gradwyn and they planned to pursue it together. That's why, after more than thirty years, she decided to have the scar removed and chose to have the operation here. That's why Robin was here both on her first visit and when she came for the operation. The plan was, of course, ridiculous but there were facts which might make it believable. That's why I went to Toronto to see Grace Holmes, who was with my father when he died. And I had a second reason for the visit: to pay her a lump sum in lieu of the pension I felt she deserved. I didn't tell my brother what Gradwyn and Robin were planning. I had sufficient evidence to charge them both with blackmail, if that's what they intended. But I decided to play along until Robin was thoroughly implicated and then enjoy the pleasure of disabusing him and taking my revenge.

'I asked him to meet me in the old pantry. The lid of the freezer was shut. I asked what sort of arrangement he proposed and he said that he had a moral right to a third of the estate. If that were paid over there would be no future demand. I pointed out that he could hardly divulge that I'd falsified the date of death without himself being accused of blackmail. He admitted that we were in each other's power. I offered one quarter of the estate with five thousand as a start. I said it was in cash in the freezer. I needed his fingerprints on the lid and I knew that he was too greedy to resist. He might have doubted but he had to look. We moved over to the freezer and when he lifted the lid I suddenly grasped him by the legs and toppled him in. I'm a swimmer with strong shoulders and arms and he wasn't a heavy man. I closed the lid and fastened the clasp. I felt an extraordinary exhaustion and was breathing hard, but I couldn't have been tired. It was as easy as toppling a child. I could hear the sounds from inside the freezer, shouts, banging, muffled pleading. I stood there for a few minutes leaning on the freezer, listening to his cries. Then I went next door and made a pot of tea. The sounds grew fainter and when they stopped I went into the pantry to let him out. He was dead. I meant only to terrify him but I think now, trying to be totally honest – and which of us can ever be that? – that I was glad to find that he was dead.

'I can't feel sorry for either of my victims. Rhoda Gradwyn subverted a genuine talent and caused hurt and distress to vulnerable people, and Robin Boyton was a gadfly, an insignificant, mildly amusing nonentity. I doubt whether either of them will be mourned or missed.

'That's all I have to say, except to make it plain that at all times I worked entirely alone. I told no one, consulted no one, asked for no one's help, involved no one else either in the acts or in my subsequent lies. I shall die with no regrets and with no fear. I shall leave this tape where I can be confident that it will be found. Sharon will tell her story and you already suspected the truth. I hope that all goes well with her. For myself, I have no hope and no fear.'

Dalgliesh clicked off the tape player. The three of them leaned back and Kate found that she was breathing deeply as if recovering from some ordeal. Then, without speaking, Dalgliesh brought the cafetière to the table and, taking it, Benton filled the three cups and pushed forward the milk and sugar.

Dalgliesh said, 'Given what Jeremy Coxon told me last night, how much of that confession do we believe?'

After a moment's thought it was Kate who answered. 'We know she killed Miss Gradwyn, one fact alone proves that. No one at the Manor was told that we had evidence that the latex gloves were cut up and flushed down the lavatory. And that death wasn't manslaughter. You don't go to the victim wearing gloves if your object is only to frighten. Then there's the attack on Sharon. That wasn't faked. She was intending to kill.'

Dalgliesh said, 'Was she? I wonder. She killed both Rhoda Gradwyn and Robin Boyton and she has given us her motive. The question is whether the coroner and the jury, if he chooses to sit with one, will believe it.'

Benton spoke. 'Does the motive matter now, sir? I mean, it would if the case came to court. Juries want a motive and so do we. But you've always said that physical evidence, hard facts not motive, prove the case. Motive will always remain mysterious. We can't see into another's mind. Candace Westhall has given us hers. It may seem inadequate, but a motive for murder always is. I don't see how we can rebut what she says.'

'I'm not proposing to, Benton, at least not officially. She has made what is essentially a deathbed confession, credible, supported by evidence. My difficulty is in believing it. The case hasn't exactly been a triumph for us. It's over now, or will be after the inquest. There are a number of odd things that come to mind about her account of Boyton's death. Let's take that part of the tape first.'

Benton couldn't resist the temptation to break in. 'Why did she need to tell it all again? We already had her statement about Boyton's suspicions and her decision to string him along.'

Kate said, 'It's as if she needed to record it on the tape. And she spends more time on describing how Boyton died than she does on Rhoda Gradwyn's murder. Is she trying to divert attention from something far more damaging than Boyton's ridiculous suspicion about the freezer?'

Dalgliesh said, 'I think she is. She was determined that no one should suspect forgery. That's why it was vital for her that the tape should be found. To leave it in the car or on a heap of clothes on the beach would have risked its loss. So she dies with it clamped in her hand.'

Benton looked at Dalgliesh. 'Are you going to challenge this tape, sir?'

'To what point, Benton? We may have our suspicions, our own theories about motive, and they may be rational, but it's all circumstantial evidence and none of it can be proved. You can't interrogate or charge the dead. Perhaps it's arrogant, this need to know the truth.'

Benton said, 'It takes courage to kill yourself with a lie on your lips, but perhaps that's my religious education intruding. It tends to at inconvenient times.'

Dalgliesh said, 'I have this appointment tomorrow with Philip Kershaw. Officially, with the suicide tape, the investigation is over. You should be able to get away by tomorrow afternoon.'

He didn't add, *and perhaps by tomorrow afternoon the investigation will be over for me.* This one might well be his last. He could have wished that it had ended differently, but at least it still had a hope of ending with as much of the truth as anyone other than Candace Westhall could hope to know.

7

By midday on Friday, Benton and Kate had made their farewells. George Chandler-Powell had gathered together the household in the library and all had shaken hands and either muttered their farewells or spoken them clearly with, Kate felt, varying degrees of sincerity. She knew without resentment that the air of the Manor would feel newly cleansed once they had departed. Perhaps this group goodbye had been arranged by Mr Chandler-Powell to get a necessary polite-ness over with a minimum of fuss. They had had a warmer farewell from Wisteria House, where they were treated by the Shepherds as if they had been regular and welcome guests. In any investigation there were places or people which remained happily in memory and for Kate the Shepherds and Wisteria House would be one.

Dalgliesh, she knew, would be tied up for part of the morning with his interview with the coroner's officer, and saying his good-byes to the Chief Constable and expressing his gratitude for the help and co-operation his force had provided, particularly DC Warren. Then he planned to drive to Bournemouth for his inter-view with Philip Kershaw. He had already made his formal good-byes to Mr Chandler-Powell and the small group at the Manor, but he would be returning to the Old Police Cottage to collect his bag-gage. Now Kate asked Benton to stop there and wait in the car so that she could check that the Dorset police had removed all their equipment. She knew that the kitchen would need no checking to ensure that it was clean and, going upstairs, she saw that the bed had been stripped and the bedclothes neatly folded. During the years she and Dalgliesh had worked together she had always experienced this slight twinge of nostalgic regret when a case was over and the place in which they had met, sat and talked at the end of the day, however short their stay, was finally left vacant.

Dalgliesh's grip was downstairs, ready packed, and she knew that his murder bag would be with him in the car. The only equipment remaining to be moved was the computer, and on impulse she typed in her own password. A single e-mail came up on the screen.

Dearest Kate. An e-mail is an inappropriate way in which to convey something important but I have to be sure that this reaches you and, if you reject it, it will be less permanent than a letter. I have been living like a monk for the last six months to prove something to myself and I know now that you were right. Life is too precious and too short to waste time on people we don't care for, and much too precious to give up on love. There are two things I want to say which I didn't say when you said goodbye because they would have sounded like excuses. I suppose that's what they are, but I need you to know. The girl you saw me with was the first and last since we became lovers. You know I never lie to you.

The beds in a monastery are very hard and lonely and the food is terrible.

My love, Piers.

She sat for a moment in silence which must have lasted longer than she thought because it was broken by the hooting of Benton's car. But she didn't need to pause for more than a second. Smiling, she tapped in her reply.

Your message received and understood. The case here is finished, although not happily, and I shall be back in Wapping by seven. Why not say goodbye to the Abbot and come home?

Kate.

8

Huntingdon Lodge, standing on a high cliff some three miles west of Bournemouth, was approached by a short drive which curved between cedar trees and rhododendron bushes to an impressively pillared front door. Its otherwise agreeable proportions were spoilt by a modern extension and a large parking lot to the left. Care had been taken not to distress visitors by displaying any notice bearing the words 'retirement', 'elderly', 'nursing' or 'home'. A bronze plaque, highly polished and discreetly placed on the wall beside the iron gates, merely bore the name of the house. The doorbell was answered quickly by a manservant in a short white jacket who directed Dalgliesh to a reception desk at the end of the hall. Here a grey-haired woman, impeccably coiffed and wearing a twinset and pearls, checked his name in the book of expected visitors and smilingly told him that Mr Kershaw was expecting him and would be found in Seaview, the front room on the first floor. Would Mr Dalgliesh prefer the stairs or the lift? Charles would take him up.

Opting for the stairs, Dalgliesh followed the young man, who had opened the door, up the wide mahogany stairs. The walls of the staircase and corridor above were hung with watercolours, prints and one or two lithographs, and on small tables placed against the wall were vases of flowers and carefully arranged china ornaments, most of a cloying sentimentality. Everything about Huntingdon Lodge in its shiny cleanliness was impersonal and, to Dalgliesh, depressing. For him any institution which segregated people from one another, however necessary or benign, evoked an unease which he could trace back to his prep-school days.

His escort had no need to knock at the door of Seaview. It was already open with Philip Kershaw, balanced on a crutch, awaiting him. Charles made a discreet exit. Kershaw shook hands and, standing aside, said, 'Please come in. You're here, of course, to talk about Candace Westhall's death. I haven't been shown her confession but Marcus telephoned our office in Poole and my brother rang me. It was good of you to telephone in advance. With the approach of death one loses the taste for surprise. I usually sit in this armchair beside the fireplace. If you care to draw up a second easy chair, I think you'll find it comfortable.'

They seated themselves and Dalgliesh placed his briefcase on the table between them. It seemed to Dalgliesh that Philip Kershaw was prematurely aged by his illness. The sparse hair was carefully combed over a skull marked with scars, perhaps the evidence of old falls. His yellow skin was stretched across the sharp bones of his face, which might once have been handsome but was now mottled and criss-crossed as if with the hieroglyphics of age. He was as carefully dressed as an elderly bridegroom but the shrivelled neck rose from a pristine white collar which was at least a size too large. He looked both vulnerable and pitiable but his handshake, although cold, had been firm and, when he spoke, his voice was low but the sentences formed without apparent strain.

Neither the size of the room nor the quality and variety of the discordant pieces of furniture could disguise the fact that this was a sickroom. There was a single bed set against the wall to the right of the windows and a screen which, seen from the door, didn't completely conceal the oxygen cylinder and drugs cabinet. Close to the bed was a door which, Dalgliesh surmised, must lead to the bathroom. There was only one top window open but the air was odourless, without even the faint tinge of a sickroom, a sterility which Dalgliesh found more discomforting than the smell of disinfectant would have been. There was no fire in the grate, not surprisingly in the sickroom of an unsteady patient, but the room was warm, uncomfortably so. The central heating must be on full blast. But the empty grate was cheerless, the mantelshelf bore only the porcelain figure of a crinolined and bonneted woman incongruously holding a garden hoe, an ornament which Dalgliesh doubted was Kershaw's choice. But there were worse rooms in which to endure house arrest, or something like it. The only item of furniture which Dalgliesh thought Kershaw had brought with him was a long oak bookcase, the volumes so tightly packed that they looked glued together.

Glancing at the window, Dalgliesh said, 'You have an impressive view.'

'Indeed yes. As I am frequently reminded, I'm regarded as fortunate to have this room; fortunate, too, in being able to afford this place. Unlike some other nursing homes they graciously condescend to care for one, if necessary, until death. Perhaps you'd like to take a closer look at the view.'

It was an unusual suggestion but Dalgliesh followed Kershaw's painful steps to the bay window with two smaller windows flanking it, which gave a panorama of the English Channel. The morning was grey with rare and fitful sunlight, the horizon a poorly discerned line between the sea and sky. Under the windows was a stone patio with three wooden benches regularly placed. Beneath them the ground fell away some seventy feet to the sea in a tumble of entwined trees and bushes, thick with the strong glossy leaves of evergreens. Only where the bushes thinned could Dalgliesh glimpse the occasional strollers on the promenade, walking like passing shadows on silent feet.

Kershaw said, 'I can only see the view if I stand and that is now something of an effort. I've become too familiar with the seasonal changes, the sky, the sea, the trees, some of the bushes. Human life is below me, out of reach. Since I have no wish to concern myself with these almost invisible figures, why do I feel deprived of companionship which I do nothing to invite and would strongly dislike? My fellow guests – we do not refer to patients in Huntingdon Lodge – have long exhausted the few subjects which they have any interest in discussing: the food, the weather, the staff, last night's television and each other's irritating foibles. It's a mistake to live until you greet each morning's light, not with relief and certainly not with joy, but with disappointment and a regret that's sometimes close to despair. I have not quite reached that stage, but it's coming. As, of course, is the final darkness. I mention death, not to introduce a morbid note into our conversation or, God forbid, to invite pity. But it's as well before we talk to know where we stand. Inevitably you and I, Mr Dalgliesh, will see things differently. But you're not here to discuss the view. Perhaps we should get down to business.'

Dalgliesh opened his briefcase and placed on the table Robin Boyton's copy of Peregrine Westhall's will. He said, 'It's good of you to see me. Please say if I tire you.'

'I think it unlikely, Commander, that you will either tire or bore me beyond endurance.'

It was the first time he had used Dalgliesh's rank. Dalgliesh said, 'My understanding is that you acted for the Westhall family in the matter of both the grandfather's and father's wills.'

'Not I, the family firm. Since my admission here eleven months ago the routine work has been done by my younger brother in the office in Poole. He did, however, keep me informed.'

'So you weren't present when this will was drawn up or signed.'

'No member of the firm was. A copy wasn't sent to us at the time it was made, and neither we nor the family were aware of its existence until three days after Peregrine Westhall died, when Candace found it in a locked drawer in a cabinet in the bedroom where the old man kept confidential papers. As you may have been told, Peregrine Westhall was given to drawing up wills when he was in the same nursing home as his late father. Most were codicils in his own hand and witnessed by the nurses. He seemed to have taken as much pleasure in destroying them as he did in writing them. I imagine the activity was designed to impress upon his family that he had power at any time to change his mind.'

'So the will wasn't hidden?'

'Apparently not. Candace said there was a sealed envelope in a drawer in the bedroom cabinet to which he kept the key under his pillow.'

Dalgliesh said, 'At the time it was signed, was her father still able to get out of bed unaided to put it there?'

'He must have been, unless one of the servants or a visitor placed it there at his request. No one in the family or household admits to knowledge of it. Of course, we have no idea when it was actually placed in the drawer. It could have been shortly after it was drawn up, when Peregrine Westhall was certainly capable of walking unaided.'

'To whom was the envelope addressed?'

'No envelope was produced. Candace said she'd thrown it away.'

'But you were sent a copy of the will?'

'Yes, by my brother. He knew that I would be interested in anything concerning my old clients. Perhaps he wanted to make me feel I was still involved. This is getting close to a cross-examination, Commander. Please don't think I'm objecting. It's some time since I was required to use my wits.'

'And when you saw the will you had no doubt about its validity?'

'None. And I have none now. Why should I? As I expect you know, a holograph will is as valid as any other, provided it's signed, dated and witnessed, and no one familiar with Peregrine Westhall's hand could possibly doubt that he wrote this will. The provisions are precisely those made in a previous will, not the one immediately preceding this, but one which was typed in my office in 1995, taken by me to the house in which he was then living and witnessed by two of my staff who came with me for that purpose. The provisions were eminently reasonable. With the exception of his library, which was left to his school if they wanted it, but otherwise was to be sold, all that he possessed was left in equal shares to Marcus, his son, and his daughter, Candace. So in this he was just to the despised sex. I had some influence on him while I was in practice. I exercised it.'

'Was there any other will which preceded this for which probate has now been granted?'

'Yes, one made in the month before Peregrine Westhall left the nursing home and moved to Stone Cottage with Candace and Marcus. You may as well have a sight of it. This, too, was handwritten. It will give you the opportunity to compare the writing. If you'll kindly unlock the bureau and lift the lid you'll find a black deed box. It's the only one I have brought with me. Perhaps I needed it as a kind of talisman, an assurance that one day I might be working again.'

He insinuated his long deformed fingers in an inner pocket and produced a key. Dalgliesh brought over the deed box and placed it before him. The smaller key on the same ring unlocked it.

The solicitor said, 'Here, as you will see, he revokes the previous will and leaves half the estate to his nephew Robin Boyton, the remaining half to be divided equally between Marcus and Candace. If you compare the handwriting on both these wills, I think you will find it's by the same hand.'

As with the later will, the writing was strong, black and distinctive, surprisingly so from an old man, the letters tall, the downward strokes heavy, the upward lines thin. Dalgliesh said, 'And of course neither you nor any member of your firm would have notified Robin Boyton of his prospective good fortune?'

'It would have been seriously unprofessional. As far as I know he neither knew nor enquired.'

'And even if he had known, he could hardly challenge the later will once probate had been granted.'

'And nor, I suggest, can you, Commander.' After a pause he went on, 'I have submitted to your questions, now there is one I need to ask. Are you completely satisfied that Candace Westhall murdered both Robin Boyton and Rhoda Gradwyn and attempted to murder Sharon Bateman?'

Dalgliesh said, 'Yes to the first part of your question. I don't believe the confession in its entirety, but in one respect it's true. She both murdered Miss Gradwyn and was responsible for the death of Mr Boyton. She has confessed to planning the murder of Sharon Bateman. By then she must have made up her mind to kill herself. Once she suspected that I knew the truth about the last will, she couldn't risk a cross-examination in court.'

Philip Kershaw said, 'The truth about the last will. I thought we would come to that. But do you know the truth? And even if you do, would it stand up in court? If she were alive and were convicted of forging the signatures, both of her father and the two witnesses, the legal complications over the will, with Boyton dead, would be considerable. It's a pity I can't discuss some of them with my colleagues.'

He seemed almost animated for the first time since Dalgliesh had entered the room. Dalgliesh asked, 'And what, under oath, would you have said?'

'About the will? That I regarded it as valid and had no suspicions about the signatures either of the testator or of the witnesses. Compare the writing on these two wills. Can there be any doubt that they are by the same hand? Commander, there is nothing you can do and nothing you need to do. This will could only have been challenged by Robin Boyton, and Boyton is dead. Neither you nor the Metropolitan Police have any *locus standi* in this matter. You have your confession. You have your murderess. The case is closed. The money was bequeathed to the two people who had the best right to it.'

Dalgliesh said, 'I accept that, given the confession, nothing more can reasonably be done. But I don't like unfinished business. I needed to know if I was right and if possible to understand. You have been very helpful. Now I know the truth insofar as it can be known, and I think I understand why she did it. Or is that too arrogant a claim?'

'To know the truth and to understand it? Yes, with respect, Commander, I think it is. An arrogance and, perhaps, an impertinence. How we scrap around in the lives of the famous dead, like squawking chickens pecking at every piece of gossip and scandal. And now I have a question for you. Would you be willing to break the law if by doing so you could right a wrong or benefit a person you loved?'

Dalgliesh said, 'I'm prevaricating, but the question is hypothetical. It must depend on the importance and reasonableness of the law I would be breaking and whether the good to the mythical loved person, or indeed the public good, would in my judgement be greater than the harm of breaking the law. With certain crimes – murder and rape, for example – how could it ever be? The question can't be considered in the abstract. I'm a police officer, not a moral theologian or an ethicist.'

'Oh but you are, Commander. With the death of what Sydney Smith described as rational religion and the proponents of what remains sending out such confusing and uncertain messages, all civilised people have to be ethicists. We must work out our own salvation with diligence based on what we believe. So tell me, are there any circumstances in which you would break the law to benefit another?'

'Benefit in what way?'

'In any way a benefit can be conferred. To satisfy a need. To protect. To right a wrong.'

Dalgliesh said, 'Then, put so crudely, I think the answer must be yes. I could, for example, see myself helping someone I loved to a merciful death if she were being stretched out on Shakespeare's rack of this tough world, and every breath was drawn in agony. I hope I wouldn't need to. But since you're posing the question, yes, I can see myself breaking the law to advantage someone I loved. I'm not so sure about righting a wrong. That supposes I would have the wisdom to decide what is in fact right and what is wrong, and the humility to consider whether any action I could take would make things better or worse. Now I could put a question to you. Forgive me if you find it impertinent. Would the loved person, for you, be Candace Westhall?'

Kershaw got painfully to his feet and, grasping his crutch, moved over to the window and stood for some moments looking out as if there were a world outside where such a question would never be put, or, if put, would require no answer. Dalgliesh waited. Then Kershaw turned back to him and Dalgliesh watched while, like someone learning for the first time how to walk, he made his way with uncertain steps back to his chair.

He said, 'I'm going to tell you something that I have never told another human being and never shall. I do that because I believe that with you it will be safe. And perhaps there comes a time at the end of life when a secret becomes a burden which one longs to place on another's shoulders, as if the mere fact that someone else knows it and will share in its keeping somehow lessens the weight. I suppose that's why religious people go to confession. What an extraordinary ritual cleansing that must be. However, that's not open to me and I don't propose to change a lifetime's non-belief for what to me would be a spurious comfort at the end. So I shall tell you. It will impose no burden on you and no distress, and I am speaking to Adam Dalgliesh the poet, not Adam Dalgliesh the detective.'

Dalgliesh said, 'At the moment there can be no difference between them.'

'Not in your mind, Commander, but there can be in mine. And there's another reason for speaking, not admirable, but then which of them is? I can't tell you what a pleasure it is to talk to a civilised man about something other than the state of my health. The first thing the staff or any visitor asks, and the last, is how I am feeling. That's how I'm defined now, by sickness and mortality. No doubt you find it difficult to be polite when people insist on talking about your poetry.'

'I try to be gracious since they mean to be kind, but I hate it and it isn't easy.'

'So I'll keep off the poetry if you will keep off the state of my liver.'

He laughed, a high but harsh expelling of breath cut short. It sounded more like a cry of pain. Dalgliesh waited without speaking. Kershaw seemed to be gathering his strength, to be settling his skeletal form back more comfortably in his chair.

He said, 'Basically it's a commonplace story. It happens everywhere. There's nothing unusual or interesting about it except to the people concerned. Twenty-five years ago when I was thirty-eight and Candace was eighteen, she had my child. I had recently become a partner in the firm, and it was I who took over Peregrine Westhall's concerns. They weren't particularly arduous or interesting, but I did visit often enough to see what was happening in that large stone house in the Cotswolds where the family then lived. The frail pretty wife who made illness a defence against her husband, the silent frightened daughter, the withdrawn young son. I think at the time I fancied myself as someone interested in people, sensitive of human emotions. Perhaps I was. And when I say that Candace was frightened, I'm not suggesting that her father abused or struck her. He had only one weapon and that the deadliest – his tongue. I doubt whether he ever touched her, certainly not in affection. He was a man who disliked women. Candace was a disappointment to him from the moment of birth. I don't want to give you the impression that he was a deliberately cruel man. I knew him as a distinguished academic. I wasn't frightened of him. I could talk to him, Candace never could. He would have respected her if only she'd stood up to him. He hated subservience. And, of course, it would have helped if she'd been pretty. Doesn't it always with daughters?'

Dalgliesh said, 'It's difficult to stand up to someone if you've been frightened of them since early childhood.'

Without apparently hearing the comment, Kershaw went on. 'Our relationship – and I am not talking of a love affair – began when I was in Blackwell's bookshop in Oxford and saw Candace. She had come up in the Michaelmas term. She seemed anxious to chat, which was unusual, and I invited her to have coffee with me. Without her father she seemed to come alive. She talked and I listened. We agreed to meet again and it became something of a habit for me to drive to Oxford when she was there and take her for lunch outside the city. We were both energetic walkers and I looked forward to those autumnal meetings and our drives into the Cotswolds. We only had sex once, on an unusually warm afternoon, lying in the wood under a canopy of sunlit trees when I suppose a combination of beauty and the seclusion of the trees, the warmth, our contentment after what had been a good lunch, led to the first kiss and from that to the inevitable seduction. I think afterwards we both knew it was a mistake. And we were perceptive enough about ourselves to know how it had happened. She'd had a bad week at college and was in need of comfort, and the power to confer comfort is seductive – and I don't mean merely physically. She was feeling sexually inadequate, alienated from her peers and, whether she realised it or not, was looking for an opportunity to lose her virginity. I was older, kind, fond of her, available, the ideal partner for a first sexual experience, which she both wanted and feared. She could feel safe with me.

'And when, too late for an abortion, she told me about the pregnancy, we both knew that her family must never be told, particularly her father. She said that he despised her and would despise her more, not for the sex itself, which probably wouldn't worry him, but because it had been with the wrong person and she had been a fool in getting pregnant. She could tell me exactly what he would say, and it disgusted and horrified me. I was approaching middle age and unmarried. I had no wish to take responsibility for a child. I see now, when it is too late to put anything right, that we treated the baby as if she was some kind of malignant growth which had to be cut out, or at any rate got rid of, and then could be forgotten. If we're thinking in terms of a sin – and you, so I've heard, are the son of a priest and no doubt family influence still means something – then that was our sin. She kept the pregnancy secret and, when there was a risk of discovery, she went abroad, then came back and had the baby in a London nursing home. It wasn't difficult for me to arrange for private fostering followed by adoption. I was a lawyer; I had the knowledge and the money. And things were less controlled in those days.

'Candace was stoical throughout. If she loved her child, she managed to conceal it. Candace and I didn't see each other after the adoption. I suppose there was no true relationship on which we could build, and even to meet was to invite embarrassment, shame, the memory of inconvenience, of lies told, careers disrupted. Later she made up her time at Oxford. I suppose she read Classics in an attempt to win her father's love. All I know is that she didn't succeed. She didn't see Annabel again – even her name was chosen by the prospective foster parents – until she was eighteen but I think she must have kept in touch, however indirectly, and without ever acknowledging that the child was hers. She obviously discovered to which university Annabel had gained admission and took a job there, although it wasn't a natural choice for a classicist and one with a DPhil.'

Dalgliesh asked, 'Did you see Candace again?'

'Once only, and for the first time after twenty-five years. It was also the last. On Friday the 7th of December, she came back from visiting the old nurse, Grace Holmes, in Canada. Mrs Holmes is the only surviving witness to Peregrine's will. Candace went out to pay her a sum of money – I think she said ten thousand pounds – to thank her for the help she gave in nursing Peregrine Westhall. The other witness, Elizabeth Barnes, was a retired member of the Westhall household and had been receiving a small pension which, of course, ended with her death. Candace felt that Grace Holmes shouldn't go unrewarded. She was also anxious to have the nurse's evidence about the date of her father's death. She told me about Robin Boyton's ludicrous allegation that the dead body was concealed in a freezer until twenty-eight days after the grandfather's death had elapsed. Here is the letter Grace Holmes wrote and gave to her. She wanted me to have a copy, perhaps as insurance. If necessary I would pass it on to the head of the firm.'

He lifted the copy of the will and took from beneath it a sheet of writing paper which he passed to Dalgliesh. The letter was dated Wednesday 5 December 2007. The writing was large, the letters round and carefully formed.

Dear Sir,
Miss Candace Westhall has asked me to send you a letter confirm-
ing the date of the death of her father, Dr Peregrine Westhall. This
occurred on 5 March 2007. He had been getting much worse
during the two preceding days and Dr Stenhouse saw him on
3 March but did not prescribe any fresh medicines. Professor
Westhall said that he wanted to see the local clergyman, the
Reverend Matheson, and he came at once. He was driven by his
sister. I was in the house at the time but not in the sickroom. I
could hear the Professor shouting but not what Mr Matheson was
saying. They did not stay very long and the Reverend looked
distressed when they left. Dr Westhall died two days later and I
was in the house with his son and Miss Westhall when he passed
away. I was the one who laid him out.

I also witnessed his last will, which was in his own hand-writing. This was some time in the summer of 2005, but I don't remember the date. This was the last Will I witnessed, although Professor Westhall did make others during the preceding weeks, which Elizabeth Barnes and I witnessed, but which I believe he tore up.

All I have written is true.

Yours sincerely, Grace Holmes.

Dalgliesh said, 'She was asked to confirm the date of his death, so why, I wonder, the paragraph referring to the will?'

'Since Boyton had raised doubts about the date his uncle died, perhaps she thought it important to mention anything concerned with Peregrine's death which might later be questioned.'

'But the will never was questioned, was it? And why should Candace Westhall feel it necessary to fly to Toronto and see Grace Holmes in person? The financial arrangements didn't need a visit and the other information about the date of death could be given by telephone. And why did she need it? She knew that the Reverend Matheson had seen her father two days before he died. The evidence of Matheson and his sister would be enough.'

'You're suggesting that the ten thousand pounds was a payment for this letter?'

Dalgliesh said, 'For the last paragraph in the letter. I think it possible that Candace Westhall wanted to ensure that there would be no risk of disclosure from the only living witness to her father's will. Grace Holmes had helped nurse Peregrine Westhall and knew what his daughter had endured at his hands. I think she would be happy to see justice done in the end to Candace and Marcus. And, of course, she did take the ten thousand pounds. And what was she asked to do? Merely to say she had witnessed a handwritten will and couldn't remember on what date. Do you think for a moment that she will ever be persuaded to change her story, to say more than that? And she didn't witness the previous will. She would know nothing about the injustice to Robin Boyton. She could probably convince herself that she was speaking the truth.'

For nearly a minute they sat in silence, then Dalgliesh said, 'If I asked you whether Candace Westhall on that last visit to you discussed the truth about her father's will, would you answer me?'

'No, and I don't suppose you'd expect me to. That's why you won't ask. But I can tell you this, Commander. She was not a woman to burden me with more than I needed to know. She wanted me to have Grace Holmes's letter, but that was the least important part of the visit. She told me that our daughter had died, and how. We had unfinished business. There were things both of us needed to say. I would like to think that when she left me much of the bitterness of the last twenty-five years had seeped away, but that would be a romantic sophism. We had done each other too much damage. I think she died happier because she knew she could trust me. That was all there was between us and all there had ever been, not love but trust.'

But Dalgliesh had one last question. He asked, 'When I telephoned and you agreed to meet me, did you tell Candace Westhall that I was coming?'

Kershaw looked him in the face and said quickly, 'I telephoned and told her. And now, if you'll excuse me, I need to rest. I'm glad you came, but we won't see each other again. If you'd be good enough to press that bell by the bed, Charles will escort you to the front door.'

He held out his hand. The grasp was still firm but the blaze in the eyes had died. Something had been shut down. With Charles waiting for him at the open door, Dalgliesh turned to take a last look at Kershaw. He was sitting in his chair, staring in silence at the empty grate.

Dalgliesh had hardly clipped on his seatbelt when his mobile rang. It was Detective Inspector Andy Howard. The note of triumph in his voice was disciplined but unmistakable.

'We've got him, sir. A local lad, as we suspected. Been questioned four times previously about sex attacks but never charged. The justice department will be relieved that it's not another illegal immigrant or someone released on bail. And, of course, we've got his DNA. I'm a bit worried about the way in which we keep the

DNA if there's no charge, but this isn't the first case in which it's been useful.'

'Congratulations, Inspector. Do you know if there's a chance he may plead guilty? It would be good to spare Annie the ordeal of a trial.'

'Every chance, I'd say, sir. The DNA isn't the only evidence we've got but it's clinching, and it'll be quite a time before that lass is fit to stand in any witness box.'

It was with a lighter heart that Dalgliesh shut his mobile. And now he needed to find a place where he could sit for a time alone and in peace.

He drove westwards from Bournemouth until, taking the coast road, he found a place where he could stop the car and look out to sea over Poole Harbour. In the last week his mind and energies had been occupied only with the deaths of Rhoda Gradwyn and Robin Boyton, but now there was his future to face. Choices had been placed before him, most of them demanding or interesting, but until now he had given them little thought. Only one life-changing thing was certain: his marriage to Emma, and about that there was no doubt, nothing but the certainty of joy.

And at last he knew the truth about those two deaths. Perhaps Philip Kershaw had been right: there was an arrogance in wanting always to know the truth, particularly the truth about human motives, the mysterious working of another's mind. He was convinced that Candace Westhall had never intended to murder Sharon. She must have encouraged the girl in her fantasy, perhaps when they were alone and Sharon was helping with the books. But what Candace had wanted and planned for was the one sure way of convincing the world that she and she alone had killed Gradwyn and Boyton. Given her confession, the coroner's verdict was inevitable. The case would be closed and his responsibilities over. There was nothing further he could do, or wanted to do.

Like every investigation, this one would leave him with memories, people who would, without any particular wish on his part, establish themselves as silent presences in his mind and thoughts for years but who could be brought to life by a place, a stranger's face, a voice. He had no wish regularly to relive the past but these brief visitations left him curious to know why particular people were lodged in his memory and what their lives had become. They were seldom the most important part of the investigations and he thought he knew which people from the past week would remain in memory. Father Curtis and his fair-haired brood of children, Stephen Collinsby and Lettie Frensham. During the past years, how many lives had briefly affected his, often in horror and tragedy, in terror and anguish? Without knowing it they had inspired some of his best poetry. What inspiration would he find in bureaucracy or the fruits of office?

But it was time to get back to the Old Police Cottage, to collect his bags and to be on his way. He had said his goodbyes to everyone at the Manor and had called at Wisteria House to thank the Shepherds for their hospitality to his team. There was only one person now whom he longed to see.

Arriving at the cottage, he opened the door. The fire had been relit but the room was in darkness except for one lamp on a table beside the fireside chair. Emma got up and came towards him, her face and dark hair burnished by the firelight.

She said, 'You've heard the news? Inspector Howard has made an arrest. We don't have to picture him out there somewhere, perhaps doing it again. And Annie is going to get better.'

Dalgliesh said, 'Andy Howard rang me. My darling, it's wonderful news, especially about Annie.'

Moving into his arms, she said, 'Benton and Kate met me at Wareham before they left for London. I thought you might like company on the drive home.'

BOOK FIVE

Spring
Dorset, Cambridge

On the first official day of spring, George Chandler-Powell and Helena Cressett sat side by side at the office desk. For three hours they had studied and discussed a succession of figures, schedules and architects' plans and now, as if by silent agreement, both stretched out a hand to switch off the computer.

Leaning back in his chair, Chandler-Powell said, 'So financially it's possible. Of course it depends on my keeping well and increasing the list of private patients at St Angela's. The income from the restaurant won't even maintain the garden, not at first anyway.'

Helena was folding the plans away. She said, 'We've been cautious over the St Angela's income. Even with your present sessions you've achieved two-thirds of the figures in our estimate over the past three years. Agreed, converting the stable block is more expensive than you'd planned, but the architect has done a good job and it should come in slightly below cost. With your Far East shares doing well, you could cover the cost from the portfolio, or take a bank loan.'

'Do we have to mention the restaurant on the gate?'

'Not necessarily. But we must have a notice somewhere with the times of opening. You can't be too fastidious, George. You're either running a commercial enterprise or you're not.'

Chandler-Powell said, 'Dean and Kimberley Bostock seem happy about it all, but there has to be a limit to what they can do.'

Helena said, 'That's why we've allowed for part-time helpers and an extra cook after the restaurant gets established. And with no patients – and they've always been demanding at the Manor – they'll only be cooking for you, when you're here, the resident staff and me. Dean is euphoric. What we're planning is ambitious, a first-class restaurant, not a teahouse, one that will attract customers from the fringes of the county and beyond. Dean is a fine chef. You're not going to keep him if you can't offer him scope for his skill. With Kimberley happily pregnant and Dean helping me to plan a restaurant he can feel is his own, I've never known him so happy or so settled. And the child will be no problem. The Manor needs a child.'

Chandler-Powell got up and stretched his arms above his head. He said, 'Let's walk down to the stones. It's too good a day to sit at a desk.'

In silence they put on their jackets and left by the west door. The operating suite had already been demolished and the last of the medical equipment removed. Helena said, 'You'll need to give thought to what you want done with the west wing.'

'We'll leave the suites as they are. If we need additional staff they'll come in useful. But you're glad the clinic's gone, aren't you? You never approved of it.'

'Did I make it so obvious? I'm sorry, but it was always an anomaly. It didn't belong here.'

'And in a hundred years it will be forgotten.'

'I doubt that, it will be part of the history of the Manor. And I don't think anyone will ever forget your last private patient.'

He said, 'Candace warned me about her. She never wanted her here. And if I had operated on her in London she wouldn't have died and all our lives would be different.'

She said, 'Different, but not necessarily better. Did you believe Candace's confession?'

'The first part, killing Rhoda, yes I did.'

'Murder or manslaughter?'

'I believe she did lose her temper, but she wasn't threatened or provoked. I think a jury would return a verdict of murder.'

She said, 'If the case ever came to court. Commander Dalgliesh hadn't even enough evidence to make an arrest.'

'I think he was close to it.'

'Then he was taking a risk. What evidence had he? There were no forensics. Any one of us could have done it. Without the attack on Sharon and Candace's confession the case would never have been solved.'

'That is, of course, if it has been solved.'

Helena said, 'You think she could be lying to protect someone else?'

'No, that's ludicrous, and who would she do it for except her brother? No, she killed Rhoda Gradwyn and I think she intended to murder Robin Boyton too. She's admitted as much.'

'But why? What did he really know or guess that made him so dangerous? And before she attacked Sharon, was she really in any danger? If she were accused of murdering Gradwyn and Boyton, any competent lawyer could convince a jury that there was reasonable doubt. It was the attack on Sharon that proved her guilt. So why did she do it? She says it was because Sharon had seen her leaving the Manor on that Friday night. But why not lie about that? Who would believe Sharon's story if Candace denied it? And that attack on Sharon. How could she hope to get away with it?'

George said, 'I think Candace had had enough. She wanted an end.'

'An end to what? To continued suspicion and uncertainty, to the risk that someone might believe her brother was responsible, to clear the rest of us? That seems unlikely.'

'An end to herself. I don't think she found her world worth living in.'

Helena said, 'We all feel that at times.'

'But it passes, it isn't real, we know it isn't real. I'd have to be in constant unbearable pain, my mind failing, my independence gone, my job gone, this place lost to me before I felt that.'

'I think her mind was failing. I think she knew she was mad. Let's go to the stone circle. She's dead and now all I feel is pity for her.'

Suddenly his voice was harsh. 'Pity? I don't feel pity. She killed my patient. I did a good job on that scar.'

She looked at him, then turned away, but he had caught in that fleeting glance something uncomfortably close to a mixture of surprise and amused understanding.

She said, 'The last private patient here at the Manor. Well she was that all right. She was private. What did any of us know about her? What did you?'

He said quietly, 'Only that she wanted a scar removed because she no longer had need of it.'

They began slowly pacing side by side down the lime avenue. The buds were open and the trees still showed the first transitory green of spring. Chandler-Powell said, 'The plans for the restaurant – of course everything depends on your being willing to stay on.'

'You'll need someone to take charge – administrator, general organiser, housekeeper, secretary. Essentially the job won't greatly change. I could certainly stay on until you find the right person.'

They walked on in silence. Then, without stopping, he said, 'I was thinking of something more permanent, more demanding I suppose. You may say less attractive, at least for you. For me, it's been something too important to risk disappointment. That's why I haven't spoken before. I'm asking you to marry me. I believe we could be happy together.'

'You haven't spoken the word love, that's honest of you.'

'I suppose it's because I've never really understood what it means. I thought I was in love with Selina when I married her. It was a kind of madness. I like you. I respect and admire you. We've worked together now for six years. I want to make love to you, but then any heterosexual man would feel that. I'm never bored or irritated when we're together, we share the same passion for the house, and when I return here and you're not about I feel an unease which is difficult to explain. It's a sense that there's something lacking, something missing.'

'In the house?'

'No, in myself.' Again there was silence. Then he asked, 'Can you call that love? Is it enough? It is for me, is it for you? Do you want time to think about it?'

And now she turned to him. 'Asking for time would be play-acting. It is enough.'

He didn't touch her. He felt like a man invigorated but one who was standing on delicate ground. He mustn't be gauche. She would despise him if he did the obvious thing, the thing he wanted to do, to take her into his arms. They stood facing each other. Then he said quietly, 'Thank you.'

They had reached the stones now. She said, 'When I was a child we used to pace round the circle and gently kick each stone. It was for luck.'

'Then perhaps we should do it now.'

They walked round together. He gently struck each stone in turn.

Returning to the lime walk, he said, 'What about Lettie? Do you want her to stay on?'

'If she's willing. Frankly it would be difficult at first to do without her. But she won't want to live in the Manor once we're married, and it wouldn't suit us. We could offer her Stone Cottage once it's been cleared and redecorated. Of course, she'd enjoy having a hand in that. And she'd take pleasure in doing something with the garden.'

Chandler-Powell said, 'We could offer to give her the cottage. I mean legally, make it over to her. With its reputation it won't otherwise be easy to sell. That way she'll have some security for her old age. Who else would want it? Would she? It seems to smell of murder, unhappiness, death.'

Helena said, 'Lettie has her defences against those things. I think she'd be content in Stone Cottage but she wouldn't want it as a gift. I'm sure she'd prefer to buy.'

'Could she afford to?'

'I think so. She's always been a saver. And it would be cheap. After all, as you've said, with its history Stone Cottage is hardly saleable. Anyway, I could try her. If she moves into the cottage she'll need an increase in salary.'

'Won't that be a difficulty?'

Helena smiled. 'You're forgetting that I have money. After all, we've agreed that the restaurant will be my investment. Guy may have been an unfaithful bastard but he wasn't a mean bastard.'

So that problem was settled. Chandler-Powell thought that this would probably be the pattern of his married life. A difficulty acknowledged, a reasonable solution proposed, no particular action necessary on his part.

He said easily, 'As we can't very well do without her, at least at first, that all seems sensible.'

'It's I who can't do without her. Haven't you noticed? She's my moral compass.'

They walked on. Chandler-Powell could see now that much of his life was going to be planned for him. The thought caused him no disquiet and much satisfaction. He would have to work hard to keep both the London flat and the Manor, but he had always worked hard. Work was his life. He wasn't entirely sure about the restaurant, but it was time that something was done to reinstate the stable block and the restaurant customers wouldn't need to enter the Manor. And it was important to keep Dean and Kimberley. Helena knew what she was doing.

She said, 'Have you heard anything about Sharon, where she is, what job they've found for her?'

'Nothing. She came out of nothingness and went back to nothingness. She isn't my responsibility, thank God.'

'And Marcus?'

'I had a letter yesterday. He seems to be settling down well in Africa. It's probably the best place for him. He couldn't hope to recover from Candace's suicide while working here. If she wanted to separate us, she certainly went about it the right way.'

But he spoke without rancour, almost without interest. After the inquest they had rarely talked about Candace's suicide, and always with unease. Why, she wondered, had he chosen this moment, this walk together, to revisit the painful past? Was it his way of making some kind of formal closure, of saying that it was now time for the talking and speculation to stop?

'And Flavia? Is she, like Sharon, out of your mind?'

'No, we've been in touch. She's getting married.'

'So soon?'

'Someone she contacted on the Internet. She writes that he's a solicitor, widowed two years ago with a daughter aged three.

About forty, lonely, looking for a wife who loves children. She says she's very happy. At least she's getting what she wanted. It shows considerable wisdom to know what you want in life and then to direct all your energies towards getting it.'

They had left the avenue now and were re-entering the west door. Glancing at her, he caught her secret smile.

She said, 'Yes, she was very wise. That's how I've always acted myself.'

2

Helena had broken the news to Lettie in the library. She said, 'You disapprove, don't you?'

'I have no right to disapprove, only the right to be fearful for you. You don't love him.'

'Perhaps not now, not yet totally, but it will come. All marriages are a process of falling in or out of love. Don't worry, we shall suit each other very well in bed and out, and this marriage will last.'

'And the Cressett flag will be raised again over the Manor, and in time a child of yours will choose to live here.'

'Dear Lettie, how well you understand me.'

And now Lettie was alone, thinking over the offer that Helena had made to her before they parted, pacing through the gardens but seeing nothing, and now at last, as so often happened, walking slowly down the lime walk to the stones. Looking back at the windows of the west wing, her mind turned to that private patient whose murder had changed the lives of all who, innocent or guilty, had been touched by it. But wasn't that what violence always did? Whatever that scar had meant to Rhoda Gradwyn – an expiation, her personal *noli me tangere*, defiance, a memento – she had, for some reason which no one at the Manor knew or would ever know, found the will to get rid of it and change the course of her life. She had been robbed of that hope; it was the lives of others that would be irrevocably changed.

Rhoda Gradwyn had been young, of course, younger than she, Lettie, who at sixty knew that she looked older. But she might have twenty relatively active years ahead. Was it time to settle for the safety and comfort of the Manor? She contemplated what that life would be. A cottage she could call her own, decorated as she chose, a garden that she could make and cherish, a useful job that she could do without strain with people she respected, her books and music, the library at the Manor available to her, daily to breathe English air in one of the loveliest of counties, perhaps the pleasure of seeing a child of Helena's growing up. And what of the remote future? Twenty years perhaps of useful and relatively independent life before she began to become a liability, in her eyes and perhaps in Helena's. But they would be good years.

She knew that already she had become used to viewing the wider world beyond the Manor as essentially hostile and alien: an England she could no longer recognise, the earth itself a dying planet where millions of people were constantly moving like a black stain of human locusts, invading, consuming, corrupting, destroying the air of once remote and beautiful places now rancid with human breath. But it was still her world, the one she had been born into. She was part of its corruption as she was part of its splendours and its joys. How much of it had she ever experienced in those years of living behind the mock-Gothic walls of the prestigious girls' school at which she had taught? How many people had she really engaged with other than her own kind, her own class, people who shared her own values and prejudices, who spoke the same language?

But it wasn't too late. A different world, different faces, different voices were out there to be discovered. There were still places rarely visited, paths not hardened by millions of pounding feet, fabled cities which were at peace in those quiet hours before the first light and the visitors swarmed out of their hotels. She would travel by boat, train, bus and on foot, leaving the shallowest of carbon footprints. She had saved enough to spend three years away and still have enough to buy a remote cottage somewhere in England. And she was strong and well qualified. In Asia, Africa and South America there could be useful work for her. For years, travelling with a colleague, she had had to journey in the school holidays, the worst and busiest time. This journey, taken on her own, would be different. She would have called it a voyage of self-discovery, but rejected the words as more pretentious than true. After sixty years she knew who and what she was. This would be a voyage, not of self-confirmation, but of change.

Finally, she turned at the stones and walked briskly back to the Manor.

Helena said, 'I'm sorry, but you know best, you always did. But if I need you . . .'

Lettie said quietly, 'You won't.'

'None of the usual platitudes need saying between us, but I'll miss you. And the Manor will still be here. If you get tired of wandering you can always come home.'

But the words, genuine as they knew them to be, were perfunctory. Lettie saw that Helena's eyes were fixed on the stable block where the morning sunlight was moving over the stone like a golden stain. Already she was planning how the reconstruction could be carried out; seeing in imagination the guests arriving, consulting with Dean over the menu, the possibility of a Michelin star, perhaps two, the restaurant well in profit and Dean ensconced for ever at the Manor to George's content; standing there happily dreaming, looking to the future.

3

In Cambridge the wedding service was over and the guests were beginning to move into the antechapel. Clara and Annie stayed seated, listening to the organ. The Bach and Vivaldi had been played and now the organist indulged himself and the congregation with a variation on a Bach fugue. Before the service, waiting in the sunshine with a small group of other early arrivals, people had introduced themselves, including a girl in a summer dress with short light-brown hair framing an attractive and intelligent face. She had come forward smiling to say that she was Kate Miskin, a member of Mr Dalgliesh's squad, and to introduce the young man with her, Piers Tarrant, and a handsome young Indian who was a detective sergeant in Adam's squad. Others had joined them, Adam's publisher, fellow poets and writers, a few of Emma's college colleagues. It had been a happy and friendly group, lingering as if reluctant to exchange the beauty of stone walls and great lawn lit by the May sunshine for the cool austerity of the antechapel.

The service had been short with music but no homily. Perhaps bride and groom had felt that the age-old liturgy said all that was necessary without the competition of the usual commonplace injunctions, and Emma's father had been seated in a front pew, clearly having rejected the old symbolism of the passing of possessions into another's keeping. Emma, in her cream wedding dress, a chaplet of roses in her gleaming upswept hair, had walked slowly up the aisle alone. At the sight of her composed and solitary beauty, Annie's eyes had filled with tears. And there had been another break with tradition. Instead of facing the altar with his back to his bride, Adam had turned and, smiling, had held out his hand.

And now only a few guests remained listening to the Bach. Clara said quietly, 'As a wedding I think this can be counted a success. One tends to think of our clever Emma rising above common female conventions. It's reassuring to find that she shares the apparent ambition of all brides on their wedding day, to make the congregation catch its breath.'

'I don't think she was bothering about the congregation.'

Clara said, 'Jane Austen would seem appropriate. Do you remember Mrs Elton's comments in the last chapter of *Emma*? *Very little white satin, very few lace veils; a most pitiful business!*'

'But remember how the novel ends. *But in spite of these deficiencies, the wishes, the hopes, the confidence, the predictions of the small band of true friends who witnessed the ceremony, were fully answered in the perfect happiness of the union.*'

Clara said, 'Perfect happiness is asking for a lot. But they will be happy. And at least, unlike poor Mr Knightley, Adam won't have to live with his father-in-law. Darling, your hand feels cold. Let's join the others in the sunlight. I need a drink and some food. Why does emotion make one hungry? Knowing the bride and groom and the quality of the food from the college kitchen, we shan't be disappointed. No limp canapés and warm white wine.'

But Annie wasn't yet ready to cope with fresh introductions, the meeting of new people, the babble of congratulations and the laughter of a congregation released from the solemnity of a church wedding. She whispered, 'Let's stay until the music ends.'

There were images she needed to face and thoughts which had come unbidden which she needed to deal with here in this austere and peaceful place. She was back with Clara at the Old Bailey. She thought of the young man who had attacked her and of that moment when she turned her eyes to the dock and faced him. She couldn't remember what she had expected, but it was not this ordinary-looking lad, obviously ill at ease in the suit worn to impress the court, standing there without apparent emotion. He pleaded guilty in a sullen unemphatic voice and expressed no remorse. He didn't look at her. They were two strangers linked for ever by one moment of time, one act. She could feel nothing, not pity, not forgiveness, nothing. It wasn't possible to understand him or to forgive, and she didn't think in those terms. But she told herself that it was possible not to cherish unforgiveness, or find vengeful consolation in the contemplation of his imprisonment. It was for her, not him, to decide how much she had been harmed by him. He could have no lasting power over her without her connivance. And now a verse of scripture remembered from childhood spoke to her with a clear note of truth: *Whatsoever thing from without entereth into the man, it cannot defile him; Because it entereth not into his heart.*

And she had Clara. She slipped her hand into Clara's and felt the comfort of her responsive squeeze. She thought, *The world is a beautiful and terrible place. Deeds of horror are committed every minute and in the end those we love die. If the screams of all earth's living creatures were one scream of pain, surely it would shake the stars. But we have love. It may seem a frail defence against the horrors of the world but we must hold fast and believe in it, for it is all that we have.*

Also by P. D. James

ff

The Mistletoe Murder and Other Stories

As the acknowledged Queen of Crime, P. D. James was frequently commissioned by newspapers and magazines to write a short story for Christmas, and four of the best have been drawn from the archives and published here together for the first time. From the title story about a strained country-house Christmas party, to another about an illicit affair that ends in murder, plus two cases for detective Adam Dalgliesh, these are masterfully atmospheric stories, with the lure of a mystery to be solved.

'A box of crackers.' *Guardian* Books of the Year

'What a pleasure to encounter P. D. James again at the top of her form.' Shirley Hughes

'There are very few writers who can compete with P. D. James at her best.' *Spectator*

ff

An Unsuitable Job for a Woman

Meet Cordelia Gray: twenty-two years-old, tough, intelligent and now sole inheritor of the Pryde Detective Agency. Her first assignment finds her hired by Sir Ronald Callender to investigate the death of his son Mark, a young Cambridge student found hanged in mysterious circumstances. Required to delve into the hidden secrets of the Callender family, Cordelia soon realises it is not a case of suicide, and that the truth is entirely more sinister.

'P. D. James is an addictive writer, [with] a quality of intelligence, a genuine curiosity about character, and an ability to describe the density of little known lives.' Anita Brookner

'One of the most compulsive and acutely observed thrillers of the year . . . a study of the complex motives that makes up the cold mind of a killer.' *Daily Express*

'A top-rated puzzle of peril that holds you all the way.' *New York Times*

ff

The Skull Beneath the Skin

Hired to protect a beautiful but neurotic actress, Cordelia Gray soon becomes embroiled in a case as dangerous to her own life as it is mysterious. Clarissa Lisle hopes to make a spectacular comeback in a production of *The Duchess of Malfi*, to be performed in Ambrose Gorringe's sinister castle at Courcy Island. Cordelia is there to ensure her safety following the appearance of a number of poison-pen letters. But it soon becomes clear that all are in danger. Trapped within the walls of the Gothic castle, the treacherous past of the island re-emerges, and everyone seems to have a motive for sending Clarissa 'down, down to hell'.

'A masterly version of the clue-and-alibi game . . . Five-star entertainment.' *Guardian*

'A fine novel . . . From its very first pages you feel you are in marvellously sure hands.' *The Times*

ff

The Children of Men

The year is 2021. No child has been born for twenty-five years. The human race faces extinction. Under the despotic rule of Xan Lyppiatt, the Warden of England, the old are despairing and the young cruel. Theo Faren, a cousin of the Warden, lives a solitary life in this ominous atmosphere. That is, until a chance encounter with a young woman leads him into contact with a group of dissenters. Suddenly his life is changed irrevocably as he faces agonising choices which could affect the future of mankind.

'Taut, terrifying and convincing.' *Daily Mail*

'Extraordinary . . . P. D. James stretches her considerable talents in this daring novel.' *New York Times*

'Spare and disturbing.' *Independent*

ff

Cover Her Face

St Cedd's Chruch fête has been held in the grounds of Martingale manor house for generations. As if organising stalls, as well as presiding over luncheon, the bishop and the tea tent, were not enough for Mrs Maxie on that mellow July afternoon, she also has to contend with the news of her son's sudden engagement to her new parlour maid, Sally Jupp. On the following morning Martingale and the village are shocked by the discover of Sally's body.

Investigating the violent death at the manor house, Detective Chief-Inspector Adam Dalgliesh is embroiled in the complicated passions beneath the calm surface of English village life.

'A classic story of English rural murder.' *The Times*

'There are very few thriller writers who can compete with P. D. James at her best.' *Spectator*